Haak drained his b
we hav

"Two enemies, sir? As in the armies of Casimir and Sanque?"

The major shook his head. "No. I mean the armies of Casimir and Sanque in one hand, and . . . something else entirely in the other."

Peter felt his throat tighten. "Sir, if I may beg your pardon, please speak plainly with me. What is going on here?"

But Haak just smiled a smile that was part sadness, part derangement.

"If you can answer that question, Lieutenant, you will be a popular man."

By Richard Swan

EMPIRE OF THE WOLF

The Justice of Kings
The Tyranny of Faith
The Trials of Empire

THE GREAT SILENCE

Grave Empire

GRAVE EMPIRE

The Great Silence: Book One

RICHARD SWAN

orbitbooks.net

Copyright © 2025 by Richard Swan
Excerpt from *The Radiant King* copyright © 2025 by David Dalglish

Cover design by Ben Prior | LBBG
Cover illustration by Philip Harris
Map by Tim Paul
Author photograph by Matthew Duchesne

Orbit
Hachette Book Group
1290 Avenue of the Americas
New York, NY 10104
orbitbooks.net

First Edition: February 2025
Simultaneously published in Great Britain by Orbit

Orbit is an imprint of Hachette Book Group.
The Orbit name and logo are registered trademarks of Little, Brown
Book Group Limited.

The publisher is not responsible for websites (or their content)
that are not owned by the publisher.

The Hachette Speakers Bureau provides a wide range of authors for speaking events. To find out more, go to hachettespeakersbureau.com or email HachetteSpeakers@hbgusa.com.

Orbit books may be purchased in bulk for business, educational, or promotional use. For information, please contact your local bookseller or the Hachette Book Group Special Markets Department at special.markets@hbgusa.com.

Library of Congress Control Number: 2024947370

ISBNs: 9780316577007 (trade paperback), 9780316577021 (ebook)

Printed in the United States of America

LSC-C

Printing 1, 2024

GRAVE EMPIRE

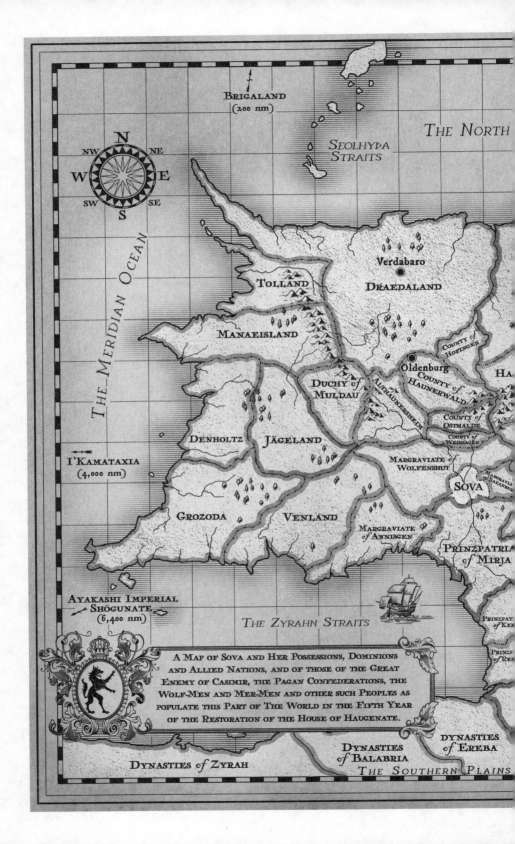

THE NORTH

BRIGALAND
(200 nm)

SEOLHYÞA
STRAITS

Verdabaro

TOLLAND

DRAEDALAND

MANAEISLAND

COUNTY of
HOFINGEN

Oldenburg

COUNTY of
HAUNERWALD

HA

DUCHY of
MULDAU

ALTHAUNERSHEIM

COUNTY of
OSTHALDE

DENHOLTZ

JÄGELAND

COUNTY of
WEISHAGEN

MARGRAVIATE of
WOLFENSHUT

MARGRAVIA
of SALANRU

SOVA

GROZODA

VENLAND

MARGRAVIATE
of ANNISGEN

PRINZPATRIA
of MIRJA

AYAKASHI IMPERIAL
SHŌGUNATE
(6,400 nm)

THE ZYRAHN STRAITS

PRINZPAT
of KE

PRINZI
of RE

A MAP OF SOVA AND HER POSSESSIONS, DOMINIONS
AND ALLIED NATIONS, AND OF THOSE OF THE GREAT
ENEMY OF CASIMIR, THE PAGAN CONFEDERATIONS, THE
WOLF-MEN AND MER-MEN AND OTHER SUCH PEOPLES AS
POPULATE THIS PART OF THE WORLD IN THE FIFTH YEAR
OF THE RESTORATION OF THE HOUSE OF HAUGENATE.

DYNASTIES
of BALABRIA

DYNASTIES
of EREBA

DYNASTIES of ZYRAH

THE SOUTHERN PLAINS

THE MERIDIAN OCEAN

I'KAMATAXIA
(4,000 nm)

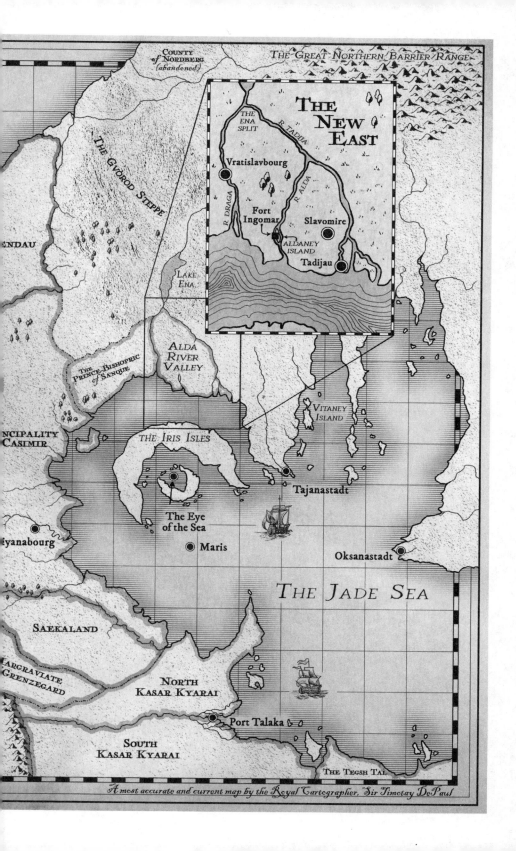

COUNTY
of NORDBERG
(abandoned)

THE GREAT NORTHERN BARRIER RANGE

THE
NEW
EAST

THE
ENA
SPLIT

R. TADIIA

Vratislavbourg

R. DRAGA

Fort
Ingomar

R. ALDA

Slavomire

ALDANEY
ISLAND

Tadijau

THE GVOROD STEPPE

NDAU

LAKE
ENA

ALDA
RIVER
VALLEY

THE
PRINCE-BISHOPRIC
of SANQUE

VITANEY
ISLAND

NCIPALITY
CASIMIR

THE IRIS ISLES

The Eye
of the Sea

Tajanastadt

yanabourg

Maris

Oksanastadt

THE JADE SEA

SAEKALAND

ARGRAVIATE
GRENZEGARD

NORTH
KASAR KYARAI

Port Talaka

SOUTH
KASAR KYARAI

THE TEGSH TAL

A most accurate and current map by the Royal Cartographer, Sir Timotay DePaul

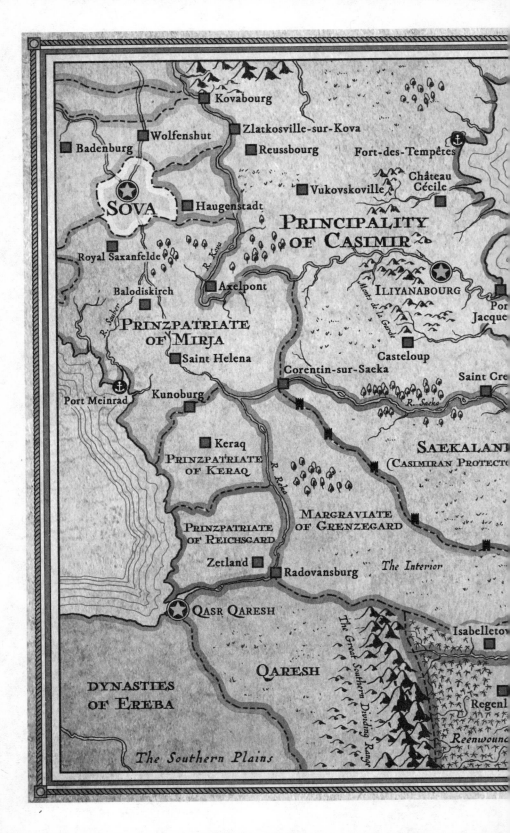

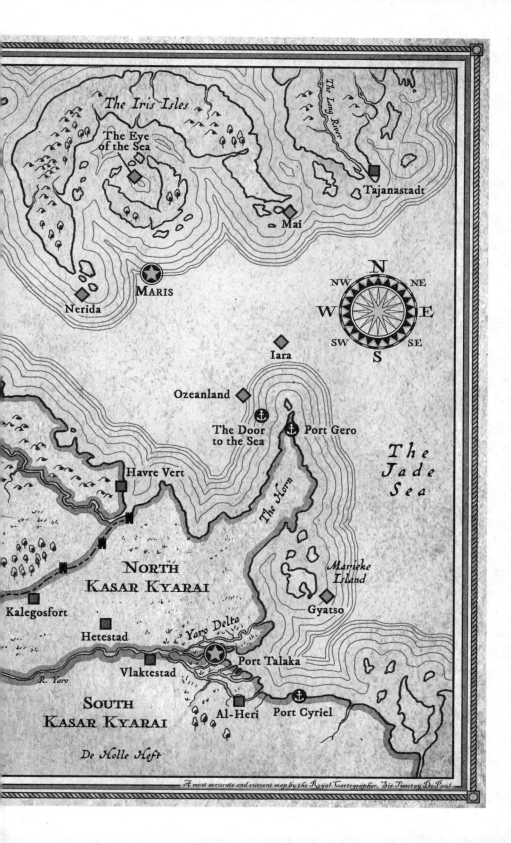

The Iris Isles

The Eye
of the Sea

The Long River

Tajanastadt

Mai

Nerida

MARIS

Iara

N
NW   NE
W   E
SW   SE
S

Ozeanland

The Door
to the Sea

Port Gero

The
Jade
Sea

Havre Vert

The Horn

NORTH
KASAR KYARAI

Marieke
Island

Kalegosfort

Gyatso

Hetestad

Yaro Delta

Vlaktestad

Port Talaka

R. Yaro

SOUTH
KASAR KYARAI

Al-Heri

Port Cyriel

De Holle Heft

A most accurate and current map by the Royal Cartographer, Sir Timotay DePaul

Table of Contents

GRAVE
EMPIRE

Prologue

The Fort at the End of the World

"Watch for when the leaves grow, when the trees blossom into life and birdsong returns to the air. The sound you hear on the horizon is not the thunder of late spring: 'tis cannon! 'Tis drumming, and shot! As with the sowing and the harvest, so we have made seasons of warfare. ''Tis the fighting season', it will be announced, and the men march off to be reaped."

FROM CHUN PARSIFAL'S
THE INFINITE STATE

Sovan Territory

ALDA RIVER VALLEY

Dear Father,

Well. I am a long way from home.

I have spent some time calculating it; the crossing over the Stygion Sea will take the better part of a week. This letter is my attempt to focus my mind on something except seasickness.

It was five hundred miles to get out of Sova herself, and the abutting Prinzpatriate of Mirja (there is little of note there except the cathedral at Balodiskirch, which is rather magnificent). It was another five hundred to get halfway through the Margraviate of Grenzegard. The locals refer to it simply as "The Interior", and it is a much benighted land, filled with mines, earthworks, smelters, the air thick with the poisonous fog of industry.

We kept well clear of Saekaland for our own safety, for the pagans there have taken to testing the Sigismund Line weekly; then we clipped the northernmost foothills of the Great Southern Dividing Range. I had hoped to see some of the rainforest greenery of the Reenwound, but it is all coal and iron ore mines and logging stations there, and the earth is turned and compacted and being excavated for the new canal system. I did, however, see the thaumaturgic wind generators being installed by teams of engineers, though they were not yet working. They are a modern marvel, though it seems there is no part of the Empire now untouched by the fires of industry, and much of the natural beauty of the world – to say nothing of the native peoples within it – is being excised at an alarming rate.

We detoured at the last moment to Kalegosfort, and I had thought we might see some pagan Saekas there, but we remained unmolested. A mercenary company was added to our caravan, and then we tracked across the (hot!) countryside to that easternmost spur of land of the contiguous Sovan Empire to Port Gero. A journey of a thousand miles – and that is only halfway. One wonders how the Empress hopes to govern such an enormous and increasingly disparate nation; even leaving aside the discontent of the subjugated, the distances alone make an incredible challenge for Imperial logisticians.

We spent three days in Port Gero before I caught sight of the vessel we were to take across the Stygion Sea. It was a rather remarkable ship, a forty-two-gun frigate called the Lord Ansobert, though the fellows with me thought it very shabby indeed. We embarked on the 1st of the month, an apparently auspicious date, though to me it seemed like any other. As I sit here in the hold, we are five days into an anticipated seven and neither hair nor hide of a mer-man, though they are known to be in these waters. My candle is almost burned to the nub, so I shall return to this letter once the picture for the rest of my journey becomes clearer.

{Two days later – the 8th}

Well, Father, some ~~drama~~ excitement on the journey. The planned debarkation point had been the colonial town of Tajanastadt, at the southernmost tip of the peninsula where the Long River meets the Stygion Sea. Instead, a storm put us well off course and nearly dis-masted the ship. Instead we have travelled north through the Haraldan Strait, which sits between Maretsburg – our new destination – and Vitaney Island. The latter I have been examining through the first mate's spyglass, which I troubled him to lend me, for many hours. So many whaling stations and ships you never did see, nor so many gulls. The latter are vermin, covering the island with their guano. They pluck at the offcuts of whale-meat, though it seems to me that very little of the corpses are wasted. A fascinating industry, though with so many of the wretches pulled from the ocean it is a wonder there are any left. One can see readily why it exercises the mer-men so (still not one sighting! The first mate tells me they are a reclusive mob).

We are due in Maretsburg at first light. Then it is another several hundred miles of travel west across the peninsula to Slavomire, the largest Imperial town in the ~~fiercely contested~~ Alda River Valley. I know you wished a safe posting for me, and I shall endeavour to remain in Slavomire if I can, perhaps in some sort of supply role. I do not think the town itself has been under any sort of attack for several years now.

I shall write again soon.

{Five days later – the 13th}

Dear Father,

A little more on this letter before I seal it. I have been recommended to do so before I leave Slavomire on account of the irregular postal collection further west.

We moved across the countryside by mule. For most of the journey I was more or less alone save the company of my guide, a mountain tribesman who spoke good Saxan. The New East is a gloomy place, there can be no question of that. I had been told many times that the most dangerous part of my journey was the crossing of the Stygion Sea, though now I am in and amongst the pine forests and hills and mountains here, I am thoroughly unsettled. Our Great Enemy, the armies of Casimir and their allies in Sanque, are supposed to have no claim to these lands east of the Line of Demarcation, but there are a great many confederations of mountain tribesmen whose loyalties are unclear at the very best of times. ~~Even though we saw no one or thing, I felt many pairs of eyes watching me.~~

I had hoped to remain in Slavomire – no such luck. The colonel there ordered me immediately on to Fort Romauld, though even that is not my final destination. That misfortune belongs to Fort Ingomar, the so-called "fort at the end of the world". It sits on Aldaney Island, a little piece of land which bifurcates the River Alda for which the valley is named. This is the closest fort to the enemy and almost the centrepiece of the entire disputed country. ~~I confess, Father, that I am frightened at such a prospect.~~

~~I fear such a long journey has given me much too much time to think. It had seemed to me so much more exciting in the regimental headquarters in Badenburg. But after several days in the New East, I feel very much under the yoke of homesickness. I have heard so many rumours of spirits and ghosts and witches and drudes in these forests. They were easy~~

to dismiss in Sova, but it is not so easy to dismiss now. I fear I have acted in haste in

I have no doubt I shall remain safe. Major Haak, who runs Fort Ingomar, commands a fine reputation and is not known for squandering his forces. I shall endeavour to "keep my head on my shoulders" per your injunction and write whenever my time permits me. Kiss Mother for me and wish Osbeorn and Aldhard luck with all their endeavours. Tell Leonie I shall write to her separately and assure her of my affections.

Yours in unanticipated haste,

Peter

Too much time to think – and still more of it now. That had been, and remained, the problem.

It was difficult to know who had first floated the idea of Peter joining the Sovan Army. It had been a couple of years ago now. He had never been especially enthused about it, but when his father had purchased him a commission, and laid out a feast in his honour, and forced his elder and younger brothers to endure it – young men who were both more interesting and talented than Peter had ever been – he'd been swept up in the excitement of it all.

His father might have purchased him the commission, but had it been his *idea*? He cared for Peter dearly. It seemed unlikely he would be pleased with the prospect of him fighting Casimirs and Sanques in the New East.

Where, then, had the idea germinated? His beau, Leonie? Her interest in him had been steadily drying up to the point where her affection was almost exhausted. But seeing him in the uniform of the 166th Badenburg Regiment had turned her around somewhat. He had been much too pleased with the resumption of their courtship to appreciate just how skin-deep her affections were. His mother, too – a cold woman who seemed to much prefer his brothers – had wept tears of pride in seeing him so turned out. Perhaps the blame lay with one, or both, of them?

His friends, a collection of clerks and novice bankers and market speculators, had affected jealousy. He was going to the land of the wolfmen, he was going to sail across the Stygion Sea – perhaps he'd see a mer-man! – he was going to *see* the New East and Sova's holdings there and give the Casimirs and Sanques and their pagan allies a good thrashing. They slapped him on the shoulder, red-faced and perspiring in the city taverns around the Imperial Bank of Sova and the South Seas Trading Company. It was *exciting*, daring, bold and brave, and after several glasses of wine and several more of brandy, he too had given in to these seductive ideas.

Now he remembered those drinking sessions with contempt. His friends' enthusiasm had been nothing but a hollow salve, designed to soothe his nerves. Oh, they were happy enough to bet on the price of furs from Valerija, or whale oil from Vitaney Island; but the idea of travelling to the colonies and traipsing through hundreds of miles of empty mountain forest to trap furs, or bludgeon a mer-man to death with the butt of a musket to wrench the whalebone from his hands so that a pampered Sovan woman could have her stay firmly braced – well, suddenly it didn't seem so glorious or exciting. They would never taste the reality of it.

But Peter would.

Too much time to think, and too many rumours about this place. The fighting here was not like the civilised land wars up and down the length of the River Kova, which separated the Sovan Empire from Casimir. The war in this rugged terrain was one of traps and ambushes, dirty tricks and terror tactics. And if the colonists in Slavomire were to be believed, it was a place in which men simply vanished, never to be seen or heard from again.

He could well believe it. As he moved through the Alda River Valley, he could not take his eyes off the gloomy forest around him. It was filled with foetid pools and dark nooks and tangled outcrops of rock throttled with grasping vines. Ahead of him, his guide, a man of middling age with milk-pale skin and faded blue geometric tattoos running down the sides of his neck, led him and their mule down a path that was indistinguishable from the surrounding earth. Above, the trees were so thick that the sun hardly penetrated the canopy.

He swore as his right boot disappeared into a bog. Nema Victoria, what was he *doing* here? How had he accepted the tub-thumping bombast of his fellow officers back in Badenburg so readily? The closer he got to Fort Ingomar, the more he wanted to turn back. It was miserable enough without the enemy. The air was filled with constant drizzle, whilst the rattle of woodpeckers' beaks and the thrashing of rabbits through the carpet of leaves set him on edge. Every defile and outcrop and log looked as though it concealed interlopers. The feeling of being observed was so acute it was tangible—

He came up short. The guide had stopped, and he had almost walked into the back of the mule. The mule's ass – there was a pun fit for the officers' mess.

"What's the matter?" he asked. He sounded testy, in a way that only haughty Sovan officers could sound, but it was born of tension. He was deeply anxious.

The guide, a gregarious man, looked suddenly nervous.

"*Mi preĝas, ke temas ne pri kathomo,*" the man muttered.

"What?" Peter hissed.

"Please, Mister Kleist," the guide said, motioning for him to be quiet.

Peter fell silent. They waited for a long, excruciating minute. "Death," the man said. He took a large sniff, and scooped the air up under his nose in an exaggerated manner. "Smell."

Peter could smell nothing except the petrichor of the pine forest. Nonetheless, he pulled his pistol out of its sash.

The guide noticed this and seemed uneasy. "No, no," he said, holding out a hand. "Put away. Make angry. Yes?"

Peter had no idea what he meant, and shook his head. He felt his palm begin to sweat around the pistol's grip.

The guide sucked his teeth, scanning the foliage with a practised eye. "Come," he said. "Quick."

"The mule—" Peter started, but the guide simply grabbed him by the wrist and pulled him along.

Peter's heart raced as they dived into the brush. The forest was thick with low-hanging branches and carpeted with ferns, roots and leaf litter. Somewhere to the north he heard a noise, an animal cry, but not one he was familiar with.

"Low, here." The guide pointed to the floor, and Peter dropped. The guide removed Peter's tricorn. "Lower," he said urgently. "Hide."

Peter felt sick. The two of them crouched in the gloom, waiting. Ahead, the forest air thickened with mist. There was . . . *something* out there. For the first time Peter smelt the death the guide had mentioned. It was not unlike decaying fruit and vegetables left out in the sun, a sickly, cloying scent.

They waited there for a very long time, an hour at least. Every time Peter moved to shift his weight, the guide gripped his shoulder and quietly shushed him. Every time he tried to ask what was happening, the man simply shook his head and would not be drawn. Peter wondered whether he should assert himself more and insist the man give him answers, in keeping with what his superiors would expect. But the guide was terrified, and so Peter was too.

Eventually the danger passed, and they pressed themselves up. Peter was soaking from the damp earth. He kept his pistol in his hand, though the damp was likely to have fouled the powder by now.

The guide said nothing, but rather motioned for him to follow. His gestures were not frantic, but there was an expression of . . . it was difficult to tell. Concern? Possibly even excitement. Peter felt wary again. He turned around, but there was nothing behind him. Just tens of miles of pristine forest wilderness clothed in veils of mist. The Great Northern Barrier Range rose gigantically in the distance, snow-capped grey peaks gutting the low cloud layer like knives in a belly. That was a place so infamously impassable – its terrain so treacherous, the storms so violent – that no modern Sovan argonauts had made it across.

The guide did not wait, and Peter swore as he moved after him. He chased him down a rocky slope tangled with ferns, twice nearly turning his ankle on a moss-covered rock. "Slow down, damn you," he called after him, though the man did not.

Peter felt very conscious that they were leaving the putative trail and the mule even further behind, and was increasingly concerned that the guide was in fact an enemy agent who was going to lead him off and cut his throat. But then a dreadful smell hit him, and he heard the buzzing of flies, and knew immediately that the man had led him to a body.

"Nema Victoria," he breathed, trying to get the rotten vegetable stink out of his nose. The guide had led him to a small clearing which abutted a brisk, fast-running stream, and he stood at the edge of it, pointing to the centre. There lay three bodies, twisted and broken, their necks and chests laid open and now the preserve of hundreds of flies. All three men had been violently decapitated, and one of those heads had been skewered on a pole which itself had been thrust into the earth upright. Bits of torn uniform and viscera lay strewn about the clearing, and Peter saw the unmistakable black fabric, silver frogging and polished pewter buttons of Sovan soldiers.

"What happened?!" he demanded of the guide, his nerves thrumming like plucked harp strings. The man was what the Sovans called a "mountain tribesman", a native of this part of the world. Some of the tribes had allied with the Sovans; some had allied with the Casimirs and the Sanques. Some had allied with neither, and killed indiscriminately. At first blush this grisly tableau looked to be the work of savage pagans – but the claw marks suggested otherwise.

The guide shrugged warily. He clearly had *some* idea, though he would not say it out loud. He pulled a small blade from a pouch mounted on the back of his belt, and with a deftness which belied his age clambered up the trunk of a nearby tree. There he cut down the body of a fourth man that Peter had not even noticed. It squelched grossly into the undergrowth.

"Where are their heads?" Peter asked, swallowing down his rising gorge. His heart was pounding, and his legs felt weak. He wanted desperately to sit down. "This is Sovan territory! This is supposed to be pacified land!"

The guide winced at him. "Come," he said in Saxan. "No path. Walk now."

"Who did this?!" Peter snapped. Or perhaps more to the point, *what* had done it? He might have thought it the work of canister given the bodies' ferocious disassembly, though there was no sign of shot anywhere. And besides, the corpses had clearly been rent and mauled.

"You tell the major," the guide said. He scanned the forest again, listening, searching, smelling. "Time to go now."

"Wait," Peter said, letting out a long, shaky breath. "Just . . . hold on a minute, damn you."

He went up to the corpses of the four men. With hands trembling and bile in his gullet, he rummaged through the blood-soaked clothes and took a few things – letters, a monogrammed pocket watch – and stuffed them in his haversack, bloodying the contents as he did so. Then, pleased with this thinking in spite of the circumstances, he rejoined the guide.

"What about the mule?" he asked, looking back up the slope.

The man shook his head. "It wait here." Then he turned and picked out a route amongst the undergrowth.

Peter swore under his breath. A very large part of him was tempted to desert. To turn back. To resign his commission, to sell it, and return to his family home in Imastadt. It would be in disgrace – but at least he'd be alive. But fear of embarrassment, of being judged by his friends and family and peers, meant that he could not.

And so with his heart and belly full of fear, he cast one last forlorn look at the corpses, now certain that a similar fate awaited him; and then he followed the guide to the fort at the end of the world.

I

An Urgent Message for the Secretary to the Ambassador

"Armed conflict is a wellspring of certain misery, but is not to be avoided at any cost. There is such thing as an intolerable peace. The diplomat finds himself at the nexus of these two states. Their mission is an unenviable one: to avert both the former and the latter."

FROM MANAGOLD'S
THE THIRD WAY

The Imperial Office

SOVA

They were no strangers to the sound of pounding footsteps in the Imperial Office. Messengers bearing urgent dispatches rattled through the place daily. They were the same children who hounded people on the streets to buy pamphlets and newspapers and political polemics – and indeed the same children who coalesced into gangs and trapped well-to-do Sovans in back alleys and threatened them with knives. They were a bloody menace, though Renata had to respect their tenacity. Sova, after all, did a very good job of crushing the poor beneath its boot heel.

The scurrying footsteps were normally confined to the upper floors of the Imperial Office, where the more important diplomatic suites lay. There, entire staffs dedicated to the different peoples of the known world languished in opulence. There was the Office of the Western Kingdoms Alliance, the Office of the Principality of Casimir – the "Great Enemy" – the Office of the Kova Confederation. There were even offices for the pagans to the north and south, countries like Tolland and Draedaland, Manaeisland and Saekaland, mysterious, closed-off places which had once been part of the Sovan Empire. The Zyrahn Dynasties of the Southern Plains, Qaresh, the wolfmen of the Kasar Kyarai, the colonies of the distant New East – all of them had an extravagant office, a host of tame analysts, and a diplomatic staff.

Not so Renata's office. This was a dingy place in the basement, what looked like a hare-brained professor's study. Overstuffed bookshelves and framed nautical artworks lined every wall, whilst maps of the Jade Sea cluttered every surface. Where there was space, paraphernalia from that submarine realm lay scattered about – a jar of iridescent oyster pearls from Ozeanland, a hunting spear from the Iris Isles, and the *pièce de résistance*, the wrought-coral battle helm of Old Scar-Eye himself, the largest white shark known to mankind.

The place had the musty quality of an abandoned library. Natural light came in through a small blurry window at street level, and thanks to the contrivance of mirrors filled the chamber. Pipes, which gurgled frequently, ran across the junction of the wall and ceiling. In winter they wore coats and gloves and drank brandy-infused coffee constantly; in summer the air was so thick they could barely breathe.

Renata shared this place with her superior, His Excellency

the Ambassador Didacus Maruska. On warm spring days like this one, it felt as though their combined breath filled half the chamber.

"Where do you think?"

Renata looked up from her copy of the *Superior Dialecta Stygio*. Maruska, a beacon of colour in his orange-and-red Qareshian kaftan, squinted at her.

She thought for a moment. "The Kasari Office," she said.

Maruska stroked his formidable beard. It was greying by the day. "A safe choice," he allowed.

It was a game they played. Each slamming office door had its own distinct timbre which resonated through the building, and they liked to guess who had received the dispatch.

Renata smiled, her expression wry. "Where else do the messengers go these days? The country is weeks from collapse."

Maruska considered this – or pretended to. "Yes. I expect you are right." He tapped the front of his newspaper. "And the gold-mark with it."

They listened for the inevitable thump of the heavy oak double doors of the Kasari office. But to Renata's surprise, the footsteps continued. Now came the telltale slap of sandal against stone step.

She met Maruska's eye. "Downstairs?"

"Probably got lost."

He pulled out his pipe and began to thumb in tobacco leaf. He struck a match against the desk, next to where a newspaper lay. The headline, which took up much of the cover, read: *WOLFMEN ROUT! NORTHERN KYARAI WEEKS FROM BEING OVERRUN. GOLDMARK TUMBLES, IMPERIAL BANK DESPAIRS!*

"They're coming closer," Renata said in a sing-song voice as the footsteps grew in volume.

"Here, then," the ambassador replied, filling the chamber with the sweet scent of Qareshian pipe smoke. Renata complained that it took all the air out of the room, though secretly she loved the smell of it.

"That doesn't count as your guess," she said.

Maruska winked at her. A moment later, there was a sharp rap at their door.

Renata stood and walked over to it, and pulled it open. There stood a young girl, perhaps ten years old, her face ruddy and perspiring from exertion. "Is this the . . . 'Stygion Mer-men Office'?" she asked in gutter Saxan.

Renata nodded, still unconvinced. They hardly received letters at all, let alone urgent ones. "Yes."

"Urgent message for Renata Rainer." The girl held the letter out as though it would poison her if she held it any longer.

"Thank you," Renata replied, taking it and giving her a penny.

"Well?" Maruska said, once the door was closed.

Renata opened and read the letter with an expression of bemusement. "This is Imperial letterhead," she muttered. "From the Office of the Royal Court. They want me to report to Zobryv Gardens – immediately."

"The embassy district? Why?"

"I don't know," Renata said. She put her shoes on and grabbed her purse. "But I'd better go. Are you coming?"

"It's not addressed to me, is it?"

"No."

He shrugged. "Well then, off you go."

Renata walked quickly through the basement corridor of the Imperial Office, and then up several flights of stairs and into the main entrance hall. This was an imposing place of schach-pattern flooring and statues and portraits of famous ambassadorial staff. Above the main entrance was an enormous painting of the wolfman Zuberi, the "Saviour of Sova" – so named for some centuries-old battle in the city. His watchful lupine eyes never failed to elicit a shiver from her.

She exited the office directly on to Admiralty Square, where the desiccated grass crunched under her feet, and immediately turned left and then left again, passing down a narrow, bustling street between the Library of Sova and the Imperial Office. She cut over a bridge which crossed the westernmost branch of the brown River Sauber, covering her nose as she did so. It was coming to the time of year when the Sauber really began to smell, ripe as it was with effluents and iridescent with industrial outflow.

Zobryv Gardens itself was largely empty, though it would soon be full of the promenading wealthy and workers taking their lunch. It was a pleasant green space of broad walkways shaded by old-growth oaks, and grass lawns and flower beds ensconced in ornate iron railings. It was a pretty little corner of the city, quiet for somewhere so central, overlooked by the rear of a long terrace of foreign embassies along the Veleurian Road.

The letter had stipulated she hurry to a small walled garden near the centre of the park, and she moved quickly in spite of the spring warmth. She was intercepted for the last hundred yards by a well-dressed gentleman whom she felt she recognised, a young man in a spring suit of plain black cloth. He wore an urgent countenance. "Ms Rainer!" he said breathlessly. "Please, quickly, this way. There is a pressing matter which requires your expertise."

"Yes, of course – lead on," she replied, trying not to sound as breathless as she felt. She followed the man at a fast walk into the walled garden, a pleasant structure overgrown with intricate knots of ivy. Ahead and in the centre was a cluster of besuited gentlemen, all craning to see something at the edge of a fountain pond.

"I have her!" her escort called out to the group.

"Nema Victoria!"

"Thank goodness!"

"Over here, Secretary Rainer! Quick!"

Overcome with curiosity, Renata hurried into the centre of the group. A man was crouched down, and in his hands was a bizarre creature; half frog, half fish, and grafted together so expertly the thing writhed and wriggled in a deathless agony, with neither air to drink nor water to breathe.

The man looked at her sharply, wearing a wide, disingenuous grin. "It's the Stygion ambassador, Miss Rainer!" he exclaimed. "He's looking a little green around the gills!"

There was about three seconds of silence as the clot of men – all of whom she now realised were colleagues from the Imperial Office – studied her with idiot expressions of glee. Then a second man snatched something from his pocket and held it out. It was an elongated black shell, redolent of seawater.

"I think he's pulled a mussel!"

And then all of them exploded into fits of red-faced, thigh-slapping laughter.

She met her half-sister in one of the kaffeehauses which sat in a row on Gooseneck Street. To the south was the enormous Imperial Stocks Exchange, and at lunchtime the place disgorged its occupants like an upturned waste bin. They filled the public houses which themselves filled the surrounding area like symbiotic fish, demanding beef steaks and ale and brandy and making as many deals there as they did in the Exchange itself.

The kaffeehaus was a dingy place filled with dark wood. In one corner, placed prominently, was a chalkboard with exchange rates for foreign currencies and the price of various commodities – furs, cotton, tobacco, silk. Once, this had been the preserve of the nouveau riche, who had come to ostentatiously drink expensive coffee filled with teaspoons of expensive sugar; now, like the surrounding taverns, it was a place of business for the merchant classes.

"And then they made a pun. *Two* puns," Renata muttered. She had been careful not to give the men – boys, really, in spirit – the satisfaction of her ire. Instead she had simply rolled her eyes and left, biting down the fury which had filled her.

"What were the puns?" her half-sister asked. She was a beautiful woman. Where Renata had inherited her mother's paper-pale skin, Amara had their father's light brown colouring. She was a postgraduate student at the University of Sova, a talented linguist and secret pamphleteer, intelligent and headstrong and roguish. She fought off suitors daily – men and women alike – and affected to tire of it.

"Something about gills. One of them took out a mollusc and suggested the wretched creature had pulled a mussel."

Amara put her hand over her mouth.

Renata squinted at her. "It's not funny."

"No," Amara said, taking a long sip of coffee. "What utter beasts. What was the creature?"

Renata waved her off. "Some vivisectionist from the University had spliced a fish and a frog together. The thing cannot have lived for long after."

"Still, not a bad likeness. For a mer-man, I mean. I know you have your whole . . . *thing* going on, but they are a little bit ghastly, Ren."

Renata set her teeth. "I deal with enough of that in the Imperial Office. I don't want to deal with it with you."

"Sorry," Amara said, though she wasn't.

Renata sighed. "All this bloody . . . *war*. War in the Kyarai, war with Casimir. Everyone's idea of diplomacy is to threaten, to shoot, to *bludgeon* terms out of your enemy. Capitulation is the only acceptable outcome. And I look around the streets and no one even seems to be that bothered about it. Parades of soldiers down the Petran Highway, lists of medal awards in the newspapers, pamphlets – there's a new row of flags on Aleksandra the Valiant Boulevard, have you seen it?"

Amara inclined her head.

"Just dozens of them tied to the lamps, all the different regimental banners. It's vulgar. I remember a time when 'blackcoat' was an insult. When did the city become so . . . *martial*?"

"Since Zelenka Haugenate took the throne?"

"Oh, don't get me started on her. Our *glorious* new Empress. It's still extraordinary to me how the Senate just . . . " Renata snapped her fingers, "*decided* to reinstitute the monarchy."

"I am absolutely not going to get you started," Amara said impishly. She had heard this diatribe before, many times. "I told you I can put you in touch with the pacifists up in Pike's Bend."

"No, I told *you*. It's a proscribed organisation. I'll lose my job."

Amara shrugged slowly. "Well then."

"Well then what? Put up or shut up?"

"Goodness me, you are prickly today. All because of some absurd lark. Really, Ren, this is precisely what they were . . . *angling* for."

"Amara!" Renata snapped, but her sister was so pleased with the pun she spent a good few moments in hearty, silent laughter, and eventually Renata found herself coaxed into laughing as well.

After they had both calmed down, Renata finished the last of her coffee. The sugar had settled at the bottom, the last mouthful tepid and much too sweet. "How are you, anyway?" she asked when her sister had recovered herself. "How is Father?"

Amara waved a hand dismissively. "Fine. He's fine. Off to the south to search for gold in the Reenwound."

Their father, a successful and eccentric Zyrahn prospector, had made his fortune in diamond mining in the western half of the Kyarai – the country of the wolfmen – and had supplied all of his many children – of whom Renata and Amara were the eldest – with generous funds to pursue their interests. Renata almost never saw him, especially since her mother had died.

"And is there anyone you are seeing?"

"Do you mean have I been successfully wooed?" Amara winked. "No. Everyone bores me. The men and women of the University are such a dull lot. What about you? How is Alistair?"

Renata thought of her putative beau, a young poet whom she

had met in a public house in Creusgate several months before. The man was lovely, but much too intense, and she had quickly tired of him. The fact that she worked for the Sovan state, too, was a source of near-endless argument. Sometimes it ended in lovemaking; more often it ended in resentful silence. Renata kept meaning to break it off, but she had been preoccupied, and their relationship had limped on like a dog with a broken leg.

"I'm sure he's fine."

"Oh dear. Who *will* be enough to tame the great Renata Rainer?" Amara said playfully. "Perhaps you could strap your legs up and learn to breathe underwater and marry a—"

"Oh, shut up," Renata said, throwing her napkin at her sister. She looked around the kaffeehaus, at all the ruddy-faced merchants talking loudly to one another. A member of the establishment was updating the commodities prices on the chalk-board, which had prompted a fresh round of loud, excited chatter. It made conversation practically impossible.

"Well, I should be getting back," she half shouted.

Amara reached across the table and took Renata's hand in her own. The levity had gone; concern was writ large on her features. "Are you all right, Ren?"

"Why do you ask?" Renata replied. Such questions always put her back up.

"You always seem so highly strung. Sensitive to the goings-on of the world. I hate to think of those wretches in the Imperial Office making fun of you, especially given how hard you work."

Amara's sympathy came from a place of genuine affection, and so Renata made an effort to reciprocate her sincerity. Many made the mistake of thinking Amara a superficial creature.

"I'm afraid until someone discovers coal or iron or gold at the bottom of the Stygion Sea, the mer-men will always be little more than a curiosity to the Empire. And that is in the best case."

"Don't the mer-men have a thing about whales? I heard they boarded that whaling ship in the night. What was it called?"

Amara snapped her fingers. "The *Sophia Juras*. Killed everyone on it."

"That's a silly rumour," Renata lied.

Amara sighed. "Well. The important thing is you are all right. Do not spend your life thinking about mer-men, please. Have you even *met* one yet?"

"The ambassador is preparing an expedition for next year."

"Ren," Amara said gently. "The ambassador has been 'preparing an expedition' for as long as you have worked there. You might as well have remained at the University with me."

"I never had your talent for languages."

"You must speak Loxica pretty fluently."

Renata snorted. "It's mostly sign language."

Amara grinned. "Show me something. How do you say 'Amara is the best sister a lady could hope for'?"

Renata considered the question, and after a moment's pause performed a silly flourish followed by a middle finger.

Amara's eyes widened, then she snorted so loudly she clapped her hand over her mouth, and the two of them fell about laughing again, so long and hard that by the end Renata was crying tears of mirth.

"Now I really do need to get back to the office," she said once they had calmed down. Around them, obese traders in groaning jackets and breeches eyed them with a mixture of lust and contempt.

Amara sighed. "Let's do lunch next week, yes? Let's get oysters like we used to when you lived in that ghastly apartment near the Creusgate magazine."

"I still live there."

"Oh, for Nema's sake," Amara said.

"Goodbye Amara."

Renata could still hear her sister laughing as she left the kaffeehaus.

The bankers had returned to their banks by the time she crossed Gooseneck Street again. She stopped outside the Board of Trade building, where a Grozodan baker offered her a sweet bun from his cart, and she bought two – one for Maruska – then made her way back across Admiralty Square and into the Imperial Office. She ducked in just as an afternoon shower started in earnest, sloughing away the dust and dirt from the Sovan streets, and made her way back down to the basement, where Maruska sat in his chair, snoring lightly. She pursed her lips.

"I got you a pastry," she said loudly. The old ambassador didn't startle awake; he simply opened his eyes slowly.

"Thank you," he said, taking the Grozodan sweet bun from her. He examined it, though there was no hint of honey or ground walnuts and pistachios such as he might have bought in Qaresh. Still, he managed to eat it.

Renata watched the rain splatter down into the streets, sending dirty streaks down the office's solitary window. When it was cloudy, the room became very dingy indeed.

"You aren't going to ask me what the message was?" she said eventually.

"What was the message?" Maruska asked.

"It was a lampoon. Men from upstairs, making fun of me. Making fun of us."

"It is as it has ever been."

"Doesn't it bother you?" she asked, trying to affect nonchalance. "To be a laughing stock? To be . . ." she searched the office, "a joke?"

"We are not a joke, Ms Rainer."

"Yes, well." She waved him off. "Sometimes it feels like it." She thought of her sister's words, words spoken with affection but which had hit on Renata's private fears. "I've not even met a mer-man."

"To be a joke and to be perceived as a joke are two different things."

In spite of her best efforts – she was a diplomat after all – she felt her anger briefly boil over. It was anger she should have spent on the men in Zobryv Gardens. "Spare me your mental gymnastics, Didi. It was humiliating."

Maruska shifted in his chair. A moment later she heard the strike of a match, and the familiar smell of rosemary-and-sandalwood-scented tobacco.

"Do you know what the problem with the Imperial Office is?" he asked.

"There is only one?"

"Have you naught left to learn?" Maruska asked sharply.

Renata forced herself to relax again. She had run into the curtain wall of Maruska's patience. Many regretted surmounting it.

Maruska pointed the bit of his pipe at her. "The problem with the Imperial Office is that it views every race of people on this world as a problem to be solved. A dog to be brought to heel. It thinks in terms of administrative ledgers, accounts, mathematical equations, supply trains and tons of powder. It sees the Kasar and the pagans and the Casimirs and the mer-men not as pieces in a common lot, but either as tools or as enemies. Does the gardener negotiate with the rake? Does the farmer *entreat* the ploughshare?"

"N—"

"Nay!" Maruska suddenly thundered, slamming a fist on the desktop. "He commands them! He bends them to his will, for they are naught but tools. And what of those he considers pests? The rats, the foxes, the wild dogs and pigs? They are killed! They are killed and they are skinned, and their meat and offal is cut out and cooked, and their bones are boiled for broth, and the blood is mixed into the soil for the plants or into the mortar for the bricks." He clapped his hands together. "The farmer does not beg the vermin to leave, he does not barter with them, he does not offer them some of his corn in return that they leave the field be. Because the farmer has the ultimate power of life and death in his hands, though he does not think in those terms. The tools he will *use*, and the pests he will *exterminate*, and the land he will claim. They perceive us as a joke not because we simply seek to speak to the animals, but in their eyes, we have dressed the fox in a day suit. We have coiffed his fur and soothed his mange, and we have bespectacled him and given him a hat and shoes and a leather satchel filled with documents he cannot understand, and we have sat him at a table in our farmhouse and set out our terms. What are the terms, Miss Rainer?"

"Please leave the chickens be?"

Now Maruska laughed, a throaty sound enriched by years of smoke and brandy. "Precisely. Why are we here in this basement whilst our peers enjoy opulence? Because they see the Stygion as a dressed fox; something which should be shot or snared and clubbed, or otherwise cowed. Look at the way they use the Kasar in the northern Kyarai, not as equals, but as living weapons to claw and stab and shoot their compatriots in the south. Look at the way the gangs tour Sungate and round up wolfmen there to press into the Legions. Look how Sova seizes the lands in the east from the mountain tribesmen and turns them on each other."

Renata collapsed into her chair opposite him. "Why do we bother? I mean, really, what is the point in all this?" She gestured to the stacks of waxed papers on the desk in front of her, messages to their Stygion counterparts a thousand miles away. They were little more than correspondents, maintaining a diplomatic channel because it was only slightly more expedient for the Sovans than to not do so. Certainly if Renata didn't have a source of private funds, she would not be able to survive in her current role. The Imperial Office paid poverty wages because it traded on prestige. Perversely it meant that the place was overstuffed with the privately wealthy, scions of noble houses who were much too haughty and arrogant to make effective diplomatic negotiators. They were people who had never had to compromise, and, with the backing of the entire state apparatus, saw no reason to start now.

"Because no one else will," Maruska said simply. "It is better to be a voice of dissent on the inside than on the outside. There is a saying in Qaresh. 'There are two ways to blunt a blade; one is in its scabbard, the other is in the belly of your enemy.'"

"You Qareshians are very fond of your aphorisms, aren't you?"

Maruska's laugh rumbled throughout the office again. A moment later he stopped, cocking his head to one side; the thump of footsteps was once again sounding through the corridors. "Come; let us have one last game, and then I think we can be done for the afternoon."

Renata blew out her lips as she listened. "The Kasar again."

Maruska tutted. "Listen, that is the carpet in the Matria Paulaskas hallway. Listen how it softens the step."

Renata smiled gamely, but the truth was she just wanted to go home now. "Fine; the Grozodans, then."

"You are only saying that because you bought a Grozodan sweet bun earlier."

Renata lapsed to silence. But once again they exchanged a look of surprise as the footsteps slapped against the stone steps leading down into the basement, and then across the undressed wooden floor of the corridor outside.

"Give me strength," she muttered, pressing herself to her feet as there came another knock at the door. She yanked it open to see a different messenger this time, a lad in his teens who doffed his cap at the sight of her.

"Urgent message for the ambassador—"

"Oh, piss off," she muttered.

The messenger said and did nothing for a moment, his face an expression of absolute bafflement.

"But it's . . . from the Empre—"

"Yes, very good," Renata muttered. She snatched her coat off its hook next to the door. "See you tomorrow, Didi," she called over her shoulder, and, pushing past the messenger, made her way out of the building.

II

All Manner of
Auditory Tricks

*"Warfare is the achievement of one's political aims through
the application of armed force. In the same way we might lever
a stubborn door open with an iron bar, so too might we lever
open our enemy's interests and degrade or destroy them. The
trick, always, is knowing when and where to insert the bar."*

FROM MANAGOLD'S
THE THIRD WAY

Fort Ingomar

ALDA RIVER VALLEY

Peter had seen bodies before. Accidents on the streets of Sova,
or the victims of knife fights and duels. Communicable disease
sometimes left entire sections of the city locked down and overstuffed with corpses. He'd had a sister, too, younger than him but
older than his youngest brother, who had died from a pox. Her
funeral was the only time he'd seen his father weep.

But to see the victims of such extravagant murder – even
if it did form part of a broader picture of warfare – made him

nauseous with fear. He knew he would be a target, but *what* a target he presented: white breeches, black coat with its white facings, silver frogging and polished pewter buttons, his black tricorn with its red, yellow and blue pompoms. So much of what he carried was valuable: his pistol and sabre and waxed greatcoat, his leather haversack filled with powder cartridges and food and a few scant personal effects. Even he himself was useful. He carried information in his brain, letters and orders from the officers in Maretsburg and Slavomire, and he was an officer and so could be ransomed. He would pass as neither frontiersman nor native. He was as conspicuous as it was possible to be, with no option for subterfuge, and useful as a corpse or a hostage to a great many people. The thought soured his guts and made him want to fold in on himself.

He followed his guide through the Alda River Valley. This was a broad, fractured country of some thirty thousand square miles, split down the middle by the Line of Demarcation, a boundary that had been established years before between the colonial settlers of Sova and those of Casimir and its client state, Sanque. The latter nation directly abutted the river valley to the west and funnelled a steady supply of men and arms into the basin. Only the proxy war that Sova and Casimir were fighting in the land of the wolfmen – the Kyarai – was preventing the valley from becoming one huge battlefield.

This was a place of treacherous mountain slopes and passes, of thick pine forests, of impenetrable clouds of rolling fog, of endless rain, of wolves and bears and sabrecats and tenacious, doughty natives. It was also a place of great natural wealth: endless timber for the Imperial Sovan Navy and for the furnaces of industry; furs, fish and meat, whalebone and oil; and if the latest surveys were to be believed, great seams of coal and iron ore, too. Sovan colonies to the east – Tajanastadt, Maretsburg, Linasburg, Valerija and Davorstadt – were already on the verge of self-sustaining, trading endlessly with the Kyarai and the Sovan Empire in return for manufactured goods. If the river valley could be tamed, then Sova could lay claim to one contiguous stretch of territory around the entire northern seaboard of the Jade Sea.

Peter was not filled with confidence. If Sova's war in the Kyarai failed – and it increasingly looked like it would – then thousands of Casimirs would be diverted north. The valley would be entirely invested with the enemy, mere weeks after his arrival. The timing could not have been less auspicious.

After several hours, they reached the outermost parts of Fort Ingomar. The fort itself was situated on Aldaney Island, a large piece of land which briefly parted the River Alda before it rejoined and flowed out into the Stygion Sea. The bridge was guarded, though he had no trouble passing through. From there he saw that the island had been largely cleared of undergrowth to create a long, sloped glacis thick with grass; the trees had been cut down for stakes and permanent structures within the walls.

Fort Ingomar was an outwardly impressive place. It was surrounded by an earthen redoubt impregnated with sharpened stakes, which preceded a ditch; and behind that rose the scarp, a sloped wall twenty feet high which had been revetted with stone. The scarp was itself crowned by a parapet twelve feet deep; behind it, standing on the banquette, he could see Sovan soldiers watching him approach. Cannons, eight-pounders, were mounted at embrasures cut into the parapet, too. In the centre of the fort were several buildings – quarters, a powder magazine, stabling for the mules, an infirmary and a storehouse.

The men and women here were a miserable bunch. They made the most minimal obeisance to him as he moved through the fort. Those who were not patrolling the walls were sitting on the rain-skinned stone of the marshalling yard, hunched in their waxed greatcoats. Many of them were drinking, their faces grey and gaunt. It seemed that the dress code, something Peter had been given to believe was inviolable, held little sway here; their uniforms were the subject of many modifications and idiosyncrasies, to say nothing of the men's beards.

After finding out where the commanding officer was quartered, Peter made his way quickly to the man's office, which lay at the corner of one of the larger of the fort's buildings. The man in question was Major Haak, a Southern Plainsman from the look of him – for his skin was the colour of mahogany – and when he spoke, Zyrahn and Saxan accents battled each other for control of his voice. He spent a long time finishing off a piece of correspondence before he addressed Peter.

"So. Colonial Command has sent you here to take the place of Captain Hulderic," he said in a rumbling basso, with neither preamble nor eye contact. "Yet you are not a captain."

Peter felt his stomach drop. His orders had been to report to Fort Ingomar, nothing more. He had no idea he was filling a dead man's shoes – a captain's shoes, at that.

"Sir, I . . . On the way here . . ." he began, gabbling as though he had a hot coin in his mouth.

"Stop. Start again."

Peter started again. "En route, sir, the guide and I came across the bodies of four Sovan men."

Haak looked at him sharply. Immediately he was tense. "Where? When?" he demanded.

"I . . . uh . . ." Peter thought for a moment, trying to trace the route they had taken through the unfamiliar country. "Perhaps halfway between Fort Romauld and the river, just before we left the trail behind. A good couple of hours of hard going. Forgive me, sir, I am unaccustomed to—"

"What was the state of the bodies? Describe it to me."

Peter searched his mind for the right words. Haak's attention was like a physical force. It took him a great deal of effort not to wilt under the man's gaze. "They had been violently dismembered."

Haak thought for a moment. "It will be Kristo." He took a deep breath, and sighed. "I *told* him not to go so far, damn him." He looked up at Peter. "Did you search them for any effects?"

"Yes," Peter said, relieved that he had. He fumbled in his haversack, produced the things he had taken. The major examined them for a quiet minute. He muttered a couple more names which Peter didn't catch.

"Describe to me the wounds," he said quietly, rolling a blood-stained locket between his thumb and forefinger.

Peter thought back to the bodies he had seen. He tried to think of them like barber-surgeon's cadavers, or like detailed drawings from an anatomical textbook – anything but living, breathing men with names and widows and bereaved children. "Like great . . . rents. Each man was decapitated, or near enough. Their necks and chests were laid open and their clothing was torn. It looked for all the world like a wild animal attack, but for a creature to have bested four armed men is—"

"Unthinkable." Haak stood and turned and looked out of the window behind him, lost in thought. Beyond the panes the weather had closed in. Fresh rain pattered against the glass. "This is a difficult country, Mister Kleist," he said eventually.

"I have heard so, sir."

Haak shook his head, but he did not turn around. "I am not talking about the Sanques, nor the Casimirs, nor even the pagans."

There was another long, uncomfortable silence.

"What *are* you talking about, sir?"

Haak clacked his tongue. He did not answer the question. "It is too late to go now. And the forest . . . It is best to avoid it after dark." He turned back to Peter. Then he opened his desk drawer and pulled out two small crystal tumblers and a bottle of brandy that was two thirds empty. He poured them both a generous measure, and Peter accepted the proffered glass not with gratitude but with trepidation. "You are to mount an expedition at dawn. Take ten from the light company. Bring the bodies back here." He pulled out a map, folded and well worn, and handed it to Peter, who accepted it like one might accept his own death warrant. "Do you understand?"

Peter's stomach felt as though someone had filled it with a cupful of molten copper. The very last thing he wanted to do was venture out into the woods again, though he had enough of his wits about him to accept this mission with silence.

"What . . . Do you have any sense of the . . . " He paused, trying to think of the right words. "What killed them, sir? A bear? Or wolves?" But it could not have been, he knew that. Bears and wolves did not impale decapitated heads on poles.

Haak drained his brandy. "Here in the New East, we have two enemies."

"Two enemies, sir? As in the armies of Casimir and Sanque?"

The major shook his head. "No. I mean the armies of Casimir and Sanque in one hand, and . . . something else entirely in the other."

Peter felt his throat tighten. "Sir, if I may beg your pardon, please speak plainly with me. What is going on here?"

But Haak just smiled a smile that was part sadness, part derangement. "If you can answer that question, Lieutenant, you will be a popular man."

It was an unhappy evening. Peter felt the eyes of every man and woman in that place on him as Haak's aide, one of the company ensigns, escorted him from the major's office and showed him around the rest of the fort.

The soldiers watched him from the banquettes, from the marshalling yard, from the windows of the barracks, the quartermaster's store, the infirmary and the stables. He fancied their eyes gleamed like an alley cat's caught in the light of a brazier. They were a surly, intractable mob, who offered him little of the deference he was entitled to as an officer. He battled constantly with himself as to whether he should remonstrate with some of the more obviously disrespectful, but it seemed ill-advised. He doubted he'd be able to lead these people in parade drill, let alone into combat.

He deposited his meagre possessions in his quarters and then made his way to a tiny common room which doubled as a mess. It was a far cry from the banqueting hall at the regimental head-quarters in Badenburg; this was a small, basic chamber, ten feet to a side and with no concession to ornament. There was one trestle table, and he sat at it tentatively. No one, not even Haak's aide, had explained the eating arrangements to him.

Eventually a large, moustachioed man entered. He smelt of powder and damp, and his greatcoat was wet and mildewed. From his uniform he had to be Captain Furlan, the commander of the small artillery detachment that manned the fort's eight-pounders.

"You are wet," he said gruffly. He dumped a small cloth parcel on the table, which turned out to contain some mutton and bread.

Peter blinked a few times. "Yes, sir."

"Soaked through. To the bone."

Peter examined himself. He was indeed wet through.

"It rains here, a lot. It is more or less constant. Wet men become sick men."

"Yes, sir."

"Forget the dress regulations." Furlan pointed a gloved finger at him. "If it rains, put on your coat. If you get too hot – and you will, in summer – you may remove your jacket."

"Yes, sir."

"You must also take extra care of your powder. The men have learnt the hard way. Even when it is not raining, it is damp and will degrade. Do you have a horn?"

Peter did indeed have an engraved powder horn, a gift from his brothers in anticipation of his promotion to lieutenant. It could be used to efficiently add more powder to the priming pan without tearing into a new cartridge and so – hopefully – ignite the damp gunpowder in the barrel. He hated the horn because it had the badge of his old regiment inscribed on it – that of the Imperial 2nd Legion, one of the prestigious Guards regiments headquartered in the capital. He had transferred to the 166th Badenburg once it had become clear that his father would not be able to afford his lieutenancy there.

Furlan grunted his approval. He took a long draw from a flask which by the smell of it contained almost neat brandy. There was a long silence. Eventually he said, "There is no one here to wait on you. If you want food, you'll have to fetch it yourself from the store."

"I'm not very hungry," Peter lied.

"So, what? You thought to sit in here alone and do nothing?"

There was another silence in which Peter felt acutely embarrassed.

Eventually Furlan took a bite of bread and grumbled, through his mouthful, "How was your journey here?"

"Long."

"Hm. We are a long way from Sova. A long way. I have heard about you. You have come from the Legions?"

"The 2nd."

"You were the standard bearer during your ensignship?"

"Yes, sir."

"And then you transferred to the regiment at Badenburg?"

"Sir."

"For want of funds?"

Peter stopped himself from gritting his teeth. It was a source of deep shame for him and his family. "Yes, sir."

"And you were stationed there?"

"For a long time, yes, sir. I was supposed to join Captain Braddock at Davorstadt, but by the time the orders came through, the battalion was already coming home."

"And so you ended up here."

"Yes, sir."

"Poor bastard."

Peter couldn't tell whether the man was joking, and smiled weakly.

Furlan sighed. "May I give you a piece of advice, Lieutenant?"

"By all means."

"This is a difficult country. A difficult country with a difficult enemy. You will see strange things, hear strange noises. Some of them will frighten and disturb you. You must keep your wits about you, yes? Especially in front of the men. We need strong leadership." He tapped his own chest. "Hearts of iron."

Peter managed to nod, though he was not sure he managed to conceal just how uneasy these words had made him. He was frightened enough simply to face a regular human enemy. Now here he was, and all the officers were doing little except lend credence to the silly rumours and gossip which bedevilled postings to the colonies – talk of drudes and demons, forest sprites and bog witches. Many were convinced the mountain tribesman could shapeshift, which struck Peter as complete nonsense. Why be afraid of what was plainly untrue when the truth was frightening enough?

"Might I ask a question, sir?"

"I don't know, might you?"

"Where are the rest of the men? I had expected to see a battalion—"

He stopped as Furlan let out a choking, rumbling sound which rattled in his lungs and turned out to be laughter.

"I know not what you heard from the colonial bumpkins in Slavomire, Kleist, but we barely have a brace of companies to rub together, nor the powder to sustain them. You'd do well to wring two hundred fighting men from this place. We had the bloody cooks standing-to last month."

Peter did his best to keep his composure, but his expression must have betrayed him, for Furlan clapped him on the shoulder.

"Don't look so glum. You'll be all right. Here, I shall give you one last piece of advice."

"Sir?"

"You will find sleeping here difficult. Try wadding your ears with cloth, or wax. And drink helps."

"Why will sleep be difficult?"

"You'll see." Furlan chuckled darkly, patting him on the shoulder again. Then he gathered up the remains of his dinner and left.

Peter retired to his own quarters shortly afterwards, his stomach growling. Around him the fort felt eerily quiet. At any given time, one of the companies would be off rotation, foraging for food, chopping wood, preparing meals, repairing the fortress, mending their uniforms, et cetera. But there was nothing, not even low voices and the rattle of dice against stone. All this activity, if it was happening at all, was happening in silence.

With Furlan's cryptic advice still ringing in his ears, and thoughts of his impending expedition back to the site of the bodies souring his guts, the last thing he wanted to do was sleep. But after such a long journey, exhaustion prevailed. He undressed and hung his clothes in the wardrobe by the light of a single candle, and then extinguished it and climbed into bed.

It was too cloudy for moonlight, and rain still pattered against the walls and roof. He felt profoundly homesick, and pressed the pillow over his face, preparing to quietly weep at this incredible stroke of misfortune.

Then he heard a scream.

"Nema Victoria," he breathed, his heart racing. The scream had sounded far away, emanating from somewhere in the depths of the woods. It was not a human scream – more like a fox or a wolf – but there was enough of a human quality to it to make it a frightening, wretched sound.

He went to the window, but he could see nothing; just the dark shapes of the soldiers huddled in their greatcoats at the parapet, or drinking and gambling quietly in the marshalling yard. A couple of the Qareshians were bent forward in Inalabric prayer, murmuring quietly. Either no one else had heard the scream, or no one was troubled by it.

He returned to his bed uneasily, trying to convince himself that what he had heard was simply an animal cry. But perhaps fifteen or twenty minutes later, just as he was drifting off, the scream came once more, and then the sound of weeping.

He sat up sharply, straining to hear. There it was again! The unmistakable sound of a person crying. The scream he might have fooled himself into thinking was the mating cry of a fox, or the screech of an owl, but not the weeping. Only people wept.

He swung his legs out of bed and walked quickly to the door, pulling it open. But there was no one in the passageway, nor had opening the door made any difference to the clarity and volume of the sound.

He stood peering into the dark and cold corridor for a long time; then, profoundly uneasy, he closed the door and returned to his bed.

"Good gods!" he cried as another scream ripped through the night, and then more crying, now from multiple people, overlapping wailing, snivelling, sobbing. Sometimes it was loud, other times barely perceptible. But it was constant, that mad, sourceless weeping.

Nerves. A fit of the nerves. Not enough food, too much to drink, and poor moral fibre, he decided. The pillow over his head made no difference at all, and so, mindful of Captain Furlan's advice, he took some of the warm, malleable wax from his candle and moulded it into two earplugs.

They blocked out some of the sound, but not all of it.

He was roused at dawn after a dreadful and fearful night's sleep. He looked out of the window to see a wet green and grey landscape wreathed in mist. His heart sank. Finding his way back to the bodies would have been difficult enough without this inclement weather.

He dressed into his uniform and, remembering Furlan's injunction, donned his waxed greatcoat too. Even though he felt slightly too warm, he dared not remove his jacket in spite of the captain's permission.

He strapped on his sabre and pistol, affixed his tricorn, and then made his way outside, stopping briefly by the storeroom to snatch a fist-sized hunk of sourdough. In the marshalling yard in the centre of the fort, a group of ten men and women from the fort's light company had assembled. He was pleased that he had not had to choose, although he felt as though that task should nonetheless have fallen to him.

He cleared his throat. The soldiers eyed him unkindly, though they touched their foreheads in salute. Almost all of them looked older than him, some significantly so. They appeared gaunt and hard-bitten, the men's faces shadowed with stubble and impermissible beards and moustaches. Some of them would have been here in the colonies for years, whilst thousands of miles away their children grew into adults and their husbands and wives quietly laboured in their absence, their only connexion to these distant spouses their wage packets.

"I am Lieutenant Peter Kleist," he said. His voice carried none of the effortless authority of Haak and Furlan. "On my way here yesterday I discovered the bodies of four men about half a day due east. Major Haak has tasked us with locating the corpses so that we may divine the nature of their demise and recover them." He pulled the map that Haak had given him from his greatcoat pocket and unfolded it. "Around here, I would say," he said, tapping the location.

"The *nature* of their demise?" one of the men said with incredulity. The rest murmured their agreement. Peter was sure he heard one of them mutter the word "demon".

"What is your name?" he demanded of the man in a sudden fit of courage.

The soldier shifted on his feet, but answered. "Schuhart."

"Sir."

"Schuhart, sir."

"You have an opinion you would like to share?"

"No, sir."

"I did not address you."

"No, sir," the man said, insouciant.

Peter gritted his teeth. He hoped desperately that he was not going to be forced to discipline them. "The bodies were found off the trail between Ingomar and Romauld. If we make for the latter, I should be able to retrace my steps. I'm unfamiliar with the country here; does anyone here know the best route?"

For an excruciating few seconds he was worried that no one would answer; then, eventually, another man put his hand up.

"Right then. You can lead us."

The man managed to touch the rim of his tricorn in silent acknowledgement. It was becoming increasingly clear that the soldiers' surliness was not entirely down to their dislike of Peter; they truly did not want to venture beyond the fortress walls. He wondered if they had heard the screaming and crying the night before, too. Perhaps it had plagued them over the course of months. One night of it was intolerable; a year of it would unravel a person's mind.

He looked up; above, dark clouds gathered.

"All right. Let's get on with it, shall we?"

Picking their way through the forest was long and arduous; and yet, if he had not been feeling so uneasy, Peter might have enjoyed the scenery. The valley was beautiful, filled with great escarpments of moss-covered grey rock and rolling forests of pine. Ferns and wildflowers covered the forest floor in a riot of colour: foxgloves, wild lilies, the dark purple leaves of hanged man's tongue. The constant babbling of streams and the roar of distant waterfalls filled the air alongside the song of sparrows and larks and the occasional shriek of an eagle. The place reminded him of the landscape in Wolfenshut, the margraviate to the west of Sova, which had long been the playground for wealthy Sovan nobles and their extravagant hunts. The thought stoked the fires of his homesickness.

As Furlan had warned, rain pattered down constantly. Peter worried about their powder more than anything, though everyone had stowed their cartridges in such a way that they were well sheltered. As for the soldiers themselves, they moved steadily through the undergrowth, seemingly untroubled by the many obstacles in their path. Peter slipped on wet moss constantly, or found his tricorn knocked off by low-hanging branches, or his scabbard or the strap of his haversack becoming ensnared in the undergrowth.

It was late morning by the time he picked up the route he recognised from the day before. Here was the westernmost part of the rocky escarpment which he and the guide had clambered down perhaps three or four miles further east. He examined the map briefly.

"We'll follow the line of this crest," he said, folding the map away and taking on some water from his flask. Everyone else seemed to be drinking watered wine or brandy. He pointed to where the escarpment tapered off into a steep but traversable hill carpeted in ferns. "A few miles to go, then I think we shall be there."

No one said anything. The soldiers drank too, and then they continued on wordlessly.

They found it. It was a little further on than Peter had thought, several hours of hiking. They only picked it up because someone spotted the mule tracks from the day before, and they doubled back until the tracks stopped. Already the place seemed gloomy and unfamiliar, but one of the men descended to check it out.

"Do you see anything?" Peter called out.

Everyone rounded on him angrily.

"Nema Victoria, be quiet!" hissed the nearest soldier. "Sir," she added.

Peter cursed himself a thousand times. Suddenly the forced silence made complete sense. It was nothing to do with them being churlish; it was about *stealth*. Even though all the maps proclaimed this half of the Alda River Valley a Sovan possession, it did not mean it was not rife with interlopers. The bodies themselves were testament to that. And here he was, a new officer in a new country, shouting like an idiot. He might as well have sent up a bugle call.

He managed to resist the urge to apologise – to admit fault as an officer was unthinkable – and instead began to descend. "You two, stay here and watch our rear," he ordered the closest two soldiers, which seemed like a sensible instruction.

He reached the bodies after several minutes of clumsy scrabbling down the hill. Those whom he had not ordered to stay joined him in the clearing. The site had not changed from the day before, though some of the bodies had been disturbed by wild animals.

Peter affected not to be troubled by the gruesome spectacle, though he felt light-headed at the sight, and crouched down next to the nearest headless corpse. "What happened here?"

He looked up at a tapping sound, and saw that one of the men was thrumming a long, straight pole which was sticking rigidly out of the trunk of a tree. "Ramrod," the man said quietly.

Another soldier picked up the musket of the corpse next to Peter, and examined the hand that gripped it. It was blackened like a coal miner's, the fingernails torn and ragged. "Too much powder." He cocked the hammer and pulled back the frizzen to expose the pan. The whole mechanism was fouled with tremendous quantities of powder. "Far too much." He removed the flint, blew the powder away, and fired off the action; then he tested the weight. "Must be at least three balls in there."

"Here. Look at this."

Everyone turned to the soldier who had spoken. She stood at the far end of the clearing, holding a musket which had been cleaved almost in two. The lock was blown clean off and the barrel was bent free from the splintered stock; the soldier pulled out from the broken end several charred wads.

"Can one of you explain the significance of this?" Peter asked. Clearly no one was going to volunteer the information.

"They were scared shitless, sir," the man nearest him said.

"Aye, and who could blame them?" another responded.

"Please elaborate," Peter said patiently.

"One of them accidentally shot his ramrod. At least two of them overstuffed the barrels. Loaded, fired, nothing happened, re-primed, loaded again, and so on. Two, three times? These were not men thinking clearly. This man has spilled enough powder to fire an eight-pounder."

Peter thought of the four men frantically ramming home wadding and musket balls one after the other into a barrel that was already jammed up, trying desperately to shoot at an enemy they couldn't see. What had done this? What had frightened them so much that they had lost their wits?

"Here we go," the far-away soldier said. She picked up a third musket, and Peter saw that it was a burned, splintered ruin where the overcharged barrel had finally touched off and exploded. The woman dropped it to the floor.

There was a long silence as all of them considered what horror had taken place here. Peter looked up at the sky to where the sun had disappeared behind the clouds once more. It was going to be a wet, gloomy afternoon.

"What is out there?" he asked quietly. "What did this?"

"If you can answer that question, sir, you'll be a popular man," the nearest soldier said, parroting Haak's words from the day before.

Peter gritted his teeth. "Collect the bodies. Let's get back before we lose the light."

He examined the trees around them. He could not shake the feeling that they were being watched.

III

A Most
Extraordinary Tale

*"Truth is found at the bottom of the brandy
glass and the top of the scaffold."*

SOVAN PROVERB

Creusgate Magazine

SOVA

Renata lived in a small rooftop apartment in the lee of the redundant Guelan Wall. It had once been fifty feet high; now, like
much of the rest of the fortifications which surrounded the old
city, it had been significantly reduced, its stone salvaged for other
construction projects.

To the north of her was the Creusgate Magazine, an army
logistics hub which looked out over the city's western approaches,
whilst to the east was the fischmarkt, an enormous seafood
market which filled the air with its brackish scent – reek, if she
was feeling uncharitable – something that seemed somehow
appropriate given her line of work. It was a noisy, bustling and

relaxed precinct, filled with artists and poets united in their disdain for Imperial Sova and its expansionist politics.

She fetched a pail from the apartment and returned to the street pump for water – just in time, too, for a long queue was already forming behind her. She filled it quickly, paranoid that Alistair would see her in the street, and then returned upstairs. From the windows in her apartment she could see over the Guelan Wall to where a vast tangle of houses and residential apartment blocks stretched into the distance, filling the late-afternoon sky with chimney smoke. There was something so . . . *alluring* about Sova. Many decried it as an overlarge, overstuffed city, one filled with cut-throats and thieves, frequently the subject of riot and disease. But for Renata, there was nowhere else in the world she would rather be. Many of the things other people hated about it were the things she loved. It was a melting pot of civilisations, the trading nexus of the known world, a place where anyone could be and do anything.

She made herself a cup of tea and cut a thick slice of fruit bread, and sat in the drawing room, allowing her thoughts to wander. A part of her still detested those obnoxious man-children from the Imperial Office who had made fun of her – *her*, and not the ambassador, whom they would not dare offend; and yet another part of her knew that there was a kernel of truth to their mockery. She had never seen a Stygion. She could speak and sign their language – Loxica – but had only ever laid eyes on sketches and drawings. She had been trained in their ways, but they were enigmatic and savage and reclusive, and surfaced only to attack Sovan whaling ships. Even Maruska did not know more than the scholars at the University. His practical knowledge was based on several fleeting diplomatic missions, and there was little scope to expand their relationship. The mer-men were not a serious trading partner. The only thing they could really lay claim to were cuts of meat and bone from whales and sharks and herring dogs, and they did not want to give those up for any price. They prized pearls as much as humans did, but Sovan oystermen did not barter for those; they took them at will, and even clubbed and shot at the Stygion who tried to stop them.

No, there was something quite ridiculous about the Stygion Office. And that was what cut her. It was not that the other diplomats were cruel; it was that they were *right*.

She tossed the fruit bread back down on to the plate, disgusted with herself. It was much too early to turn in, otherwise she might have been tempted to simply go to sleep and write the rest of the day off as a failure. There was a pile of Alistair's verse on the table, which she idly leafed through, but she found it embarrassing – much of it was about her – and overwrought, and couldn't bring herself to read it. Instead she spent the balance of the day reading through some diplomatic treatise from the University, until even the candles in her apartment were not enough to stave off the gloom. Then she prepared herself for sleep, and climbed into bed.

She had barely closed her eyes when there came a violent pounding at the door. Such was her shock that she actually cried out; then, when the pounding continued, she climbed out of bed and put on a robe, and approached the front door.

"Who is it?" she demanded. She cast about the place for a makeshift weapon, and decided that one of the fireplace pokers would do should it come to it.

"Secretary Rainer!" a gruff voice shouted. "Open this door in the name of the Empress!"

"Who is it?" she snapped again, annoyed. "It's after dark and I'm not expecting anyone."

There was an audible sigh from beyond the threshold. Between them was a stout oak door with several locks; it would take a very determined intruder to gain access.

"Sergeant Engilram, ma'am. You were summoned this afternoon to attend Colonel Glaser of the 1st Sovan Legion."

"I . . . what?"

"I need not tell you, ma'am, that in spite of your position, ignoring an Imperial summons is a *crime*."

Renata swore loudly and yanked the door open. Before her was a burly sergeant, red-faced from his ascension to the top floor. But he was no ordinary soldier; he was from the 1st Sovan Legion, the so-called "Imperial Life Guards", the foremost of the élite Guards regiments headquartered in the capital. Even Renata, ignorant as she was of matters martial, recognised the man's white coat with its royal-blue facings.

"The letter for the ambassador? From the messenger boy? That was real?"

"I'm afraid so, ma'am. You have been expected for several hours now."

"Nema Victoria," Renata muttered, suddenly feeling ill. "I thought it was a joke."

The sergeant's features creased in confusion. "Why would you think that?"

Renata waved him off. "I need to get dressed," she said.

"Quickly—" Engilram started, but she slammed the door in his face.

In spite of the late hour, the streets of the capital were still thronged with people. She followed Engilram outside, to where there was a collection of six or seven soldiers waiting by the street pump, each armed with a musket. In this part of the city, sandwiched between bohemian Creusgate and the academic quarter – for just across the Klaran Road was the University – they were a very unwelcome sight indeed. Those still out and about jeered and decried them as blackcoats and warmongers, though none were so bold as to test themselves against the soldiers' bayonets.

Renata found herself being whisked through the dark, rain-glossed streets. They travelled briskly down the Sofijan Highway past the fischmarkt, where sellers tried desperately to hawk the last of their stocks as their ice melted and the fish began to ripen in the warm night air; then they turned due east down the Creus Road. As they crossed over the main branch of the Sauber, the Imperial Palace hove into view. It was a colossal structure, an enormous obsidian-dark pyramid rendered in old Saxan gothick, an architectural tradition which had been since supplanted by the baroque style. Sova had once been a place of magick, centuries before, and some of the enormous structures in the capital owed their size not to the wit of masons but to the arcane abilities of sorcerers. But magick had long since been outlawed, and only the Corps of Engineers had been made privy to certain thaumaturgical practices which enabled them to maintain the runes and sigils holding these colossi aloft.

The Imperial Life Guards were barracked by the Old East Battery at Sungate, in and amongst the great organs of state. Engilram took her quickly inside, and eventually to an office on the north-eastern corner. He knocked quietly on the door, and heard from inside "Enter!" and they did.

Beyond the threshold was a large chamber, well appointed with all the martial bric-a-brac Renata would have expected: busts, oil paintings, the regimental colours. Sitting at a desk in front of the large windows – they afforded little in the way of view except for the facade of the Imperial Institute for the Scientific Arts – was Colonel Glaser himself.

"Aha," he said as he laid eyes on her. He was perhaps fifty or so, white-skinned, his hair thick but greying. He wore a more ostentatious version of the uniform Sergeant Engilram wore, and a less ostentatious version of Sergeant Engilram's moustache. "The fabled secretary."

Renata inclined her head. "Colonel Glaser," she said, politely, professionally. "You must excuse me—"

"It is no matter. We already had the hen." He gestured to Maruska, who was sitting in front of Glaser at the desk. "Now we have her egg."

"And should the egg take a seat?" Renata asked gamely.

Glaser laughed, surprising himself. "Very good, madam. Please."

She took a seat as bade. She caught Maruska's eye, and though he did not seem to be annoyed with her directly, something was clearly troubling him.

"I have already spoken to His Excellency here on the nature of our problem, and I am not in the habit of repeating myself," Glaser said. Renata inclined her head; she believed him. "But since I now have the full brace of Stygion diplomats, I shall give you the précis ahead of the second part of our meeting."

"Thank you, Colonel. I'm grateful," Renata said, feeling her pulse quicken. She was about to add some humorous addendum, but it seemed that the mood had shifted, and levity was now inappropriate.

Glaser drew in a deep breath, and released it. "This morning, two men presented themselves to the Royal Petitioner. They were Neman monks of one sort or another, and most peculiar fellows. They insisted on meeting the Empress, which of course was impossible."

"Of course."

"Over the course of the day they found themselves in front of, among others, myself, as a member of a committee of the Privy Council. We were discussing the impending failure of our efforts in the northern Kyarai." Glaser's expression curdled into one of distaste. "It was decided, for reasons beyond my grasp, that we were the best placed to listen to their entreaties."

"What did they say?" Renata asked.

"They gave a most extraordinary tale," Glaser said. "They hail from an old fortress in the south called Zetland, in the very southernmost part of the Prinzpatriate of Reichsgard. I know the region, of course, and the fortress's historic significance, but I'm not directly familiar with it."

"It is just over the border from Qasr Qaresh," Maruska said. "An old Sovan Templar fortress, at least partly in ruin."

"And yet, apparently inhabited. The men belong to a religious sect called the 'Bruta Sarkan'. A spiritual successor to the Templar order, but with no mandate and *certainly* no martial capability."

"Surely the *raison d'être* of the Templars," Renata said.

"Quite. Though precisely who they would make war on escapes me. After all, we are firm friends with the Qareshians, are we not, Ambassador?"

Maruska inclined his head. "I like to think so, Colonel."

Glaser steepled his fingers. "Whatever the state of their lodgings, the monks brought with them some most unwelcome news, the first part of which was that, pursuant to their particular and peculiar brand of Nemanism, they practise the art of séance."

Renata considered this carefully. "Séance is illegal," she said eventually.

"It is," Colonel Glaser agreed. "And for a very good reason."

He did not need to say why. The attempt by a rogue army of Templars to overthrow the then Emperor using stolen magicks was a well-known episode in Sova's mediaeval history. The attack had been thwarted after a costly battle in the capital, and had resulted in the prohibition of all magickal practice – and particularly the arts of séance and necromancy – across the Empire. Now, two hundred years later, only a small cadre of individuals in the Corps of Engineers were permitted access to the ancient sorceries, to examine their scientific applications. As for any interaction with the afterlife, such was strictly forbidden.

"But they have been doing it nonetheless," Renata said. Unlike most Sovans, who were unfamiliar with, and afraid of, the arcana, Renata was more ambivalent. The Stygion, after all, routinely practised magick.

"They have."

"Are they to be shot?"

"They may yet be."

"Yet they came," Maruska said. "They came knowing that they could be executed, and informed you anyway. That surely speaks to the credibility of their claims."

"And what precisely *are* their claims?" Renata asked.

"Well, now we get to the nub of it," Glaser said. "For the last two hundred years, these monks have been conversing with the spirits of the dead, along with the other creatures of the afterlife – sprites, angels, demons, et cetera. I know not the taxonomy of these things, nor is it permitted for me to know."

"But something has gone awry with the practice," Maruska prompted.

"Indeed. The monks speak of an old prophecy known as the 'Great Silence'. It certainly does not form part of the Nema Victorian orthodoxy that I am aware of."

"It sounds like Conformism," Renata said warily.

"For what it's worth, I agree with you," Glaser said. "I'm not sure the monks themselves see it in those terms, but it is all beside the point. The point *is*, this prophecy postulates that one day the afterlife will fall silent. The spirits, the angels and so on will all vanish." He shrugged. "It is supposed to herald the End of Days."

"Blimey," Renata said.

"May I?" Maruska asked, gesturing to Glaser with his pipe.

"Yes, yes," the colonel said, waving him away.

Maruska packed it, and Colonel Glaser pulled out his own pipe and did the same, and then leant forward and lit both of them with a match. Smoke quickly filled the chamber, and Glaser idly pushed one of the windows behind him open.

"What precisely *is* the Great Silence?" Renata asked.

"The monks do not know. What they *do* know is that up until a few weeks ago they were able to speak to the dead, and now they cannot. It has all . . . gone quiet."

"Silent, even," Maruska said.

Glaser looked at him pointedly. "Indeed."

Renata thought a moment. "Well, that is certainly very interesting, Colonel. What I do not fully yet grasp is where His Excellency and I fit in to this."

"That brings me neatly to the second part of this meeting," Glaser said. "Excuse me a moment."

He stood and walked over to a section of wall to the left, and pressed a concealed switch. A hidden doorway popped open, and Renata exchanged a brief glance with Maruska.

"Impressive," she said quietly.

"I'll say."

Glaser returned a moment later with the two monks. One was older, perhaps the same age as Maruska, whilst the younger one was probably the same age as Renata – an amusing mirror-image of the two of them. The older one was fatter, grey-haired, and wore a white habit and surcoat embroidered with a black cross, whilst the younger was olive-skinned and dark-haired – likely Grozodan – and his clothes consisted of a simple dark brown robe. Both had tonsured hair and a diffident air about them – possibly the result of the death sentence they now faced.

"This is Brother Herschel," Glaser said, gesturing to the older man, "and this is Brother Guillot." Now he turned to the two diplomats. "This is His Excellency Didacus Maruska, and his deputy ambassador, Secretary Renata Rainer." The monks, who seemed to be very much out of their depth, bowed low. Maruska and Renata inclined their heads in reciprocation.

"I have given them the skin of it," Glaser said to Herschel and Guillot. "What we want to know now is what you need Stygion ambassadors for."

For a moment it seemed as though neither man would say anything at all. They looked like a pair of nervous students who had been asked to give a presentation. Renata smiled in an encouraging way, and eventually Herschel said, "If you will indulge me, Colonel, it will be easier if I—"

"Just get on with it, man. We have indulged you this far."

Herschel wilted, but nonetheless found his voice. "We have struggled to discover precisely what the Great Silence is," he said, clearing his throat several times in successive efforts to speak louder. "Those volumes which would have been written on the subject are likely to have been lost in a fire which gutted the library in Keraq some centuries ago."

"Why don't you tell us what it is you *do* know?" Glaser said with a hint of impatience.

"What we *do* know is that the Great Silence is either the extinction of every spiritual force in the afterlife, or a mass relocation to some deeper plane unreachable to us. Either of these eventualities suggests the interference of a third, uh, entity."

"You are saying that they are either being killed by something or running away from something?" Renata asked.

"Precisely."

"What are they running away from?" Glaser asked. "Or being killed by?"

"We do not know."

"Then how have you arrived at this conclusion?"

"Because the spirits themselves have made no mention of any such abdication or upheaval. We must believe that their sudden extinguishment was born either of surprise or calamity – or indeed, both."

"Why do you know about it?" Maruska asked.

"What do you mean?"

"I mean, why do *you* have knowledge of this? And why did the spirits not know of it and prepare accordingly?"

"That's an excellent question," Glaser said, turning back to the monks.

Herschel looked uncomfortable. "You must understand, Excellency, that the Neman Creed is full of these sorts of prophecies. The Prophecies of Zabriel, for example, form an apocrypha which is explicitly rejected by the Victorian Orthodoxy."

"So you *are* Conformists?" Renata asked.

"We are not Conformists. We are not religious at all, at least, not in that sense."

"You are monks, though?"

"It is you called us monks. We do not refer to ourselves as such."

"Let us not debate nomenclature," Glaser said.

Herschel cleared his throat yet again. "In answer to your question, Excellency, I could point you in the direction of a dozen such prophecies. The older volumes of the Creed are full of them."

"I see. And so, as each has failed to reach fruition, they have been disregarded accordingly," Maruska said.

"Correct."

"And you believe, in the event, erroneously."

"Certainly in the present instance."

"And – forgive the question – you are certain it is not your *methods* which are at fault?"

Herschel shook his head, though he seemed not the least bit offended. "The rituals have remained the same for centuries. We are very adept at the practice. We have changed nothing."

"Perhaps therein lies the issue?"

Again the man shook his head. "We do not believe that to be the case."

"Have you considered the possibility that the spirits are no longer interested in speaking with you?" Renata asked. She kept her tone light, so as not to offend them.

Herschel actually chuckled. "Every time we conduct a séance, Madam Secretary, the difficulty is not in finding a willing participant, but in cutting through the clamour. We have never wanted for conversation."

"What is it all in aid of?" Renata asked.

"What do you mean?"

"I mean, why do you speak with them?" *If indeed you do,* she might have added.

"Would you not, given the opportunity?" Herschel asked gently. "The chance to speak to a deceased loved one, or a figure from ancient history, or an elemental being?"

There was a pause. Renata didn't know what to think. She knew that the afterlife was a real place where one's life essence travelled; the weight and breadth of historic record and the modern practice of magick – albeit in a limited form – was testament to that. And besides, she herself might have been a rare sight in temple, but she was a practising Neman. Her faith obliged her to believe in it, even if nothing else did.

Even so, it was all so far removed from her daily life that it felt too abstract to be compelling. It was like hearing about some catastrophe in a country on the other side of the world; she had no trouble in accepting the truth of it, but it was not something that would affect her daily dealings.

As though Herschel could read her thoughts, he said, "Colonel, please. I know that it all sounds far-fetched to you . . ."

"Something of an understatement."

" . . . but we would not have come here, knowing our lives would be forfeit, if we did not think it was a matter of the utmost urgency. This does not concern just the Bruta Sarkan; it concerns every man, woman and child on this earth, human and otherwise. What affects the afterlife inevitably affects the mortal plane."

"Let us at least hear your proposal," Renata said, heading off Glaser, who looked as though he were about to shoot the pair.

"Of course," Herschel said, sensing, probably correctly, that he had more of an ally in Renata than Glaser. "As we all know, there are several other practitioners of the magickal arts in the region. The Kasar, who have their Spiritsraad, and the Stygion, who have the Psychic Conclave."

"I thought the Spiritsraad was a building," Glaser said.

"It refers to both the temple and the congress of magickal practitioners within," Herschel said.

For the first time since she arrived, Renata was beginning to form an idea of where this all might be heading.

"What magicks do the Stygion practise?" Glaser asked.

"A great many, Colonel," Maruska said. "Selachomancy, channelling, séance, to name but a few. The Stygion are the most magickally gifted of all earthly races. It was through the Eye of the Sea, after all, that magick first entered the world."

"You are talking about the epicentre of the Great Cataclysm," Glaser said, rubbing his chin. "I'm trying to remember my lessons from temple school."

"Precisely, Colonel," Herschel said eagerly, sensing Glaser's latent interest and trying to husband it. "The Great Cataclysm concerned the conjunction of the mortal plane and the afterlife, the point in time at which, thousands of years ago, magick came to our realm. And because it entered via the Eye of the Sea, the magick there was the strongest and most intense."

"And it made the Stygion."

"Right. And the Kasar. And dozens of other hybrid races besides, though of course, their bloodlines did not stabilise and they have not survived into the modern age."

"Of course."

"The Eye of the Sea, that crucial gateway, lies at the centre of the Iris Isles, many tens of fathoms below the surface. The Iris Isles are of course part of the Stygion Sea, and well within the Stygion borders."

"Well, you need to be careful with that. I am not sure the Empire recognises the 'Stygion borders' such as they are claimed," Glaser said, a warning note in his voice.

"It does not," Maruska said tonelessly.

"Stygion-controlled territory, then," Herschel offered.

"We shall make a diplomat of you yet," Renata said, and they all shared a muted chuckle.

"So . . . what?" Glaser asked. "You want to use Sovan ambassadors to entreat the mer-men to open the Eye?"

"Nema, no!" the monk erupted, making them all start.

"Bloody hell!" Glaser said angrily.

Herschel looked horrified. "I am sorry, Colonel, but – to be clear – the Eye of the Sea must remain closed *for ever*. It is the portal through which demonic entities would enter our realm and—"

"Yes, all right, I think we all get the picture," Glaser muttered.

Herschel collected himself. "Colonel, I know that Sova requires you to reject these heresies, but I can assure you that these matters are as real as you and I."

Glaser thought a moment. Just as Renata did not have the measure of her own feelings, so too did Glaser seem to be wrestling with his. For all he affected disdain for the monks and their story, it was clear he was grappling with how to proceed. If they would only give him a fig leaf, something that didn't sound like lunacy, so that he could keep a straight face if questioned by a political rival on the subject.

"So it's a fact-finding mission, then? You wish to find out if the Stygion, as the foremost magickal practitioners in the world, have sensed anything awry, and you need the ambassador to do it?"

"Precisely that, Colonel," Herschel said encouragingly. "Guillot here can speak Kasarsprek and so we have no need of a formal diplomatic legation to the Kyarai, but we do not know the Stygion at all, and nor does anyone else within the Bruta Sarkan. They are an enigmatic people."

"The Kyarai is a war zone, Brother Herschel," Colonel Glaser said pointedly. "If your plan is to visit the Spiritsraad in Port Talaka first – which it seems to be – you are very unlikely to make it before Casimir takes the capital. Even if you left presently, you would likely be arriving at the same time as the enemy. A day or two ahead, at most."

"That is a risk we shall have to take, Colonel," the monk said.

Glaser quirked an eyebrow. "Well. You do not want for courage, I will say that of you."

"Believe me when I say, Colonel, that I am frightened: both of the enormity of our task and of the consequences of failure. But someone must do something. We have to *do* something."

"Indeed," Glaser said, now with a measure of respect. "We could use a few Herschels on the general staff, I daresay."

The monk offered a weak smile. "The final point I would make is this: if I am wrong – and I pray that I am – then we have nothing to lose in the attempt."

"Except the sum total of our diplomatic mission to the Stygion," Glaser remarked.

"A scant forfeiture," Maruska said, winking. Glaser snorted. "I would add, Colonel, that we have not mounted an expedition for some years now. Even if it transpires that there is nothing to this 'Great Silence' theory, the journey will not be without diplomatic value."

"I agree," Renata said. She was not particularly keen to travel with these strange monks; she was even less keen to accept the truth of their story, for to do so was to admit that the entire world was teetering on the brink of oblivion. But she was desperate to put her diplomatic training into practice. If this mission was the best current opportunity to do so, then she was going to take it.

"I do not doubt it," Glaser said wryly. "I am more concerned with diverting men and matériel to escort you."

"Oh, I shouldn't think—" Maruska began, but Glaser held up a hand.

"Mark this: if we are going to do it, Excellency, we are going to do it properly. Authorising this mission means accepting at least the *possibility* of the prophecy. And I do not go in for half-measures."

Maruska inclined his head tactfully. "Of course, Colonel."

There was another pause as Glaser thought again, though Renata no longer seriously considered that he would refuse.

"Let us for a moment assume I will indulge this request," he said. "Who do we have in reserve? And what I mean by that is, what happens if the mission goes wrong and the pair of you are killed?"

"There is a man at the University who is well versed in all matters Stygion. We exchange notes frequently. He would be the natural choice to replace us," Maruska said.

"And that is it?"

"He will have students, naturally. But the Stygion are not considered to be of great value to the Empire, and the diplomatic apparatus is *scaled* accordingly."

"Well," Glaser said thoughtfully, missing the pun. "Perhaps that is something we shall have to remedy."

"Nothing would please me more, Colonel."

Glaser sighed. "I must say, Brother Herschel, I do not know what to make of this. A part of me – and it is a sizeable part – thinks I should have you both shot. And yet . . ." He fell once again into a brief reverie. "And yet, there is some attraction to the argument that we have little to lose in the attempt. The risk of doing nothing does seem to me to be the greater."

Both Herschel and his mute companion breathed out great sighs of relief. "Thank you, Colonel," Herschel said.

"Do not thank me," Glaser said. "It is likely I have just sent all of you to your deaths." He turned to Maruska. "How soon can you be ready to leave?"

"I would say two days," the ambassador replied.

"And you, Madam Secretary?"

"Two days," she agreed, though she would have left there and then had it been necessary.

"Very well. I shall have my adjutant make the arrangements. I will be in touch." The colonel wrote something down on a piece of paper in front of him, applied a dribble of wax, sealed it with his signet ring, and gave it to Herschel. "You two can quarter with me. This is my address. Go there now; my husband is called Velimir. Tell him I sent you."

"H-he will not mind?" Herschel asked.

"Oh, he has seen stranger things," Glaser said offhandedly.

"I doubt that," Renata murmured under her breath. Maruska stifled a smile.

Glaser gestured to the door. "Right. All of you out, now. It is late, and saving the world is one of many things I have to attend to this evening."

IV

A Treacherous Country

*"One's enemy makes up only a fraction of the hazards
faced by a soldier. Inclement weather, hunger, thirst,
difficult terrain, wet feet, wild animals, and indeed more,
all conspire to rob the warrior of his fighting spirit."*

FROM LUGOS'
PRIMER FOR THE SOVAN INFANTRYMAN

Fort Ingomar

ALDA RIVER VALLEY

Dear Father,

*I am writing this as I sit in my quarters at Fort Ingomar.
Time passes strangely in this place; I can only have been here for
a few weeks, though already it feels like much longer.*

*Let me make a clean breast of it: I fear I have made a mistake in
joining the Sovan Army. I had long thought that some wellspring
of courage would appear within me the moment I was faced with
hardship; instead, my life in the Legions, and latterly Badenburg –
the life which you gave me, one of luxury and privilege – has left
me ill-equipped for the difficult realities of campaigning.*

This is a treacherous country. Major Haak and Captain Furlan have been at pains these past weeks to instil in me the severe nature of the Alda River Valley. It is not just the Great Enemy of Casimir we are to be concerned with; the soldiers speak constantly of ghouls and sprites in the forests, and I am certain they fear supernatural misadventure more than the enemy's muskets. Once I might have written this off as silly folklore, but there is some quality to this land which is difficult to describe. It is a gloomy place, full of mist and rain, with storms quick to form and dissipate. At night the forest plays all manner of auditory tricks ~~and by day I cannot shake the feeling of being watched constantly. I have heard screams which seem to emanate from a place which is at once distant and yet close, insofar as a sound can be so described. These noises penetrate me like a spade through sod, unearthing my fears like a veteran grave robber. I find I am frightened all the time.~~

Doubtless it is the contrivance of animals, for I have heard a fox's shriek and a wolf's howl and this is not dissimilar, ~~though some of the men report a curious aethereal weeping sound, too, which is less easily explained, and which I myself have heard on occasion, though I do not like to admit it.~~

The fort itself is a joyless place. I have made something of a friend of Captain Furlan who commands the artillery here, though it seems the other officers have written him off as a sot. Either way, we are but two companies, the 8th which is a line company, and the 10th which is a light company and which is now at my beck (I have been breveted to captain, though they shall not increase my pay!). Taking command of nearly one hundred men is a somewhat heady experience and I hope to acquit myself well, though I am certain I am unfit for the task. The women and men are all my elder and must store together the better part of one thousand years' experience, against my two. To make matters worse, I am sure they resent my having *transferred from the 2nd Legion. The Guards regiments have different reputations to different people, but in the New East they are considered overly favoured, their reputation as élite warriors ill-deserved.*

The unhappy task of instructing these soldiers on how best to engage the enemy now falls to me. With the support of the officers in the regimental headquarters, such seemed surmountable; out here on the fringes of the New East, I am found very much wanting. My charges do not warm to me, and though they do obey my instructions, it is with great recalcitrance. Major Haak provides little support, and even my friend Captain Furlan is interested mostly in self-preservation, though he does occasionally offer me advice. Of the captain of the 8th, Beckert: he has only disdain for me, and we have exchanged nothing in the way of conversation this past fortnight.

I hope you do not think me ungrateful. I know that my commission cost a significant sum of goldmark, and I will do everything in my power to earn the trust and faith of our household. It is my hope that one day my name will be included on the roll of honour in the regimental headquarters. ~~It is more likely my name shall be found on the regimental cenotaph.~~

For now I will keep my head on my shoulders, and hope that the Casimirs and the Sanques present themselves soon so that I may earn myself some glory.

Peter looked at this last sentence askance. It was not true in the slightest; indeed, it was the very last thing he wanted. The thought of it alone made his guts sour. He would have been perfectly happy to spend a year in the fort doing nothing at all. Then he could return to Sova to sell his commission and do something entirely ordinary for the rest of his life.

He finished off the letter and placed it into its envelope; then he melted a little wax by the solitary candle in his quarters and sealed it, and placed it at the bottom of the strongbox under his desk to languish.

He looked at his correspondence kit and wondered whether he should pen a letter to Leonie. He tried to think of some florid, sentimental verse of the kind which was very in vogue with officers at the moment. But that font of inspiration had run dry. Correspondence, for him, was about catharsis. And he could not achieve it spouting out saccharine nonsense. He imagined his mother and brothers and Leonie in the drawing room in their house in Imastadt, listening to his words being read out. His brothers would affect jealousy, though they would be privately pleased that they were not risking their lives. His mother would be shedding tears of pride, each glistening in the firelight like citrine gems, for Peter would have finally done something of note in her eyes. And Leonie? Leonie would be rapt—

But it was such an absurd image he immediately dissociated himself from his own reverie. The only expression he could conjure in his mind of both his mother and Leonie was one of incredible boredom.

Perhaps he *should* write more extravagant letters. He imagined accounts of heroism, in which Casimirs had dragged heavy cannon through the forests at night and breached the fort and he led a ragged and desperate defence against waves of those brutes from the likes of Vukovskoville and Kolfort and Vratislavbourg. He imagined his sabre biting into the flesh of his enemies to the cheers of his soldiers, having finally earned their respect. He tried to conjure up a positive emotion that might naturally flow from such a feat. Instead it just made him despondent.

He stood to undress, for it was late in the evening and the screaming and weeping would begin soon. How utterly insane it was that that had become simply another part of the routine: standing-to, cleaning and maintaining their muskets, organising patrols, ensuring there was enough food and water for the men, corresponding with distant generals, listening to the deranged weeping and screaming of invisible entities all around them, stoppering his ears with wax and turning in for the night.

This time, however, there came not the slow escalation of madness; instead, from nowhere, a bloodcurdling banshee-shriek ripped through the still night air.

Peter dropped to the floorboards in the same way he would when under fire from roundshot.

"Nema's fucking blood," he whispered, heart pounding so violently it felt as though it were about to crack his breastbone. He lay there prostrate, gasping for air, waiting.

But there was no more.

He pressed himself up slowly, sweating and shaking, extinguished the candle and approached the window. He squinted into the darkness beyond. On the banquette he could make out the dim shapes of members of the line company who were on rotation, the white facings and silver frogging of their coats catching what little ambient light there was. But the forest beyond was dark and quiet, the only sound coming from the river where it flowed in two large channels either side of Aldaney Island.

He waited for a long time, his head cocked, barely breathing. It had to have been an animal. A passing barn owl. They made awful shrieks in the dead of night. He was certain of it.

Except that he *wasn't* certain of it. It hadn't sounded like a barn owl at all. And there had been something at least partly human about it. It was a bizarre, troubling, unsettling thought, but it was an invasive and persistent one all the same.

There it came again! A scream, a long moaning wail that sounded much too close to have come from beyond the walls of the fort, and yet much too distant, as though it were echoing down a long tunnel.

He gritted his teeth. There was no commotion outside, no consternation. Night attacks were vanishingly rare due to their chaotic and unpredictable nature – and besides, no one was rushing to stand-to, or tolling the alarum bell, or doing anything out of the ordinary at all.

He buckled his sabre back on, unboxed his pistol and stuffed it into his sash, snatched up his tricorn and made his way back outside into the staging area. He would not cower in his quarters. He was resolved to cut to the heart of the matter this time.

It really was profoundly dark. There was just a hint of drizzle so fine it could have been heavy mist in the air, and the subtle, constant background flow of the River Alda. The smell of moss and damp stone filled his nostrils.

There was a small barracks in Fort Ingomar, but there were still plenty of soldiers encamped in the lee of the wall. They ate hunks of cold sausage and stale bread and drank from skins of watered-down brandy. Those who saw him touched their hats or foreheads in salute.

"You there," Peter said as he approached a private perhaps two or three years his senior. The woman was lying on her back in the crook of the wall, her haversack a makeshift pillow; when she saw him, she lurched to her feet and touched her forehead. She did not seem to be particularly pleased to be roused.

"Aye, sir?" She cast a glance at Peter's midriff. "You're armed, sir?"

He ignored the question. "I heard something. It sounded like a scream. Have you heard anything?"

The woman did not look pleased with the question, as though by speaking of these bizarre occurrences they would manifest. "Sometimes there are noises, aye, sir," she said to the floor.

"What do you mean by that?"

"Just that, sir. Noises."

"Screams, moans, cries?"

" . . . Aye, sir," the private mumbled.

"Are they wounded men?"

She shook her head. "No, sir. Everyone is accounted for. We've not had a visit from the enemy for some time now."

"The mountain pagans, then?"

"Could be, sir. But . . . "

"But what?"

"Nothing ever turns up in the patrols. And the hounds do not smell blood."

Peter clacked his tongue. Every minute he spent trying to prise answers from this woman was a minute in which his courage slowly leaked away. "But you all hear these noises?" he asked, tapping his foot impatiently.

She nodded, so subtly that in the damp darkness Peter nearly missed it.

"For the whole time you have been here? How long have you been here?"

"Eight months, sir. I don't think it's been the whole time. It's certainly started to get worse recently."

Peter began to feel angry, but it was an anger born of fear. "And no one has thought to try and explore the source of these strange noises?"

The private was clearly unhappy with that prospect. "Major Haak's orders, sir, are to remain inside the confines of the fort at night. We have not mounted an expedition beyond the walls after dusk for many weeks now. Well before your arrival, sir. You would not have known," she added, careful not to embarrass Peter by implying his ignorance of a standing order.

Peter thought for a moment. "Fine. That will be all," he said eventually.

"Aye, sir," the woman replied, relieved to return to her lean-to.

Peter left her and surmounted a nearby set of steps which led up to the wall. He stopped next to one of the eight-pounders, the enormous iron cannon exuding a quiet aura of lethality. He rested his hand on the barrel, to find it slightly warm to the touch. Through the embrasure, the pine forest loomed. What strangeness lay beyond the redoubt? What aethereal horrors?

He gasped, flinching and grasping the parapet to steady himself. Another violent shriek had cut through the air several paces to his right. Instinctively he lurched in that direction, searching in the darkness for what he presumed was a freshly wounded soldier; and there, slouched against the wall, was a man. His legs were missing, and about the stumps was an enormous slick of blood.

"W-what happened?" Peter asked, breathless with horror. There had been no explosion, no report, no shot from beyond the wall. Perhaps an attack by a wild creature, the same thing that had shredded those men in the forest the day of his arrival? But no one else was moving or shouting or saying anything. And besides, what titanic beast could maul a man in such a way as to remove both of his legs?

The man, whom he did not recognise, looked ghastly pale.

"The . . ." he said. "Th-the . . . G-g . . ."

"Nema Victoria, just . . . Wait a moment, I'll fetch a physician!"

The man beckoned Peter to move closer. His hands trembled, and there was blood burbling from his mouth. Peter looked down to see that his entire midsection was laid open too, and great handfuls of viscera were spilling out on to the floor. He paused; a moment before, the man's injuries had been confined to his legs. From where had come these fresh contusions?

"You must run," the man gurgled, his voice a rough, hoarse whisper. His eyes were wide with terror. "They are coming. You must get away from here . . . *Ack!*"

He expired. Peter, as baffled as he was horrified, shouted frantically for men to attend him. A moment later, the bootsteps of a dozen soldiers converged on his position.

"Sir?" they clamoured as they crowded round him. "What is the matter?"

"Quick! This man needs—" Peter started, and then stopped. He had turned back to where the disassembled soldier had lain; but there was . . . there was *nothing* there.

"No . . ." he breathed. "How is that . . . how is that possible? I just saw . . ." He looked over the edge of the banquette, to see if the corpse had tipped over the side, but the ground there was completely clear too. And there was no blood, either. The stone was as clean as if it had been scoured by fresh rain.

He examined his hands; there was no blood on them, either.

"Sir?"

Peter cast about the banquette, but it was clear even in the poor light that there was nothing there.

"I don't understand," he said. Nonetheless, he stopped scrabbling about on the floor like a madman. He looked as though he had lost his mind. "I saw a wounded man here – a dying man. None of you have seen anything?"

"No, sir," came the muttered chorus of responses, though the soldiers looked dejected and fearful rather than contemptuous.

Could it really have been just a ghastly hallucination? Such things were confined to fever dreams. He had never seen a vision with such incredible clarity before. He could see and smell and *feel* the man; the blood, the viscera, the shit in his breeches.

He looked out across the ditch, and over to the redoubt. There was nothing. Just the sound of the river and the cold breeze cutting through the pines.

"Just . . . everybody get back to your posts," he muttered, and made his way to his quarters.

Major Haak summoned him at first light. Beyond the window was another misty grey morning, though there was a hint of blue on the horizon. Perhaps the sun would touch Fort Ingomar today.

"Fit of the nerves?" Haak asked him. He was bespectacled and looking at a supply ledger which the quartermaster had provided him with. In the distance Peter heard the crack of a rifle – hunters, bringing in some game.

"Sir?"

"I heard you lost your head at the parapet."

Peter flushed with embarrassment. He felt a sudden urge to loosen his stock collars and get some air to his neck.

"I thought I heard a scream beyond the wall," he said. "When I went to investigate, I suffered . . . a hallucination."

"What manner of hallucination?" Haak asked. His voice was level, his attention still apparently on the ledger in front of him.

"I saw a wounded man. He had lost his legs, and latterly his midsection. He spoke to me."

For the first time, Haak looked up. He wore a curious expression. "Well? What did he say?"

Peter thought back to the ghastly vision, though his brain had done its best to eradicate it from his memory. "He told me we had to run. That 'they' were coming."

"He did not clarify who 'they' were?"

Peter shook as head. "No, sir. And then he vanished."

"No one else saw it?"

"I alone."

He had expected the major to dismiss this ludicrous story out of hand. At best it was the trick of a stressed mind; at worst it was a confection designed to imply insanity, and therefore unfitness for duty and a return to Sova. An ignominious return, but a return nonetheless.

Instead, Haak mulled it over for a while, his expression dark.

"I told you this was a strange place," he said.

"You did, sir."

The major kept his seat, but turned and looked out the window. "I consider myself to be a careful man, Mister Kleist. I have tried to cultivate a reputation for prudence over the years. I trouble myself to *listen* to what I am told, to weigh it and examine it – and if necessary to disregard it. Many of my contemporaries are not of the same mind. They require blind obedience at every turn, and get a great many men killed in the process."

Peter didn't quite know how to respond to that, and so said nothing.

"When reports first crossed my desk of visions and sightings of . . . *ghouls* and strange noises in the night, we first thought it was an attempt by the enemy to penetrate the fortress. The pagans of the mountain confederations are skilled infiltrators, and Casimir has gone to great pains to cultivate their assistance as mercenaries." He was quiet for a moment, briefly lost in his own thoughts. Eventually he turned back to his desk. He looked tired. "But it was not the enemy. What else do you think we might have considered?"

"Malingering," Peter said, a little too quickly.

The major nodded. "Precisely. We had men flogged for it, of course. Trying to appear insensible, and so perhaps be returned to Badenburg. As though we might have the men and mules and matériel – to say nothing of the inclination – to go to the trouble of shipping the insane back off to Sova, rather than just shooting them." His lip curled in a sneer. "But the weight of evidence is too great to ignore."

"The . . . weight of evidence, sir?"

"All of these goings-on have a common root. I have become somewhat inured to it, but your arrival here, your fresh eyes and experiences, have set it as firmly in my mind as that scarp. We can no longer ignore the fact that there is some scheme afoot to lure us out of the fortress."

It was not the conclusion Peter had been expecting. "The men consider the problem to be supernatural in nature."

Haak paused, taking the measure of him. "Sova was once home to the practice of sorceries," he said carefully. "Death magicks."

Peter, like almost all of his contemporaries in the Army, was a keen student of history. "I have read Parsifal," he said tactfully. "But it is all unlawful now, save for the Engineers."

"The proscription of a practice, and its eradication, are two different things."

Peter cleared his throat. "Yes," he said, suddenly uncomfortable with the tenor and direction of the conversation. He wanted to hear he was being ridiculous, that he was suffering from a psychological malady. He wanted his fears to be dismissed out of hand, not confirmed. "Notwithstanding . . . " he added, weakly.

"You yourself have heard things. Seen things which cannot be explained through rational means?"

"Yes, sir, including the matters to which I have drawn your attention this morning. But like you say, perhaps it was just a trick of the mind."

Something shifted in Haak's expression, and Peter sensed he had failed some sort of test. "Perhaps," he grunted. "Perhaps there is something more at work here."

"It seems unlikely—"

"Does it? The whole company is plagued with these auditory manifestations. I myself have heard them. We cannot reject such compelling evidence."

Peter's heart was pounding. "What do you mean to do?"

Haak gave him a lopsided grin. "Spring the trap."

"The trap, sir?"

"When you first arrived, you came across the corpses of several men who had been the subject of great violence, yes?"

"Yes."

"The medical officer examined the bodies and is convinced they are claw marks."

Peter's vision swam. "What kind of claw, sir?"

"That is what I want you to find out, Mister Kleist."

He felt his throat tighten. "Sir, I am of course at your disposal, but perhaps Captain Beckert, with his superior experience and greater familiarity with the Alda country, might be better—"

"No," Haak said simply. "The 8th is a line company and better suited to garrison the fort."

Peter wondered if there was anything else he could say which would excuse him from this expedition. "Yes, naturally," he settled on, which didn't take him much further at all.

Haak picked up a letter from his desk. "I have had word from

Major Kulkani in Fort Romauld; apparently a detachment of Casimirs and Sanques is moving north up the Alda. Pagans have already begun preparing the ground at the point where the Rivers Tadija and Alda bifurcate."

"That's—"

"Seventy-five miles away."

Peter managed to keep a grip on himself. "What do they plan to do there?"

"My guess is to establish a fort to the east of the old Line of Demarcation and from there begin to stake claims to the land all the way up to the Long River. Sova agrees. They probably want to cut off the whole peninsula and prevent our northwards expansion – that, or force a confrontation."

Peter thought about the country Haak was talking about: thousands of miles of forest, and then the end of the New East – the Great Northern Barrier Range. That was a truly wild place, unexplored and unpopulated.

He suppressed a shudder. "Which of these two matters should I prioritise?"

"The orders stipulate that engaging and destroying this Casimiran force and reducing the fortress – if indeed there is one – takes priority over all other matters."

With one hundred men?! Peter wanted to scream, though greatly mismatched engagements were nothing new in the Alda River Valley, and in such treacherous terrain weight of numbers counted for little.

"I understand, sir," he said, his mouth dry.

"That is what the *orders* stipulate," Haak continued carefully. "But I would like you to give equal weight to investigating this . . . separate matter. I want to know what it is that is killing the men and women under my command. I want to know what it is that is infecting their minds. I want to know what it is that is plaguing this fort. Do you understand, Mister Kleist? The opportunity to examine the valley, the country, and unearth its secrets is too good to pass up." There was a sense of urgency about the major's entreaty, the smallest spark of derangement in his eye.

"I understand," Peter said again, as a great sense of resentment settled like a cannonball in his stomach. "When shall we leave?"

"Today," Haak said. "Ensure you have enough store for two weeks there and another two back, though I do not think it will take you that long. Oh, and one last thing."

"Yes, sir?" Peter asked miserably.

Haak tapped a letter on his desk. "I've received word from Sova of a plague spreading through Draedaland. They are hoping to contain it along the Haunerwald border. Anyone attempting to cross into Imperial territory will be shot on sight."

"Is that so?" Peter said, unsure what to do with this information.

"No word yet on how it affects a person. Just keep an eye out for any sort of malaise, yes? We are not so far from the pagans here. The last thing we need is a pox spreading through the fort."

"I understand."

"Thank you, Mister Kleist. Good hunting. That will be all."

V

Unexpected Violence

*"War does not hold a monopoly over desolation. Missionary
evangelism has turned the Principality of Casimir from
a thriving nation into one beggared of rational thought.
An entire polity turned to Neman Conformism, drinking
its poisonous milk as though from a great demonic
teat. I can think of no better way of reducing a state to
intellectual rubble than with religious dogma."*

FROM GROSSO'S
THE GREAT ROT: THE RISE OF NEMAN CONFORMISM

Creusgate Fischmarkt

SOVA

It took the full two days to lay the preparations for the diplomatic
mission. Although Maruska was the ambassador, the reality was
that it was Colonel Glaser and his men who were orchestrating
matters. As a result, it felt less like political outreach to Renata
and more like a raiding party.

Deciding who exactly would join them was the first order of
business. Obviously Maruska and Renata were the kernel around
which the rest of the mission was to be formed, and for oversight

and protection there would be an accompaniment of cavalrymen from the 1st Sovan Legion. The two monks of the Bruta Sarkan would naturally accompany them, too, but there was still a feeling that the expedition was missing something – or rather, someone.

On the second day after the meeting with Glaser, Renata met with Amara at the Creusgate Fischmarkt. It was hot and dry and dusty as they walked up the Sofijan Highway, all the way from the Argonauts' Society building to where the University of Sova blotted out the spring sunlight. Amara's nose was permanently wrinkled, though as a scholar of linguistics she spent a great deal of time in the University and should have been used to the smell. Still, thanks to the contrivance of heat and breeze, the whaling ships docked in Shank's Harbour filled the air with a gross stench, as the beasts themselves were rendered down for their fat and oil and meat and bone. Above, gulls flocked constantly, dousing the warehouse roofs white with guano.

Adding to this was the pungent scent of the fish market itself. Arm in arm, Renata and her half-sister moved with purpose up the length of the road, keeping out of the way of the hundreds of carts as they loaded up with wares from the docklands. The place was a hive of activity as fresh goods were transported down a maze of one-way streets as quickly as possible: exotic meats to the Fleichfelder livestock markets to the north-east; piles of dung and barrels of blood and urine for the tanneries in the unsociable trades district. Some went south down the Aleksandra the Valiant Boulevard to the Victorygate Getreidemarkt, wagons and carts filled with aniseeds and almonds and grain.

"How long do you think you'll be gone?" Amara asked as they moved into the fish market itself, ducking between stalls and sellers and merchants looking to get fresh pieces for their taverns. Every type of sea creature was in abundance: eels, crabs, octopuses, lobsters, pickled herrings and anchovies, fresh oysters – sold by the dozen, with vinegar or lemon and bread-and-butter – and every type of white and red fish one could imagine, to say nothing of the whale and shark meat.

"A good few weeks. Perhaps a month or two. It is difficult to know how the going will be."

"How will you travel?"

"By stagecoach."

Amara drew up sharply against an enormous white shark which had been hung up by its tailfin and which several people were marvelling over. A fishmonger was about to fillet it, but was happy to let the crowd marvel a little longer. Renata looked at the markings above the shark's gills. There were indentations where armoured segmenta had sat, meaningless to a layman but as plain as day to her.

"What's the matter?" Amara asked her.

"This was a Spear-mount," Renata said disgustedly.

"What's that?"

She shook her head. "Nothing. Come on. I know somewhere we can get fresh oysters."

They made their way through the market to a place that sat in the shadow of the Council of Bishops. There, a fishwife brought them a basket of oysters, as well as some freshly baked bread, a trivet of butter and a pewter pot of lemon slices. She shucked them a dozen each, and the sisters took a moment to eat.

"What about in Grenzegard?" Amara asked. "I doubt there are many staging posts in that part of the world."

Renata shrugged. "If we can use the canals, we will. If not, I suppose we will walk. And by that I mean ride."

"It is a long journey."

"It is an important journey."

"You finally get to meet your fishmen." Amara was trying to be wry, but Renata was preoccupied. In spite of herself, and of Glaser's incredulity, she thought frequently of the monks and their prophecy. And besides, she was supposed to be helping Maruska, and was conscious of the time.

"Please don't call them that," she muttered.

Amara took Renata's hand in hers. "You will be careful, Ren, won't you? The places you are talking about are not safe places."

Renata was about to respond when they were interrupted.

"Madam Secretary?"

They both looked up, to see an adolescent girl clad in the livery of one of the city's messenger companies.

"Yes?"

"An urgent summons from Colonel Glaser, ma'am." She handed over the letter, and Renata took it, opened and examined it.

"Did he send a coach?" she asked.

"Yes, ma'am, just over here on the side of the highway."

Renata sighed. "Thank you," she said.

The girl touched her forehead and scurried off. Unlike the street urchins, the liveried messengers were well paid, and she did not wait for a tip.

"Sorry," Renata said, smiling apologetically at Amara.

"Oh, that's all right," Amara replied reassuringly. "I shall wring out of you another quarter-hour's company en route."

Together they left the oyster house and entered the coach, and the driver urged the horses into motion. Inside it was gloomy; it was a two-horse stagecoach from the Imperial Office pool, and they had tinted windows and thicker blinds to protect the privacy of the occupants.

"Feels very fancy," Amara said, tracing the fine upholstery with her fingers. "I wonder if I shall be mistaken for someone important?"

"Oh, I doubt that in my company," Renata said idly.

Amara *tsked*. "Sometimes I think you save all of your cheer for your colleagues and clients and leave me with nothing but the morbid dregs."

Renata forced herself to smile. "I'm sorry, Amara. My mind is elsewhere."

"You *really* can't tell me why you are going?"

She shook her head. "It is a most sensitive state secret."

There was a pause, taken up by the squeaking and clattering of the coach and the incredible bustle of the Creus Road. They made good time down the highway, and it wasn't long before they were travelling past the Senate and the adjacent Royal Exhibition Centre.

"Still," Amara said encouragingly, "you must be pleased. You have always wanted to be part of something like this. Ever since you joined the office?"

Not like this, Renata might have said. "No, you are quite right. I should be more grateful. Listen; when was the last time you went to temple?"

Amara's brow furrowed. She opened her mouth, and then closed it again. "I . . . don't know. A few weeks ago?"

"Will you go again soon? Speak to a confessor?"

Amara's confusion deepened. "Ren, what on *earth* are you talking about?"

Renata made a frustrated noise. "I know it sounds peculiar, but I think it is worth just . . . bringing your spiritual well-being up to date. Keeping current with it. If you take my meaning."

"I most certainly do not take your meaning," Amara said, chuckling. "Is it the hair shirt next? You aren't exactly ascetic yourself, unless you made up those stories about Alistair's oddly shaped cock."

"For Nema's sake, Amara, why can't you ever just listen to me?" Renata shouted – at precisely the same moment there was an enormous explosion.

At first she felt as though the coach had hit a deep rut in the road, for there was a single loud bang like a large firework going off and a propulsive jolt which sent her knees into her chest. But in the space of an eyeblink, the interior was filled with thick white smoke and flying splinters of wood, and her ears were ringing and her teeth hurt and she could taste blood in her mouth.

There were several seconds of absolute stillness and silence as the world slowly returned to her.

"Amara!" she grunted. She fumbled instinctively for the coach door and pushed it open, filling the interior with sunlight and the sound of screaming. She felt as though she had been kicked in the breastbone by a horse. Her heart thrummed and fluttered painfully in her chest, and every part of her felt weak and shaky.

With the door open, the smoke cleared somewhat and she saw Amara sitting across from her, dazed and mute, eyes wide and swivelling around in shock. Two runnels of blood trickled from her nostrils and on to her dress.

"Amara!" Renata slurred again, reaching out for her sister's hand. Then she turned; there was a shadow on the cobbles outside, and movement over her right shoulder, and she had the briefest glimpse of a pistol held in a gloved hand.

"N—!" she shouted abortively, before there was a second thunderous report and Amara's left shoulder disintegrated in a great spray of red.

Renata screamed; Amara pitched forwards. Renata caught her, but the dead weight and her own acute shock conspired to send them both sprawling heavily on to the highway.

The air filled with shouts:

"I say!"

"Stop that man!"

"Get him, he's over there!"

"Fetch constables, quick!"

People crowded around her. Renata fended them off, crawling across the dusty, filthy cobbles to where her half-sister lay. The colour was draining from Amara's skin already, and her lips looked blue. A pool of blood was spreading underneath her shoulder, mixing with the dirt of the road.

"Somebody help me!" Renata screamed insensibly at the stunned onlookers. Her ears felt as though they were stuffed with wadding. A Neman nun snatched off her wimple and pressed it firmly against Amara's shoulder. Renata saw that the musket ball had clipped the very top of her sister's shoulder, just above the clavicle, blowing open the muscle there but leaving the bone intact. She could even see it where the flesh was laid open, a white spar amongst the red. On the floor, a flattened disc the size of a goldmark coin lay in a little pool of blood.

The nun was shouting at her nearby sisters. Other people descended on the scene too. One was a naval officer, by his uniform, who had been enjoying some smoked calamari wrapped in greasepaper.

"Here," he shouted to his men through his mouthful. "We can take her to the RNH."

The Royal Naval Hospital was a few miles to the south-west. Renata found herself suddenly redundant as the men flagged down a nearby carriage and carried Amara into it with the practised urgency of sailors. A part of her felt very strongly that she should accompany her to hospital; but as the dust – literally – began to settle, and her thoughts coalesced and crystallised, her fury flared to incandescence. Her anxiety and stress over the past few days had, like a bolt of lightning, been seeking somewhere to ground itself – and had found a place in her would-be murderer.

She pushed herself to her feet, and, in spite of the protestations of the crowd, lurched off down the Haugen Highway.

"Ms Rainer! Ms Rainer! By Nema, are you all right?"

She turned to see Colonel Glaser running down the road after her. Beyond him, soldiers from the Life Guards barracks were flooding the street, and the carriage was billowing smoke as it slowly caught fire.

"Good gods," Glaser said as he caught up with her, noting the state of her face and clothes. "Let's sit you down," he said, reaching out to take her by the arm.

"No, damn you!" Renata shouted, and whirled away and resumed her hobbling run. The day was hot, the air leaden, and in her spring dress and with her grenade-blasted lungs it was difficult to catch her breath. She wanted to cry for the injury done to her sister, but she wanted to throttle the person who had tried to kill her more.

"Ms Rainer, this is lunacy!"

"Either help me or go away!" Renata shouted.

Glaser swore in exasperation, turned away and began to shout out to his soldiers.

Renata limped on, slowly regaining herself until she was able to run without looking like a drunk. She paused to take stock. She had more or less reached Sungate. On her right was the Kasari enclave within Sova, a place known informally as "Wolfsland". Historically, the only Kasar in the city had been the Imperial Warden, the traditional bodyguard of the old Haugenate emperors. Now, displaced by colonial proxy war, they were ten a goldmark bit. It was strange; the place was a dilapidated, overcrowded slum, and yet each Kasar had the strength of two grown men. Such large, powerful creatures did not belong in six-storey tenements, eking out a living along with the rest of Sova's human poor.

Renata tried to think. She was feeling increasingly frantic. She did not think her attacker had come this way. No; the crowd had pointed west, towards the Dynast's Palace. In her addled state she had come too far.

With her breath labouring in her throat, she resumed her run, tugging at the front of her dress to try and get some air in her lungs. She ducked down a back alley that was sandwiched between a long row of tall terraced houses and a motley stack of stones – the old mediaeval boundary of this part of the city. Here the ground was laid with illegal outflows, tangles of rusting pipes and puddles of effluent winding their way towards the Sauber like a pile of dead snakes.

"Move!" she shouted as she thumped her way through a cluster of holy men and women who were enjoying the lunchtime sun. She ran past a soot-stained temple on the riverbank, then cut right up the embankment – what had once been a promenade, until the river became too rancid and the humours too noxious – back into Wolfsland and towards the Kasari embassy.

She slowed to a stop, and bent double to catch her breath.

It was hopeless.

"I think he went into the Dynast's Palace," Glaser called out from behind her. She turned sharply, to see the colonel running up the embankment, tracing the same route she had taken. Like her, he was not wearing clothes conducive to heavy exercise, and was red-faced and sweating in the hot lunchtime sun.

"Then let's go!" Renata declared, re-energised, but found herself arrested by Glaser's hand on her right arm.

"Wait a moment," he said, panting. "I have sent men around the eastern side to block the exit, and there are constables moving up the Miran Bridge to head off the road there. You should go to the watch house and wait for this to be resolved."

"To hell with that!" Renata snarled, and tried to pull away, but his grip was firm.

"Madam Secretary, you are much too important to risk your life—"

"Just . . . " she struggled against his grip, "*stop!*" She steadied her breathing. "Colonel, with respect, please just shut up. He shot my sister. I am not going anywhere."

Glaser sighed mightily, rubbing his face with his hands. "For Nema's sake, stay behind me, then," he muttered angrily, and shouldered past her.

The Dynast's Palace was an enormous structure of glass and iron, a gift from the Kasar to the Sovan state in celebration of the two nations' historic ties. The dome itself rose forty feet into the air, and inside were pleasant geometric water gardens designed to mimic the streets of Port Talaka. It was also a place dense with lush exotic vegetation; in the same way the gardens were designed to mimic the Kasari capital, so the trees and plants were designed to mimic the Reenwound, the enormous rainforest that dominated the western half of the Kyarai. It was a pleasant, if stiflingly hot place, and open to the entire Sovan public, though more often than not it languished empty.

They entered slowly, carefully, as a hunter might enter a forest in search of a sabrecat. Down the centre of the palace was a straight channel of water gurgling with fountains, and branching off it were square pools each thirty feet to a side. The air was soup-thick and intolerably humid.

"Can you see anything?" Renata whispered.

Glaser shook his head, peering through the emerald gloom. His pistol was in his right hand, primed and ready to fire. Renata could see the black stains the gunpowder had left on his glove.

"Do you have a weapon for me?"

He quickly and quietly withdrew a small folding knife from his pocket and handed it to her. She had hoped to be given his sabre, which was a ridiculous thing to hope for in the circumstances, and accepted and wielded the knife like a back-alley cut-throat.

"Stay behind me," Glaser said quietly, guiding her with his right hand so that she was indeed behind him. Renata found her bravado abandoning her; it was one thing to chase a person through the streets for action's sake and privately, secretly consider their capture impossible; it was quite another to trap them in a corner and make combat all but a certainty.

They moved around another square pool, this one dominated by a large three-tiered fountain rendered from sandstone. Ahead, the palace stretched enormously and vertiginously, the building easily two thousand feet long.

Renata saw the gun too late. It was off to their right, the figure crouched behind a low wall. What part of the person was not concealed by the flora was covered over with a heavy woollen cloak.

"Watch—!" she shouted, but was cut off by the report of the pistol. The ball whizzed through the air like a hornet and shattered against the head of one of the fountain's gargoyles.

The figure ran. Suddenly overconfident, Renata darted after

him, certain she could bring him to heel with a few quick slices of the knife. But the man was fast, springing away with incredible agility, and after a few moments she realised she had managed to lose herself amongst the foliage. Perhaps – it dawned on her too late – that had been the plan. The assailant could easily have made good his escape after the explosion had failed to kill her. Had he now led her into this labyrinthine rainforest greenhouse to make good his assassination?

"Colonel?" she called out, her throat dry. She whirled around, disoriented. Now eager to escape the Dynast's Palace entirely, she ran in the wrong direction, ending up in a dense arboretum. "Shit," she breathed, holding on to one of the trees, its trunk covered in tangles of brown fibres like hair. "Colonel," she whispered. "Colonel?"

She didn't see the figure until he was almost on her; he had moved quietly through the trees, and was now a dozen paces away and closing fast. Gone was the pistol; she would be killed silently by a dirk so as not to attract attention – "the gambler's end", as it was known in Sova.

"No!" she shrieked instinctively, clumsily raising the pocket-knife. But a moment later, a second figure crashed into the side of her, and she went flying, knocking her head against the side of the tree. She lost consciousness for several seconds, fading to the sound of swearing, grunting, and steel on steel; then she propped herself up against the foot of the trunk, touching her forehead with a shaking hand to find there was blood there. She felt suddenly nauseous, and in desperate need of water.

"That way!" she heard a voice shout. Through blurred vision she saw a man – her saviour – pointing to the rear of the Dynast's Palace. But she could not make out who it was.

She collapsed backwards, resting against the tree. Blood dripped on to her dress. She thought randomly of the difficulty and cost of getting it successfully washed out of the fabric.

She thought of the Great Silence.

She jolted awake as Colonel Glaser appeared next to her. "Ms Rainer! Are you all right?" he asked, his voice an echo, crouching down and turning her head roughly to the side to examine the wound there.

"Who was that?" she asked faintly, squinting into the greenery.

"I didn't get a look at him," Glaser muttered, pressing some makeshift bandage against her forehead. "Now, enough of this bloody nonsense. We need to get you in front of a physician."

VI

The Grey Eminence

"There is something so contemptible about newsmen. Their salt is misery, their butter woe. Their job is to distil the wretchedness of millions into inches on a sheet, and capture its most despondent and salacious essence. A dozen such stories are so reduced, each an oyster of despair waiting to slip down the gullet of ready consumers. But if the newsman is worthy of contempt, the news-reader bears an equal burden of scorn. A person who makes it their business to read the news every day, wallowing in matters which he could not possibly hope to affect, is a foolish wretch. There is no end to human unhappiness, and so there is no end to his unhappiness."

SATIRIST AND PAMPHLETEER BILIOUS JOSEPH

The Dynast's Palace

SOVA

"Bloody fool, bloody bastard fool," Count Lamprecht von Oldenburg muttered repeatedly as he exited the Dynast's Palace at its easternmost extremity. "Bloody fucking Nema-damned ass."

He sweated as he jogged west down the Creus Road. It was

lousy with soldiers and a large crowd of idiots staring goggle-eyed at the fire engulfing the remains of the ambassadors' coach.

"My lord count?" Someone tried to accost him.

"Nema Victoria and all the thrice-damned and blasted saints," he wheezed, keeping his head down. The Senate House was on his right and the Royal Imperial Courts of Justice on his left. There was no other place in the city – in the world – with a higher concentration of people who recognised him on sight. He should have come a different route.

"Lamprecht, is that you?" someone called from across the road.

"Can't stop," he muttered.

A great fat drop of sweat fell from his forehead. A wound on his hand – a day-old, self-inflicted bite mark – throbbed painfully as his blood rose to meet the demands of this most unhappy exercise. His clothes, now damp and in no way designed to accommodate rapid movement, chafed his groin and armpits and neck.

"Count von Oldenburg, a moment of your time—"

"Later, damn you," von Oldenburg shouted over his shoulder. He snatched a newspaper from a stand, throwing a coin at the stallkeeper – a hundred times the value of the paper – and brought it up about his face to conceal it.

He cut north up the Baden Highway, now slowing to a walk. Here the Schwartzheide lay to his right, an unpleasant stretch of parkland sitting between the Sauber and Assembly Square. He thought to take a moment to catch his breath there, but some mob was gathered in the square. Instead he pressed on at a fast walk, over the Baden Bridge and past the imposing facade of Guildhall where some other gaggle of reprobates had gathered to complain. His lip curled into a sneer. The commonfolk – the bloody *commonfolk*, complaining, *always*, endlessly complaining, and looting and rioting and fucking each other and breeding more looters and rioters. They filled the city with a sense of unspent energy. He grew nauseous with the thought of them, swelling and bloating Sova like maggots in the body of a dead badger. And the heat, Prince of Hell, the spring *heat*, thickening the air until it was as hot as a smith's workshop—

"My lord?"

"Piss off!"

Finally the Court of Nobles reared into view, a large, palatial building on the south-east corner of the Summit of the Prefects – itself an enormous urban promontory in the north-west of the old city. He hastened across the final stretch of road to the mule-driven elevator, which as a member of the Empire's governing aristocracy he was entitled to use. Everyone else who wanted to enter the Court had to go further north and either walk or be walked up the long and winding road. No effort whatever had been made to make that journey even slightly easier.

It took about a minute to be winched to the top. From there he hurried into the Court itself, through the main doors, through the courtyard beyond, and up several sets of stairs. The Court of Nobles was set out a little like the Imperial Office, with different parts of the building dedicated to the various duchies, counties, baronies and margraviates that made up the broader provinces of the Empire.

He entered his office and closed the door behind him. The place was quiet; even leaving aside the fact that it was the Senate's spring recess, the nobles did not trouble themselves to spend much time in the Court. They much preferred their country fortresses and estates.

He pulled the glove from his right hand.

"Shit," he muttered. The bite mark between his index finger and thumb was red and throbbing, and had not subsided mean-ingfully in the past day. He fumbled into his jacket pocket and took out a half-empty bottle of tonic, took a long swig of the bitter liquid, swallowed down the inevitable surfeit of saliva, and then dabbed his lips with a handkerchief.

With this ritual complete, he moved through the office and snatched a decanter of brandy from a drinks cabinet next to his desk, unstoppering it and taking a long draw. Then he took another, and another, until he felt the first stirrings of inebriation. He needed water, but that could come later.

He unbuckled his sabre and tossed it unceremoniously to the floor, then his jacket, then sat down heavily at his desk and yanked his collar open, gasping for air like a fish plucked from the ocean.

He tried to rally his racing thoughts. Matters had overtaken him quickly, slipping through his fingers like grains of sand. Such a risk – such a bloody stupid risk – to present himself, his *person*, in the Dynast's Palace. Without thinking, he raised his right hand and bit furiously into the scarred and calloused flesh there, opening the day-old scab which had formed at the junction of his thumb and index finger.

"Kasivar, Prince of *Hell!*" he erupted, thumping the desk and scattering trinkets and papers laid there, flecking them with blood. There would be an investigation. The great legal apparatus of Sova would be turned to the task. Lawyers and constables and – most detestable – journalists. *Pamphleteers.* He groaned. He should not have intervened directly in this nonsense. He *knew* it.

There was a knock at the door.

"Fuck off!" he roared.

"It's Broz."

Von Oldenburg gritted his teeth. "In, quickly."

The door opened and a man stepped in. He had the dark skin of a Southern Plainsman and a fashionable moustache, and was clad in poor man's rags – though he was not poor. Indeed, as one of von Oldenburg's foremost agents, his salary eclipsed that of most minor lords. He was also flushed and sweating profusely.

"Did you catch him?" von Oldenburg asked.

Broz shook his head curtly. He looked at von Oldenburg's bleeding hand briefly. "No, my lord. I lost him in the grain market."

Von Oldenburg took a deep breath through flared nostrils,

and released it. He poured another measure of brandy and offered it to Broz, who sat and accepted the glass, though he did not drink.

"Most vexing," von Oldenburg said after a little while.

"I agree."

"What did you find up at Pike's Bend?"

Broz reached into his pocket and produced a pamphlet. It was badly burned, and much of it was missing, but the headline was still visible. It read:

!PLAGUE IN DRAEDALAND!
AVOID ALL TRAVEL NORTH OF SOVA

"A dozen reams. All burnt," Broz said. "Along with half the press. Valentina is dead."

"Murdered?"

Broz tapped his throat.

Von Oldenburg bit back a spectacular sequence of oaths. "This was yesterday?"

"Aye."

"What about the presses on Blood Street?"

Broz shrugged. "No one will touch the story now. Word gets around."

"And the Imperial Household?"

"It was the Privy Council, my lord, who commissioned the pamphlets."

"What about the Army?"

"Preoccupied with the Kyarai."

"Town criers?"

"I haven't confirmed it yet, but I'm almost certain Hüber is dead, too."

Von Oldenburg lifted his hand to bite it again, but stopped himself at the last moment. The wound was already much too deep. Instead he tugged his glove back on.

"It is beyond doubt then. The Selureii are throttling the news. Trying to stop word of the plague spreading."

Broz inclined his head. "Is the answer, my lord, not to spread the word yourself?"

Von Oldenburg waved him off. "I have informed the Palatinate of Nordenkova," he said brusquely, referring to the political confederation of four counties sitting between Sova and Draedaland. "The borders are already closed. That is enough for now."

There was a pause as both men considered matters.

"And now this business with the diplomats," Broz said.

"Aye. I do not think the woman was the target, though. It would have been the ambassador himself. A case of mistaken identity."

"They have hitherto acted with a measure of care."

"Today was very clumsy," von Oldenburg agreed. "Very amateurish. I did not think they would go that far, not with the city as lousy with yeomanry as it is."

"Do you think anybody saw you outside the palace?"

"No." Von Oldenburg did not need to ask the same of Broz; the man was a talented infiltrator. He rubbed his chin. "We must assume the two matters are linked."

"The news of the plague and the attempt on the diplomat's life?"

"Yes. Though quite what the connexion is escapes me. My contact in the Imperial Office tells me they are travelling south, to see the mer-men. I must make it my business to find out why. Rather, I must make it *your* business to find out why. I intend to return to Haunerwald, and then likely on to Verdabaro."

"You mean to go today?"

"I mean to leave immediately. Make the necessary preparations."

"Aye, my lord."

"Oh," von Oldenburg said as Broz stood, "I was due to meet Pasko Marušić at the South Seas Trading Company today."

"Yes, my lord."

Von Oldenburg checked the time. He snorted. "Over four hours ago."

"Shall I track him down, sir?"

"He'll still be there. He owes me ten thousand goldmark."

"Shall I have him taken care of in the usual way?"

"Mm," von Oldenburg grunted through a mouthful of brandy, shaking his head. "No. He may yet make the sum back. Just put his eyes out."

Broz inclined his head. "As you wish, sir."

"And wait until I'm out of the city before you do it," von Oldenburg added, rubbing his bandaged hand where he had bitten it.

It was really quite tender.

It was a long, arduous week in a four-horse stagecoach up the winding Hauner Road to his home, and von Oldenburg's health deteriorated steadily over the course of the trip.

The route was indirect and often treacherous. The interposition of the Hassian Mountains, which bifurcated the County of Osthalde from the east, and the Tollish Marches, which reached their rocky fingers deep into Althaunersheim from the west, forced them to follow the Sauber all the way out of Wolfenshut until it turned into the River Gale. From there, they paused at Castle Weisbaum so that von Oldenburg could take dinner with Count Hangmar – though he felt too unwell to do the same again at Castle Osterlen.

They passed through the heart of Haunerwald. This was von Oldenburg's county, a rocky, hilly, mountainous place, though the north was given over to vast swathes of old-growth forest. Here the county's natural beauty had been spared the Imperial Navy's voracious need for timber; they took that from conquered lands or those further south. Still, parts of it, like Draedaland to the north, were bleak and damp and marshy, and it was noticeably colder half a thousand miles north of Sova.

They arrived at Castle Oldenburg at dusk on the seventh day.

It was an enormous fortification of grey stone that sat atop a huge and steep natural hill, capped with dozens of conical turrets which sprouted from the structure like mushrooms. At the foot of the hill was the town of Oldenburg, which lay next to the River Braun. It was home to a population one thousandth of the size of the capital's, a quiet and gloomy settlement sagging under the weight of their lord's infamy.

Eventually they reached the main entrance. Von Oldenburg's entire right hand and arm felt as though they were aflame. The bite mark pulsed painfully with each beat of his heart, his breath was laboured, and he perspired great quantities of sweat into his clothes.

"Are you all right, my lord count?" the doorman asked him as he staggered out the back of the stagecoach, light-headed and nauseous.

"Yelena," he muttered, bending over, hands on his thighs. "Fetch me Yelena immediately."

"At once my lord."

He was determined to enter Castle Oldenburg unaided, a tradition stretching back many centuries. But he was so febrile and confused that he must have fallen unconscious before he reached the threshold; for the next thing he knew, he was lying in bed, more or less spreadeagled, and completely naked.

He was not alone.

A woman sat astride him, riding him to the hilt. She too was naked, and her milk-pale skin was covered in an intricate network of geometric tattoos. She moved not with the wild passion of a young woman in love, nor with the false overexuberance of a prostitute; rather, she did so deliberately and with great concentration, chanting in a low voice in rhythm to the rise and fall of her hips, each slap of her buttocks against his thighs a drumbeat.

Von Oldenburg looked down to see that there was a great red line running from his hand, all the way up his arm, down his chest and stomach, and up the length of his cock. It flared with burning agony, as though it had been imprinted on his skin with a brand. Each time the woman landed, a great pulse of pain shot from the bite mark on his hand and down the line.

She moved more quickly as he felt himself being brought to climax. Now that he was fully conscious, it was not a slow process; the woman was an undeniable beauty, her body svelte, her breasts bouncing in a most pleasing manner. For her, this was – not business, exactly, but something falling within her professional remit; for him, however, and in spite of the pain he felt, it was an undeniable pleasure.

That was, until he came.

"*Eniru min!*" the woman shouted as he finished, except instead of a pleasant sensation, it was one of incredible agony. He tried to buck her off as he came, each expulsion one of boiling, foaming magma; but she gripped him tightly, her thigh muscles like iron.

"Nema damn fuck and blast!" he roared as she clamped on to him like a limpet, draining him in the same way a surgeon might lance a boil. Then, once this sorry episode was complete, she bent over the side of the bed to where a large metal bowl had been set, and vomited up a great stream of black ectoplasm.

"Blood of gods," von Oldenburg muttered, aghast, scrabbling back and away from her up the bed. She bucked once, twice, her body clenching to expel this foul fluid. Then, once she was done, she reached a trembling hand for a goblet of wine. She took a mouthful and swilled it around her cheeks, then spat that, too, into the bowl.

"How do you feel?" she asked him in accented Saxan.

Von Oldenburg examined the wound on his right hand. The inflammation had vanished. His skin was dry and the pain and dizziness had gone. In fact, he felt . . .

"Perfectly fine," he remarked, and then chuckled delightedly. "Nema, Yelena, you are a bloody marvel."

"Hm," she grunted. She stood up next to the bed, her pale skin glistening with sweat in the moonlight. The tattoos covering her body seemed to flicker and flash, as though charged with lightning. She put on a robe, and then picked up the bowl of oil-black sputum. "We have much to discuss," she said.

"Aye," von Oldenburg said, breathing heavily.

"You should eat. Restore your energy. Then we can talk."

"If you—" von Oldenburg began.

But she had already left.

"So. You are returned."

Von Oldenburg looked up from his brandy. It was an hour later, and he had eaten ravenously, with no regard for propriety at all. With his wound healed, and his belly full of meat, pastry and wine, he felt greatly restored – though in body only. Now that his base requirements had been sated, his mind was clouded with the weight of the tasks before him.

"I am returned," he agreed.

Yelena stepped into the drawing room – or what had once been a drawing room. Now it was part study, part library, part museum and part laboratory. The place was overstuffed with books and curios, and priceless antique tables and desks had been transformed into workbenches. The chamber would not have looked out of place in the Corps of Engineers building. It was a collection that had taken decades to assemble and tens of thousands in goldmark – to say nothing of the human cost.

"You should not do that."

Von Oldenburg examined the faded red bite mark on his hand. What should have been a thin web of flesh connecting his thumb and forefinger was thick with callous.

"I know," he said, sighing.

"It was utterly malignant. It might easily have killed you."

"I knew you would be able to cure it."

"I might not have been," she chided. She walked slowly across the chamber. She was an undeniably beautiful woman, imperious and regal in spite of her lowborn origins. Like von Oldenburg, she was in her fifties, but thanks to a decade living off a castle larder, the only lines that marked her skin were the faded geometric tattoos of a Draedist. Even clad in a blouse patterned with embroidered wildflowers and a simple blue kirtle – peasant clothing – she looked more like a queen in the midst of some act of subterfuge, rather than the pagan witch-healer she was.

She came to a stop at a table where several items lay. She picked one up idly, a hinged sphere of brass and gold which rattled as some mechanism within shifted.

"Be careful with that."

She looked sharply at von Oldenburg. There was a silence in which she examined him with a faint air of contempt.

"You have spent too long in Sova," she remarked, holding the sphere with no more or less care. "You have spent three months dealing with subordinates, fools and simpletons, and you forget what it is to respect a person."

Von Oldenburg pinched the bridge of his nose, his anger uncoiling. "You are right. It has been a long and tiresome journey. And I am greatly preoccupied."

Yelena placed the sphere back in its cradle with precisely the level of carelessness designed to provoke him, and took a seat opposite. "What progress have you made? Are the Selureii in Sova?"

"The Selureii are indeed in Sova. They have been there for some weeks. I know not how many – at least two. They have been trying to strangle news of the plague from spreading, setting fire to presses, killing pamphleteers and town criers. The day I quit the city, Broz and I followed one of them all the way from Shank's Harbour down the Creus Road. The bloody fool tried to blow up one of the Stygion diplomats, right outside the Life Guards' barracks."

Yelena's eyes widened slightly. "To what end?"

Von Oldenburg shrugged. "That is what I intend to find out."

"Did no one apprehend him?"

"The diplomat woman – her name escapes me, 'Rainier' or something – gave chase. Followed him into the Dynast's Palace with an officer from the Life Guards. The Legionary Prefect." He shook his head. "Utterly reckless."

"She was killed?"

"No. Broz saved her life."

"Did anybody see you?" Yelena asked.

"Not in the palace itself. Nor leaving it."

"But Broz could not apprehend the assassin? *Would-be* assassin." She thought for a moment. "And you are certain it was the Selureii?"

"I am," he said. He looked up at her. "Tell me about them."

She shrugged. "There is not much to tell that you do not already know. They are a death cult. A severe and didactic group. They are not well liked by my fellow Draedists except amongst the conservative and orthodox. They are singularly focused on death magick. They make it their business to commune with the dead. And they preach endlessly."

"And they are based in Verdabaro?"

Yelena nodded once.

Von Oldenburg thought a moment. "I thought all shamans in Draedaland communed with the dead."

"They do."

"So what is the difference?"

"There is being a practitioner, and there is obsession with the practice. The two are not the same."

"Hm."

"What is the connexion between the attempt on the life of the Stygion ambassador and the plague in Draedaland?"

"Thinking about it logically, I would imagine the mer-men have some . . . special knowledge of, or perhaps even a solution to, the plague. Knowledge the Selureii are seeking to deny to Sova."

He took a deep breath, and released it slowly. "That suggests in itself the knowledge is magickal in nature."

"Ah," Yelena said playfully, though to von Oldenburg it sounded sarcastic. "So *that* is why you are interested."

"I have made no secret of my interests," he said, gesturing pointedly to the magickal paraphernalia scattered about the chamber.

"To *me*. If Sova knew of this—"

"But Sova does *not* know of this." He worked his tongue around his mouth like a ball of gristle. "It is funny; I have spent many years in and amongst the Draedists, learning their ways, their magicks. In other circumstances the Selureii and I might have been allies. Friends even."

From her expression, he could tell Yelena did not like that sentiment. "You were never interested in my people. Just their talents."

"Aye. That is true. Although your 'people', if they can so be called, were but a few generations ago Imperial subjects themselves."

"A few centuries more like," she replied, but von Oldenburg wasn't listening.

"Imagine it," he said wistfully. "Draedaland, Manaeisland, Tolland, all of the Western Kingdoms . . . all of them once Sovan possessions. Conquered by might, governed by right, the people kept to heel with magicks."

"You yearn for the Empire's restoration, I understand that," Yelena said, unwilling to hear this particular speech again.

"Sova has denied *itself* magick," von Oldenburg replied, raising his voice. "No other nation or race in the known world has hamstrung itself so absurdly. The pagans practise. The wolfmen practise. The mer-men practise. Who knows what secrets and powers they have unlocked?"

"Well, you do, for one."

"I alone!" von Oldenburg suddenly thundered. "I alone have made it my business to research that which the Empire has given up freely. And I do so entirely *without* the confines of the law. You jest, but if it was made known what I have here, what objects and artefacts and lore I have unearthed, what expeditions I have led and what pagans I have been treating with, they would shoot me. Do you realise that?"

Yelena nodded her head slowly. "I do. But I have warned you before against speaking to the Selureii."

"They could grant me access to their death magicks."

"A poisoned chalice if ever there was one."

"I could pay them great sums of goldmark."

"Scant reward in a world that they apparently contrive to end."

Von Oldenburg lapsed to silence. He did not like it when Yelena spoke sense, but it was also why she was so valuable to him.

Eventually, he said, "I must explore the nature of this plague in Draedaland."

"That is a venture fraught with risk."

"The same could be said of practically everything I undertake."

She looked at him, her expression serious. "Do not ask me to return to Draedaland. Not after what they did to me."

"I shan't ask you to," von Oldenburg replied, though he could not hide his disappointment. "I shall miss your talents, though."

She quirked an eyebrow. "Which ones?"

He laughed, a slow, rumbling, booming noise. Outside, a light rain began to patter against the glass windows of the drawing room. Beyond, the country was dark and silent. "Gods, I have missed you, Lena," he muttered.

"Is that so?"

"Aye. 'Tis so."

She bent forward in her chair and gripped the hem of her kirtle, pulling it up until she had exposed herself.

"Prove it."

VII

Monsters in the Night

"A man with two masters makes an enemy of all the world."

SOVAN PROVERB

Line of Demarcation

ALDA RIVER VALLEY

Dear Father,

Well. We have left the "Fort at the End of the World".

I have made no secret of the difficult nature of this country. Not only am I – are we – plagued by all manner of curious sounds at night, which I had hoped to ascribe to the local wildlife (but which I cannot), but the weather itself conspires against us too. The day we left on this miserable expedition north, the sky was rent by the most unnaturally calamitous thunderstorm I have ever witnessed. The soldiers were not perturbed, but this did not comfort me. Rather, I am concerned that they have become inured to the strange nature of this place.

We have set out north with one hundred men, the entirety of the light company under my command as brevet captain and fully half of the garrison. Our journey is one of seventy-five miles across particularly treacherous country. At some point we must trouble ourselves to cross over the Line of Demarcation, too, and thereafter make war on the Great Enemy of Casimir. I must confess, even in spite of the difficult living conditions at Fort Ingomar and all of its spectral goings-on, I had become accustomed to the routine. It was a hard life, stripped of all comfort, but the walls were thick and robust, and I quickly lost any sense of ~~mortal~~ danger.

I am heartened to note that we are joined by Captain Furlan and enough artillerymen to man two eight-pounders, which have been disassembled for the journey. There was a long debate about whether we should trouble ourselves to bring guns at all, given the obvious difficulties of freighting them and their limbers, but should the fort at the Ena Split be in any state of readiness, then we shall have nothing to breach it with whatever. I anticipate that the mules and men dragging the guns will shortly fall well behind, though the men of the light company seem perfectly happy to keep pace with them. I am certainly not alone in my reluctance to undertake this operation.

As well as the Sovans, who of course make up the body of our mission, we have several pagan guides who know the country intimately. They herald from a tribal confederation known as the "Black Mountain" (there is a Draedic word for it, but should I attempt to spell it I would run out of ink). They seem like agreeable fellows, though the men treat them callously, which I find surprising given that they have allied themselves to us at great personal cost.

We have tried to keep the baggage train to a minimum, though supplying over a hundred soldiers with victuals is no mean feat, and the gun limbers are filled with shot and powder and all manner of accoutrements which must between them weigh the better part of two tonnes. Captain Furlan is the most senior officer present by rank, but is responsible only for the artillery, and will not assist me beyond what is strictly required of him. Such an assemblage of persons and matériel is well beyond my ability to govern – though govern them I must.

At the moment, it is all I can do to govern myself.

I shall write again soon.

Your loving son,

Peter

They covered barely seven miles on the first day. The ground, which was fractured and rocky in the best of conditions, had become a quagmire thanks to the sudden torrent. Had they more time, they could have requisitioned some Imperial engineers from Fort Romauld and cut themselves a road, or even built rafts to take up the River Alda. Instead, they hitched the wagons to their limited supply of mules, and together with the soldiers, who had stripped to the waist, pushed and pulled and dragged the heavy cannon and supply carts through the mud. The going was so difficult and their labours so exhausting that on the second day Peter was tempted to call off the expedition altogether and wait for the weather to improve.

Captain Furlan simply laughed at the prospect.

"It *doesn't* improve," he said, smoking a pipe as he watched the artillerymen and a dozen filthy, sweating soldiers strain against the back of a gun carriage to try and get the thing over a mound that could not have been more than six feet high. The mules hee-hawed their displeasure as they were whipped bloody, whilst a great cacophony of swearing and grunting filled the air. A little way ahead, one of the pagans, a pale-skinned, pale-haired woman with a blue tattoo across her face like a swashbuckler's mask, scanned the forest. She wore a brocade poncho over a . . . Peter didn't know how to describe it. It was like a spring dress, but sleeveless and cut above the knee, scandalously high by Sovan mores. His gaze lingered.

"The sun must touch this place at some point in the year," he said absently. The woman turned, briefly locked eyes with him, and then darted off ahead. Peter felt his cheeks redden.

Furlan out a great exhalation of smoke. "It does. It gets exceedingly hot. Stinking hot." He took a long draw of watered brandy. "In a few months you will not recognise the place, and the bloodsuckers will outnumber us a thousand to one. But the rain – the rain never stops." He pointed to the north-east, where the foothills to the enormous Northern Barrier Range dominated the horizon. "It's the mountains."

Peter grunted. He didn't want a lesson on climatology. "Major Haak has given us two weeks to reach the Ena Split."

"By my reckoning we have made seven miles today. Seven miles a day, eleven days? If anything, we shall be there early."

There was something infectious about Furlan's easy manner.

"Yes, well. I suppose when you put it like that . . . "

"What other way is there to put it?" Furlan said, extinguishing his pipe. Then he left Peter, and went to shout at his men.

They travelled for another two days, putting fifteen miles between themselves and Fort Ingomar. They spent the time in silence, picking their way through the country quietly for fear of unearthing pagan interlopers and – much more pressingly, at least insofar as the soldiers were concerned – malevolent sprites. Peter had decided to head due north until they reached the junction of the River Alda and the River Tadija. The latter was broader and slower, and they could construct rafts to move the guns easily and, more importantly, quickly. Morale would hold only for so long. Every moment they spent beyond the safe confines of the fortress was like an unnameable itch, a feeling of slow, saturating horror, a formless acid dread in the pit of the stomach. It made them all twitchy and irritable. Sovan soldiers were famously disciplined, but in the gloomy confines of the valley, tempers flared and fights erupted with alarming frequency. Matters reached the point where Peter reluctantly authorised the flogging of one man, which put an end to the unrest, though it increased the weight of resentment against him tenfold.

"Their respect is yours by right," Furlan said disapprovingly, as Peter unburdened himself of the matters which he had hitherto confined to his letters home. It was a miserable, wet night, and they sat huddled together in their waxed greatcoats whilst rain thundered down around them. "You need not earn it."

"Notwithstanding," Peter said, wanting to prolong the conversation. He had been suffering from an unsettling nightmare for the past few nights, one in which his body from the feet upwards slowly vanished, and he was putting off sleep. "There must be some way to speed up the process."

"Captain Hulderic was well liked. Most of the men I'm sure would rather have left his shoes unfilled. Which is of course preposterous," Furlan added, catching Peter's expression. "But there it is. And you are young. And this is a difficult posting. Grow some whiskers, that might help."

Peter rubbed his smooth chin, which he had been at pains to shave daily as per the regimental dress-code ordinances. He could grow a beard, thankfully; he was young and inexperienced, but he was not baby-faced. There was some mercy in that.

"I suppose so," he said eventually.

Furlan sighed. His breath smelt strongly of alcohol "If it is advice you are after, then here is mine: you are not their friend. And you never will be. It is human nature to want people to like you, but your position makes you inherently unlikable. What they need is someone who will deploy them strategically, with one eye on defeating the enemy and the other on preserving their lives. Respect is earned in battle, and you have not been in one. Do not rush the process."

Even though the advice was good, Peter still resented having to ask for it. How did leadership come so naturally to some people and not others?

Somewhere in the distance there was a ghostly, aethereal shriek. It set Peter's heart to racing.

"It's getting worse, isn't it?" he said after a while.

Furlan sniffed, and nodded. "It is."

"Worse than it was at Ingomar."

"It is," Furlan said again.

"What is going *on* out here?"

Furlan grunted, and pressed himself up. He stood in the darkness, the rain pattering off his tricorn and greatcoat.

"If you can answer that question, Lieutenant—"

"I'll be a popular man?"

Furlan chuckled. "Now you're getting it."

That night Peter was awoken from a broken and unsatisfactory sleep by a blood-curdling scream – a real one this time. The rain had stopped, though the trees dripped so persistently that it might as well not have.

Convinced they were under attack, he leapt out of his tent, grabbed his sabre and pistol, and began moving directly to the source of the noise, bleary-eyed and fuzzy-headed. It was still an hour or two off dawn, and the forest was profoundly dark – as he discovered shortly after walking headlong into a tree.

"Nema," he muttered, blinking away stars. There were other shouts now – even the discharging of muskets, which crashed calamitously into the night.

"Cease fire!" someone – Furlan – was shouting, but then there was a tremendous flash and report as another musket was fired. The ball very clearly impacted a thick tree branch not twenty paces away. "Cease firing, damn your eyes!"

The flash had crazed Peter's vision with dancing splotches of colour, and he staggered around like a blind man with a leg injury. There was one more explosion of sound and light as another soldier fired her musket. It killed off the very last vestiges of his night vision, but it had the effect of branding a starkly lit image of the local forest on the insides of his eyelids.

He blinked furiously as he reached the outermost position of the encampment.

And then he saw—

He blinked again, and again, jamming his fists into his face as though he might print the image directly on to his eyeballs. He examined the pulsing after-image there as though scrutinising a painting in an art gallery, except this one would only exist for a handful more seconds.

Surely that wasn't—

Eyes.

A pair of eyes in the forest, discorporate in the darkness, having caught the light from the muzzle flash and reflected it back – brightly enough to have been captured with almost perfect clarity on his retinas.

More blinking only hastened the dissolution of the image, until it was gone completely.

Peter felt sick with fear.

"What's the matter?" he demanded as he reached the source of the scream. The place was in disarray now as men and women were preparing their muskets for a volley of fire into the darkness.

A man was gibbering like a lunatic in the undergrowth. Two more soldiers were holding him down, one searching for a wound. But there was no injury, no blood. By the brief, scant moonlight, Peter could see that, unlike the ghastly vision he had suffered in Fort Ingomar, this man was intact.

"Bloody hell," Furlan muttered, crouching down. He slapped the thrashing soldier sharply across the cheek. "Govern yourself, man!" he snapped. "What is the *matter*?"

"A monster, I saw a monster!"

"There are no monsters," Furlan said, but even though he spoke in his gruff and unsympathetic way, there was a trace of doubt in his voice. Did anyone believe that out here?

"It was . . . I . . . It was close, it smelt me, I could feel its breath!"

"Be quiet!" Furlan snapped. "Be quiet, for the gods' sake. If you start a panic in this company, I will shoot you myself."

The man swallowed, nodding vigorously. "Aye, sir."

Peter felt as though he really ought to take charge of the situation – or at least say something. But he just couldn't. Couldn't find an appropriate time to speak – which had almost certainly passed anyway – couldn't summon the necessary authority, couldn't overcome the fear he himself felt. For in spite of Captain Furlan's insistence to the contrary, he had seen . . .

What had he seen? What exactly *had* he seen? Eyes. A pair of eyes. What did that mean? An owl? A jaguar? A sabrecat? A bear? A wolf? It could have been any one of those things. What was more likely, a wild animal, many thousands of which inhabited the forest, or a monster?

What was more likely?

"Just a wild cat," he heard himself say, codifying the lie. He said it again more forcefully. "Just a wild cat. I saw it myself. You'll have half the bloody Casimirs down on our heads with your raving, to say nothing of the pagans!" He himself was shouting now, making more noise than the frightened soldier. At least his shouting sounded like the sort of berating an angry officer might produce, and not someone venting their over-heated nerves.

Furlan retreated, happy to divest himself of the reins of command. Now it was just Peter and a gaggle of nervous soldiers. In their quiet midnight terror, the dynamic shifted firmly in Peter's favour.

He pretended to examine the sky, but it was thick with cloud again, the appearance of the moon always a fleeting thing. There was no way to tell the time beyond his innate sense of its passage.

"Right," he said quietly, more to himself than anyone else. "Just . . . as you were."

Then he repaired to his tent.

A few minutes later, it began to rain again.

On their sixth day out of Fort Ingomar, one of the Black Mountain pagans – not the woman, but a man, Cathassach – returned to inform them that they would achieve the River Tadija by the evening. He led Peter and Furlan to a sheer escarpment of rock easily forty feet high, which jutted out of the forest like an enormous grey tooth. Beyond, Peter realised with a dismal feeling, stretched the last few miles of Sovan territory within the Alda River Valley. From this vantage point, and assisted by a spyglass, he could just make out the Ena Split itself, nearly thirty miles to the north-west. Beyond that was the enormous Lake Ena – and beyond *that*, thousands of miles of uncharted forest and mountain. It felt much more like the end of the world than Fort Ingomar ever had.

Getting the eight-pounders down the escarpment, which seemed to stretch for many miles in both directions was going to be extremely difficult; but after that, reaching the Split would be straightforward. The River Tadija was wide and slow, and Furlan assured Peter that he and his sergeant knew how to make suitable rafts for the guns.

Peter ordered a picket line to be established by the light company, and the pagan guides led two dozen of the most capable men down the rock face. It wasn't sheer, but it was treacherously steep. Then, in spite of a lashing of cold spring rain, everyone stripped to the waist and began the difficult task of tying and lowering down the mules, gun limbers, carriages and barrels, and the rest of the baggage train.

For the entire day Peter suffered the compulsion to assist, but Furlan told him quietly and firmly that his solitary role was to direct matters. The mules went over first, tied under the legs and singularly unhappy. One man was kicked, fortunately only in the thigh. At the shallowest point of the slope, the wagons were lowered slowly as though it were merely a steep road. The men strained to keep the tension in the ropes, conscious that failure meant the destruction of their food stores. Peter tried to occupy his mind with maps of the river valley and possible approaches to the Split – though more often than not his eyes and attention settled on the female pagan, whose name transpired to be Olwin. But by the mid-afternoon, his nerves had frayed irreparably. As the last cannon barrel was lowered down the cliff face, he succumbed to the temptation to take on some of Furlan's brandy.

"Did you see anything last night?" he asked the captain as he handed back the flask.

"What do you mean?"

"During the . . . incident. The firing."

Furlan pulled an expression of distaste. "No," he said. It felt like a lie.

"I thought I saw someone watching us." Some*thing*.

"Probably just a wolf chancing its arm on some scraps," Furlan replied. "Nema knows it isn't the Casimirs. Not a hair nor hide of them."

"Probably," Peter murmured, thinking of the wide-eyed soldiers from the night before, their tangible fear. It rose off the valley ahead of them like mist, a great cloud of unease, saturating the air. He wanted to say more, but instead began to fuss about the little trestle table that he and Furlan had erected to examine and annotate their maps. As he did so, someone whispered in his ear.

"*Pistu.*"

He turned sharply, expecting to see one of the pagans – preferably Olwin – standing at his elbow.

But there was no one there.

His brow furrowed, and he was about to say something when

he was distracted by a creaking, groaning sound. At first he thought it might be a failing bough, for Nema knew the forest was tested by the weather often enough. Then he realised with a plunging feeling in his gut that it was the ropes holding the cannon barrel – all thousand pounds of it.

"Get clear!" he roared, at precisely the same time one of the ropes snapped with the sound of a gunshot. One line of soldiers suddenly toppled over as the tension was released, whilst the other fell to the ground a second later, hands smoking, as they were suddenly and briefly saddled with an extra five hundred pounds of weight.

A single scream, and then a great collective groan, went up from the foot of the rock face.

Peter approached the edge, swallowing, legs weak. There on the forest floor was a member of the light company, spreadeagled on his back. The barrel was lying on him perfectly vertically, from groin to head. There was something gruesomely comedic about it, the sort of caricature image one would find printed on a pamphlet in Sova.

Furlan joined Peter at the precipice, looking at the grisly scene and wincing.

"Well," he said, putting the bit of his pipe in his mouth. "He might just have saved the barrel."

They made camp quarter of a mile away from where the man had been crushed. Peter had felt compelled to oversee the retrieval of the body. It was a testament to the skill of the regimental clothiers that the man's uniform had not torn, but rather had contained the explosive disassembly of his body.

The accident crushed morale as surely as the cannon barrel had crushed its victim. Crossing over the Line of Demarcation had also set the company on edge, though it seemed to Peter that they had been in as much danger in the Sovan half of the valley.

That they had not come across any ambush or enemy force was entirely by luck rather than design.

Furlan seemed untroubled by the accident. If anything he seemed pleased that they had only lost one man, and with nothing except minor injuries sustained by the rest of the company – a case of rope burn, a turned ankle, a woman who had taken a splinter to the eye but who could still see.

As they ate their evening meal together, Peter once again took the time to unburden himself, wary that he was treating Furlan like a Neman confessor.

"The first casualty under my command," he said.

Furlan grunted, tiring of this dynamic. "There will be others."

"You seem uniquely inured to it."

"Is that what you think?"

"Well, yes," Peter said, doubtfully. "Perhaps not."

"Perhaps not indeed."

There was an awkward pause. "You know, moments before the accident, I heard something."

"What do you mean?"

"A voice whispered in my ear."

Furlan considered this for a moment. "What did it say?" he asked, in a tone of voice which suggested he didn't particularly want to know the answer. His lips glistened with brandy in the light from the cookfire.

"I'm not sure," Peter admitted. "Pea-stool. Pistol?" He spoke each combination aloud, but shook his head. "Pea soup?" He snorted bitterly. "No. I cannot recall."

"*Pistu*," said a voice, to his sudden horror. But this time it was Cathassach. The man had been loitering in the shadows near the two officers, a sort of unofficial close protection detail. Like Olwin, he was pale and tattooed, though he wore a Sovan waxed greatcoat over his mountain confederation garb. The pagans, after all, liked to remain dry as much as the next person.

"What did you say?" Peter demanded.

Cathassach, ghostly in the twilight, simply repeated it. *"Pistu."*

"Yes," Peter said. "That's the word. What does it mean?"

The man thought for a moment. "Crush," he said.

There was a long pause. Peter and Furlan exchanged a glance. "Interesting," the captain said after a while.

Neither of them felt much like talking after that.

❧

That night, Peter found himself roused from a fitful sleep once again. But there had been no noise, no shouts of desperation or call to arms. He lay in his tent in silence, waiting for something to happen, though it did not.

Propelled by a lingering sense of unease, he retrieved his sabre and pistol and climbed out of the tent. He walked amongst the tents and trees, acknowledging the brief and subtle obeisances of those soldiers who were awake or on sentry duty.

There was something definitely . . . *off.* An intangible sense of wrongness that set his heart to fluttering and his guts to churning. A susurrus of wind sounded more like whispering than the rustling of trees. The air had a strange quality to it, almost as though it *smelt* wrong, as if he had stepped through an invisible boundary into another place entirely.

He performed a long, slow loop of the encampment, trying to work out what it was that had roused him. And then he saw movement perhaps fifty paces beyond the line. It was a relatively well-lit night, though it was still dark, and he knew immediately that it was not a natural movement – the shaking of a tree branch in the breeze, the skulking of a fox, the rain dislodging a rock. It was a purposeful, man-made movement. A sentry taking a shit?

"Is anyone out there?" he asked the nearest soldier on rotation.

The man shook his head in the darkness. "Not that I know of, sir."

Peter sucked his teeth. "Just come with me a moment," he

⦿ 114 ⦿

said, and the man pressed himself to his feet and grabbed his musket.

Peter walked slowly to where he had seen the movement. He stopped frequently, even though the distance was not that great, looking and listening for any sign of a person.

"Do you hear that?" he asked the soldier.

"The, uh, weeping, sir?"

"Yes."

"Aye. I hear it."

Peter set his jaw. "Wait here."

He approached what he saw now was a dark mass on the floor. At first it looked like it could be a large pile of mule shit, or perhaps a small crop of stones and rocks. But there was an unmistakable smell rising off it – not of excrement, but of blood and offal.

He squinted in the darkness, and then approached and squatted down next to the pile.

Immediately he recoiled with revulsion, so suddenly and energetically that he kicked himself clumsily on to his buttocks.

It was viscera. Vital organs, arranged in a very specific way. Brain, heart and lungs, liver, kidneys, bladder and intestines, testes. Placed as though every other part of the body, bones and skin and muscle, had simply vanished. Some of the organs were badly damaged. The stomach was torn, the heart and lungs ripped where splintered bones had torn into them. Peter realised with horrifying clarity that these were the organs of the man who had been crushed that day. And someone had set them out in this very grotesque, very specific way.

"What in the name of Nema Victoria," he breathed. He pressed himself to his feet and looked around, peering into the profound darkness, trying to see if anyone was there.

In the distance, he caught the glint of a pair of eyes.

VIII

An Assemblage
of Persons

"This has given rise to a modern phenomenon where the bankers trade not in physical commodities (such as lumber, or coal, or iron ore, or furs) but rather – exempli gratia – intangible slices of a company's value, or the speculated future price of a given asset, or even the forthcoming option to be bound by a sales contract. Absent a scrying orb, such valuations have no basis except in utter fancy. So positioned, a person can generate an income – or a spectacular loss! – based on numbers conjured from thin air. The former he keeps for himself; the latter he is at pains to pass on to his broker, stockholders, and most commonly and easily, the taxpayer."

FROM LASKA'S *INTANGIBLE INSTRUMENTS: THE PLAGUE OF THE MODERN SOVAN TRADER*

Royal Naval Hospital

SOVA

They found Amara in a private chamber in the Royal Naval Hospital. The hospital sat on the waterfront, where the westernmost branch of the River Sauber had been diverted to create a canal and large artificial naval docks. Through the window in the chamber, Renata could see the South Battery, an enormous artillery emplacement built into the mural tower at the southwest corner of the old Guelan Wall.

Amara was unconscious, exhausted from the pain and sedated. She looked ashen in the late-afternoon light. The Royal Naval Hospital was both a hospital and a research institution, home to the most skilled surgeons in the Empire – men and women who had spent decades amputating limbs and removing musket balls, shrapnel and splinters the size of stakes from soldiers and sailors. But in spite of this, Renata was heartsick with worry. She sat next to her sister, holding and stroking her hand in the dying light, whilst outside she heard a constant stream of muffled conversation where Colonel Glaser and a gaggle of Life Guards, yeomen and city constables congregated to pick over the ruins of the day.

The door opened, and a moustachioed, pipe-smoking naval surgeon walked in. He wore a dark blue jacket with polished brass buttons and high black stock collars, and his sleeves were rolled up to the elbow. He was rubbing his hands with a large damp rag that smelt strongly of surgical spirit.

"You are the sister?" he asked, moving briskly past Renata. "I am Mister Lilic." He threw the rag over his shoulder and took the pipe out of his mouth, pressing the bit of it into the bandages around Amara's shoulder. She stirred, whimpering.

"What are you doing?" Renata demanded.

The surgeon looked at her irritably, but said nothing. He put the pipe back into his mouth and began to unravel the bandages. His brow furrowed.

"What's wrong?" Renata asked. "Please?"

"Wait a minute," Lilic said. He peeled back the last layer. They had removed the bone fragments and stitched up the wound, for the pistol ball had laid open a good portion of Amara's shoulder. But the whole area was a bright shade of purple, yellow and red, striking in its virulence.

"Is that . . . What does that mean? Is that bad?"

Lilic ignored her, pressing the backs of his fingers against the wound. He pressed it harder, and a trickle of foul-smelling liquid erupted from between the stitches. In spite of herself and her love for her sister, Renata found herself repulsed.

"Is that normal?" When the surgeon continued to ignore her, she said, "Nema damn you man, answer me!"

Even then Lilic took his time. He pressed his rough, calloused hand against Amara's forehead, where perspiration glistened in the afternoon sunlight.

"The wound is badly infected," he declared. "Which is surprising."

"Why is it surprising?" Renata asked, feeling her stomach drop. She remembered being relieved – *relieved* – that Amara had been shot in the shoulder. Not the brain or heart or lungs, and not in the gut, or anywhere in the abdomen really. The shoulder was nothing, just a lump of flesh. She knew that being struck on the bone could be mortal if a fragment of it was explosively propelled further into the body. And bones themselves, it seemed, could be infected, though that was really at the outer limits of her knowledge on the subject. But the shoulder? Surely a more harmless flesh wound did not exist.

"Infections are common in wounds such as these. Bits of detritus – in this case her dress – get carried deep into the flesh. But although the ball here has laid open much of the shoulder – and that is to do with the close proximity of the pistol – I have applied counter-sepsis solution and removed the fragmented bone, and closed the wound. And the ball was not lodged inside." He rubbed his moustache with a thumb and forefinger. "Infection is always a risk, but I would not have expected it to be this virulent this quickly. Not in light of the measures I have taken."

Renata gripped Amara's hand tightly, holding it to her breast as though she might transmit some of her own life force to her sister.

"I don't understand," she said, though she did. She understood perfectly. It was true that in the chaos of the afternoon her mind had become largely impervious to new information, but this she grasped perfectly.

"Where were you when the shot was fired?"

"On the Creus Road. In a coach. Is that relevant?"

"No," the surgeon decided. "It might have been had you been somewhere else – a tannery perhaps."

Renata swallowed hard. She did not want to cry – she had never been one to weep, particularly. But she had not been confronted with the spectre of untimely bereavement since the death of her mother when she was child. And she was still unsure she had fully come to terms with that.

"What is the solution?"

"Carbolic acid?"

Renata shook her head. "No, I mean the solution to the *problem*. She cannot . . ." *Die.* She didn't even want to say the word out loud.

The surgeon regarded Amara for a long while. "I shall discuss the matter with my colleagues. I expect the answer in the short term will be to reopen the wound, debride it and allow it to suppurate. There are other techniques which we may attempt, including leaving the wound open. Some of my fellows have had success in letting wounds such as these take on air for a period of hours and even days. Maggots, too, can be used to consume the dead flesh." Renata winced in revulsion. "It is an inexact science, I am afraid. Take solace in the fact that there is no place better equipped in the Empire to deal with it."

She took a moment to compose herself. "I thank you for your time and attention," she said, giving her best diplomatic smile.

The surgeon accepted this with a weary grace. "We shall have to begin remedial action shortly." He looked at her meaningfully. "I shall give you the same advice I give everyone in your position: if you have anything to say to your sister, I should say it now."

He left the room to spare Renata the embarrassment of breaking down in front of him – for there was no cure for Sovan awkwardness – though in the event she did not. The fact of the matter was, for all she was upset, she did not truly believe that Amara would die. Infections were routinely survived. A few days of unpleasant fever, certainly, but not the death sentence they had once been. Besides, Amara was the flipside of Renata: vivacious, exuberant, irrepressible. She would survive through sheer force of will, Renata was absolutely certain of it.

"Right," she said, placing Amara's hand back on the bed. "You just listen to me. I love you. All right?" She took her sister's hand back into hers. "I love you and I need you. I need your . . . *unruliness*. Do you understand me? I need it in my life. Because life will be a lot quieter and less colourful without you. And I could not bear that." She squeezed Amara's hand tightly. "So please, Nema, come back to me. Please?"

And then, finally, she did cry.

They were ushered out of the Naval Hospital and repaired to Colonel Glaser's house. Although the Life Guards were barracked at the junction of the Creus Road and Haugen Highway, Glaser himself, as a Privy Councillor, was entitled to an ostentatious manse atop the Summit of the Prefects.

It was now well into the evening, and they took a carriage; Glaser, Renata and Maruska, the latter having been summoned from the Imperial Office and apprised. Although they were colleagues, they were also close friends, and Maruska comforted Renata with tenderness for the duration of the journey.

Glaser's husband, an independently wealthy and urbane man by the name of Velimir, greeted them at the front door. All around him reared an enormous turreted mansion of grey stone, the brickwork lost under a vast network of perennial creeping vines.

"I heard the news," he called out to them as they approached. "Is anyone injured?"

"No, we're fine," Glaser said. "But we'll need food – and drink."

"Zorica has already laid out dinner," Velimir said. "In the main hall. I daresay it's cold . . . "

"Don't fuss so, mother hen. We'll be fine."

"Hm," Velimir grunted disapprovingly. "Are you all right, my dear?"

Renata nodded, though she was not. She had no stomach for these deadly intrigues.

"Some brandy will see her right," Glaser said over his shoulder, sweeping through the entrance hall.

"She's going to need more than a bloody drink," Velimir shot back. He turned to her. "Though it's usually a good place to start, eh?" he added conspiratorially.

Renata smiled weakly. "I suppose you are right."

It was not long before Glaser, Renata and Maruska were arranged in the manse's drawing room, rather than its great hall, where a profligate feast languished uneaten. Here in the low light, amongst an abundance of hunting trophies, rugs and tapestries – to say nothing of the Legionary paraphernalia – they swilled glasses of amber-coloured brandy in silence, each waiting for someone else to speak first.

"Well. I talked to the sheriff," Glaser said after a while. "They did not apprehend the man in the end."

Renata felt her stomach drop. "He is still at large?" In the excitement of the day, she had spared little thought for her would-be murderer.

"I am afraid so."

"I thought you said you had him cold in the Dynast's Palace?" Maruska rumbled disapprovingly.

"'Tis not so. I lost him in the foliage. It was someone else, a passer-by, who saved Ms Rainer's life."

"So you saw neither the perpetrator nor the saviour?"

Glaser scoffed. "Ambassador, if you are suggesting—"

"Please, stop it, the pair of you," Renata murmured, her hand tracing the lump on her forehead where she had been thrown into the tree. She set the glass of brandy down; it was making her feel nauseous.

Maruska sighed. "So the sheriff and his constables had no luck? Nor the yeomanry?"

Glaser made a frustrated noise. "I do not know what it is you want me to tell you, Ambassador. The man was not apprehended."

"And Renata's rescuer; he has not presented himself to give an account?"

"No."

Maruska muttered something in Qareshian. "If he is at large, he will strike again."

"Yes. I expect so," Glaser said into his glass.

The three of them were silent as they considered matters for a moment.

"There is a question of timing," Maruska said after a while. He spoke carefully, in a considered manner. "The arrival of the Bruta Sarkan monks. The preparation for the diplomatic mission. The attempt on Renata's life. These things are unlikely to be unconnected."

"Hm," Glaser said, nodding. "The thought had crossed my mind."

"You have spoken to Brother Herschel?"

"I have. He had nothing useful to offer, save that the matters are 'likely to be connected'."

"But the attempted assassination is evidence that we are cutting to the heart of something, do you not think?" Maruska pressed. "If what Herschel told us is even partly correct, such prophecies tend to attract a great number of undesirables: profiteers, the zealous, the insane. For every Brother Herschel and

Guillot, there will be some doomsday cultist whose aims lie in opposition to ours."

"That is a rather remarkable piece of conjecture," Glaser said, though there was a note – rare, Renata imagined – of uncertainty in his voice.

Maruska shrugged.

Glaser sighed, and drained the last of his brandy. "Let the constables and lawmen do their jobs, and we shall do ours. We shall leave Sova at first light."

"*We*, Colonel?" Renata asked in a brief moment of lucidity. She could feel herself falling asleep as the weight of the warmth, the comfortable chair, the brandy, and the events of the day crushed her into a state of exhaustion.

"Yes. I have decided to accompany you," Glaser said, though he did not seem to be happy at the prospect. "This matter, especially in light of the day's events, is beginning to vex me. *Greatly*. And besides, it is not entirely born of altruism. I have been considering a trip to the Kyarai for some time now. Here is an opportunity to take care of a number of matters concurrently."

"A happy coincidence," Maruska said levelly.

"Indeed." Glaser nodded to the door. "I suggest you retire. If you have anything you require from either the Imperial Office or your residences, have my men gather it for you. Is that understood? I don't want anybody gallivanting about the street without at the very least an armed escort."

Maruska nodded. Renata nodded too, though it was because she had drifted into unconsciousness and slumped forwards. She jolted awake as she dropped the dregs of her brandy on the floor.

"I'm sorry," she muttered, but Glaser waved her off.

"Get you to bed. We shall reconvene in the morning."

That night she dreamt of an enormous wall. Not enormous like the mediaeval fortifications which encircled the old city of Sova; a wall ten times bigger. A hundred times bigger. So large that each stone was the height of a grown man, and the bottom could not be seen from where she stood at the embrasure.

It reared into the twilight like the slope of an unfathomable ziggurat. Above her, the deep blue sky roiled with white and grey cloud. Beyond the wall stretched a vast carpet of mist. In the distance, the sun was setting.

The silence was profound. At this height, she should have been buffeted by constant cold winds, but nothing stirred in that bizarre, airless space.

"Hello?" she called out.

"Ren?" came the response from the mist. The voice was unmistakably Amara's, but there was no sign of anyone else atop the wall. And yet it sounded as though it had come from a couple of feet away. "Ren, is that you?"

Renata's heart lurched. "Amara? Where are you? I can't see you."

"I'm frightened, Ren. What is this place?"

Renata's skin broke out in gooseflesh. "It's a dream," she said, more to herself than to her half-sister. She held out her hands and touched the stone merlon of the wall, as though she were a blind woman feeling her way along a corridor. "It's a dream. Just a dream." She began to walk across the top of the wall, her footsteps feeling sluggish and phantasmic.

"They're coming Ren," Amara said.

"Who's coming?"

"Gods, I'm frightened!"

"Who is coming? Amara? Amara!"

Renata was running now, but it was like running through syrup. No matter how much she pumped her arms and legs, she could move no faster than a slow walk, as though she were merely promenading in this bizarre liminal space.

"Amara, I can't see you. Where are you? Talk to me!"

"Oh, it's coming, Ren!" Her sister was hysterical now, the depth of her fear chillingly animalistic. "Oh my sweet saints in heaven, they are coming! Nema Victoria preserve me!"

"Amara! Amara? Amara! Where are you, for Nema's sake! A—!"

❧

"—mara!" she shouted into the empty, dark chamber.

No: not empty. There was someone standing at the door.

Renata's blood turned to ice. The assassin. The murderer. They had found her, *here*, in the safety of Glaser's manse.

"No! Help! Somebody help me!" she shrieked.

"Madam Secretary! Madam Secretary! Ms *Rainer*!"

Renata stopped screaming. It was Velimir.

"Nema, I am ... so sorry," she spluttered breathlessly, acutely embarrassed. She looked over to the window sharply, suddenly fearing she had overslept; but by the dull grey penumbra around the curtains, it could not have been long past dawn – as early as five o'clock in those long spring days.

"Oh, don't worry about me," Velimir said generously, waving her off. He was clad in a fine silk dressing gown, his arms folded against the morning chill. "I'm probably one of the few people in this vipers' nest you can speak plainly with."

"I hardly think my screaming lunacy counts as speaking plainly," Renata muttered. "But thank you for your indulgence." She looked at him askance. "Was there something ...?"

"Yes. My apologies for waking you; everybody is up and break-fast is being laid out."

"Ah. Well. Thank you for letting me know," Renata said.

"I wouldn't normally personally rouse the guests," Velimir said by way of explanation, for his presence as the head of the household was unusual to say the least. "But a message has just this minute arrived for you, and in the circumstances, I thought it best to give it to you by hand."

"The ... circumstances?" Renata asked blearily. But as he

handed her the note, she could see why; it was on the letterhead of the Office of the Kammerfräulein – one of the Empress's most senior ladies-in-waiting. "Ah," she said quietly. "Thank you for your discretion."

Velimir inclined his head. "I take my leave," he said, and left.

Renata's heart was still thumping as she opened the letter with a shaking hand. It read:

M. Secretary

We are given to understand from the Colonial Committee of the Privy Council that you shall shortly be journeying south to, inter alia loca, *the Kasar Kyarai. As representatives of the Imperial Crown, We wish you every success in your endeavours.*

From what We have been told of your plans, it may be that you call upon the assistance of one Capt. Joseph Lyzander. Capt. Lyzander was in the recent past a staple of the Imperial Court but has recently returned to his regiment within the Kyarai.

If, during the course of your mission, you and Capt. Lyzander should cross paths, it would be of the greatest assistance to the Imperial Court if you would deliver to him the enclosed letter.

Her Most Excellent Imperial Majesty

Z.H.I.

"Zelenka Haugenate Imperatrix," Renata breathed. A letter from the Empress herself, written by her own hand. From within it, a smaller, sealed envelope tumbled out on to the bedclothes. Renata examined it, bemused. Was it . . . *perfumed?*

And then she heard her name being called, and scrambled out of bed to prepare for the journey.

It wasn't until the middle of the morning that they were marshalled in the Nastjan Fields Artillery Ground, a large green space in the lee of Victorygate, waiting for the final members of the expedition to arrive. Here was assembled an escort of Life Guards, ten cavalrymen resplendent in their fur-trimmed green-and-gold pelisses and black busby hats. But the uniforms were where the similarities ended; like the rest of the élite Legions, this microcosm of Imperial might was human motley, an aggregate of creeds, colours and sexes.

Renata, tired and irritable after a poor night's sleep and pre-occupied with thoughts of her sister, the attempt on her life, and now this curious letter from the Empress – to say nothing of the Great Silence – sat in the back of a carriage alongside Maruska. A small crowd had gathered on the Aleksandra the Valiant Boulevard to gawp, and Renata, who did not much enjoy being the centre of attention, pulled the blind down over the coach window.

"She will be fine," Maruska said gently.

"Hm?"

"Amara will be fine. A ball to the shoulder is not fatal. I knew a man once lose half his brain to roundshot. Lived another ten years with a flat skull. Apparently the only thing that changed about him was his tolerance for spice. Imagine that."

"The surgeon said the wound was already badly infected," Renata said, immune to any attempt at comfort. She looked suddenly at Maruska. When she spoke, it was matter-of-factly. "If she dies, I will be adrift."

"She is not going to die," Maruska chided. "Here. Let us speak about our plan. We have much to rehearse this coming week – not least our Loxica, which is much out of practice."

Renata sighed. "Not now, Didi. Please? Soon, I promise. I slept poorly and my mind is elsewhere."

"*I* slept poorly," Maruska said, stifling a yawn. "Curious dreams."

"I had a strange dream," Renata murmured. "A nightmare." She thought of the enormous wall, and the deep-seated feeling of dread which still had the power to rough her skin into gooseflesh all these hours later. What was it that required such an enormous fastness to keep out? *What* had Amara seen?

"Just nerves. Anticipation," Maruska said. "We have much to anticipate."

They both turned as the door to the carriage opened. Renata's heart sank; she had hoped for news from the Royal Naval Hospital. Instead, Herschel and Guillot stood in the entranceway.

"Your clothes have changed," Maruska observed. Both monks had been issued spring jackets of black cloth, high-collared shirts fastened with silk cravats, and breeches and fashionable riding boots. The effect was transformative – though their tonsured hair spoiled the effect slightly.

"Aye," Herschel said, wincing as he pulled himself up the carriage steps. He sat down heavily opposite them, massaging the flesh above his knee with his thumbs. Guillot came in afterwards, apparently too nervous even to enunciate a greeting. A sort of breathy half-word escaped his lips and he sat down next to his senior.

"What of your robes?"

"These fine fellows decided we looked too conspicuous." Herschel gestured to the cavalry outside.

"Well. I think you both look exquisite," Maruska said.

"Would that such subtleties not be necessary," Herschel said. "I have been thinking more about your misadventure in the Dynast's Palace yesterday. It is unlikely to be unrelated to the upheaval in the heavens."

"Yes, well. That wound is still raw," Maruska said pointedly. "Perhaps we can discuss it a little later."

Herschel took the hint. "I should well imagine. Still, it is good that we are getting under way. We've not a moment to lose." Out of the presence of Glaser, he seemed a different man; a little fussy, but he spoke and acted with none of the diffidence that Renata had come to expect. The younger man, Guillot, too, seemed more affable, though shy.

They all turned as the final member of the diplomatic mission opened the door with great violence. A stout Hauner woman stood there, no more than five feet tall. She had a commanding, self-possessed air, clad in a beaten brown leather duster which reached her ankles, and fingerless calfskin gloves. About her waist was strapped a stack of three books which were bound in a cross of padlocked chains.

She nodded brusquely to the company in front of her, sparing a glance only for the bizarre hairstyling of the two monks, before pulling herself heavily into the carriage. "Shift over, would you?" she muttered to Guillot – definitely a Hauner, Renata noted from her accent – and then sat down next to the younger monk. The carriage rolled and creaked like a ship riding a swell.

"Madam Ozolinsh, I presume?" Maruska asked, smiling brightly. "From the Corps of Engineers?"

"Aye," she said, sighing and fidgeting to get herself comfortable. "And who might you be?"

Maruska introduced everybody. Ozolinsh looked decidedly unimpressed with the company.

"Well. I have been given some notion of what it is we are doing, but I hope one of you will elaborate. Nema knows we will have enough time if our destination is the Interior."

Maruska cleared his throat. "Our destination, madam, is Port Talaka."

"I thought we were going to see the fishmen?"

"The Spiritsraad, first," Maruska said, nodding to Herschel.

Ozolinsh shook her head. "I admire your optimism, Ambassador, but the entire northern Kyarai will be in Casimiran hands before the month is out. We will be lucky to make Kalegosfort." She sniffed, readjusting herself. Her legs splayed out wide, forcing Guillot to press his knees together like a maid. "If you want my opinion—"

"I am confident you will share it irrespective," Maruska said.

Ozolinsh paused, squinting. "Are you being rude to me?"

"I would not dream of it, madam."

"If you want to see the dogs, Wolfsland is less than a mile east. In *my* opinion, we will have to excise the Kyarai from the itinerary entirely. Take the canals to the tip of the Reenwound. Follow the Sigismund Line to Port Gero." She shrugged. "Might see a few Saekas en route, but better the odd pagan than the Great Enemy, eh?"

No one said anything for a little while. "Well. I think you should expect the plan to remain unchanged in the first instance," Maruska said eventually.

Ozolinsh shrugged again. "Makes no difference to me." She nodded to Renata. "What's the matter with her? Does she not speak?"

Renata felt her cheeks colour. She opened her mouth to remonstrate with this brash newcomer, but Maruska cut her off.

"Her sister is gravely wounded. She was shot in the shoulder with a pistol yesterday, and her convalescence threatens to be a difficult one."

"Blimey," Ozolinsh said. "Well. I am sorry to hear that, though I cannot say I am surprised, with the way Sova is at the moment. Going to the dogs, it is. Literally – ha!" She paused, thinking a moment. "I knew someone shot in the shoulder once." She sniffed. "They died."

Even the monks looked aghast at this. But before anyone could say anything, there came the sound of horses whinnying, and the coach jolted and lurched forward. Outside, they heard a man barking instructions, and a moment later the sound of dozens of hooves clattering across the cobbles filled the air. The assembled commonfolk cheered this spectacle idiotically, having not the faintest idea where the cavalry and this mysterious stagecoach were going or what they were doing.

"Off we go, then!" Ozolinsh said brightly, and pulled out a sandwich from a parcel of greasepaper she had packed for the journey.

IX

Red Cove

*"The state is an entity that is distinct from the people which
comprise it, and which is represented by the government.
There is no more pressing purpose than for the government
to act as a foil. Where the choler of the people rises, the
government must be a soothing balm. Where the people
must be roused into action, the government must be
fire and bombast. But predominantly, the government's
role is to be dull and serious, a constant to the people's
capriciousness, and utterly, exuberantly preoccupied with
the welfare of its citizens above all other considerations."*

FROM CHUN PARSIFAL'S
THE INFINITE STATE

Ena Split

ALDA RIVER VALLEY

Dear Father,
    This may be my last letter.
    *Whatever supernatural thing ails this place, there is no
denying that there is truly mortal danger, too.*
    My Black Mountain scouts have finally laid eyes on

the Great Enemy. Our orders were to investigate a new fortification where the rivers Alda and Draga bifurcate (the "Ena Split", so named for Lake Ena, which drains there) and if necessary, reduce it.

We have spent the better part of two weeks navigating our way here. The going has been slow to say the very least. Through the contrivance of rafts, mules and tow ropes, we have been able to transport the cannon and their limbers, as well as the balance of our supplies, and this has alleviated the physical burden on the soldiers. But their minds remain very much taxed. There is nothing quite like back-breaking physical labour to occupy one's thoughts. With that removed, I fear that the light company has become even more ruminative than before, forever looking inwards, too frightened of this place and its strange goings-on to focus on our enemy.

I can hardly claim superiority for my own part. I have told no one of the arrangement of viscera I saw in the forest, not even Captain Furlan. I have already burdened him with too much, too many matters which I should have been keeping to myself (or indeed, confined to these letters). I have been overfamiliar, sharing private concerns which have unmanned me. I fear the man's indulgence will wane any day. Already it feels as though he is seeking to distance himself from me, though he was never a garrulous man.

Either way, my mind is now turned to real and tangible enemies, enemies armed with firelocks and cannon. We have finally laid eyes on them. Considering we have been travelling through Casimir territory for over a week, I had expected to be plagued by bluecoats. But it is only now that we have reached the Ena Split – or rather, several miles short of it – that we have seen the rude fortification which is to become Casimir's base of operations.

I say Casimir, but it is of course the Sanques who are in the greater abundance here. Numbers are apparently difficult to

*gauge for the pagan confederate, but the construction of a fort
and redoubt can hardly be achieved with a handful of men. They
have their own pagan allies, too, whom our Black Mountain
scouts informed me belong to the "Red Cove" confederation. I am
given to understand this is a particularly martial host, famed for
their savagery. I hope, like so many things in the New East, this
is an exaggeration. I fear it is not.*

*Our plan is to mount a raid as soon as possible. Every day
that we delay is a day that the fortification grows stronger. And
besides, I have my second task to think about, too – to find out
just what it is that is tearing up men like wet paper.*

*I have a feeling that the person or creature which laid out my
dead soldier's offal so carefully is at least part of the answer.*

Such a gloomy note to end on, but I have written it now.

Wish me luck.

Your loving son,

Peter

The Ena Split was a quiet place, which was strange given the
many thousands of tonnes of moving water. Here the River Alda
was broad and slow-moving, a distant cousin to its southern half,
which roared and foamed through the valley and crashed into
the Jade Sea like an avalanche. To the west was the even broader
and shallower River Draga, upon which was built Vratislavbourg,
capital of the Prince-Bishopric of Sanque. Sanque was functionally
a Casimiran possession, and seemed to exist as little more than
a mercenary state from which could be extracted a ready source
of allies to garrison the river valley.

"There is a fort," Cathassach was telling Peter and Furlan.
They were standing underneath a hastily strung shelter of waxed
fabric, protecting them from the worst of the afternoon's rain.
Around them, men dithered, with no orders yet to make camp.
Rain made gunpowder warfare practically impossible, and so no

one was paying particularly close attention to the forests – though sabres and hand-axes cared little for the wet.

Peter examined the sketch the scout had provided him with.

"This is an outer ring of breastworks?" he asked.

"*Jes*," Cathassach replied. "Logs, and piles of stone," he added in moderate Saxan. He was about forty, Peter guessed, and the tattoos encircling his mouth and eyes were reminiscent of a skull. His hair, obsidian-black, was cut into a single line running the length of the top of his scalp.

"And here is ... what, a scarp?" Furlan asked, pointing to the sketch.

The pagan considered this a moment. "Earth. Soil, with cut logs. Stone, here."

"They must have laid the foundation," Peter said.

"Agreed," Furlan replied. "An earthen rampart, not yet revetted." He turned to the pagan. "You said there was stone? A quarry?"

The scout nodded. "*Jes*. Here. And they cut fifty yards *ligno* in every way."

"*Ligno*?" Peter asked.

"Wood," Furlan replied, not taking his eyes from the sketch.

"Rear of fort is against the ... *ĝemeloj*." Cathassach snapped his fingers.

"The Split?" Peter said.

"*Jes*."

"What's this?" Furlan asked, running his finger down a line leading to the south-west.

"That's a portage road," Peter said.

"And what about this one?"

"That is *ponto*," the scout said, referring to a line running from the central axis of the split across the River Alda.

"A pontoon?"

"Bridge."

"So they are venturing east, then?"

A shrug.

"What's this here? A wall?"

"That's the rampart we were just talking about," Peter said.

Furlan clacked his tongue. "Are there any structures within?" He drew clumsy outlines of larger buildings in the air. "Like houses? Barracks?"

"One. Log house."

"How many men?" Peter asked.

"We counted over fifty."

"Regulars?"

"*Jes*. And Red Coves."

"Any cannon?"

The scout nodded. "Six. *Sur rulafustoj*," he added, when he caught the look on Peter's face.

"In wagons? Limbered?"

"Aye."

"They are not in a state of readiness, then?"

The scout considered this for a moment. "No."

"'Tis no wonder. I cannot think of the last expedition that came this far north," Furlan rumbled, looking up and in the direction of the lake. Interposed between their position and that of the enemy were several miles of forest, whilst immediately to their right, the River Alda thrummed with rain. To the east, the foothills of the Great Northern Barrier Range looked very close indeed. This was a wild country.

"We should unload the cannon," Peter said to Furlan quietly. "And have the men find a good route through. We are likely going to need to cut our way through at least some of this forest."

"I agree." Furlan turned to the scout. "Find me a good route through this mess. I should like to bring the guns to the forest line."

"There is a road west—" Cathassach began, but Furlan spoke over him.

"A quagmire in this weather. And it will be watched." He shook his head. "No. We'll bring them up under cover of darkness.

Brief the rest of your Black Mountain scouts. We will begin immediately."

Cathassach dipped his head, and then he was gone.

Furlan sighed mightily. "Tomorrow morning, then."

Peter eyed the forest ahead. He did not fancy cutting his way through it, especially not at night, in the rain, and with an enemy at the end of it. But if Cathassach was right – and they had no reason to think he was wrong – they were better off moving quickly.

"Tomorrow morning," he agreed, and they folded away their maps and pencils and began issuing orders.

It was a difficult night. The men cut their way through the forest as quietly as possible, uprooting ferns, chalking roots, cutting away branches and smaller trees. The rain kept up until past midnight, providing a blanket of noise to mask the chopping of hand-axes and the grunting of men and mules. But by the small hours the forest was silent, save for the dripping of old rainwater. The gun limbers were moved up slowly on wheels caked in grease to prevent their squeaking.

At one point in the night Peter was presented with the head of a Red Cove scout; the woman's skull had been split by a hand-axe.

"Are there any more?" he asked Cathassach quietly, so nervous he felt sick.

"We are looking," Cathassach replied.

By the time dawn broke, they had approached a place set back twenty yards or so from the forest edge. Here to the east was a natural defile running next to the River Alda, and they could see the pontoon bridge spanning the width of the river, a decent and solid construction which led directly into the fort itself to the south-east. There was no wall there; instead, the Sanques had relied on the escarpment at the point of the Split itself to provide a temporary natural defence.

Peter turned to Furlan where they crouched amongst a thicket of dripping ferns. He was sweating heavily under his greatcoat.

"We could use the rafts to cross the river," he said quietly. "Double back over the pontoon. Strike them in the rear."

Furlan sucked his teeth. "Good," he said after a moment's thought. "That's a long dash, though, a hundred yards at least – and completely out in the open."

Peter was firm. He had to put his stamp on this engagement. He had to earn the respect of the men. "I think we should do it."

Furlan nodded. "Twenty men ought to be right."

The necessary orders were issued, and twenty men and women disappeared back down the way they had come to find the rafts and cross the river somewhere out of sight. The rest of the light company was situated appropriately: twenty to the portage road, forty into the defile to the east, and a final twenty to remain in reserve. The cannons were quietly and carefully unlimbered by Furlan's artillerymen and prepared to fire.

Peter eyed the nascent fortification. In front of them, and faithful to Cathassach's diagram, was the breastwork dug out of the cake-soft earth, which was fronted by stakes. Behind that was a half-hexagon of stone foundation, itself behind a ditch and defended by an undressed earthen rampart. There were piles of quarried stone and cut logs everywhere, and it was clear that, for all the present set-up provided an obstacle, the Sanques had staked the success of their defence on not being discovered in the first place. At the rear of the fort, sitting in a natural defilade, was a large but crude log-house barracks with enough space for perhaps thirty men. As Cathassach had said, it was the only standing structure in the fort.

There were Sanques posted to the earthworks and Red Coves moving idly through the cleared space, but the Sovans were undetected. Peter and Furlan signalled to one another when they had achieved their final positions, and the opening volley took the enemy completely by surprise. The first roundshot from the eight-pounders blasted the head clean off a Sanque at the redoubt and thumped into the earth behind, sending a great plume of mud up into the air. The second hit one of the thick wooden stakes planted in the ground in front of the ditch, shattering it and sending wicked splinters into the men around it.

Peter had delegated command of the two flanking detachments to his sergeants, and the first musket volleys crackled in the cold morning air. Away to his left at the portage road, he watched a great cloud of white smoke billow from a mass of twenty muskets. Not quite twenty, he noted; the damp had got into some of the powder, and he saw the frantic movements of several soldiers as they worked to clear stoppages.

The acrid smell of igniting gunpowder filled the clearing.

A great clamour went up as men were roused violently from their torpor. The Sanques at the earthworks organised themselves quickly, and much more measuredly than Peter would have expected from the lesser of their enemies. The scouting reports seemed to have been accurate, for about sixty or seventy soldiers manned the fort, as well as several dozen Red Coves. The pagans, clad in simple homespun clothes, did not form up in the same way as the Sanques; rather, they dispersed with their muskets immediately into the forest, and, taking cover, began to fire in the manner of skirmishers.

Peter moved with the main body of men up the defile running to the east of the open space between the redoubt and the fortress proper. He flinched as Furlan's cannon fired again; both shots thumped into the stakes and earth of the redoubt and caved in a large section of it – it was not well made – and already Sanques were moving to abandon it for the safety of the rampart behind.

Peter clutched his sabre in his right hand, gripping it so tightly he felt his fingers might buckle. But amazingly, although his heart was pounding forcefully and his blood was singing, he found that the situation was not quite as awful as he had expected. In his mind, in his nightmares and imaginings, he had lacked all agency.

The battle was something that happened *to* him, something to be endured whilst his nerves frayed irreparably. He had been quietly terrified that the sound of shots fired in anger would unman him completely, freeze him in place like a statue, and probably get him a court-martial to boot. Now that he was actually here, surrounded by Sovans and damp earth and the stink of burning gunpowder, he found he was able to move between the ranks with something approaching confidence.

This isn't so bad, he thought, imagining himself as some great general striding in front of ranks of Sovan legionaries, or perhaps even atop a wonderful white palfrey—

And then a musket ball clipped the outside of his shoulder.

"Shit, fuck and blast," he shouted, clutching the wound. "Nema Victoria!" he added – except there was no wound, just a great rip, a busted seam, his left epaulette flapping like a poorly secured sail. Not a drop of blood had been taken from him, but still his voice faltered in his throat. Men stood in the defile waiting for orders. Now was the time to press the attack, for the outer redoubt was almost completely abandoned and they could use it as cover. Instead, Peter found himself shouting, "Fire by ranks!" – a ludicrous order, for there were no ranks – and the men simply shrugged and began shooting at will, thrashed into order by the sergeants.

With the initial surprise now expended, and with the Sanques behind the rampart, they began to exchange mostly ineffective musket fire across a distance of no more than fifty yards. Balls thumped into the wet earth, cutting down ferns, blasting out chunks of tree bark, buzzing through the tepid air like hornets. The musket balls were fat, three quarters of an inch in diameter, and travelled – in ordnance terms – slowly. They did not cut *through* a person, but rather flattened and mushroomed inside them, causing catastrophic damage. A man close to Peter took one directly above his right eye, which caused the top quarter of his skull to explode outwards in a great spray of brain matter.

The man to his left wiped the blood off the side of his face, then took aim and killed the man's killer.

"Move up!" someone was shouting from far away. "Move up, damn you!"

An explosion of cannon fire thundered through the air as the eight-pounders fired in tandem. One battered into the scarp's foundation with a great clang like the tolling of a church bell, sending up a cloud of stone chips; another thumped softly into the rampart, achieving nothing. Furlan's artillerymen worked frantically, sponging, charging, loading. Another two roundshot ploughed into the enemy. One hit the same part of the rampart again, causing a minor avalanche of soil but nothing useful; the other took a Red Cove square in the breastbone and blasted him to bits.

"Move up!" someone shouted again. Peter realised it was Furlan. He was standing at the forest's edge now, more or less in the open, his pipe in his mouth, pointing with one of his huge gloved fingers to the north. "Mister Kleist! Move *up*!"

Peter swallowed. He did not want to move up. The defile provided almost perfect cover. He turned to see if he could spot his soldiers on the rafts; and to his surprise saw that the rafts had been left on the far side of the River Alda, and twenty Sovans were crouched on the far bank, waiting to move across the pontoon.

The cannon fired again. A section of the rampart towards the centre, loosened by the rain, suddenly collapsed downwards. Stakes from the temporary palisade dislodged, rolling away.

"Lieutenant Kleist! Breach! Get *into* that *breach*!" Furlan was bellowing.

Peter gripped the handle of his sabre. He was paralysed with indecision. Everybody was shouting. He looked over sharply to see that the Red Coves on the portage road had engaged the men there in hand-to-hand fighting; axes and bayonets and musket barrels clattered into one another. Bodies littered the open space beyond the redoubt. Occasionally someone added to the tally. Furlan directed the men in the reserve to move up and start taking shots at the pagans in their rear, even though he was not the officer commanding the engagement. Then, after a moment, he ordered them to commit, so that the Red Coves were out-flanked and forced to retreat.

Peter was sweating incredibly and struggling to breathe. His arm ached where the musket ball had clipped it, though there was no injury there whatever. He wanted nothing more than to grip it and sit down for a moment, but that would not possibly do. In spite of his mortal fear, he was more concerned with what the men around him thought of him and his stock of courage than with the battle itself. His body, his mind, the parts of it that operated without conscious thought, were screaming at him to flee. They knew better than he the terrible danger of battle. And yet he was going to override that primordial instinct in case some-one should brand him a coward. He would *die* to avoid being so labelled. It was absurd.

He looked over to the pontoon. At the western end of it were two great stacks of stone waiting to revet the scarp, and Sanques had taken up positions behind them, ready to shoot anyone trying to cross the bridge. His plan to outflank the enemy, which had seemed so clever earlier in the morning, now seemed utterly ridiculous.

He gritted his teeth. The Sanques there were exposed from their right, and there were not many of them. He looked back to the place where Furlan had breached the rampart. Enemy engi-neers were busy plugging the gap with logs and sacks of soil. The opportunity to storm the breach seemed to have passed already, and he knew there would be recrimination later unless he could salvage the situation.

"I need ten men with me!" he announced. He had an idea, but he was going to need to act quickly before he thought about it for too much longer.

He collared the northernmost section of the main force and led them up the defile to where it intersected with the redoubt.

Here it had been completely abandoned, and they clambered over the wet soil, using the stakes as handholds, and behind the breastworks. A few scattered shots chased them, but none landed.

"Shoot those men there!" he directed inexpertly, pointing his sabre at the Sanques at the eastern end of the fort. They were thirty yards away, at an elevation of perhaps twenty feet, their white coats blending well into the hazy, cloudy sky beyond.

To his amazement, the men and women around him actually followed his orders. They took aim and fired, hitting the Sanques in their right flank. Two were killed outright, leaving great splatters of blood against the stone; the rest, seeing that they were being fired upon, beat a hasty retreat to the barracks.

Suffused with a sudden feeling of mad elation, Peter scrambled to the east, moving quickly through the trench and down to the water's edge just south of the pontoon. Here the Alda was a good hundred yards across, though the bridge had been well constructed, a solid span of wooden planks sitting on twenty or thirty boats gently bobbing on the currents. He signalled frantically to the soldiers opposite to make their approach; and then, as they did so, he called his own little detachment up to begin firing upon the easternmost position of the fort again.

The commanding Sanque officer noticed what he was doing, a captain by the markings on his uniform, and was in the process of directing more of his own men to defend the pontoon when a roundshot struck him in the right shoulder, compressing his entire midsection to the width of a sheet of paper for a split second before cutting him completely in two and sending the top half of him spinning away like a pile of wet laundry. The effect it had on the enemy force was marked, to say nothing of the effect on Peter, who swallowed down his gorge before he could vomit.

He was not given time to dwell on it. Another roundshot, expertly aimed, struck the nascent breach again. It punched a wicked hole through the logs laid there and sprayed the enemy engineers with a devastating cloud of splinters. Then Furlan ordered the surviving infantry on the portage road – for they had defeated the Red Coves there and were now exchanging musket fire with the Sanques behind the earthen rampart – up into the breach.

Peter's mind was once again thrown into disarray. He should have ordered his own men, the larger body, into the breach. Already he was battling with imagined accusations of cowardice; already he was thinking of how he would justify his actions to Furlan. He could easily claim that he had not heard the captain's orders; he could even claim that his own plan had appeared better to him at the time. Sometimes it was better to appear obstinate than indecisive.

He shook his head, and was opening his mouth to issue orders when suddenly a great shriek went up from the ground ahead. Peter ducked instinctively as a hastily aimed volley of musket fire smacked into the earth and trees around him; then looked up to see a detachment of a dozen Red Coves moving on his position. They had abandoned the south-eastern rampart entirely in favour of storming Peter and his ten soldiers.

They were coming to kill *him*, he realised. The commanding officer. With his sabre and pistol and rank signifiers, he was clearly the commander of these men. Perhaps not in spirit, but he certainly had the right uniform for it.

"Uh," he said, stupidly, wretchedly, as his courage deserted him. Perversely, he was so frozen in place with fear that to an observer it looked as though he were standing his ground with great stoicism.

The pagans appeared terrifying as they descended. Their tattoos, unlike those of the Black Mountain tribe, were red, and against their milk-white skin they looked more like incisions than inks. Het up on narcotics and wielding hand-axes carved from bone and flint, they screamed across the open space like berserkers.

"In the name of Nema," Peter breathed. Some force external to himself, some aethereal sense of purpose, compelled his left hand to draw his pistol and fire it. He managed to strike one of the pagans in the chest, laying open a great flap of skin just beneath the man's left nipple and felling him. Then he pulled a second pistol as his men unleashed a volley of fire from close range. It was the only shooting they would do; a moment later, the Red Coves were on them like a pack of wolves.

Peter instinctively brought his sabre down in a short, slashing motion. The man who had approached him directly was not a tall one, though he was stripped to the waist and stocky with muscle. Peter's sabre bit into his left forearm, sticking fast into the bone there. With a thunderous roar, the pagan brought his right hand across to jam his hand-axe into Peter's ribs, but one of the infantrymen skewered him underneath his right armpit with twenty-three inches of steel and pinned him to the redoubt.

Peter was about to breathlessly thank the man when with a great shriek another Red Cove swooped in and effortlessly chopped the back of the Sovan's neck with his axe, severing the man's spine and killing him instantly. He dropped without a sound, and Peter aimed and fired his second pistol into the pagan's face at point-blank range. The ball went into the man's eye, glanced off the curve of the back of his skull, and ricocheted back out the front of his neck. The deformed ball bounced harmlessly off the front of Peter's jacket with the force of a firm poke from an index finger.

He couldn't possibly say how long this encounter lasted; a minute, perhaps two at most? The Red Coves were killed to a man, but they took five of Peter's detachment with them, men and women who had but moments before been living, breathing Sovans.

Panting heavily, Peter leant against the back of the redoubt. Furlan had deconstructed about a quarter of the rampart atop the scarp now, though the cannons had finally fallen quiet as forty Sovans stormed the wall of earth. A chaotic melee was taking place within the footprint of the fortress proper, and Peter could see the remaining Sanques – as well as a few blue-coated Casimirs – retreating into the log house-barracks to take up firing positions out of the windows there.

"Come on," he breathed, secretly pleased that the worst of the engagement seemed to not only be over, but more or less decided in their favour. Having survived the brief but brutal struggle with the Red Coves, he felt somewhat reckless, and took his remaining five men to the north-east of the outer wall, where they once again clambered up the claggy earth. Here they linked up with the twenty men who had successfully crossed the pontoon bridge, and together they shot, stabbed, mutilated and killed the remaining defenders in that part of the fort.

Peter took a moment to catch his breath. Here, on the other side of the rampart, the fort was a simple wide hexagon of pavement, leading down to the natural escarpment which overlooked Lake Ena. To the south, bodies lay in great abundance, many half buried in collapsed portions of earth and bristling with splinters. More Sanques were scattered across the pavement. Those who had been hit by the roundshot from the eight-pounders were in incredible states of disassembly – and this was a light engagement, the whole thing involving fewer than two hundred men. What horrors were to be found on a battlefield of tens of thousands?

"Get it open!" Furlan was shouting, directing a group of men who were smashing an enormous log into the door of the barracks like mediaeval soldiers battering down the castle gate. "Come on, you craven doghearts! Get it down!" More Sovans still were smashing the windows with the butts of their muskets, and a dreadful tussle ensued for control of the structure.

The position of the Sanques, however, was hopeless. A few minutes later they had surrendered. Only a handful of men remained, and most of those were gravely wounded; they begged for quarter, and Peter ordered that it be given.

Furlan appeared at his side, sweating profusely, and slapped him roughly on the shoulder. "The morning is ours," he announced humourlessly. "Well done."

Peter sucked in several deep lungfuls of air. It was still early; the entire engagement had taken perhaps an hour, though he felt as though he had been fighting for a whole day. A great burden of administration now fell on his shoulders, for there were the wounded to tend to, prisoners to interrogate, men to feed and water, and of course the position itself needed to be secured. They would billet in the barracks that night, of that he had no doubt; then he needed to consult with Furlan about their next moves. The forces of Casimir and Sanque were unlikely to let this raid go unanswered, after all, but they had no engineers with them to finish construction of the fort, nor men enough to garrison it.

And besides, this was only one half of his mission. Now that his blood was cooling, he was already thinking about the investigation that Major Haak had tasked him with. In every way that mattered, this fight at the Ena Split was merely a pretext.

No. The danger had not passed.

In fact, Peter had the sense that his troubles were only just beginning.

X

On the Nature of Diplomacy

"One of the most acute issues facing the diplomatic practitioner is overcoming the 'blood debt cycle'. This is especially problematic in older conflicts, in which tit-for-tat killings and so-called 'brush fire' skirmishes have continued for so long they have obfuscated the war's genesis. Such conflicts will inevitably require one side to unilaterally cease hostilities, and in so doing let the blood debt go unanswered. Thus we often run headlong into the retaining wall of foreign policy: requiring a human polity to act in spite of their human instincts."

FROM J. P. COOK'S
IMPERIAL FOREIGN POLICY & INTERNATIONAL RELATIONS

The Old Pilgrim Path

PRINZPATRIATE OF MIRJA

The first day of the journey took them out of the Province of Sova and into the Prinzpatriate of Mirja. They paused at the boundary, some seventy miles south-east, mostly following the line of the Sauber. In the distance, to the west, they could just make out the tallest towers of the Royal City of Saxanfelde. It was an enormous metropolis that was traditionally the seat of the Empress' third child, though the newly elected Zelenka Haugenate did not even have a husband, let alone children – in spite of the urgings of the Senate.

They made good time. The stagecoach was as good as modern industry could make it. The struts where the wheels were connected to the frame were cushioned by steel springs, and the interior was expertly upholstered, so at least they would be travelling in comfort. The horses, too, came from endurance stock husbanded by many generations of Sovan breeders, and could sometimes cover up to twenty miles in a stretch if they were well watered, fed and rested.

Renata's sour mood had settled in the stagecoach like a patina, and no one felt much like talking. Ozolinsh grumbled about the rocking motion of the carriage, which apparently made her feel nauseous. She had forced one of the monks to sit in the middle so that she could take some air next to the window, and stuck her finger in her ear constantly as though trying to dislodge something. But that was the sum of the scintillating conversation that had taken place on the first day.

They stopped frequently at staging stations to change the horses – four times on the first day. At first Renata enjoyed stretching her legs and taking some air, but these pauses quickly became tiresome. The troop of Life Guards already seemed like more trouble than they were worth, given how much care and attention their animals seemed to require – no human was so well tended – and how frequently they too required changing. Still, Sova's merchant travel infrastructure was very well developed. The roads were good and kept in an excellent state of repair, and the stations were often small towns in themselves, where cottage industries had sprung up around the vast stables – veterinarians, wheelers, repairmen, coach gunners, liveried messenger companies, and of course, the perennial need for inns and taverns.

"Gunpowder, coffee and brandy!" was a frequent refrain across the Empire.

They started early on the second day, having spent a damp night in the best inn they could find – which had turned out to be not very good at all. They left just after dawn, waiting for Maruska to finish his breakfast. They had all been offered onion-infused porridge, which only the old Qareshian had gamely accepted, and which he had declared to be "excellent". Maruska took the opportunity to hone his diplomatic craft whenever he could.

It was a warm spring morning, and the sun was out, and with over a hundred miles between them and Sova by lunchtime, Renata found her anxiety for Amara was being slowly replaced with preoccupation about the mission.

"So," Ozolinsh said through a mouthful of cured sausage. Renata had no idea where she had procured it from; it had not been available at the inn. "Why do you think the end of the world is coming?" She did not seem particularly fazed. "What was your name again?"

"Viktor Herschel," the older monk said, holding out his hand.

"So you do have a Neman name," Ozolinsh said, shaking it.

"Not that anybody seems to be interested in it," Guillot muttered. He looked uncomfortable in his spring jacket.

"You were briefed before we left," Maruska said, somewhat pointedly.

"I was told that these two" – she gestured to the monks – "had been speaking with the dead."

"We have."

"That is illegal."

"We know."

Ozolinsh looked at Maruska and Renata. She pointed at them with her half-gloved fingers. "You both knew this?"

"Madam, the Empress herself knows it," Maruska said.

"Hm." Ozolinsh chewed in silence for a while. "You know, you could have spoken to us first."

"Us?" Herschel asked.

"Us. The Corps of Engineers."

"Why should we have done that?"

"Well, during my briefing I was told that the reason for the diplomatic mission was because you need to speak with magickal practitioners. The mer-men and wolfmen and so forth."

"That is correct."

"But we do still practise – well, I am going to call it thaumaturgy, since saying 'magicks' makes us sound like children at a birthday party; what is it that you think the Corps of Engineers does?"

Herschel snorted. Renata had not thought him capable of derision, but there it was. "Madam, with the greatest respect, you are a caretaker of a few ancient wards. I am talking about actual death magick. The afterlife. Access to the holy dimensions, where all manner of spirits and creatures and demons and gods dwell . . ."

He trailed off, withering under Ozolinsh's stare.

"Caretaker?" she said icily.

"I'm just calling it what it—"

"I'll have you know that without me, the greatest buildings in the capital would collapse!"

"Here," Maruska said. "Let us have a bit of peace for a moment whilst I finish this letter. By my reckoning we will be stopping again soon."

It was a lie, Renata realised a little later, simply to get them to shut up, for the coach did not stop for another two hours. It was early evening, and the penultimate staging station for the day. They had been travelling across open countryside for some time, with nothing but the Sauber for feature. Now they pulled into a small town and debarked from the coach, stretching legs and backs and arms. Maruska bustled off to send another handful of correspondence via liveried company.

"How is everything in there?" Colonel Glaser asked, framed by the afternoon sunlight. He looked somewhat rakish atop his horse, which he dismounted and handed over to ostlers.

"Oh, just getting to know each other," Renata said.

Glaser smiled, and winked at her. "Only three weeks to go."

"Brandy, sir," one of the cavalrymen said, appearing at his elbow.

"Oh, thank you," Glaser replied. He turned back to Renata. "One more stop," he said brightly. "Then a bath and sleep."

"Don't threaten me with a good time, Colonel," Renata said absently, watching as the sweating horses were unhitched from the stagecoach and more were brought out of the stables beyond.

"Yes, well," Glaser said. "You wouldn't want to trade places with me. It'll be saddle sores for the lot of us before this journey is through."

Renata winced. "You have my sympathies," she said, and she meant it.

"Well. Sometimes we have to endure some personal discomfort for the good of the realm," Glaser said, a little too pointedly.

But he left to speak to the Life Guards before she could answer.

Halfway through the morning of the following day, Maruska downed his quill and stoppered his ink pot. "Renata."

"Yes?" she said, jolting from her reverie. The constant swaying, rocking motion of the stagecoach was the most powerful soporific she had ever encountered.

"I do not know about you, but given that we shall soon be grappling with the sharp end of our work, I am feeling somewhat out of practice."

She looked at the two monks and Ozolinsh opposite. All three of them briefly met her gaze, but turned away, uninterested.

"As am I," she murmured.

"Why don't you give me Managold's five tenets? We can work through them together."

Renata nodded. She knew that something like this, some scholarly revision, had been in the offing, though she felt unenthusiastic at the prospect. If it had been just her and the ambassador, she might have tried to wrangle another day of silent introspection; but with the other three in the stagecoach, she could not afford to be so churlish.

"Credibility in authority," she said. She cleared her throat. "Offer only what you can afford; demand only that which you can take."

"What about bluffing?" Ozolinsh asked immediately.

"Bluffing is for amateurs," Maruska said with contempt. "Look where it got the fools in the Kasari Office."

Ozolinsh shrugged. "Just asking a question."

"Credibility in authority," Maruska said, directing his attention back to Renata. "*Authority*. Our authority must be credible. How do we ensure it is?"

"The Army," Renata said. "We have the largest standing army in the world. Both our allies and our enemies know this."

"What else?"

"The goldmark. Trade. Embargo, blockade, sanction. Economic warfare is just as effective – if not more effective – than actual warfare."

"Gold before gunpowder," Maruska said, nodding sagely.

"Certainly it is not thaumaturgy," Ozolinsh muttered. She waggled her fingers. "Magicks!"

"Blood once turned the wheels of empire; now it is *money*," Maruska quoted, ignoring the engineer. "We can threaten to shoot our enemies, but it is much cheaper to pay them."

"What's a fishman going to do with gold?" Ozolinsh demanded. "I thought they traded in oyster pearls or something equally ridiculous."

"Pearls can be *exchanged* for gold," Renata said patiently.

"Aye, so can a musket ball."

Maruska sighed. "Give me the next one," he said to Renata.

"Clarity of will," Renata replied. She had caught the interest of the monks now. "We must know our own objectives intimately. One cannot expect a third party – a *foreign* third party – to understand what we are trying to achieve if we do not understand it ourselves."

"Number one: stop the end of the world!" Ozolinsh said cheerfully through a mouthful of sausage.

"Madam, you are incorrigible," Maruska said.

"Thank you," Ozolinsh replied.

"Next one, Renata," the ambassador sighed.

There was a short pause as Renata marshalled her thoughts. "Beware the intolerable peace."

"Never be cowed by the severity of armed intervention if your cause is just," Maruska murmured, as though it were a responsorial psalm.

"Conflict is expensive both in blood and treasure, but sometimes it is better to grapple with a matter early, and prevent a greater and more damaging conflict in the future."

"And what did Managold call it?"

"Pre-emptive self-defence," Renata said without missing a beat.

"Incredible," Guillot muttered, his breath fogging the window that he stared fixedly out of.

Everyone looked at him briefly, but the younger monk did not seem to be interested in developing the thought.

"Two more," Maruska said, squinting slightly at Guillot.

"Fraternalism," Renata continued. "Accepting that the different customary behaviours of a foreign people are not intrinsically wrong simply because they do not align with the customary behaviours of a native people. The effective diplomat respects the pluralism of empire—"

"What's pluralism?" Ozolinsh asked, her face a mask of distaste. Before anyone could answer her, she said, "You know what they taught us on day one at the thaumaturgical engineering college?"

When it became clear that the question was not rhetorical, Maruska said, "No."

"Never use a big word when a small one will do." She pointed to Renata. "You can stick that advice under your 'clarity of will' point."

"Madam," Maruska said patiently, but Ozolinsh waved him off before he could go on.

"Yes, I know, shut up," she muttered. Her gaze lingered on Renata for a few moments, before she turned to look out of the window.

Renata gritted her teeth. "Fraternalism—"

"And that's a Sovan doctrine, is it?"

Renata looked sharply at Guillot, for it was he who had spoken. "Do not interrupt me again," she said, her irritation spilling over.

But the young monk was not cowed. "You seem perfectly happy to indulge *her*," he said, gesturing to Ozolinsh.

Before Renata could retort, Maruska said, "Yes. Fraternalism is one of the core tenets of international diplomacy as espoused by Managold."

"And who's he, then?"

"Managold is widely regarded as the grandfather of the modern academic field," Maruska said patiently.

Guillot gestured to Renata. "And these are his words? What you two are saying? These tenets? That you cleave to?"

"Brother," Herschel murmured, startled by his junior's direct manner.

"We do our best," Renata said.

"It's called the Sovan *Empire*," Guillot said. "Not the Sovan ... *Fraternal* ..." he threw his hands up, as though he might be able to pluck the words out of the air, "Compact of Nations. These places were invaded. The native peoples were subjugated and killed. Look at what the Empire is doing in the New East. Look at what it has achieved in the Kyarai."

"I rather think that is your field, is it not?" Renata said stonily. "The wolfmen were corrupted by religion. By Conformism."

"I thought the Kasar were corrupted by Sovan missionaries?" Ozolinsh said.

"The *southern* Kasar – whom we call the Sudreiks – were converted by Casimiran missionaries to Neman Conformism. The *northern* Kasar were converted to Neman *Victorianism* by *Sovan* missionaries," Maruska explained. "There followed inter-necine war."

"There's one of your big words again."

"The two religious factions within the Kyarai went to war with one another," Maruska said. He seemed happy to continue for as long as it defused the tension in the stagecoach. "Sova pledged to protect the Victorianists in the north—"

"And Casimir the south, yes; this I do know," Ozolinsh said. "'Tis all as tangled as a merkin."

"Succinctly put, madam."

"We are neither Casimiran nor Conformists," Guillot huffed. "And in any event, it is not the priesthood which filled the nation with gunpowder and muskets and cannon and forts and turned the north against the south."

"Enough, Brother!" Herschel said, aghast. "You are speaking to representatives of the Sovan Senate; of the Imperial Crown."

Guillot shrugged. "I have said nothing untrue," he said, and there followed several long moments of silence.

"I see that leaving Sova has loosened your tongue," Renata said to Guillot, now more bewildered than irritated. "You were much more circumspect in the capital."

"His mind labours under the weight of our mission," Herschel said quickly, looking helplessly between the two diplomats. He turned back to Guillot. "Brother, apologise."

The younger man sagged slightly. He offered a brief, awkward smile. "I am sorry," he said quietly. "Brother Herschel is right; I find myself most vexed at the moment."

Maruska waved him off. "I am more than happy to have a frank exchange of views," he said. "I would just prefer that it wait until after the lesson."

Herschel nodded enthusiastically. "Indeed. It was not our intention to interrupt what is clearly important business."

There was another pause as everyone waited to see if Guillot did indeed intend to interrupt this clearly important business again, but the silence stretched.

"Well," Maruska said tiredly. "We might as well have the last one. Renata?"

"Sova in all things," Renata said. They all waited for another outburst, but Guillot simply tutted and continued to stare at the window.

"Sova in all things," Maruska echoed. "We act in Sova's Imperial national interests *at all times*, including the interests of its economy, religion and colonies."

Now he looked at Guillot.

"To the exclusion of all others."

At the end of the fourth day, they stopped at Balodiskirch. It was a beautiful place, the surrounding country once scrubby and rocky, now long since irrigated by the River Reka; a place of elegant wildflower prairies and rolling plains, whilst the town itself was charming, walled and filled with whitewashed adobe houses with terracotta roofs.

Most came to Balodiskirch for the cathedral, an enormous and imposing temple in the Saxan gothick style. It had been constructed over an old and much-neglected pilgrimage site, a place where Saint Creus – a messianic figure within the Neman orthodoxy – had received a number of immutable truths and sacred tenets from Nema herself, during a period known as the

Long Insanity. By virtue of this fact, and although Balodiskirch was a small town, it was the seat of the Bishop of Mirja, the governess of the province and a member of the senatorial Council of Bishops voting bloc. Renata had seen the bishop many times, since the council building was a stone's throw from her apartment in Sova.

Colonel Glaser arranged for them to spend the night in the bishop's palace; the woman herself was absent in the capital, but her household staff were more than willing to accommodate their party. Guillot absented himself for the evening to go and pay his respects in the cathedral, whilst Maruska dispatched his correspondence from the staging station and then retired – it was easy to forget that he was an old man, and these long journeys were hard on him. In the end it was just Ozolinsh, Herschel and Renata for dinner.

"Tell me, Mister Herschel, how it is that your Templar sect fits into the broader Neman Church, then?" Renata asked the man after a fairly lengthy and uncomfortable silence.

"Hm," Herschel said, finishing his mouthful. "A fraternal company, really," he said. "We live in the old mediaeval fortress in Zetland, but unlike the Templars who constructed it, we are not a martial order."

"Where does the name 'Bruta Sarkan' come from? It is a strange one, if you don't mind my saying."

"Oh, it comes from the Old Saxan. I think literally translated it means 'cast aside'. There are competing etymological theories."

"Oh?"

"Some of my brothers believe it means to cast aside weapons, since the Templars used to ... well, kill people. Qareshians, mostly. Like the ambassador."

"And the other theory?"

"The other theory is that we ourselves were cast aside. After the proscription of the practice of death magicks in Sova, and the formation of the old Sovan Republic."

"But you endured? As a secret order? Practising the magicks anyway?"

Herschel nodded. "Precisely that."

"And so what is it that you actually *do*?" Ozolinsh asked. "Apart from shout at ambassadors and lament the state of the Empire?"

Herschel smiled thinly. "Brother Guillot is not a bad man. In fact, that was very out of character for him. I don't know if either of you have felt it, but there is something . . . wrong. Out of joint. I don't know whether it's just myself and Brother Guillot, but—"

"No," Ozolinsh said, surprising them both. "I feel it too." She tapped the books chained to her waist. She did not go anywhere without them. "You forget, I am thaumaturgically attuned as well."

"What are you both talking about?" Renata asked.

"Something is changing. Since we have lost contact with the afterlife, there is some . . . quality to the fabric of reality which has shifted. It has left me feeling uneasy, like a mild but persistent sense of dread."

Renata was surprised to see Ozolinsh nodding along to this. "I have sensed nothing of the sort," she said, feeling distinctly uneasy.

"It is because you are not attuned," Ozolinsh said. "You have not had training in the thaumaturgic arts. We are sensitive to it."

Herschel endured this with good humour, unwilling to throw aside this surprise ally, though Renata could tell he did not consider the engineer's feelings on the matter to be as valid as his own.

"Well," she said. "I hope you both . . . feel better."

"In answer to your question, Ms Ozolinsh, we perform séances," Herschel said. "We speak with the souls and creatures that dwell in the holy dimension."

"How? What do they even *say*?"

"As to how, this is done through a combination of sacred ritual and imbibing a . . . well, I shan't go into the specifics of the concoction, but there is a special drink that we take. As to what they say? A great many things. I do confess that a lot of it is difficult to understand. We spend much more time trying to decipher the messages we receive than speaking with the dead. And sometimes . . . sometimes . . ." He paused, looking uneasy. "Well, I shan't ruin the evening. But sometimes we contact something that perhaps we ought not to."

Renata's eyes widened slightly at this. She didn't disbelieve the man; the historic use of death magicks in Sova was too well documented to be anything other than immutable fact. Indeed, the city itself was rumoured to have been subjected to some sort of demonic assault as recently as two centuries ago. Nonetheless, having never experienced the practice of thaumaturgy except in the most passive way, it was difficult for her to simply take the man at his word.

"Anyway," Herschel said. "I shall speak to Brother Guillot. Having lived in Zetland his entire life, he has seen first-hand the effects of Sovan, uh, *civilisation* in the Interior. Suffice it to say he is not a fan of Imperial methods."

"Strange, then, that he should choose to accompany you on your mission," Renata remarked.

"He is young and highly capable, and he speaks Kasarsprek. And besides, he is as invested in saving the world as anyone else."

"If that is indeed what we are doing," Ozolinsh muttered.

"What have we got to lose in the attempt?" Herschel shot back.

"Our lives, you dolt," she replied, and returned to her pie.

It was with no small amount of trepidation that Renata retired that evening. Herschel's words, spoken with quiet authority and conviction, had spooked her more than she had let on.

She returned to her bedchamber and resolved to busy herself with some work to try and take her mind off matters. The greater temptation had been to read the Empress's letter to their liaison in Port Talaka, this Joseph Lyzander, and she even contemplated using a candle to melt the wax slightly and break the seal in the manner of a spy. But in the end, professionalism won out, and she replaced the letter in her strongbox. Instead she recovered a volume of Loxican hand signs to read; but after perhaps twenty minutes, she set it to one side. Some annoying psychological trick had left her experiencing the same quiet dread which both Herschel and Ozolinsh claimed to be feeling. She had felt nothing before – morose at her sister's injury, but that was it – but now her guts pulsed with a nameless disquiet. It was akin to a prey instinct, a sensation of being observed, a prickling of the skin of the neck, gooseflesh on her forearms. She spent some time trying to calm down, willing the sensation to dissipate, but it persisted. Indeed, the more she tried to ignore it, the more prominent it became.

She sighed theatrically. "Stupid," she muttered, reaching for the volume again—

And stopped as she heard a scream.

She jolted, her heart racing. Instinctively she went to the window to see if there was perhaps some commotion on the street, but the place was quiet and dark, not served by a comprehensive network of street lamps like Sova.

The scream had seemed both close but distant, near enough to hear with great clarity but at the same time an echo from far away. It was a scream imbued with great terror, an existential scream, issued from the throat of someone who faced incomprehensible peril.

Renata stood for a long time in that quiet, gloomy chamber, waiting for another.

But there was nothing.

The journey dragged on. They passed the old ruins of Waldeburg Keep, changed horses again at Rekaburg, and spent the fifth night in Saint Helena, an old Templar fortress now home to the 19th Imperial Pioneers regiment. There they passed a rambunctious evening in the officers' mess, and spent the sixth day in silence, nursing dry mouths and sore heads.

After Saint Helena, they left the line of the Reka and entered a broad, sweeping country of enormous wildflower plains, scrubby, rocky outcrops, and dusty, dried-up lake beds. The days grew longer and hotter. The horses overheated quickly and could not be driven as fast as they had been through Sova. They were also burdened with extra water. Spring jackets and cravats were removed, stock collars were loosened, and the stagecoach windows were opened to their maximum extent in a vain effort to get some air.

After the Prinzpatriate of Mirja came the Prinzpatriate of Keraq, and after that, the Prinzpatriate of Reichsgard. These territories, once the preserve of pagan Saekas and home to little more than mediaeval Templar toeholds, had become flourishing southern provinces. Their western borders abutted the Zyrahn Straits, and the coast was lousy with whaling stations, merchant ports, naval yards, and parasitic townships. Those traders from the Southern Plains who did not land at Kormondolt Bay or take the old pilgrim path through the Interior landed here, and Imperial excise houses made a fortune off hundreds of tons of coffee beans, leather, textiles, ceramics, ebony, exotic pelts, and as much ivory as hands could be laid on.

The days blurred into one. The architectural composition of towns and cities changed. Sovan gothick and baroque gave way to whitewashed adobe; Neman cathedrals became converted pagan and Inalabric temples of pink frontier stone and copper domes. The numbers of white-skinned Sovans in their inappropriate boots and breeches and summer jackets and dresses dwindled, and dark-skinned Qareshians and Zyrahns and Saekas – to say nothing of the wolfmen – in their brightly coloured and loose-fitting garments, were in great abundance.

They passed through Agilmar, then Rudsindfurt and Hrolfbruck, and by the end of the tenth night they were nearly eight hundred miles from Sova and not far from Zetland itself, home to the Bruta Sarkan sect. Renata had assumed the monks would be pleased to see their brethren again, but, quite bafflingly, the opposite seemed to be the case.

"Change of plan; I think we will spend tomorrow night in the Bruta Sarkan temple after all," Colonel Glaser said as they sat in a small tavern just off the side of the road. The irrigated agricultural town of Hrolfbruck was a day's ride behind them, Zetland a day ahead, and there was very little of anything in between except a few staging stations. These, however, were a far cry from the well-appointed stations further north. For the first time Renata was glad of the presence of the Life Guards.

"No," Herschel said immediately. He exchanged a brief look with Guillot. "I have told you before, there is no need. I thought we agreed on this."

"It is better to head further east to Radovansburg," Guillot said.

Glaser shook his head patiently. "Radovansburg is too far for the horses."

"Aye." One of the Life Guards nodded absently.

Herschel smiled awkwardly. He let out a brief, brittle chuckle. "You will not be welcome there. We are a . . . secretive bunch."

Glaser's frown deepened. "I care not a jot whether we will be *welcome* or not," he said. "Zetland – for all your order may like to pretend otherwise – is an Imperial possession. I plan on using it."

"There are no horses there," Guillot said quickly. "No fodder."

Renata looked askance at the younger monk. She had taken a fairly intense disliking to him since his obstreperous display at the beginning of the week. "What is the matter?" she asked directly. "Why do you not want to go back?"

There was a pause in which both monks squirmed.

"It is not a matter of not wanting to go back," Herschel said.

"It's just pointless," Guillot mumbled, not taking his gaze from the table in front of them.

Renata caught Colonel Glaser's eye. "You have been away for

weeks now. Surely your brothers would like to know you are safe, and that your message is being actioned? Presumably the entire magickal apparatus of Zetland is being turned to the task?"

Herschel took a deep breath and held it, nodding. Back now was that nervousness, that diffidence. He released the breath explosively, and said, "Yes. They would." He seemed like he was going to say more, but instead lapsed to wretched silence.

"Well," Glaser said, unsure what was happening but certain he was annoyed by it. "Irrespective, that is our next stop. I suggest you all get a good night's rest—"

"Colonel, I just . . . I really don't think we should stop there," Herschel said lamely. Next to him, Guillot shook his head.

"Taken under advisement, Mister Herschel," Glaser said, now thoroughly irritated. He stood, and the Life Guards present stood with him – a little stiffly – and swept out of the room.

Renata looked at the two monks, both of whom refused to meet her gaze. "What is it we are going to find there?" she asked them.

"Honestly?" Herschel said eventually.

"Yes."

"I do not know. And that is what worries me."

Maruska had spent the days applying the theory of diplomacy and international relations to the state of modern-day Stygion society. As an exercise it felt overly scholarly and theoretical, but the sad truth of the matter was, there had been no diplomatic outreach to the mer-men for years. All of their strategies existed *in vacuo*. Nothing would be certain until they passed through the Door to the Sea.

And there was still so much to achieve before then.

It was a hot, leaden afternoon by the time the fortress of Zetland came into view. Renata and Maruska had long given up on practising their Loxica. Everyone sat in sweaty torpor whilst the carriage creaked and rocked them, pulled by increasingly exhausted and unwilling horses.

Like Saint Helena, Zetland was an old Templar castle. It was hopelessly out of date as a fortification; a moderately skilled Sovan artilleryman could have brought the curtain wall down in under an hour. Most of these old castles were either ruins or had been transformed into stately homes; Zetland, however, bucked the trend in that it was both a ruin and a home.

The stagecoach pulled to a stop quarter of a mile away. A low ceiling of thunderclouds the colour of slate had gathered overhead, pressing down on them like the palms of a strangler. The air felt charged, and not just with the threat of a spring downpour. Since her conversation with Herschel and Ozolinsh in Balodiskirch, Renata had found it difficult to ignore the subtle, gnawing sensation at the back of her mind. There was definitely something ... *wrong*. And that feeling had only grown stronger as they had drawn closer to the home of the Bruta Sarkan.

"There's a stable," she remarked, for indeed there was. There was also a large tract of cultivated land for vegetables, a henhouse, beehives, and a number of outhouses, all in the lee of the western-most wall – itself overgrown with a thorny creeping vine.

Even from where they sat, it was obvious that something had gone wrong. The animals milled about the fields, untended. The fortress felt quiet. Glaser and his cavalry rode up to the main gate and called out, but there was no answer.

Renata took in the scene for a few moments, then turned to the monks. "What happened here?" she demanded. "What aren't you telling us?"

When neither of them answered, she sighed angrily and de-barked from the stagecoach.

"Renata!" Maruska called after her. Ozolinsh followed her out.

"It's like everyone just fucked off," the engineer said. She had removed her enormous duster for the first time and looked strangely diminutive without it on.

"It is," Renata said, squinting to try and see what the Life Guards were doing. One was pulling his horse on a circuit around the fortress; the others had dismounted, and were examining the outbuildings and stables.

She and Ozolinsh approached. They had been walking for five minutes when Renata stopped and turned sharply.

"Tell me you heard that," she said to – *demanded* of – Ozolinsh.

A scream. A man screaming in the throes of incredible agony. *Again* that bizarre quality of being both close and yet far away. Had it come from the old fortress? If it had, it had not spurred the cavalry to action.

"I heard it," Ozolinsh said. She looked distinctly unhappy. "I think we should go back to the coach."

Renata gritted her teeth. "This is ridiculous," she muttered, and quickened her pace.

"Madam Secretary," Ozolinsh said, now ten paces behind her. That the bolshy, phlegmatic engineer was unsettled should have been enough of a warning, but Renata was feeling dramatic, and not a little tired of these supernatural intrigues.

Colonel Glaser intercepted her five minutes later, still atop his courser. She was only a few hundred yards from the front gates now, and she could make out the message written there.

"Whatever happened here, I think we missed it," Glaser said, his features grim-set.

Renata did not take her eyes off the words on the gates.

"Has anyone looked inside?" she murmured.

"No," Glaser replied. He glanced behind him, but the Life Guards had finished circumnavigating the fortress, and were now busy slaughtering the chickens and ransacking the stables. "I think discretion is the better part of valour here." He nodded to the stagecoach. Renata turned, to see Ozolinsh making her way toward it. "Have they said anything? The monks?"

She shook her head. "Not yet, at any rate."

"Well, they shall have some explaining to do after this."

"I'll say," Renata murmured. She scanned the vast open plains around them. A long way to the north was a single figure on a horse, unmoving – watching them. There was no one else. "Perhaps he knows something," she muttered, nodding to the distant interloper.

"Hm," Glaser grunted, uninterested. "Go back, would you? We'll finish having a poke around here, and then we'd better get moving." He examined the clouds above. "I don't want to get caught out in the open in this storm."

"Where will we go?"

He sucked his teeth, wincing. "We'll press on to Radovansburg," he said. "We'll just have to take it slow, for the animals' sake. It's another twenty miles at least."

He said nothing more; just pulled his horse around and had it take him back to the castle. Beyond, the air filled with the frantic clucking of condemned chickens.

Renata took one last look at the words daubed on the gate before turning back to the coach. They read, in large white letters:

DO NOT ENTER
ALL DEAD INSIDE

XI

Striking North

*"Imagine it for a moment. To die, to be permanently,
irretrievably killed, the balance of your life spent in one painful
instant, for the sake of a length of soil. For the stroke of the
cartographer's pen. For the fleeting satisfaction of a carousel of
general staff. For the mutable appreciation of some distant king.
Imagine participating in such a scheme willingly. Imagine it."*

FROM CHUN PARSIFAL'S

THE INFINITE STATE

Castle Oldenburg

COUNTY OF HAUNERWALD

In spite of her initial protestations, Yelena agreed to go with him.
Von Oldenburg was pleased for that; the pagans in Draedaland
were a surly, intractable lot, a miserable people living in a wet,
cold, desolate country. He could speak a little Old Saxan, though
she was a native, and for all he prided himself on his familiarity
with their Draedist sorceries, he could hardly count himself a
practitioner. Yelena, on the other hand, was a witch – and an
accomplished one at that.

He made preparations to leave, setting many men to the task. Von Oldenburg belonged to a voting bloc within the Council of Nobles called the Palatinate of Nordenkova, a collection of provinces which lay to the north of Sova and which bordered the River Kova to the east. They generally made a nuisance of themselves, bandying about unhelpful accusations, being disruptive in the Senate, killing off progressive legislation and hoarding both private wealth and the wealth of their counties. He wrote letters to the Counts of Hofingen, Osthalde and Weishagen, letting them know that he was leading a secret expedition north, and reminding them of a number of political contingencies they had in place should he be killed.

Indeed, it seemed like the risk of being killed was fairly high. Certainly Sovans were not welcome in Draedaland, and there was the perennial risk of highway robbery to contend with, too. But unlike Sova and its provinces, magicks were practised openly there. They did not just need to keep a keen eye out for knives and guns, swords and cannon – as if the pagans would have even the first clue how to operate one! – they needed to be aware of sorceries. And those were by their very nature invisible.

His convalescence was spurred on by eating and drinking heartily and several more spirited fucks with Yelena. That she had missed him was beyond question. That she loved him was much more doubtful. Von Oldenburg had never truly, fully trusted her, but, notwithstanding, he had brought her into his confidence. He wondered – probably too frequently – if he could kill her if the need ever arose. If he would be able to. As a younger man, he would have done it without a moment's hesitation; in his advancing age, he was a little more cautious.

But only a little.

"What *do* you know of the plague?" she asked him over breakfast the morning of their departure. Outside, a collection of soldiers from the 15th Imperial Fusiliers, a regiment he had co-opted to fortify the northern border of Haunerwald – quite outside the bounds of his authority, though he was not worried about that block-brained marionette Zelenka Haugenate – prepared themselves for the expedition.

"Very little, thanks to the schemes of your countrymen." She looked irritated at this pointless barb. He sighed at her lack of humour, and popped a boiled quail's egg in his mouth. "I haven't learnt anything new on the subject. Have you heard anything more, in my absence? It is having a curious effect on its victims, is it not?"

"It's affecting their minds," Yelena replied. She disdained the hearty fare laid out before them, preferring instead to sip a steaming hot mug of herbal tea. "Rendering them insensible."

"An affliction of the mind," von Oldenburg mused. "Transmitted how, I wonder? A pox? One that affects the brain?"

Yelena shrugged. "Possibly."

He chewed thoughtfully for a moment. "Or something else? Something arcane? That at least would explain the activities of the Selureii, who are trying to contain the news."

"What do you think?"

Von Oldenburg saw off the last of his watered-down brandy, which he liked to drink with his breakfast. "No sense in speculating. We shall have to take precautions, though. You will bring your magickal accoutrements?"

"Mm. And you have yours." She nodded to the spherical brass mechanism he had brought to the breakfast table with him.

"You never know," he said, stroking the orb.

"What is its purpose?"

"I am trying to create a thaumaturgic amplifier," he said brusquely, and did not elaborate.

"You know," Yelena said, idly tracing a pattern on the table surface, "the safest thing to do would be to not go at all."

"Well, I am not interested in the safest thing. I'm interested in the most profitable thing. And sickness, plague, a pox is bad for business. Mm – that reminds me," he said, standing and pocketing the mechanism. "I need to send a letter to Broz before we go."

※

He wrote to Broz, his banks and his trading companies, spending perhaps an hour on the task. Then, finally, with Yelena and the fusiliers prepared, they set out.

For von Oldenburg and Yelena, it was a post-chaise, a two-person closed cabin resting on four steel-sprung wheels, drawn by four horses and driven by a postilion. For the fusiliers, it was a long, gruelling march. They had anticipated a journey of eleven days to reach Verdabaro, for that was where the Selureii were based. But the destination was less important than the journey. Their first priority was seeing how far south in Draedaland the sickness had spread, and in so doing discover its precise nature.

"Do you have everything you need?" von Oldenburg asked Yelena quietly as they moved through the open countryside north of Castle Oldenburg. Spring in Haunerwald was much chillier than it was in the capital, and they were swaddled in large overcoats.

"For what?" she asked.

"To perform . . ." he leant in close, "*magicks*."

"Yes," she replied, irritated.

"Your potions and so forth?" He hated this. He had ruthlessly pruned everything from his life that he was not an expert in, or that he could not make himself expert in. But for all of his study and examination of sorcerous artefacts, he was still a rank amateur in matters of the arcane. It was a source of limitless frustration.

The ghost of a smile played across her lips. "I have my potions, aye. I could perform the necessary rites with a corpse, as well, if needs be."

Von Oldenburg sat back, as if physically repulsed. "Well," he murmured, looking out across the countryside. "Let us hope it shall not come to that."

They crossed over the border at Fort Walaric, the only bastion fort in the entire county. This was an impressive fastness of sloped grey stone, giving the garrison a commanding view of the Southmark of Draedaland. Here, von Oldenburg paused to speak to the commanding officer, a captain from the 160th Kovan Guards who had himself only arrived the day before. But after a brief evening meal with the man, it quickly transpired that no pagans had attempted the border.

He saw Yelena later that night. She was quiet as she came in, but von Oldenburg had not been asleep.

"What was it this time?" he asked her in the black darkness of the bedchamber. "For information? Or fun?"

She said nothing as she stripped off her clothes and climbed into bed next to him.

"Could you at least be more discreet?" he pressed.

"My business is my own," she muttered.

"You are not to do that further north. Nema Victoria knows what poxes you will contract."

"I shall do as I please."

Von Oldenburg felt his choler rise. "You seek to humiliate me? In my own county?"

"I seek to do no such thing."

"My humiliation is the only corollary!"

She shrugged. "That is something for you to grapple with. Not me. Our arrangement is as it has ever been."

He was quiet for a moment. His hands balled into fists. "Not again. Not on this journey. Save your entertainments for when I'm gone, if you must do it."

"I shall do as I please," she repeated.

Von Oldenburg's blood surged. He let out a cry of anger, and raised his hand ready to strike her.

But he pulled the blow at the last moment.

"Touch me," she said icily, "and I leave."

Von Oldenburg exhaled. His fist unclenched. The truth was, he was a little frightened of Yelena, and especially in the darkness. She had never revealed the full extent of her power to him. Who knew what secret hexes she might cast on him? Just because she hadn't done so yet didn't mean she couldn't.

"I am sorry," he mumbled eventually.

Yelena said nothing.

Later that night, he awoke to the sound of a woman weeping.

Von Oldenburg sighed. "I shouldn't have said anything," he muttered. "You are right, your business is your own." He laid a hand on her shoulder, and rubbed it gently. "Come now, Lena, we have an early start. You should try to sleep."

"It's not me," Yelena said. Her voice was level and calm, and cut clearly through the chilly air of the bedchamber.

"What do you mean? The weeping?" von Oldenburg said.

"It's not me," Yelena said again.

"But you can hear it?"

"I can."

There was a silence. Von Oldenburg listened intently, but the crying had stopped.

"Strange," he said eventually, enduring a brief spasm of unease. "I didn't see any women in the fort earlier today."

"There weren't any," Yelena said.

He did not sleep well after that.

They set out at dawn. It was a damp, misty day, with little sign of the sun. Some of the fusiliers had gone ahead to scout out the route. The rest of them accompanied the post-chaise carrying von Oldenburg and Yelena.

They left Fort Walaric, which faded into the fog behind them, and with it the last Sovan bastion for five hundred miles. Ahead was pagan country, old-growth forest and marshland in every direction, all the way to the North Sea. Beyond that, across another thousand miles of cold, choppy saltwater, was Brigaland – more pagans, and no friends of Sova.

Leaving the fort behind felt like more than just crossing the invisible border from Haunerwald to Draedaland. To von Oldenburg it felt profoundly inauspicious.

"Have you any notion of the auguries?" he asked Yelena, though there was little enough to divine from their surroundings. She carried things, though, little pouches of bones, flowers, twigs and saplings. He would never be a superstitious man, but he put some stock in her readings.

"Death," she said simply.

Von Oldenburg snorted. "Rubbish," he scoffed, doing as he did when faced with uncertainty. Treat the experts as partisan idiots, declare their ideas to be ludicrous untruths, shout one's own position loudly, clearly and repeatedly. It had worked in the Senate. It never worked as well on Yelena.

"You asked me what I saw, and I saw death," she said, unfazed by his rudeness. "Is it any wonder, given what you know?"

Von Oldenburg licked his lips. He glanced uncertainly at the postilion, but if the man was listening to them – unlikely over the thumping of horses' hooves, the clink and creak of leather harnesses, the rattle and knock of wood, the squeal of the steel springs – he gave no sign of it.

"Here," she said, recovering a deck of cards from a pocket in her dress. She shuffled and then fanned them. "Choose one."

"That's it?" he said, his features creasing in contempt. "There is no more ritual to be done? You have said more in the past."

"Choose one," she said, her voice as cold as the spring air.

Von Oldenburg rolled his eyes. He pulled his glove off so as not to take multiple options, and plucked one of the cards from the pack, revealing it with some trepidation. It was a faded picture of Nema Victoria, the deer-headed chief goddess of the Sovans, standing on a bank of cloud. Next to her was a herald, blowing a large trumpet. Below, lying in supplication, was a carpet of human beings.

"*Jugo*," he said with distaste. "What does that mean?"

"Judgement."

He sneered at her look of fear, and handed the card back.

She repaired it to the deck and then put the cards away.

They caught up with the Fusilier scouts and together made slow progress up a disused pedlars' path. The old Hauner Road, once a huge, paved and well-kept Imperial highway, lay in a broken, muddy ruin twenty miles to the west, completely overgrown by wild grasses and, to von Oldenburg's great lament, impassable.

"Where are we going?" he asked the postilion.

"We'll make for Toutorix," the man replied from the foremost left horse. "The plan is to be there by nightfall."

"How far is it?"

"Less than thirty miles."

The day wore on, and the mist cleared. The fusiliers moved quickly, but the going was difficult. This part of Draedaland seemed eerily quiet. There were some homesteads, tumbledown cottages with steeply sloped thatched roofs in the shape of inverted Vs; but there was no sign of occupants anywhere. Smoke from cookfires was notable in its absence. Occasionally they would see an errant cow or sheep – once they saw a fox with a bloodied chicken in its jaws. Agricultural land lay untended and uncultivated. Gates and doors were left open.

As the day wore on into evening, and the cold, briefly ameliorated by the appearance of the sun in the early afternoon, returned in force, they saw Toutorix in the distance. Like many pagan towns in the Southmark, it had once been part of the Sovan Empire, and the buildings were architecturally gothick – several centuries old, now, but still standing. These were not derelict daub cottages; they were sturdy structures of stone, brick and timber, with roofs of slate. The streets were cobbled and drained, and the town was segregated into closures per ancient guild ordinances.

It was also completely empty.

The fusiliers came to a stop half a mile from the curtain wall. Like the mediaeval wall in Sova itself, much of it had been systematically harvested for its stone, so that it looked more like an oversized boundary marker than a fortification. The town had spilled beyond, with cleared ground and skeletal timber frames outside the old border, ready to be dressed in brick and plaster.

Toutorix should been home to five thousand people and more. The streets should have been trafficked by all manner of people and their animals, the taverns should have been rowdy with pagan labourers drinking their marsh ale, the windows should have been filled with honey-coloured candlelight, and the cold air should have been redolent with supper.

But there was no one.

"I've known graveyards with more bustle," the lieutenant of the Fusiliers murmured to his men.

The sun made another brief appearance on the horizon, bathing Toutorix in a red glow. It had the effect of making the clouds look even more forbidding, almost black. There would be rain that night.

"What are your orders, my lord count?" the lieutenant called out to von Oldenburg.

Von Oldenburg examined the town as one might examine the corpse of a dead pig.

"Why don't you go and investigate?" he said. "I'd like a roof over my head tonight if at all possible."

The fusiliers exchanged looks, and then advanced on the town. Von Oldenburg dismounted and watched the men unshoulder their muskets in response to an instruction from the lieutenant he couldn't quite hear.

"Don't start shooting, you bloody fool," he murmured. He imagined them shooting a couple of townsfolk, and then a whole mob of them unlocking from the shadows and beating them all to death. But it seemed he didn't need to worry. The fusiliers crossed over the old curtain wall as the sun set, and continued into the town unopposed.

"Have you ever seen a town turned over to pox before?" he asked Yelena.

She shook her head.

"I have. In the Zyrahn Straits. There is an island there, just off the coast of the Grozodan peninsula, where they quarantine sick sailors from the Southern Plains and out to the west. An outbreak of Sigheri fever from a Balabrian ivory trader. Killed about three hundred. The whole colony. I was younger then, just a merchant, not even a master of my own ship. Spent most of my time drinking and whoring in Grallstein." He paused, thinking about it for a while. "We didn't go ashore, of course. No one was allowed ashore for about three months. Then they went in with the lime and the fire." He was quiet again. "Do you know how you can tell a town has turned over to pox?"

Again, Yelena shook her head.

"It's the smell. Even from quarter of a mile out to sea. On a still day, you can smell it. The bodies ripening. That many people, all decaying at once . . . it's potent."

"I can't smell anything," Yelena said.

Von Oldenburg shook his head. "There is no plague here."

A few moments later, the lieutenant appeared on top of the old curtain wall. "My lord count! It's safe to approach!"

❧

They approached, though whether it was safe to do so remained up for debate. Certainly their initial assessment – that the town was empty – seemed to be accurate. Every window was dark, every residence and tavern was still. No smoke, no flickering candles, no smell of . . . well, anything, let alone cooking food. Vermin moved unmolested through the streets – dogs, foxes, rats. There would once have been wild pigs, too, but it seemed that, as in Sova and its provinces, steps had been taken to eliminate them.

The southern closure of Toutorix was obviously where the merchants' road ended, for here was a market square; but although it was empty of people, there was evidence of recent activity everywhere, with fruit, vegetables, fish and meat piled high on the stalls. The vermin had congregated to pick over the leavings. Von Oldenburg saw two dogs fighting over a cow femur. A great cloud of flies had settled on a tray of rotten apples. Toward the rear of the market, a family of foxes rootled through baskets of turnips and cabbages. The smell here was cloying, the sweet, ripe smell of decaying organic matter.

Both von Oldenburg and Yelena turned sharply at the sound of splintering wood, and saw one of the fusiliers kicking in the front door to a nearby residence. They waited in silence, listening to the sound of heavy bootsteps on wooden floorboards. Eventually the man returned.

"Nothing," he said quietly to the lieutenant.

In the distance, thunder rumbled.

"All right," von Oldenburg said, vexed. "Find us some food that hasn't gone bad. We'll billet here tonight and head off in the morning."

"No," Yelena said quietly from next to him.

He rounded on her. "What's the matter?" he demanded. But he wasn't angry at her, not really. His anger was born of unease. Not *fear*, not yet. But the potential for fear was there. Oh, it was there.

"A feeling," she said, infuriatingly vague. "It is dangerous to be here."

Thunder rumbled again in the distance, but louder this time. The storm was closing in. Von Oldenburg glanced up at the sky angrily, as though the weather had conspired with Yelena to provide a dramatic coda.

"There will be rain soon," he said. "I don't want to get caught out in it."

Yelena looked around the town. "I don't like it."

"What's to like? We have two weeks of this."

"Eleven days."

Von Oldenburg gritted his teeth. "We are going to have to get used to a little danger. Just being in Draedaland is dangerous."

Yelena shivered. "Something happened here—"

"Obviously!"

"Be silent!" Yelena snapped. Von Oldenburg obliged. "I can *feel* something. There is . . . a presence here. The air is . . . " She held her hand out in front of her, rubbing her thumb and forefinger as though the matter of the air itself was coated in some patina. "Can you not *sense* that?"

"No," von Oldenburg lied.

"It's like . . . " She shivered. "It's like potential energy, thaumaturgic energy, as though the air is being overfilled. I am . . . *Oleni*, I am struggling to make sense of it."

"I'll say," von Oldenburg muttered. He thought of the tarot card, the image of Nema Victoria printed there. "Well. We shall keep our wits about us." He gestured to the soldiers. "We have men to protect us. That is their sole responsibility. And we need to keep their powder dry. Can't do that out in the rain."

He could sense Yelena softening, her resolve weakening – not that she had any kind of say in the matter, but he liked to secure her cooperation whenever he could.

"All right," she muttered eventually. "Let's find ourselves a bedchamber, then. I will want to make preparations for the night."

Von Oldenburg knew this to mean a number of different witchy superstitions: salt circles, runes carved into the door frame, the burning of sage and other rituals. It was not that he did not believe in the arcane – he knew the afterlife was a real place, and magicks were a real force in the world. What he did not have time for were the silly rituals that surrounded it. The sorceries that could be harnessed from the afterlife, the necromantic spill-over from that deathless realm, were a tangible form of energy that had a huge number of thaumaturgic applications. Centuries before, when judicial mages had wielded the magicks – and the priests of the Neman Church before them – they had done so using ill-understood forms of séance, rite and incantation. In so doing, they had all but accidentally yoked the forces of the after-life, and utilised but a fraction of the possible power.

Von Oldenburg had dedicated decades of his life to developing a mechanism, using the powers of human ingenuity, industry, and scientific endeavour, to harness and control that energy.

So. Yelena could burn incense and whisper prayers if she liked, if it made her feel better. But von Oldenburg was certain it was largely – not entirely, but largely – a hollow enterprise.

"Suit yourself," he grumbled, and with one last look at the gathering clouds, made for the nearest empty residence.

It was not the rain that woke him, though heavens knew it was loud enough, a frigid torrent that battered the slate of the roof above mercilessly and set the whole house to trickling and dripping.

It was the screaming.

He sat up in their purloined bed. Sweating, heart racing, scrab-bling back against the headboard. The world had gone mad. A thousand people, ten thousand, everyone screaming in an insane chorus of fear. Not just fear, but absolute, primal *terror*.

"Wha ..." he grunted, eyes darting around the dark bed-chamber, trying to identify the source of the noise. But there was nothing. He snatched up his sabre and ran, quite naked, to the window, throwing open the curtains. He expected to see some massacre taking place, some atrocity in the streets where soldiers were shooting and bayoneting hundreds of innocent townsfolk – to the extent that Draedist pagans could be innocent of anything. But the street was empty, occupied by a sole fusilier huddled in his waxed greatcoat.

He turned, wide-eyed and frantic, to Yelena. She too was awake, her own eyes screwed closed, hugging her knees to her chest and rocking back and forth. She looked as though she were enduring a spasm of profound pain.

"What in hell's name is going on?!" he demanded, still with his sword in his hand. His feet crunched into the salt which Yelena had sprinkled on the boards.

Suddenly she stopped rocking and looked at him sharply. Her eyes opened—

"Nema Victoria!" von Oldenburg gasped. Yelena's eyes were featureless balls of obsidian black.

"Judgement," she moaned.

"Lena?!"

"I . . ." she said, her voice trembling. Ink-black tears welled up around those black sockets and ran down her cheeks. She looked terrified. "I can see . . . " The last word failed into whisper. "They are coming. Oh my . . . Irox protect me . . . "

"Lena!" von Oldenburg thundered. "In the name of Nema, tell me what is going on!"

The screaming outside, or wherever the blasted hell it was coming from, cut out abruptly. And then Yelena was shrieking at the top of her lungs, absolutely horrified, scrabbling madly, the covers falling away. She leapt out of the bed, knocking over the side table and candle and chamber pot, and pressed herself frantically into the far wall, as though she might make herself a part of it.

"My lord count!" one of the fusiliers shouted from the hallway, pounding on the door. The latch was poorly made and the door swung open, and the soldier was confronted with the bizarre tableau of von Oldenburg and his courtesan, both naked in the darkness, the former armed and the latter terrified.

"Nema damn fuck and blast!" von Oldenburg roared.

There were several beats of silence. The screaming – all of it, real and unreal – had stopped. Von Oldenburg's hand twitched, as he realised the ridiculousness of the scene. "This is not what it looks like—" he started, but the soldier interrupted him.

"We've found the townsfolk," he said breathlessly. He was soaking and ruddy-cheeked from the cold. Rainwater was dribbling off him and pooling on the boards beneath his boots.

Von Oldenburg turned to look at Yelena, who had now fallen silent – her eyes were mercifully back to normal, though quite why he did not know – and back to the soldier.

"Well, where are they? What's . . . what are they doing?"

"It's best if you come and see, my lord."

Von Oldenburg sighed, a ragged sound. He was very aware of the figure he cut – shabby, overweight, old grey flesh, his cock and balls shrivelled in the cold – to say nothing of Yelena, who looked positively feral. "Well get out, damn you," he muttered, tossing his sabre on to the bed. In his haste, he hadn't even removed its scabbard.

"Sir," the soldier said, and ducked back outside.

The fusiliers looked frightened. It was dark, but von Oldenburg could see the fear in their faces every time lightning flashed. It framed them, burning ghoulish after-images on the backs of his eyelids. They were like ghosts.

Rain pattered and crackled off their waxed greatcoats as they moved like a funeral procession through the town. Their boots sloshed through rainwater where the ditches could not keep up with the demands of the sudden deluge. They gripped their muskets like drowning men clinging to flotsam.

Von Oldenburg and Yelena were led through the northern closure and out of the town entirely. Here was farmland, a mishmash of fields and rickety fences, the ground fractured and uneven and undulating. In one of the fields nearby, a large copse had been recently felled at head height, leaving several hundred trunks standing barren.

"Where are they?" von Oldenburg called out above the rain and thunder, freezing cold and wet.

No one answered. After a few more minutes of walking down the muddy track, they came to a stop.

"Lieutenant?"

"There," the man said, pointing.

Von Oldenburg followed the line of his finger to the copse. He blinked, squinting through the dark and rain, waiting for some lightning. He didn't have to wait long; a few moments later, several long, lingering flashes put the field in sharp relief.

"Nema Victoria," he breathed. It was not a copse; they were not trees. It was the *townsfolk*. Hundreds of them, standing still. He might have thought it some baffling art installation, or a statuary, except they were moving, only just. A twitch of a limb, a gentle sway, a shaking of a head. Men, women, children, most peasants in simple homespun clothes, but certainly some wealthier merchants there as well, insofar as a merchant class existed within Draedist society. Those that lived in the old Imperial Hauner towns tended to cleave to Sovan ways of life; the pagans in the countryside were a different breed altogether.

"What are they *doing*?" he asked. "Is this the effect of the plague?"

"I know not, my lord," the lieutenant said. He looked profoundly uneasy. "They have not moved all night. It's possible they have come from somewhere else and congregated here, but . . ." He trailed off.

The rain lightened slightly. Von Oldenburg turned to Yelena. "What do you make of it?"

"I think we should go. I think we should go back to Castle Oldenburg." She had not properly recovered from whatever it was that had ailed her in the bedchamber. Von Oldenburg had to strain to hear her above the great racket of the storm.

"Oh, for Nema's sake," he muttered. He returned his attention to the lieutenant. "You, man. Go and see what is going on."

This was clearly an unpopular instruction. "Are they not contagious?" the lieutenant asked uncertainly.

"Have you not a weapon?" von Oldenburg snapped. "Why is it you think we are here? To examine precisely these matters."

Even then, the man hesitated.

"Blood of gods, you are a Sovan soldier! What hope is there for the Empire if the sight of a few sick peasants unmans you?"

"There is too much rain for shooting—"

"You have a bayonet! Why are you still here talking to me about this? Be about it!"

Unhappily, the lieutenant and several men surmounted the fence and began to advance across the rain-saturated field to where the townsfolk stood like automatons. Von Oldenburg watched them go, his expression curdling. Uncertainty was antithetical to his existence. The state of being ill-informed, ill-appraised was intolerable to him. What were these idiot pagans doing? Why were they just standing there?

"Why are they just standing there?" he demanded of Yelena.

"I don't know," she said quietly.

He waved her off. "Useless bloody witch," he muttered.

There was another flash of lightning, and he saw that the fusiliers were now quite close to the pagans, who had not stirred even slightly.

"It is like their minds have been vacated," he mused, willing the darkness to recede. It was hours before dawn, and they had not a hope of getting any kind of torch going in this rain. "I have not known a pox like it."

Then the screaming began.

"Fuck and hell," von Oldenburg said, gripping the wooden fence in front of him. He could see nothing in the darkness. "What's happening?" he demanded of the nearest fusiliers.

"I know not, my lord," one of the soldiers said, his voice trembling.

"Well go and bloody find out!"

The men did not. The funny thing was, von Oldenburg couldn't blame them – not really. He wouldn't have gone, either.

The screaming stopped. Next to him, Yelena was rocking back and forth, profoundly unhappy. She was mumbling something in Old Saxan which von Oldenburg couldn't make out above the rain and thunder.

They waited, but the storm was passing, fading, dissipating. The lightning didn't come again, or rather it did, but in the distance beyond the hills, achieving nothing except weakly backlighting the field.

"Shit," von Oldenburg muttered. He didn't know the lieutenant's name. "Lieutenant?" he shouted. It wasn't so much a shout; more of a hesitant call. But then, the peasants clearly weren't affected by sound, or the thunder would have driven them berserk. "Lieutenant?"

But there was no answer.

❧

They stood in the field for hours, not daring to approach. Eventually the rain stopped, but the darkness endured. By the time the first cold, grey light suffused the horizon, the frigid damp had seeped deep into von Oldenburg's bones.

"There," he croaked, and cleared his throat. "There." He pointed. The peasants were a little closer now, having moved perhaps fifty paces west. At the extremity of the mass, the four fusiliers, including the lieutenant, stood gormless. Von Oldenburg noticed, too, that some of the peasants had died, for there were a dozen or so corpses in the field.

There was no sign of struggle. There was no visible injury to the soldiers. They looked a little pale, little drawn, a little grey in the morning light. But they were otherwise unharmed.

"Nema," von Oldenburg breathed.

As he said it, the nearest automaton seemed to hear him. It was a Draedist woman wearing a brown kirtle. She locked eyes with him.

And then, slowly at first, the whole mass of them began to move.

"What's going on? What's happening?" von Oldenburg murmured.

Faster, now, the vacant pagans approached them. Expressionless, soundless, they moved as though being driven by an enormous invisible hand.

"Time to go, I think," von Oldenburg said briskly, and, gripping Yelena by her upper arm, began to move quickly back to the town.

Behind them, the pagans gave chase.

XII

One's Enemy,
So Presented

"A defeated enemy is defeated; a humiliated enemy is dormant."

SOVAN ARMY APHORISM

Ena Split

ALDA RIVER VALLEY

Dear Father,

If before I was no stranger to death, then now we are firm friends.

As I write this, the last of our mortally wounded has died. It has taken three days for our most hopeful case to fail, a man struck in the leg. It is a curious thing, is it not, to think of a wound to the limb as fatal? Captain Furlan tells me that musket shot will jounce around inside a man as effortlessly as a racquet ball, so that the entry wound may be relatively slight, whilst the damage internally is catastrophic. So it was with our final death, a young man with what appeared to be a glancing blow to the side of the thigh. A sliver of the ball had hived off, so the men

*tell me, and cut into the bone of his femur and embedded there,
enpoxing the marrow quite virulently. We had neither the wit
nor the tools to take the leg off; in any event, he was febrile very
quickly and passed in the middle of last night.*

*Of the hundred of us who left Fort Ingomar, we have suffered
twelve dead, and another twenty or so wounded. Of our enemy,
we have killed close on twenty-five; no doubt they will return in
force, though not before the month is out. In the meantime, and in
the absence of any orders, we will destroy this place. The men are
calling it "Fort Kleist", which I enjoy quite secretly, though a dark
part of me knows that it is thanks to Captain Furlan that we have
prevailed. Still, I acquitted myself better than I thought I would.
What was it you used to say? 'Tis only when we are frightened
that we can be brave? You put it much more profoundly.*

He paused. His father *had* put it much more profoundly, but
now the words escaped him. Still, the notion was there.

The truth was, though, that the fighting had affected Peter
deeply. He had spent the following days in a trance leaving the
soldiers under his command to sort themselves out – it seemed
like they knew what to do anyway. He found sometimes he was
unable to catch his breath, and he would quickly go somewhere
private, hand on his chest, feeling the world closing in. It was as
though someone had tied a rope around him, underneath his
armpits, and was drawing the two ends apart, squeezing the life
out of him. His vision would fade at the edges, and he would
sweat, and the whole crushing sensation would last for perhaps
five minutes. Slowly it would recede, and he would heave in great
lungfuls of air, and he would feel weak and shaky and sick.

The only solution was to endure it. He ate, though meagrely,
and took plenty of brandy per Furlan's advice, though that did
not help either. In fact, sometimes it made the feeling worse. He
felt . . . on *edge*. Het up. Like his whole body was vibrating with
energy, thrumming like a tuning fork. Every time he tried to

relax, he found his thoughts wandering to the Red Coves, the screaming pagans who had tried to cut him down – and who had very nearly succeeded. He could not help but obsess about how *close* he had come to death; about how but for a few lucky turns of Fate's wheel, he would now be dead.

He returned to his letter, and wrote:

It is difficult to know what to do. Taking and dismantling this fort was but a pretext in Major Haak's mind for a broader investigation into the supernatural matters affecting the River Valley. How precisely I am to conduct that investigation is beyond me.

"Sir?"

Peter turned. He was sitting at a small desk at the end of the barracks. Behind him, wounded men lay in the available beds, convalescing quietly. Outside, though it was dark, men were busy tipping cut stone into the lake, demolishing the earthworks and filling in the redoubt. The clatter of logs rose through the air as the palisade walls were knocked down and the stakes were unearthed. It seemed like a shame in many ways; with some Imperial engineers, they could have turned this fortress to their own ends. But even if they finished its construction, they had not the manpower to garrison it.

He set his quill down. "Yes?"

"The prisoner is ready to speak."

"Ah. Thank you."

He made sure he had his pistol and sabre, and followed the man outside. It was gloaming, and the smell of cookfires filled the air. He looked out across the vast grey body of Lake Ena, and shivered. It was more of a sea than a lake, nearly a hundred miles long and sixty miles across at its widest point. To the north-east stretched hundreds, if not thousands of miles of uncharted forest and impassable mountain. What was *out* there?

They had only one prisoner who had survived, a sweaty, pale and frightened Sanque. Taking a pagan alive was always impossible, and what few Casimirs there had been had either died or retreated in good order into the forest.

The Sanque was being kept under guard to the western end of the fortress, propped up against a section of earthworks which had not yet been demolished. There was some blood on his white jacket, but it was not his. Judging by his uniform, he was not an officer, just an infantryman.

By a striking piece of misfortune, the Sanque did not speak a word of High nor Common Saxan, and they had no one who spoke Kòvoskan – Furlan had a few words, "whorehouse Kovan", as he called it, but nothing like enough to conduct an interrogation. The Sanque, however, did speak the pagan tongue of *Old Saxan*, and so it fell to Cathassach to translate three ways.

"What are you doing here?" Peter asked the man directly, and then gestured to Cathassach to translate. There followed a painstaking sequence of back-and-forth.

"Building a fort," the Black Mountain said without a trace of irony.

Peter exchanged a glance with Furlan.

"To what end?"

Again Cathassach spoke to the Sanque in Old Saxan.

"To . . . uh, lead? The area? East of lake?"

"You mean to – I see; he means to *govern* it, to control it," Furlan said. Then he added, slightly irritably, "We knew that already."

But before Peter could ask any more questions – or say anything at all – the Sanque had begun to babble.

"What's he saying?" Peter asked Cathassach. The pagan held up a hand to silence him so that he could concentrate.

There was a pause as Cathassach looked up at the sky. From his position on the floor, the Sanque kept talking.

"What's he saying?" Peter repeated. "Why are you looking up there?"

"Sangoluno?" Cathassach said to the Sanque.

The Sanque nodded vigorously.

Cathassach clacked his tongue. *"Kie ni povas trovi ilin?"*

"Nordoriente."

"Ĉu vi volis konstrui la fortikaĵon antaŭ la sangoluno?"

"Jes."

"Kio estus okazinta, se ili estus alvenintaj antaŭ ol la fortikaĵo estis kompleta?"

The Sanque drew a thumb across his throat. *"Ĉiuj estus mortaj."*

Peter had given up on trying to interrupt the exchange and now waited for it to reach its natural conclusion. He understood *mortaj*, at least.

"Well?" Furlan said, snatching the pipe out of his mouth. "You two hens have had enough clucking."

For the first time since Peter had met him, Cathassach looked worried.

"He say they need to build, finish building, before the blood moon."

"What's the blood moon?"

Cathassach looked again at the sky, but it was too cloudy for a moon that evening. "Red moon," he said a little impatiently, shrugging. Evidently it had some sort of ritualistic significance, but he wasn't going to get into it then and there.

"Why do they need to complete the fort before the blood moon?" Peter asked, disconcerted.

"Because attack comes on blood moon."

"Well . . . when is it?" Furlan asked.

Again Cathassach studied the sky, then moved his head from side to side as he performed some quick mental calculations. "Three days?" he settled on.

"An attack from who?" Peter said, his impatience verging on anger.

Cathassach exchanged a few more words with the Sanque. *"Ĉu monstroj?"*

"Jes."

"Ne troviĝas monstroj ĉi tiel norde."

The Sanque shrugged. Cathassach turned to Peter. "Monsters. From the north."

Furlan pinched the bridge of his nose. "They were going to finish the fort within the next three days before they were attacked by monsters?" he said, his eyes screwed closed.

Peter looked around. "They hadn't a hope of finishing this place inside of three weeks, let alone three days."

"What does he mean by monsters?" Furlan asked.

Cathassach fell into another conversation with the Sanque. The longer it went on and the more confused noises the Black Mountain made, the more Peter lost hope of achieving any sensible explanation.

"Monsters," was all Cathassach could conclude with. "He wants to leave."

"I'm sure he does," Furlan muttered.

Peter sighed. He wanted to ask the prisoner more, but they were not going to get anything sensible out of him. Indeed, the man looked quite *insensible*. However ridiculous he sounded, there was no doubting he believed in what he was saying.

Except, it *didn't* sound ridiculous. That was entirely the problem. It sounded much too plausible. Peter thought of the eyes he had seen in the forest looking at him, the pile of offal arranged so gruesomely, so artfully. And now this talk of monsters in the forest. These matters were clearly connected, and it was only the bright light of the day and the fact that he kept the company of dozens of armed men and women that meant he was not fleeing back to Fort Ingomar – and beyond.

"No wonder the rest of his compatriots were so keen to abandon this place," he muttered to Furlan as they walked back through the bones of the fort together.

"Aye," Furlan replied, smoking his pipe thoughtfully.

"I wonder what he meant by monsters?" Peter asked.

"Maybe the same things that are making this bloody racket at night," Furlan said. He cast a glance over to the north-east, to where the pontoon bridge connected the river valley to the wild and gloomy country beyond. "I have a feeling our answer lies in that direction."

Peter had had the same feeling, a feeling that manifested as a fear that bordered on mania. "We should go back," he heard himself say. He hadn't really meant to say it, not out loud.

He could see out of the corner of his eye Furlan looking at him disapprovingly, but he did not meet the older officer's gaze. "Major Haak's orders were to investigate the source of this . . ." He gestured expensively around him, indicating the matter of the air itself. "*This.*" He didn't have to say any more. The noises at night, the screams, the unnatural goings-on needed no further codification.

Peter swallowed. Haak *had* been explicit.

"Monsters," he muttered. "Attacking the fort in three days. Why?" He endured a brief surge of frustration that made him want to scream. "Why?" He rounded on Furlan. "What in the name of Nema Victoria does that . . . *mean?*"

Furlan blew out his lips. "Leave him to the Black Mountains. Let them cut his skin off until he starts making sense."

"I will not permit such savagery," Peter said quietly.

Furlan laughed. "What is war except savagery? Blowing a man's brains out with musket shot is acceptable? Cutting a dozen men in half with cannonade is all right? But when the pagans peel a man, that is somehow a problem?"

"Do not remind me," Peter muttered, his thoughts immediately returning to the Red Coves.

"Nearly did for you, did they?"

"I just said don't remind me," Peter snapped.

There was a brief silence. "It will get easier," Furlan said gently.

Peter shook his head. He didn't want comfort. He didn't want to be perceived as in need of it, which was ridiculous given the lengths to which he went to seek it out. Only Furlan and his own private correspondence knew his true feelings on the matter. Insofar as the rest of the light company was concerned, he was a prudent and brave leader. He thought it an ill-deserved reputation. He had felt nothing in the battle except fear and an incredible drive to preserve himself. He had been an opportunistic fighter, pursuing low-risk and high-reward gambits. He had, after all, avoided the centre, the breach. Furlan had not raised it after the battle, but he must have thought it.

"We shall have to press north-east, then," he said suddenly, recklessly, his sense of self-preservation once again subordinating to his need to be perceived as brave.

Furlan cocked an eyebrow. "I agree," he said. "I suggest we leave a small detachment here. Guard the wounded, finish reducing the fortress. Together they can take the cannon back to Fort Ingomar and deliver news of our expedition."

Peter nodded absently, feeling a little resentful that he had not been given time to come up with a plan himself, but knowing that he would not necessarily have thought of those matters so quickly.

"We should spend the night here," he said, wanting to wrest a little of the control back. "Set out at dawn. What do you think, thirty men?"

Furlan shrugged. "That ought to do it. We shall struggle to feed many more."

"Let us hope in the meantime that we are able to glean a little more information."

"I shouldn't count on it," Furlan muttered, and with these words, they parted company for the night.

Little more was gleaned from the Sanque; the man was wounded in an escape attempt in the dead of night, and by the time dawn came around, he was pale from blood loss and a few hours from expiry.

"Did you get anything else out of him?" Peter asked Cathassach.

"Monster country," the Black Mountain replied, pointing to the north-east, where they were to make their expedition.

"That's it?" Furlan demanded.

Cathassach nodded.

The captain sighed. "Wonderful."

With powder and supplies checked, they made their way across the pontoon bridge; thirty men and women from the light company, including a sergeant – a Southern Plainsman called Musil – plus two Black Mountain guides, Cathassach and Olwin. Once again Peter found his eyes tracing her figure.

"She'd sooner have your tongue out," Furlan said as they reached the far bank.

Peter turned to him sharply. "What are you talking about?"

The captain smiled knowingly. "Just teasing."

It was a mild spring dawn, and Lake Ena, stretching enormously away from them, was wreathed in mist. Ahead the landscape sloped upwards constantly, and in the distance vertiginously so. In fifty miles they would hit the thickly forested foothills of the Great Northern Barrier Range; in a couple of hundred they would hit the mountains themselves. The phrase "the end of the world" was bandied around a lot by soldiers stationed in the New East, but the mountains really were it insofar as Imperial cartographers were concerned.

"Perhaps we shall break some new ground," Peter murmured as they picked their way slowly over a trail-less country, now constantly on the lookout for game as well as the enemy.

"Let us hope it doesn't come to that."

They hiked and climbed and picked and scrabbled and squelched their way through the forest. It was bizarre; Peter actually found himself missing the presence of the Casimirs and the Sanques. It was one thing to fear a human enemy, knowing that they were human and therefore mortal. Here the sheer absence of the known was an enemy in itself. He could not stop turning the words of the Sanque prisoner over in his head. *Blood moon, monster country.* All the screams and whispers and talk of spirits and drudes plagued him like a psychic malaise. He had not realised quite how inured he had become to these supernatural goings-on. The threat and prosecution of real battle, with musketry and cannon fire, had conspired to rob him of his earlier fears. Now, in this desolate, quiet place, they returned tenfold.

"*Reiru.*"

"What?" Peter said, turning. There was no one next to him; the light company had spread out, forced apart by the territory. The closest man was Musil.

"What was that, sir?" the sergeant asked in what sounded like a Balabrian accent, sweating in his tricorn and jacket. The mist had cleared, and it was a muggy morning, promising thunder later in the day.

"What did you just say?" Peter asked again, but he knew the sergeant had not said anything.

"I didn't say anything, sir," he replied.

Peter waved him off. *Not again*, he thought, his guts clenching. *Not this again.*

"Actually, Sergeant?"

"Sir?"

"Fetch the pagan girl for me, would you?"

"At once, sir."

They carried on through the forest, neither hair nor hide of an animal to be seen. Their supplies, hard biscuits and a few pounds of cured meat, would not see them past more than a couple of days. That was something, Peter noted; there was no birdsong. The forest was as silent as the grave.

"*Jes?*" Olwin said as she approached, ruddy-faced from exertion. Like Cathassach, she had been scouting ahead, and it had taken perhaps half an hour to recall her.

"I heard something," Peter said. He scratched his chin; per Furlan's advice he had started to grow a beard, and now several days of stubble coated his chin and cheeks. It was the first beard he'd ever grown.

"*Jes?*" Olwin repeated. Now that she was directly in front of him, he noticed more tattoos on her face; like Cathassach's, they gave the faintest impression of a skull imprinted there. Peter considered her to be quite beautiful.

He cleared his throat. Even entertaining such thoughts was surely a betrayal of Leonie back in distant Sova.

"I heard something in my ear." He was speaking much too loudly, as though she were a simpleton, rather than simply a non-Sovan. Within the broader silence of the forest, the effect was almost aggressive. "A word. Someone spoke a word in my ear."

"*Ĉu el la etero?*"

"I don't speak . . . " Peter said, shrugging exaggeratedly.

Olwin shrugged back. "What word?" she asked in heavily accented Saxan.

He cleared his throat again. "Uh, *reiru?*"

Olwin nodded. "Means 'go back'. *Jes?* Return." She performed a little walk with her index and middle fingers. "Go away."

Peter was quiet for a few moments as he considered the implications of this.

"Someone told me to . . . go back?" he asked her.

She shrugged, apparently unfazed. Then, pausing only briefly to see if he wanted anything else, she darted to the head of the line, moving through the forest with a feline grace.

"Shit," Peter muttered, looking at the trees around him.

Once again, he could not shake the feeling of being watched.

On and on they went, each step taking them further away from the Ena Split. Even without all the bizarre goings-on, this would have been an unsettling experience. They were over a thousand miles from Sova – closer to fifteen hundred – with nothing but enemy territory at their backs and the unknown before them. Peter felt less like a soldier and more like one of those insane explorers from the Sovan Argonauts' Society.

They camped that night, having made perhaps ten miles, slept poorly thanks to the rain and their persistent nightmares, and struck camp at dawn. It was a gloomy day, the sky dark with cloud. As they moved off, Peter's foot crunched something. Thinking it to be a nest – though there were still no birds to be heard – he bent down and picked up what turned out to be a crude fetish made of twigs and bound by sapling fibres.

"You there," he said to the closest soldier.

"Yes, sir?"

Peter held the fetish in his hands, turning it.

"Fetch me ..." he murmured. Who had made this? Had it always been there, or had someone placed it there overnight? He shook his head. Someone would have spotted an interloper; they had sentries posted.

Surely?

"Fetch who, sir?" the soldier asked after a moment.

Peter shook his head. He tossed the fetish away. "Nothing," he said. It was better not to know. His sanity depended on it. "Don't worry about it."

The first of the day's rain began to fall.

On, endlessly on. The ground rose. The forest was unbroken, but the land contoured upwards as they approached the foothills of the Barrier Range. Water was in great abundance from the rain and many freshwater streams, but food was becoming an issue. They simply could not find any game. It was as though their expedition was at the centre of an enormous invisible stockade forcing all living things away.

After three days and thirty miles, Peter was about to give the order to return to Fort Ingomar when news was passed down the line that they had come across something.

"They are requesting you at the front, sir," the nearest soldier told him.

"Right," Peter said, and moved through the undergrowth up the hill to the head of the line. They were spread out over about a quarter of a mile now, and it took a little while to get to where the Black Mountain scouts were. Here was Furlan, too; the three of them were lying prone at the lip of an escarpment, overlooking a valley. Beyond, the hills – more like small mountains, really – rose into the iron-grey sky. The air smelt of pine sap and mist.

Furlan pressed his finger to his lips, and motioned for Peter to approach slowly. He crouched down, angling his sabre as he did so, and crawled to where the others lay.

"Nema Victoria," he breathed.

It was a house, a cabin – no, a *hall*. A large wooden structure, thirty feet along its longest edge. Its walls were constructed of stout beams, whilst the roof, steeply sloped and badly warped, was moss-impregnated thatch. In fact the whole thing was so overgrown that it looked as though it were being reclaimed by the forest.

"Who built this?" Peter breathed.

"*La Ruĝgolfuloj ne vojaĝas ĉi tiel norden, ĉu ne?*" Olwin asked Cathassach.

"*Ne,*" the older Black Mountain murmured.

"What's she saying?" Furlan whispered.

"No Red Coves. Not this far north," Cathassach said.

Furlan turned to look at Peter. "What do you reckon?"

Peter reckoned that he wanted to turn around and leave this place immediately. The hall, whatever it was and whenever it had been built, was clearly abandoned. It seemed to exude malign energies in the same way a sacred burial ground might. He went cross-eyed just looking at it.

"Well, I think we should at least have a look," he said.

Furlan nodded, though for the first time Peter thought he detected unease in the captain's eyes. Perhaps Furlan had secretly wanted Peter to suggest they leave. Wouldn't it be ridiculous, he mused, if all of them simply wanted to go, but no one wanted to be the one to say it. They were going to press on, likely into mortal danger, because nobody wanted to be thought of as spineless.

Furlan tutted as he looked up at the sky. "This rain is only going to get worse," he said. He pointed to the foothills across the other side of the small valley. "It's coming from the mountains, look."

"We can shelter in the hall if needs be," Peter heard himself say.

Furlan gave him a strange look, almost as though he had been betrayed. "Good thinking, Lieutenant," he said tightly.

Peter turned to Cathassach. He gestured to the hall. "Go and have a look, would you?"

The Black Mountain appeared singularly unimpressed with this instruction, but nonetheless complied. He snatched up his hand-axe and descended the escarpment into the bowl of the valley. Olwin followed shortly after, and skirted round to the north. The pagans' clothes, dark browns and greens, kept them well camouflaged against the foliage of the forest, and even their tattoos had the effect of breaking up the shapes and contours of their white faces and necks and hands. It was not long before Peter had to concentrate very hard just to be able to follow them.

"What do you reckon?" he whispered to Furlan.

"Some sort of pagan settlement. Draedists or Manaeii or Tolls, who knows?"

"Not New Easterners?"

Furlan waved him off. "You know what I mean. Some tribal confederation. Probably this whole area was settled once."

"And now what? They all died?"

The captain shrugged. "Sure. Haven't found a pound of meat in thirty miles, nor any ground that was capable of being farmed.

Maybe they starved. Maybe they just left to find food." He nodded to the hall. The two pagan scouts were at either end of it now, and peering through gaps in the planks of the wall. "Whatever happened, it happened a long time ago."

They were quiet for a few moments.

"Maybe something killed them all," Peter said.

"Aye," Furlan replied, pressing himself up. Cathassach was waving to them: the all-clear. "Maybe."

It was empty inside the hall.

The ground was laid with boards, and there was a large stone firepit in the centre. The smoke hole above was letting in a tremendous amount of rain where the gable had collapsed. There was no furniture. The place smelt strongly of mildew. The internal supports were wreathed in vines, and great lesions of moss and lichen smothered the walls in a simulacrum of plaster. It was gloomy and damp, the only light – and that was fading fast under the weight of the encroaching storm clouds – coming through the smoke hole.

Outside, the thirty men from the light company, under the direction of Sergeant Musil, set up a cordon around the valley.

"All right," Peter said, feeling an unnameable itch just from standing in this cursed place. "All right. Here's what I think. We get a fire going and we use this place as shelter for tonight. Then tomorrow we make back. We haven't got the provisions to go any further, and it's clear . . . " he thought of the crude wooden fetish he had found in the campsite, "it's clear there is no one here."

"Agreed," Furlan said, a little too quickly, and the two of them exchanged a brief, uncomfortable smile. "I'll get the men to gather some wood together before this whole place goes to rot."

It had been a little too early in the day to billet, and so they had to spend a slightly embarrassing amount of time doing nothing. Furlan and Peter pretended to be looking at maps, whilst they sent out a foraging party with the pagans for edible roots and leaves. They had all long given up hope of finding any game, and they wanted to save some of their provisions for the journey back.

It was almost a relief when the weather fully closed in and the rain was so torrential that it made anything except sentry duty pointless. They pulled the men into the hall, and by the light of the fire, they quietly diced and drank and otherwise passed the time.

Peter set himself up in one of the corners, and had begun to write another letter to his father when Furlan came up next to him.

"You write a lot," the captain remarked. He was a little drunk, but there was nothing new in that.

Peter nodded. "I do."

"Who to? Your beau?"

"Not as often as I should," Peter said. Thoughts of Leonie almost invariably soured his mood, and had been almost completely supplanted with thoughts of Olwin, by whom he was increasingly captivated. Sometimes he dreamt of taking her back to Sova with him, and presenting her to his mother as his intended. He enjoyed imagining Leonie fleeing the room in tears. The stir would be intense, the controversy ludicrous.

"Who, then?" Furlan pressed, a little too glassy-eyed to notice Peter's discomfort.

"My father."

"Ah. How is the old man?"

Peter cleared his throat. "He's dead, actually. He died some time ago."

Incomprehension wrinkled Furlan's features. "Why do you write letters to him, then?"

Peter shrugged, shaking his head. "I do not know," he settled on eventually. "A way to . . . make a clean breast of things. It's a silly thing, really."

Furlan paused, his expression softening as he finally understood. "I see," he said quietly. He sat down. "It's a rum thing, losing a father – if he's decent. There are plenty who aren't."

"Mine was a good man. I miss him dearly. It's a cold thing to say, but my mother does not hold much love for me. She much prefers my brothers. Life is hard for her, as a widow. You know what Sova is like."

Furlan nodded knowingly. "Aye. 'Tis a cruel place for those who exist without the machinery of state."

There was a pause. "One more night in this blasted country," Peter said, smiling weakly.

"Nema willing," Furlan muttered, taking another swig of brandy. His lips glistened in the firelight.

"Whatever it is that is out there, I think it is best left undisturbed."

"Or disturbed by a whole bloody regiment," Furlan said. "Linasburg, Slavomire . . . Davorstadt . . . These places are just the beginning, Peter. The New East is frontier country now, but one day it will be as thick with people as Sova."

"I daresay you are right."

Peter could hardly conceive of it, that such an inhospitable and wild country, saturated as it was with arcane energies and malign creatures, could ever be tamed. But it seemed there was very little that could stop the fires of Sovan industry these days.

He was about to say something else, but stopped when he heard a sound from outside. A scream.

"Not again," he muttered, standing and striding the length of the hall to where the door was. He threw it open and looked out into the rain – and froze.

"No," he breathed, as a dozen monstrous figures converged on the hall through the darkness. He was stuck in place, breath catching in his throat, muscles weak, mind racing. They were fast, so *fast*, and certainly, most definitely, not human.

One of their faces caught the wan firelight, and Peter saw again those eyes, the same eyes he had seen in the forest over a week before.

This was it.

This was how he died.

"To arms!" he managed to shout, throwing the door closed. "We're under attack! To arms!"

XIII

The Interior

"Do not be cowed by the severity of armed intervention if your cause is just. It is a rum thing to risk the lives of one's soldiers – to say nothing of the health of the exchequer. But any experienced foreign policymaker will attest: our enemy is a diseased limb. A swift amputation is always the safest course of action."

FROM MANAGOLD'S
THE THIRD WAY

Radovansburg

PRINZPATRIATE OF REICHSGARD

On the eleventh day of the journey, they pulled into the small walled town of Radovansburg, the last Imperial settlement before they crossed into the Interior.

The atmosphere within the stagecoach was toxic as they debarked and made their way into an inn. Glaser and the Life Guards sorted out stabling and found someone to butcher the animals they had taken from Zetland; then the colonel returned and collared Maruska, Renata and the two monks – almost physically in the latter case.

"Come with me. You: sort out our rooms."

Ozolinsh, to whom the final instruction had been directed, looked as though she had been slapped. "Absolutely not," she declared.

"Just let her come. She's going to hear about it anyway," Renata muttered. She was actually growing rather fond of Ozolinsh.

Glaser, who was clearly in no mood to argue – with them, at least – surrendered the point immediately and led them through into a back room. "See that we are not disturbed," he said, tossing a goldmark bit to the barkeep. Then he closed the door behind them and barred it.

"Sit down, everyone." This was a side of Glaser that Renata had not really seen before. He looked angry, and had had time to stew in that anger. This was the version she imagined striding up and down ranks of men on the battlefield, gesticulating with his sabre, directing them to blast enemy soldiers apart with cannonade and hails of musketry.

"May I just say—" Herschel began, but Glaser cut across him.

"Yes, I think you had better," he snapped. Both monks looked wretched.

The colonel began to pace the room.

"When we left Zetland," Herschel said quietly, "the brothers and sisters were going to . . . they were seeking to . . . " He paused. Guillot had clearly kicked him under the table.

"Right," Glaser said. He walked smartly over to Guillot and grabbed him by the scruff of his spring jacket. "*You* can wait outside."

"Get off me!" Guillot yelped, but Glaser's grip was iron, and he physically dragged the young monk to the door, opened it, and threw him out.

"Watch him," he said to the Life Guards who were playing a card game at one of the tables outside. Then he turned back in, and closed the door again. "Brother Herschel. You were about to tell me at length and with precision what has happened," he said stonily.

Herschel cleared his throat.

"After we discovered that we could no longer contact the spirits of the afterlife," he said, fiddling with his hands and staring at the table, "and after we had consulted the relevant texts and parts of the Neman Creed, and after we as an order had decided that this could be the beginnings of the Great Silence . . . "

"Yes?"

Herschel took a deep, shaky breath. "The decision to alert the Empire . . . well, it was not a common . . . we did not all think—"

"You weren't going to tell anyone," Renata said impatiently. Maruska held out a hand to steady her temper.

Herschel shook his head. "No. That's not quite right. We weren't *not* going to tell anyone; we just weren't necessarily going to . . . tell Sova."

"Why?" Glaser demanded.

"Colonel, with the greatest respect, your first instinct was to execute us. Not necessarily yours personally," he added quickly, as Glaser's expression curdled, "but *institutionally.* Sova is – has *become* – ah, rather blinkered about the employment of magicks, and it was decided that . . . well, that we would try something else. Speak to the Saekas, perhaps. And in the meantime . . . "

"And in the *meantime*?" Glaser prompted.

"And in the meantime, members of the Order were going to try and . . . Look, it's going to sound bad, but it's just a word—"

"Nema Vic*toria*, out with it, man!"

"A ritual," Herschel concluded lamely. "A special sort of ritual."

There were a few moments of silence. "What do you mean? What sort of ritual?"

"What's so bad about the word ritual? My morning coffee is a *ritual,*" Maruska said. There was a gleam in his eye as he tried to remove some of the tension from the room.

Herschel coughed, playing for time. "Well, with the failure of séance, we thought we'd try something with . . . "

"Something with a bit of chest hair?" Ozolinsh offered.

"Quite," Herschel said with a faltering smile.

"Brother Herschel, you of all people know that we are not blessed with a great deal of time," Glaser said.

Herschel sighed. "The Order was going to try not just to perform a séance, but to . . . *summon* a creature and perhaps bind it here, and then . . . "

"And then what? Sit down and have a brandy with it?"

"*Ask* what was going on. *Ask* it whether the Great Silence was – is – indeed in progress."

Glaser pinched the bridge of his nose. "Brother Herschel, I must say, this all sounds rather far-fetched."

"Attempted summonings are well documented in Sova's history," Ozolinsh said levelly. "If you know the books."

"*Attempted* summonings. I am not for one moment disputing the reality of the arcane and the afterlife, madam," Glaser said. "But even with the weight of historical record, you must admit that some of the accounts are outlandish."

"I am afraid, Colonel," Herschel said, and for a moment it seemed as though he were going to stop there. "That if we are going to make any progress on this diplomatic mission, you are going to have to suspend your incredulity somewhat."

Glaser sighed. "Tell me about it, then. The . . . summoning." Saying it out loud seemed to cause him physical pain.

"Well, that's the problem. I do not know what happened. When we summon a spirit, we are channelling energies from the holy dimensions into a host – a willing host!" Herschel added hastily as everyone's expression darkened – "and binding it there. It is not something that has been attempted in the recent history of the Order."

"A foolhardy endeavour," Ozolinsh muttered.

Glaser ignored her. "So let me see if I have this straight: you lost contact with the afterlife, took a vote as to your next steps, decided to reach out to the Saekas in the first instance, and in the meantime to conduct a summoning ritual to gather more information from the afterlife. Is that about the skin of it?"

"Aye, you have it."

"So in coming to the Empire, you broke with your brothers?"

"I have long believed that our only hope is with the assistance of the Stygion, and to a lesser extent the Kasar. But we cannot achieve anything without Sova's help. So Brother Guillot and I took it upon ourselves to leave."

"Before the summoning?"

"Before the summoning."

"Which enterprise seems to have met with failure."

Herschel nodded sadly. It was easy to forget, Renata reflected, that if everyone inside Zetland was indeed dead, then his entire order, and all of his friends and colleagues within it, had just been extinguished.

Glaser's foul temper seemed to have dissipated. Now he seemed curious more than anything else. "Who wrote the message on the door, then?"

Herschel shrugged. "One of the brothers? A passing trader? Though there were not many. Perhaps they concluded that the fortress had become enpoxed, and sought to quarantine it."

Glaser blew out his lips. "Explain to me the mechanics of it. How does the ritual of a summoning kill everybody in the Order. How many men are we talking about?"

"Men and women. Several hundred. A summoning is an extremely energy-intensive process. It is likely they turned everyone to the task. I know not the intricacies of the ritual itself, but if everyone exposed themselves, their minds, to the afterlife, made conduits of themselves, and those dimensions are indeed in the grip of an existential malaise, then . . . "

"Blimey," Ozolinsh muttered.

"But this is conjecture?" Renata asked. "Everybody was alive when you left. You do not actually *know* what happened."

"I do not," Herschel admitted.

"And so in travelling to Sova, you were acting very much outside the bounds of your authority," Glaser said.

"Insofar as I required permission from anybody except myself."

"You feared recrimination on your return?"

"Verily."

Glaser considered matters for a moment. Eventually he levelled a finger at Herschel. "Is there anything else I need to know? Anything else you have withheld?"

The old monk hung and shook his head. Renata noticed the hair in the centre of the tonsured part was growing back. It looked quite ridiculous.

"All right," Glaser murmured. He was unsure, but he was also tired, and clearly not about to put hot irons up the man. "If I find there is some other piece of information—"

"There is not, I assure you."

"Hm." His jaw worked a moment. "Madam," he said, turning to Ozolinsh. "A word in private, if you please."

"Right. Yes."

"The rest of you, do what you will. I have many things to achieve before we lose the light. Let us reconvene in the morning."

Renata went to sleep uneasily that night. The feeling of dread in her stomach had persisted throughout the evening and was at its most intense just before she slept. She could not shake it no matter what she tried: deep breathing, brandy, letter-writing. She regretted having attuned herself to it, and cursed Ozolinsh and Herschel for turning her mind to the matter in the first place. Ignorance had most assuredly been bliss.

Once again she found herself dreaming quite lucidly, trapped atop that same fortification, the enormous curtain wall so high that the top of it sat above the cloud layer. The sky was stratified into great washes of colour, a violet haze fading to pink and blue. A brilliant star field twinkled above, and in amongst the glittering haze she could see bands of kaleidoscopic astral mist.

"A-Amara?" she called out. Her voice barely travelled in that leaden non-air.

"Renata," a voice replied. But it was not Amara's; it was Maruska's.

"Didi?"

"Over here," he croaked.

She turned, and saw for the first time that behind her lay an enormous open space of paving. It was a little like being in the Sovan market, except the place was empty. Every hundred yards or so, arranged in an infinite grid pattern, were statues, housed on great boxy plinths of marble each forty foot high. But the statues themselves defied comprehension. Every time she looked at them, they shimmered and swirled and refused to be perceived.

At the base of the nearest plinth, Maruska sat propped up, his brightly coloured Qareshian robes marking him out against the fractal infinity of this bizarre place. But as she approached, Renata realised that it wasn't Maruska – or at least, it wasn't all of him. His robes were rags; his flesh was rags, too, from the waist down. Great clumps of viscera lay against the flagstones, in a pool of blood that looked like a plate of red glass. Maruska's breathing was irregular and laboured, and his face was sheened with sweat. He looked as though he had been savaged by an entire pack of wolves.

"Didi, my god," she breathed.

She tried to run, but could not. Instead she was once again relegated to fighting her way through the air, which had suddenly become treacle-thick. Maruska remained at all times twenty paces away, though in this bizarre dream dimension, his voice was as loud and clear as if he was standing right next to her. Which was just as well, because the words were little more than a feverish whisper, spoken into her ear with incredible fear and urgency.

"They are coming," he implored, an echo of the same nonsense the spectral Amara had conveyed. "They are coming for all of us."

"Who is? Nema Victoria, *who*?!" Renata shrieked. She was horrified, but she could not wake up. So great was the injury to her mind that she felt as though she were about to enter a dissociative state.

"They are right. They are right! You must listen! Do what you can to stop it. Do you understand?"

She shook her head furiously. "What are you talking about? Why won't you just—"

And then she was there, transported immediately to Maruska's side, and he was grasping at her with his bloodied hands, pawing desperately at her face and neck and shoulders, groaning and whining as his lifeblood cascaded out of the nub of his body, and then his ribs were opening and expanding outwards, splintering and breaking, and—

Renata woke up screaming.

"We have enough to focus on in the real world without stirring the tea leaves of our dreams," Maruska said after Renata had relayed to him the details of her nightmare.

"The real world?" she snorted with great derision. "Our mission is entirely preoccupied with the spirit realm."

They had reached the westernmost point of the Warinhari canal system. After several hours, in which they had stood at the prow of a freightliner watching Glaser's men, as well as a dozen stevedores, load the stagecoach and their horses aboard, the boat was finally hitched up to a team of four huge, horned plains horses, and they were off.

Here, in this part of the world, the destructive voracity of Sova was writ large. Either side of the canal the earth was laid open as though it had been flayed by an enormous whip. The ground had been excavated in great seams and trenches and piled up into mountainous spoil heaps where coal, iron ore, lead and tin were dragged from the earth by the midwife of industry. Here was the cutting edge of technology, steam-driven pumps which drained thousands of gallons of subterranean water and dumped it into the canals, and enormous posts wrapped in scaffolding which would eventually become thaumaturgic wind generators.

"I think it was more than just a dream," Renata said. "I had a similar vision with Amara."

"A dream is not a prophecy."

"But what if it *is*?"

Maruska shifted his weight uncomfortably, and mopped his brow with a kerchief. It was hot and dusty and dry here, and the air was thick with black clouds of pollution.

"It is hardly surprising you had such a dream in light of your sister's injury. You yourself were nearly killed. Such experiences leave their marks on our minds for decades. You cannot expect to overcome them so quickly and easily."

They stood in silence for a little while, taking in the scenery. The canal was busy with boats and iridescent with run-off, glittering in the bright sunlight. The towpaths either side were choked with plains horses and oxen, and the stench of their shit baking in the heat – mixed with the smell of burning wood and coal – was overpowering. Where the earth was not bored into or blown open, or buried under spoil and slag, or piles of timber, or cut away and laid with foundations and grids of scaffolding, it was little more than hot savannah stretching for tens of miles in every direction.

Slowly, a thought crystallised in Renata's mind. She turned, looking at Maruska askance. There was definitely something different about him, about his manner. He was fidgeting, and seemed anxious.

"You had a nightmare too, didn't you?" she said. "Was it the same one?"

He waved her off. "Don't be ridiculous."

She continued to examine his face – in profile, for he refused to turn to her.

"Stop looking at me like that," he said. It was not like him to be irritable.

"Then tell me why you are so het up."

He rounded on her, his features creased in anger. "Because I am trying to focus on the diplomatic mission, and my deputy is prattling on about her dreams as though they had any relevance to matters whatever!"

She actually took a step back. Maruska had never once shouted at her, for as long as she had known him.

His anger quickly melted away from his face, to be replaced by an expression of acute embarrassment. "I am . . . I am so sorry, Renata. That was . . . I am sorry."

Renata turned away from him, searching the boat for something else to look at. At the stern, she saw Ozolinsh exchanging murmured conversation with the two monks. She and the engineer briefly locked eyes, and Renata saw her own fear and uncertainty reflected back at her.

"I don't like this," she announced eventually. "Something is wrong. I think we all need to start taking this much more seriously."

"I daresay you are right," Maruska said darkly, and he walked off and left her standing there alone.

They spent three days being towed through the canal network. Renata should have used the time to read her Loxica, revise Stygion diplomatic protocols, and prepare generally to enter the Door to the Sea. Instead she brooded, her thoughts consumed by her nightmares, the dead monks, the attempt on her life, her sister, and a dozen other things.

On the fourteenth day of the journey, they passed the foothills of the great Southern Dividing Range, the enormous red mountains that separated Qaresh and the Southern Plains from the Kyarai; and then on the fifteenth day, the landscape transformed dramatically. Here in the western third of the Kyarai was the Reenwound, a vast and dense rainforest which trapped all of the rain coming off the Jade Sea and hoarded it.

The quality of the air here changed significantly. In the Interior it had been hot and dry and filled with dust where the Sovans violated the earth; here it was thick not just with the spoil of industry – though Sovan timber merchants and gold miners, Renata's father included, were exuberantly stripping the rainforest of its natural wealth – but with water too. As the Kyarai transitioned to the early months of summer, the sun boiled steam directly off the Reenwound and saturated the air with it.

It was not just the wreckage of insatiable Sovan commerce that had left its mark on the Interior. Here, Sovan Army supply trains were in great abundance, for tens of thousands of soldiers populated this part of the world as they struggled with the forces of Casimir for the soul of the wolfmen. Horses, oxen and carts filled with food, powder and other supplies trundled along next to the canals on roads jammed up with traffic, kicking up enormous clouds of red dust.

On the sixteenth day, they passed by Fort Aliprand on the Sigismund Line and repaired to the stagecoach to cross the border into the Kyarai itself; and on the seventeenth, they finally reached Kalegosfort. From there, it was only three days' travel to Port Talaka.

"Nema Victoria," Renata said, taking in the scene as they arrived.

Kalegosfort was in a frenetic state that bordered on chaos. The old mediaeval fortification, a tumbledown castle surrounded by walls of pink stone which formed the core of the town, had been commandeered as the Sovan military headquarters, whilst every lodging in the place was filled with Sovan soldiers. For the first time Renata was exposed to large numbers of wolfmen, too; they walked in and amongst their human counterparts, a full head taller, trussed up in Sovan-issue military breeches and jackets, carrying stout falchions tucked into their dynastic sashes. They looked a far cry from their poverty-stricken brethren in Wolfsland.

Glaser signalled for the stagecoach to stop, and he pulled up alongside it and dismounted. Renata wound down the window. Behind the colonel was a sign that somebody had erected, upon which was painted an arrow and the words *6th Division HQ*.

"Right," he said, wincing slightly as hot, ripe air flowed out of the cabin. "Excellency," he said, addressing Maruska, "you come with me up to the headquarters. Madam Ozolinsh, I suggest you try and find somewhere for us to billet tonight. It's going to be all arses and elbows up there." He pointed to the old castle.

"You do not need me present?" Renata asked, hot, tired, and rankling at this surprise demotion.

"No," Glaser said. "I need you to find someone for me. A man by the name of Captain Joseph Lyzander."

Renata did a double-take as her blood surged. "The Empress spoke to you, too?"

Glaser looked briefly confused. "About what?"

"Captain Lyzander," Renata said, her hand going idly to the letter she kept in her pocket.

Glaser wrinkled his nose. "Madam, I am certain I do not know what you are talking about. Captain Lyzander is a member of the 19th West Kovan Regiment." He glanced about him, and then indicated a woman in the distance. "Look for a fellow in that uniform. They will be able to point you in the right direction."

Renata squinted at the sea of soldiers in black jackets and tricorns. "Right," she murmured.

"Captain Lyzander has some experience of gaining entry into Port Talaka by clandestine means and is likely to be of assistance to us. Do your very best." He turned back to Maruska. "Come then, Excellency. It will be on foot from here."

Ozolinsh and the monks disappeared off to find them somewhere to stay, whilst Renata headed in the direction of the soldier Glaser had pointed out, shouldering her way through presses of soldiers, Kasar and bewildered civilians.

The afternoon was marching on, and the sky was closing over with banks of grey cloud. Here in Kalegosfort there was a very real sense of doom in the air, of a war on the verge of being lost, of enemies at the gates, of an existential crisis for the northern Kyarai. She was reminded of it everywhere she looked. Embedded in the walls of every building, little alcoves contained geometric stone idols of Nema, relics of an imported religion, hoarded and husbanded and protected with a ferocious zeal that surpassed anything one would find in Sova. These idols and fetishes, and the abundant shrines and temples which housed them, would be destroyed with incredible violence by the Sudreik Kasar and their Casimiran sponsors. Renata had only to blink to see the town transformed from a thriving trading settlement to a great heap of corpses and burning rubble.

"Excuse me," she said, reaching the soldier Glaser had pointed to and tapping her on the back.

"Yes, madam," the woman replied, very much preoccupied with several large sacks of flour.

"I'm looking for Captain Joseph Lyzander of the—"

"19th West Kovans? In the pits, ma'am," the soldier said over her shoulder.

"The . . . pits?" Renata said, picturing coal mines.

"Over there," the soldier said brusquely, pointing and drawing the brief conversation to a close.

Renata followed the line of the woman's finger through the narrow alleys between walls of adobe until she came out into a clearing.

"Ah," she murmured to herself in realisation. Here was a

square fighting pit, eight feet deep and thirty to a side, bedded with sandy red earth and with markings painted on the walls for a ball sport which was not currently being played. Around it stood dozens of men and women and Kasar of all colours and creeds, all uniformed members of the Sovan Army. In the pit itself, a wolfman was fighting a human man. The former was a seven-foot grey-furred brute with one ear missing; the latter was a Plainsman, a Balabrian Dynast from the look of him, with skin the same reddish-brown colour as the earth. His hair and beard were close-cropped but unkempt, and his body, taut with muscle, glistened with sweat and ran with rivulets of blood. He wore the breeches and boots of a Sovan soldier, whilst above the pit stood a man holding his shirt, jacket and musket.

Renata watched the fight progress, largely unimpressed. Fighting of any sort lay at odds with her diplomatic sensibilities, though its various forms were so prevalent in Sova it was difficult not to become inured to it. Boxing, fencing and cage fighting in the city were extremely common and extensively gambled on, and even pistol duelling had been recently re-legalised by the Empress as a sop to the Senate traditionalists.

She might have been unimpressed with the sport of fighting, but that was not to say she was unimpressed with the fighters.

She let out an involuntary gasp as the wolfman smacked the Sovan about the side of his face with incredible ferocity. Stunned, the man staggered to one side. She saw then that the wolfman's claws were sheathed in leather, though at least one of the claws had split the glove.

The wolfmen cheered; the Sovans jeered. The fight was close to being over, for what man could fight a Kasar and hope to win?

The answer, apparently, was this one. Affecting to be dazed, the Sovan suddenly pushed himself away from the wall of the pit and tackled the Kasar around the midriff. The latter, falling only by virtue of having been caught off balance, collapsed roughly to the sand and let out a great snarl of rage. Getting both feet underneath the man's midriff, he kicked him off with great violence, so that the Sovan smacked hard back into the wall. There, winded and having struck the back of his skull, he sank to the floor into a sitting position, and held up a hand. That, it seemed, signalled the end of the fight.

The assembled crowd roared their approval or disapproval depending on which way they had bet, though for Renata the smart money had always been on the wolfman. She watched as goldmark bits changed hands, notes were bundled up and stuffed into pockets, chalkboard odds were erased, and the two contenders were hauled out of the pit by their mates. The Sovan took an ill-advisedly large swig of brandy, and set to washing the blood and sweat from his torso.

Renata's gaze lingered a moment, and then she approached the cluster of men and women.

"I'm looking for Captain Joseph Lyzander," she said to the nearest soldier.

The man turned to her and gave her an unfriendly look. "Who wants to know?" he asked.

Renata's expression curdled. "Secretary Renata Rainer of the—"

"Madam Secretary," the topless and bloodied pit fighter interrupted, smiling and spitting out a great ball of crimson phlegm on to the ground. He rubbed a rag roughly over his face. "You are looking for me."

Renata's words caught in her throat. "I . . . yes. How did—"

"I received a dispatch from Colonel Glaser," he said. He pushed himself away from his supporters – most ill-advised, since he had to be caught by them a moment later. There was much laughter and, it appeared, drunkenness.

Renata pursed her lips. "You should not be speaking so freely of these matters," she began, but to her great frustration, he simply smiled and waved her off. To her greater frustration, she found herself obliging him with her silence.

"You are arrived, then." He approached a large tub filled with water, and began to liberally splash it over his torso "Let me have a wash and I shall join you."

"I . . . Right," Renata said, faltering. Her hand idly traced the letter in the right hip pocket of her dress. Suddenly it felt much heavier. "Yes. Be quick about it; you are expected at headquarters."

"Yes, yes," he muttered, and dunked his face into the tub.

It took them the better part of thirty minutes to make their way up to the old fortress, through its gates, and into the operations room which Glaser had commandeered for the afternoon. They waited quietly in the corridor as a gaggle of human and Kasari officers filed out, and then entered to see Glaser and Maruska standing in front of a large map of Port Talaka and the intervening country. Upon it were a great number of pencilled arrows and rectangles representing different military formations. Renata was no expert in matters martial, but the picture looked dismal.

"Ah," the colonel said, turning briefly. He gestured to a decanter of brandy and a few tumblers. "Help yourselves."

Renata demurred, but Lyzander poured himself an overlarge measure, which she frowned at.

He winked at her.

"No word on the shamans from the Spiritsraad," Glaser said, looking out of one of the small windows with a northern aspect. "I had written instructions for them to be evacuated, but either those instructions have not reached Port Talaka, or they have been ignored, or the shamans are dead, or . . ."

"My own letters seem to have met with the same fate," Maruska muttered.

"Aye, well. The postal service is not what it once was in this part of the world," Lyzander said. Only Renata seemed to notice the sarcasm in his voice.

Glaser sighed, and gestured vaguely to the roads around

Kalegosfort, clogged with soldiers and refugees. "We are going to have to try and enter the capital. Which is precisely what I wanted to avoid."

"Is it still in Sovan hands?" Renata asked anxiously.

"Not for much longer." He tapped a line on the map, what looked to be the southernmost distributary of the River Yaro, the delta of which Port Talaka was built astride. "Marshal Klossner is holding them here, for now."

"For now?"

Glaser nodded. "News from Till Island is that the Casimiran Navy will arrive in the next day or two to begin reducing the Sovan fortifications of the city itself. We've naught to stop them."

"What about the *Sovan* Navy?" Maruska asked.

"A good part of the Jade Sea Fleet was lost a fortnight ago off the coast of Oksanastadt. Burned in the dock."

"Nema," Renata breathed. Of course, they had missed the news, being seventeen days out of Sova. She could imagine the breathless headlines, and the chaos in the Imperial Office. "And the colony?"

Glaser shrugged. "Well, I should imagine we will lose it."

"But—"

He waved her off. "Let the colonials worry about the colonies. We need to worry about getting those priests out of the capital."

"The Kyarai is a colony in all but name," Lyzander offered, taking a long draw of brandy.

"Captain Lyzander," Glaser said as though he had only just noticed him. "Do not be facetious. The wolfmen are our allies, not our subjugates."

"Indeed," Maruska said.

"You received my dispatch?"

"I did, sir," Lyzander said, nodding. "Three days ago."

"Hm," Glaser grunted.

"So what is our plan?" Renata asked.

"Our plan is to take Captain Lyzander's advice as regards

getting into the capital and out again," Glaser said. He regarded the man, his eyes picking out every violation of the Army dress regulations one after the other. "The Empress spoke highly of you and your abilities to the Privy Council."

Renata's blood surged with a strange and uncomfortable emotion. Once again she felt the weight of the Empress's perfumed letter in her pocket. *Very highly indeed.*

Lyzander inclined his head, his expression unreadable.

"Whatever we do, we must set off shortly," Maruska said in the silence that followed.

"And travel through the night," Glaser agreed. "It is still two hundred and fifty miles to Port Talaka. We must remember that this is only the very first part of our mission, and the penultimate when ranked by importance."

"And what, if I may ask, Colonel, *is* this mission?" Lyzander asked.

Glaser picked up his own brandy, and finished it.

"You, Captain, are going to help us save the world."

XIV

A Time of Judgement

"It suits Sova to pretend that the afterlife is not a real, tangible place; that our gods, our devils, our angels and demons are but a fiction. Clothe it in the dogma of religion; make it seem risible, I say. Deal with the matter as it arises – on expiry! I should not like to go to the time, effort and expense – financial and philosophical – of reorganising our entire society so that our lives become nothing except a prelude to death."

FROM GROSSO'S
THE GREAT ROT: THE RISE OF NEMAN CONFORMISM

Toutorix

DRAEDALAND

Von Oldenburg was not accustomed to running. He was certainly not accustomed to running for his life.

Behind, the pagans followed.

It was the silence that bothered him most. He felt like they should be snarling, that writhing mass of demented, rabid humans. They should have been screeching and crying and screaming and hooting and hollering, they should have been making every fearful and angry noise the human mouth and throat could produce.

But they were silent. Just vacant automata, propelled by some residual, autonomic force.

Von Oldenburg, Yelena, and those fusiliers who remained fled back the way they had come. Von Oldenburg rumbled and grunted and sweated as his heavy frame jounced and jostled, taxing every joint in his legs. His boots became soaked through with muddy water. He stole frantic glances behind him. The pagans continued to give chase, but many were dropping to the ground and lying there motionless. The rate of attrition was quite startling.

The soldiers ran ahead and frantically readied the post-chaise and horses. One of them raised his musket and fired, and an incredible flash of light and *crack* of igniting gunpowder filled the air. The chest of one of the Draedists blew open in a great welter of blood, and he collapsed to the floor.

So, von Oldenburg reflected grimly, *they can be killed.*

The post-chaise was hitched up to the horses, and von Oldenburg and Yelena scrabbled inside. The postilion whipped the horses, and they whinnied and thundered away. They were alive to the danger in that keen, perceptive way animals tended to be.

The remaining fusiliers shouted and screamed after them, but the postilion needed no encouragement to abandon them to die.

"Leave them," von Oldenburg said anyway, to be sure, and they left them.

They rode on for an hour, slowing after perhaps ten minutes to husband the horses. The pagans could not keep up. Whatever had happened to them, they had not been blessed with superhuman speed or endurance. In fact, the opposite seemed to be the case; huge numbers of them had perished suddenly in the chase, as though each had had a limited store of energy that had been exhausted in those frantic minutes.

Von Oldenburg ruminated on it at length, turning his great

intellect and his knowledge of the arcane to the problem. Next to him, Yelena sat quietly, lost in a reverie of her own.

"Where should we go, my lord?" the postilion asked. It was a cool, grey day, the fecund green earth ripe with the smell of rain.

Von Oldenburg looked around, trying to take his bearings. There was little enough to look at, just rolling fields. To the distant west, the Tollish Marches erupted from the horizon like splintered grey teeth. Otherwise, this part of Draedaland was like any other part of it; cold, damp and desolate.

He sighed. Everything he needed, especially the thaumaturgic amplifier, he had kept locked in the post-chaise, so there was no reason to return to Toutorix. But with no protection, and little in the way of supplies, it was clear they were going to have to make their way back to Haunerwald.

"Damn and blast," he muttered. It seemed foolish to even attempt to reach Verdabaro now. The place was still the better part of nine days north, and who knew what bands of blighted pagans populated the countryside between?

His features curdled with dismay as he realised that this situation was perhaps beyond the bounds of even his capabilities. He was going to have to tell the Senate and its useless marionette Zelenka Haugenate.

And yet . . .

"There must be something we can attempt first," he said.

"What's that, sir?" the fusilier asked. He looked pale and wretched, no doubt firmly in the grip of guilt for having abandoned his comrades so readily.

"Be quiet, damn you," von Oldenburg replied, looking at the man with contempt. "Go over there for a moment."

The fusilier looked unhappy but obliged, dismounting and walking fifty paces north.

Von Oldenburg turned to Yelena. "What was that? I mean really, what *was* that? That was not a pox."

Yelena shook her head. "No," she said quietly.

"Speak up. What's the matter with you? What was that great calamity last night? Why were you screaming in bed? And what the bloody hell happened to your eyes? You said something was coming, or approaching."

Yelena said nothing.

"It is all linked, yes? I have seen and read enough to know that these matters rarely want for connexion."

Yelena looked at him, eyes red-rimmed, her expression caustic. "There is great evil here," she said eventually. "I can feel it in the air. It is . . . saturated with it."

Von Oldenburg scoffed. "Spare me," he muttered. He was angry, and not a little frightened, but he needed to stop being intransigent. He could shout and deny and dismiss these matters all he liked, but it was not making the strangeness go away. To the contrary; it was getting worse.

"Tell me, please," he said. "What do you remember of last night?"

Yelena shook her head slowly. "Little enough. Just the sensation of something approaching. And a great malignant presence. It is something I have never felt or experienced before, but being here is making it worse. The further north we travel, the more intense is the feeling."

"And it . . . frightens you?"

"It terrifies me," she said without hesitation.

Von Oldenburg did not like that. He did not like Yelena to be frightened – at least, not of the arcane. She was his tame expert. The afterlife and the thaumaturgic energy therein unsettled *him*, with their ramifications and potential; but she was supposed to be au fait with it.

"Why do you not *know*?" he demanded in a sudden eruption of anger.

"What do you think I am?" she snapped back. "I was a healer. Not some prophet, some . . . *kondukilo*, some, some *conduit* between planes. Understand? I am attuned, but that is all. Why do *you* not know? You have made it your life's work to know these things."

Von Oldenburg went to bite the callous next to his thumb as he did when he was particularly exercised. What was he to say? That the fundamental truths of the holy dimensions eluded him? That in spite of the blood and gold and intellect he had spent on unpicking the secrets of the afterlife, he had achieved very little? That he was nothing more than an enthusiastic amateur groping about in the dark?

He took a moment to take a few swigs of tonic and govern himself.

"Aye, well," he muttered, pretending she had not asked him anything. "I think we shall have to abandon our designs on Verdabaro. At this rate we shall be lucky to make Elisedd."

"You surely do not mean to keep going?" Yelena said with sudden urgency.

Von Oldenburg shrugged. "I came here to get answers about this blight. I came here to learn more about the death magicks. So far I have nothing except a host of dead men to show for my efforts. Besides, we shall need food."

"Food we can get from Castle Oldenburg."

He shook his head. He summoned the fusilier, who returned and remounted the foremost left horse. "One more town," von Oldenburg said, pleased that he had settled on a course of action. So much of life, so much of success, came down to having the courage to make a bloody *decision*. "Then we can choose what to do next."

The postilion encouraged the horses on, and soon they were making their way slowly north.

"After all," von Oldenburg said. "Toutorix may be an outlier."

Toutorix was not an outlier.

They spent a cold day and night travelling slowly north,

thirty-five miles as the crow flew. Elisedd was another former Sovan town built on the old Hauner Road, the mediaeval equivalent of a staging station with all of its attendant cottage industries. Even from a mile away, it was clear the place was dead.

"Nema Victoria and all the saints," von Oldenburg muttered, and then punched the side of the post-chaise. "Go and see what the matter is!" he shouted to the fusilier.

The soldier hesitated, perhaps realising that he had more power within this undynamic trio than he had first realised.

Von Oldenburg, unwilling to provoke a confrontation, for he had realised the same thing, added, "There's a captaincy in it for you."

The fusilier frowned. "It's two thousand goldmark, my lord."

Von Oldenburg scoffed. "Last week I lost *ten* thousand goldmark in an afternoon on coffee futures. I could make you a bloody colonel if I wanted. Now get over there and earn it."

The fusilier, as hungry for promotion as any Sovan Army officer, dismounted and walked towards the southernmost part of the town. There, a line of cottages fronted on to a small bubbling stream, with the ground itself having been completely overrun by wildflowers. Von Oldenburg and Yelena watched the man approach cautiously, and then, when he was perhaps a hundred paces away, walk with more speed and confidence. Clearly he considered the place to be empty.

"We are on a fool's errand," von Oldenburg muttered, preparing to exit the post-chaise himself.

And then he paused.

A pagan had appeared in the open doorway of the cottage nearest the fusilier. The man himself had not spotted them, preoccupied as he was with the main road through the town beyond.

Yelena was about to call out to him when von Oldenburg silenced her with a rough shove. "Shut up," he hissed. He squinted, watching the pagan carefully. "Let us see what happens."

The fusilier was now past the cottage and on to the cobbled

main street of the town itself. He was walking more cautiously again, his musket swinging back and forth in wide arcs.

The pagan began to run.

"What are you up to, then?" von Oldenburg murmured as the man charged mindlessly at the fusilier. Too late, the fusilier heard him; he turned sharply to bring his bayonet between himself and his assailant, and managed to stab the man directly through the gut so that the bayonet extruded from his back by at least ten inches. But still the pagan attacked, grasping and clawing at the soldier.

Next to von Oldenburg, Yelena jerked as though she had been slapped.

"What is it?" he demanded.

She grasped the sides of her head as though in the grip of a sudden and acute migraine.

"Can you not feel—"

Now von Oldenburg flinched as a blood-curdling shriek sounded in his left ear, as though someone had pinned him to the floor and was screaming directly at the side of his face.

"Nema fuck and blast!" he shouted, clutching at his heart, which thumped and squirmed painfully at the sudden burden of shock. He jerked away from the source of the noise, expecting to see one of the ghouls standing *right there*—

But there was nothing.

He leapt out of the post-chaise, snatching his sabre from its scabbard, checking for any sign of interlopers. But still there was no one.

He took a moment to steady himself as the world around him seemed to ripple and warp, as though the air was a transparent skin that was being stretched and pulled at. He shook his head and gritted his teeth, waiting for a sudden and obnoxious bout of nausea to pass; and then, sweaty and pale, he looked over to where the fusilier and the pagan were.

"Huh," he said to himself. The pagan was most certainly dead on the floor, his skewering on the bayonet having done for him. But now it was the fusilier who was standing motionless, as though the pox – though it was not a pox – had been transmitted instantaneously to him.

Von Oldenburg looked over to Yelena, who was still holding the sides of her head. He looked back to the fusilier. The man stood, his shoulders slightly hunched, stationary in the street. It was as if his mind had just boiled away like steam off hot water.

No. It was *not* like that. It was like it had been *stolen*, by the pagan. It was communicable, but solely by contact. Sometimes the communicator died in the attempt, but judging by the mass of vacants in Toutorix, they could obviously survive for some time. Presumably their mortal bodies, liberated from all intellectual function, perished for want of water within a matter of days.

Von Oldenburg stood there for a long time, trying to think of what to do. He knew he should tell the Senate, for the threat to the Empire was immeasurable. Given the ease with which the mind rot was transmitted, matters could escalate to uncontrollable levels extremely quickly.

And *yet*.

He could not help but think of the *potential* here. The timing of the scream, that dreadful banshee keen which had ripped through the aether at the same time the fusilier had been killed – that could not be ignored. There was clearly a supernatural element to this which required careful scrutiny. It was the perfect chance to try his thaumaturgic amplifier. Who knew what arcane secrets could be unlocked and turned to fresh industrial enterprise?

"I need a rope," he muttered to himself. "A net. Something to bind him with."

He cast about the place, but of course they had nothing suitable. He was starting to regret being so cavalier with the lives of his soldiers.

"We need ... " He made a frustrated noise, pacing back and forth in that boggy field. "We need people. We need men, soldiers." He sighed angrily. Such a fool he had been in Toutorix. Where were all the damn *people*? Not everyone could be dead.

"Help me, damn you," he called to Yelena. He began to unhitch the horses, for without a postilion they could not guide the post-chaise. Yelena did help him, in spite of the mental turmoil she was suffering. Von Oldenburg loaded up saddlebags with some provisions, ensuring not to leave his precious mechanism behind; then mounted up with a grunt.

He eyed the fusilier, standing dumbly on the main street of Elisedd.

"Come on," he muttered. "We can make our way down the old Hauner Road."

They travelled for half a day and came to the large village of Ultan, a place of rickety wooden fences, fields at the mercy of outdated agricultural practice, and dwellings of steeply sloped thatch. Here, finally, were some living, breathing Draedists.

"Tell them I need five strong men and women," von Oldenburg said to Yelena. "With rope and . . ." They obviously weren't going to have nets. Perhaps fishing nets? "Fishing nets if they have them." He craned his neck, searching about the place. "And I'll have that mule and cart, as well. And get us some food. I'll pay well for all of it."

The pagans, peasants all, their way of life not discernibly different from their distant ancestors, listened as Yelena translated his words into Old Saxan. But von Oldenburg did not need to speak Draedic to see that they were unhappy. It was hardly surprising; even in his shabby state, he cut an imperious figure, clad in his tricorn, Sovan finery and expensive greatcoat. Clearly they mistrusted him, and envied his wealth and status.

"They don't want your money," Yelena said after one of the peasants, a woman who looked to be the leader of this settlement, had finished gabbling away.

Von Oldenburg's features creased with contempt. "I've never

encountered a problem that could not be solved with money," he said. "Ask them again."

Yelena endured a brief spasm of irritation and repeated his demands. But the pagan woman was unmoved.

"They're not interested in helping you."

"Tell them—" von Oldenburg caught himself. He was tired and overwrought, and was about to resort to his default, which was to threaten everyone with death. But that was not what the situation required. He had forged a long and successful career on leveraging people. He prided himself on having the intellectual nous to know when a situation required carrot, and when it required stick.

"Tell them that I am a representative of the Sovan state, and that I have been sent here to discover the nature of the plague. Tell them my men were killed in Toutorix, and apologise for my curtness. Tell them I seek to take a specimen back to Haunerwald. Emphasise the beneficent nature of our mission."

Again he waited as Yelena translated his words. Now the crowd around the woman shifted. They fell to discussing matters between them. More pagans appeared at windows and doors and exited their dwellings, joining in the conversation. It seemed like the village decided on matters as a collective, a notion which privately appalled von Oldenburg.

Again they spoke to Yelena, and again she spoke to von Oldenburg. "They will help us," she said simply.

"That's all they said?" Von Oldenburg eyed the mass of Draedists. He looked at Yelena. "That was a lot of conversation."

"Yes, they discussed at length how much they mistrust you."

He waved her off. "Then you did well not to burden me with it. Tell them I should like to leave immediately. We do not have much time."

"They want more than just money, though."

"What, then? A commission into the Sovan Army?"

"They would like me to spend a little time attending them."

Von Oldenburg sneered. In spite of his affection for Yelena – an affection which sometimes manifested as proto-love, especially when he had gone without a good fuck for a while – he despised her great many weaknesses of character.

"For Nema's sake, be quick about it, then!"

❧

It took perhaps half an hour for the pagans and supplies to be assembled, and another hour for Yelena to ply the dullards with herbs and salves. Von Oldenburg paid them a retainer of ten goldmark, which was an obscene sum; but much like his now dead-but-alive postilion, they correctly gauged that he needed their help a lot more than they needed his money.

Three men and two women joined them, all pale-skinned, with nary a leather boot nor tailored jacket in sight. Each was hale and healthy, and, in spite of their mistrust, keen to assist. Yelena explained to him as they rode across the countryside that the villagers of Ultan were quite terrified, having of course heard a great many rumours of the plague spreading across Draedaland.

"They believe it to be the End of Days," Yelena said. "The time of judgement."

Von Oldenburg thought of the tarot card he had picked, and said nothing.

They reached Elisedd the following afternoon, slowed considerably by the donkey and wagon loaded with Draedists. Nothing had changed about the place; the vacant fusilier had become as much a fixture as the surrounding buildings, whilst the post-chaise remained precisely where they had left it.

Von Oldenburg had Yelena explain to the pagans that they needed to capture the man using the ropes and fishing nets, and that under no circumstances were they to touch him.

"I suppose it must be skin contact which is to be avoided," he mused quietly to her.

She shrugged. "I should think so."

"Get them to wrap themselves in garments. Around the neck and arms, and cover their faces as much as possible."

The pagans, now visibly frightened and extremely uncertain of this task, took some time to wrap extra clothes around themselves like rudimentary armour. Von Oldenburg allowed them to liberate his suitcases from the post-chaise for the task, though he was privately annoyed, and considered the value of the clothing was not greatly subordinate to the value of the pagans' lives.

"They look rather ridiculous," he muttered. He dismounted his horse and snatched up one end of the length of rope which they had brought. It was thirty feet long, and well made. "You there, hold the other end," he said, gesturing to the nearest woman, a thickset redhead. She obliged, and von Oldenburg carried on walking until the rope was taut between them. "Like this, see? Yelena, explain it to them. Approach the man like this, ensnare him in the middle of the rope and wrap it around him. You will need to run rings around him, like children at a maypole. Understand? Do not let him get close. No touch! Yes? No *touch*. Touch equals die!"

They practised, using one of the pagans as a stand-in.

"Thrash more!" von Oldenburg shouted at the fake thrall. "Go mad. Like you want to *kill* them!"

They practised for an hour, until the afternoon was wearing on and von Oldenburg became acutely conscious that the fusilier was going to perish from exposure, or want of water, or both. When the time came, he took his pistol out of its box and primed and loaded it, and drew his sabre, and then gestured for his ragtag team to get on with it.

They advanced on the fusilier slowly, two pairs of pagans with ropes strung between them, and the fifth with a fishing net. They approached in the same way they would approach a skittish horse.

"Steady," von Oldenburg said, though they could not understand him, and he had issued Yelena with a stern injunction to remain with the post-chaise. Self-preservation would be their guiding light now. "Steady."

He had no idea what level of proximity triggered the vacant's prey instinct, but it seemed to be about ten paces. His blood surged as the fusilier looked up and then lurched forward. The pagans gasped and shrieked, though the soldier made no sound whatever. Once again the atmosphere seemed to fray and warp, and von Oldenburg endured a brief spell of intense dizziness as all manner of bizarre and unsettling noises suffused the aether around him. When he had regained his senses, he saw the fusilier thrashing on the ground, writhing ferociously to be out from underneath the rope. The pagans were all shouting at each other in Old Saxan, pale and sweating and terrified, faces locked in rictuses, muscles straining with effort.

"Get the ... get the net over him! The *net!*" von Oldenburg shouted, unwilling to go any closer. He watched impotently as the pagans – just local peasants, not warriors – scrabbled to contain the silent ferocity of the vacant soldier. "Nema, 'tis hopeless," he muttered, gripping his pistol. He really did not want to shoot the man; it was unlikely he was going to get another opportunity like this.

The fusilier was almost up off the ground. The Draedists tried to wrap the ropes around him, but until they pinned the man's limbs to his sides, it was hopeless.

"His legs! Bind his *legs!*"

One of the pagans, in a moment of insane, reckless bravery, darted forward and hastily wound the rope around the fusilier's ankles, once, twice, and had begun the process of tying the rope into a knot when he succumbed. The fusilier grabbed his face, and the world began to dissolve; there was a bowel-loosening scream, and then—

Von Oldenburg shot the vacant pagan through the back of the head. At such close range, the musket ball did appalling damage. The other pagans screamed their anguish. Who knew what this man was to them? A friend? A lover? A beloved father, husband, son?

"Shut up, damn you, and tie him!" von Oldenburg snapped, tossing the pistol aside and bringing his sabre up. He would cut every one of these idiots down if he had to.

Weeping and screaming, the Draedist with the net threw it over the fusilier, who was quickly entangled; then the rest of them wound their ropes around him like a maypole. Once he was trussed up, and with a little encouragement from von Oldenburg's sabre, the pagans manhandled him into the wagon, where he lay thrashing noiselessly.

Von Oldenburg took a moment to recover his pistol, clean it off and reload it, and then told Yelena to dismiss the pagans.

"Lamprecht, for Nema's sake, it is a two-day hike and they have lost a—"

"Unless you know some way to get water into this man's belly," von Oldenburg replied, gesturing to the vacant in the wagon, "then I suggest you dismiss them before every single death we have suffered on this expedition is rendered in vain."

They swore at him, of course, and shouted; but they were human beings with human fears and fallibilities, and they did not want to get their brains blown out of their skulls by a pistol any more than the next person, and eventually they left.

Von Oldenburg, slightly exhilarated at having snatched a minor victory from an otherwise calamitous defeat, and looking forward to returning to Haunerwald, offered Yelena a smile. "Don't be such a misery-guts, Lena," he said. "This is going to be the beginning of something quite magnificent."

XV

Idiot Men, Dead Men

*"Was there ever a more bloodthirsty artifice than the division
of the Neman Church into Victorianism and Conformism?
Did we not have enough enemies before? Its sole purpose
seems naught but to enrage otherwise entirely sensible
men and women to acts of breathtaking savagery."*

FROM GROSSO'S
THE GREAT ROT: THE RISE OF NEMAN CONFORMISM

Uncharted Foothills

GREAT NORTHERN BARRIER RANGE

Chaos enveloped the old pagan hall.

The content of Peter's shouts would have been enough by
itself; soldiers were quick to leap to arms when faced with the
destructive potential of musketry. But the tenor with which
they were delivered – in the tone of a man who is so frightened
he borders on lunacy – had the effect of rendering the men
insensible. Instead of priming flintlocks, affixing bayonets, and
readying themselves in good order, they clamoured madly, each
trying to see what was going on. Cries of confusion filled the

air. Of everyone, only the Black Mountains readied themselves, quietly palming hand-axes and dirks and retreating into the corners of the hall.

"Get to it, you doghearts!" Furlan shouted, wide-eyed. He physically manhandled soldiers away from the walls. "What are you doing? Cowering like maids! Get up! Get those swords fixed! Load, damn you! There's time enough to rake over it later! You heard the lieutenant! To arms!"

For once Peter did not resent the captain's effortless command, buttressed at least in part by the large quantity of brandy he had taken on. Though Furlan had not seen what he had seen; perhaps even brandy would not be enough to steel the soldiers' hearts.

His hands shook wretchedly as he loaded and primed his pistol. He spilt as much powder as went into the barrel and pan, and as much again when he loaded his second. It did not matter. They were about to die, of that he was absolutely certain. Two shots, a clumsy swing, and those creatures would rip him limb from limb.

"Get on with it! Idiot men are dead men! You can prattle on about it after the action!"

Something smashed into the doors. One of the men near Peter fired wildly, the musket ball smashing into the wood and punching clean through it. The crash of it near-perforated his eardrum.

"Hold! Nema damn fuck and blast, hold!" Furlan roared.

But the other soldiers fired now. Enormous flashes of light filled the hall as gunpowder ignited and exploded. Peter flinched as a ramrod impaled the door jamb. He thought immediately of the bodies he had seen on his arrival in the New East, the four Sovan soldiers who had been utterly brutalised in the forest. He realised, with a sick heart, that that was *his* fate.

Furlan appeared next to him, sabre in hand. "So, we have answered Major Haak's question," he said grimly.

"We have answered it with our deaths," Peter replied. His guts roiled with hot acid. There was another crash into the door, another musket discharged early. They were going to set fire to the place.

"There's a thought," Furlan growled. He turned. "Cathassach! Get here, damn you!"

Everyone's vision had been crazed by the flash of gunpowder and the vast clouds of smoke that now filled the hall. Peter did not even see the pagan approach until he was right next to them.

"*Jes?*"

"Get back to Fort Ingomar," Furlan said, stabbing his index finger into the man's chest. "Peter, tell him what you saw."

"I . . . I . . ." Peter had no idea what he had seen. Monsters. Beasts.

"For Nema's sake," Furlan muttered. Then he turned and shouted into the hall. "Stop firing, you blasted idiots, there's nothing to shoot!"

"*Ni ĉiuj mortos. Mi tute ne esperas atingi la fortikaĵon.*"

"Speak Saxan, you dolt!"

Cathassach shook his head. "All die here."

"No! Not you. Escape. You must pass on the message. We need a battalion, a regiment up here. Understand? You must tell Major Haak. The answer to his question is here to the north-east. Bloody . . . beast men. Yes?"

Cathassach shrugged. "I try."

"Yes, you bloody well try."

Something hit the roof; thatch loosened. The soldiers cried out. Peter watched them fumble ineffectually with their muskets and powder. Men and women who had not even fired yet were loading second, even third balls, ramming them home. They had not a hope of achieving anything.

"This is it," he said, steeling himself. There were several of the creatures on the roof now. "This is it." He thought of his brothers, thought of Leonie, whom he had never loved and who had never loved him. He thought of his mother, too, who had never seemed to hold much love for him in her heart either. He thought of his father, who he missed dearly. He was so very far from home.

Furlan seemed to read his mind. "No need for your letters any more, lad. You can see the old man in person."

Peter offered a weak smile. He could summon little in the way of courage. Death was a frightening enough prospect in itself; now there was the added horror of entering what seemed to be a deeply broken spirit realm.

"We have to live," he said, as the sound of snarling and growling filled the hall. There were things clamouring at the smoke hole now. More men fired their muskets desperately into the opening. One exploded, killing the wielder. Peter turned to Furlan, his eyes wide with desperation. Next to them, the door bulged inwards where the flimsy planks gave way. "We have to live!"

"Don't need to tell me, boy," Furlan said.

And then the beasts were through.

There were several more explosions of gunpowder. The air became a thick, choking haze of smoke. Peter was knocked to the floor immediately. Something had hit him with the power of a runaway horse. Rain, driven by the wind, belted through the open door. Its cold wet was refreshing after the choking heat of fire and smoke and the acrid stench of ignited powder.

The doors at the back of the hall were smashed open. What remained of the gable was torn away. Screams faded, to be replaced with furious grunting in the darkness, growls and scrabbling and scratches, the sound of ripping fabric and ripping flesh, the surprised exclamation of someone having the air and life forced out of them.

Peter pressed himself up and shot at one of the dark shapes, point-blank. He had fired directly into where the thing's kidney might be, and its coal-black skin burst open like a watermelon painted with tar. It let out a howl of rage and whirled around, just as he brought his sabre sweeping across. In so doing, he accidentally cut the thing's hand off at the wrist. It was too dark and smoky to make out what it was he was fighting, but he had the impression of a tall black creature, part man, part jaguar. There was no mistaking the eyes, which glinted and gleamed like a cat's – the same eyes which had haunted him for weeks.

However strong and ferocious these creatures, nothing could survive losing so much blood so quickly, and the thing sank to the floor. Peter discarded his pistol and drew his second, looking for an enemy to shoot; but a moment later it was smashed out of his hand with such force that his whole arm went numb. He brought his sabre down clumsily, making contact with something soft and eliciting a howl of pain and anger, and then a clawed hand smacked him squarely in the nose. Pain cracked through his whole face and head. His nose snapped very audibly, and he was staggering backwards until he hit the wall. He blinked away tears of agony, choked on the suffocating smoke, and slashed again blindly, this time achieving nothing.

He heard Furlan shouting something, and there were a few more bangs of muskets being fired – or exploding, it was impossible to tell. He wiped blood from his eyes. His fingers shakily traced several bone-deep rents across his forehead and cheekbones.

Demented aethereal screaming filled the unknowable space between life and death.

"Live!" he shouted, insensible. He staggered into someone, and gripped them by the arm. "We have to live! Cathassach, get out!"

The soldier, whoever it was, mistook him for one of the creatures. One last musket shot imprinted the impression of a terrified Sovan face on to Peter's vision; then the butt of a weapon smacked into the side of his skull and knocked him clean into unconsciousness.

He was not out for long, not in the scheme of things; but however long it had been, it had been enough to end the fight. A horrible, deathly silence filled that old pagan hall, the only sound the unending torrent of rain outside.

He lay still, his mind foggy. It was like being in the grip of a fever dream. He knew that he mustn't move, for to move was to be identified as being alive, and these monstrous interlopers would soon put an end to that.

Blood trickled from his face on to the wet boards of the hall. He was quite close to the door and was being slowly soaked by the frigid rain. His blood mixed with the rainwater and created a pool of diluted crimson. The temptation to examine and finger and probe the wounds on his face was great, particularly as his senses returned – and with them, the pain of those grievous incisions. But he lay still.

A long time passed. He drifted in and out of consciousness. The fight had left him entirely now, if it had ever been in him, and all that was left was weakness and fear. Still, he had fought. That was the most important thing. He had fought, in spite of his terror, and had been *seen* to fight. If anyone else survived, if Cathassach did indeed manage to escape and make it back to Fort Ingomar – and there seemed scant prospect of that – then the report would be that Brevet Captain Peter Kleist had acquitted himself in a manner befitting a Sovan officer.

He tried to take comfort from that, but there was no hollow glory in the world that could contend with simply being *alive*. He would happily return to Sova in abject disgrace, reviled as a coward, disavowed by his family and peers; he would suffer every indignity that came with dogheartedness, if it meant being alive. There was nothing sweeter than life itself. Everything else was a problem that could be solved, or endured. Death did nothing except remove all his options.

Over time, it became clear that several of the soldiers had survived the encounter. He heard them groaning. The creatures did not kill them out of hand, as he expected. Instead they spoke to each other in a harsh, guttural language, seemingly no longer interested in slaughter. Peter could hear them moving around the hall, though he kept his eyes firmly closed. He could think about nothing except the human offal he had seen in the forest arranged so neatly. Was that his fate? To be disembowelled, and become little more than an ornament in some kind of ritualistic sacrifice?

Eventually he chanced to look. It took effort not to gasp. For a moment he thought that the wolfmen of the Kasar Kyarai had somehow established their own colony in this desolate place. A huge black figure, fur the colour of ink, loomed in the hall. Its features were unmistakably leonine, as if a jaguar and human had been melded together. It walked upright, and wore a pair of pantaloons made from dried, woven leaves. It was otherwise unadorned, save for an unsightly eruption of what looked like pustules across its shoulders.

Peter was frightened of the creature in a way that anyone would be frightened of a powerful, monstrous enemy; but there was something else, too. It seemed to exude an aura which instilled in him a special kind of dread. It was not dread in the sense of a prey instinct, but altogether more primal. It was unsettling, as if there was a singular *wrongness* about this creature. It felt as though it should not exist, as though the celestial beings which permitted the creation and existence of new life had erred.

Peter wanted to weep then, but only living things wept, and so he bit his tongue. He watched as the creatures – about five or six of them – began to manhandle the bodies of his men. Amongst them he saw Olwin, the Black Mountain pagan, though it was not clear whether she was alive or dead. Furlan's body was limp, but he groaned as he was hauled upright, and Peter's blood surged at that. He considered whether it would have been better to perish in the initial melee and so be spared the inevitable horrors of capture and ritual sacrifice; he concluded it would have been better to have not joined the Army in the first place.

He watched as one by one the living were separated from the dead. There was no sign of Cathassach; perhaps he had escaped after all. It seemed unlikely that he would have time to reach the Ena Split and return with a rescue party, let alone Fort Ingomar, which was a six-week round trip. And even if he did return, Peter and the rest of the survivors would be long gone, certainly from this dilapidated pagan hall, and more likely from the mortal plane altogether. Even their tracks would have long been lost under weeks of intervening weather.

Eventually one of the creatures bent down to examine him. In spite of his attempt at playing dead, he flinched. The catman did not seem fazed; they had probably long gauged him to be alive. That big black jaguar face sniffed around the blood from his facial wounds in the same way a hound would. The smell seemed to invigorate it. Peter winced and whimpered as the catman licked the blood from his face; and then, a moment later, he was hauled to his feet as easily as a parent lifting a young child and taken outside, where the rain had lightened off to a drizzle. It was just pre-dawn, and the forest and hills around the glade were backlit with weak grey light.

He was laid on the grass. Damp soil soaked into his uniform. All in all, it seemed perhaps five of them had survived the attack. The old pagan hall had become the expedition's mausoleum.

He briefly considered running – a wild thought considering he could barely stay awake, let alone stand. Besides, even at full clip he wouldn't make it ten paces before these catmen horrors cut him down.

He wasn't given any more time to think about it. With a sense of profound despair, he was lifted and slung over the shoulder of one of his captors, and carried even further away from everything he had ever known.

XVI

City of the Wolfmen

*"I find it extraordinary, the commonfolk's capacity for nostalgia.
It is a national psychosis, and an utter confection, this notion
that war and famine and plague was lesser in the past, both in
frequency and intensity, or had some unique generational crop
of women and men of high competence to tackle them. These
matters are like a bonfire; in times of peace and prosperity, it is
reduced to embers; in times of war or contagion, it is like a great
conflagration. But it is always there, always burning. It has
ever been the case, since the world began to spin on its axis."*

SATIRIST AND PAMPHLETEER BILIOUS JOSEPH

Kalegosfort

NORTH KYARAI

"There *is* no good way into Port Talaka," Lyzander said, after
Glaser had finished explaining to him the nature of their mission – or at least the parts of it he was willing to divulge.

He, Glaser, Maruska and Renata were standing over a detailed map of Port Talaka which had been drawn up by Sovan
engineers. The capital of the wolfmen had once been a modest
city, comfortably contained within the bounds of its mediaeval

walls, nestled in and amongst four of the many distributaries of the Yaro River. But in the past century, it had become a thoroughfare for Sovan colonists and commercial interests, and had ballooned to become the largest metropolis south of Sova itself. Here wolfmen were outnumbered by Sovans and Qareshians and Southern Plainsmen three-to-one as everyone looked to make their fortune in commodities, colonial land speculation and war profiteering.

"Try not to be coy, Mister Lyzander," Glaser said. "We do not have a great deal of time."

"I'll say," Lyzander replied, uncowed by the admonishment. "Klossner's back is against Ten Dai and he'll be pushed further north—"

"Marshal Klossner is holding against the river at Al Heri."

Lyzander shook his head. "Not so, Colonel. The *rearguard* was left at Al Heri, but Klossner is fifty miles north by now, and two regiments lighter."

"I have just had several senior officers inform me—"

"They are wrong," Lyzander said simply. "Trust me. Sir."

Glaser endured a spasm of anger. "If you speak—"

"There's so much value in having hard truths delivered directly, is there not?" Maruska interjected smoothly.

"In*deed*," Glaser muttered after a moment's silence. He sighed. "I – *we* – need to get to the Spiritsraad," he said. "I need to evacuate the Kasari shamans from there. Everything else is chaff."

"They will not leave the Spiritsraad," Lyzander replied.

"What makes you say that?" Renata asked.

"Because they have said as much. They will not abandon their holiest temple to the Sudreiks and their" – he waggled his fingers as though spooked by a ghost – "idolatrous Conformism. They would rather die."

"Nema Victoria, you are insolent," Glaser remarked. "I cannot think why the Empress recommended you so specifically and highly."

Lyzander's veneer fractured. "She mentioned me by name?" he said. He was affecting nonchalance, but his voice cracked slightly.

"He already told you that," Renata muttered. Maruska gave her a curious look.

"Focus, please," Glaser said. "If the shamans cannot be brought *out* from the Spiritsraad, then we shall have to go *in*. Either way, this liaison forms a central plank to the diplomatic mission."

"I thought the diplomatic mission was to the Stygion?"

"We are liaising with *all* extant practitioners of the old Draedist sorceries."

"But not the Saekas."

"No."

"And this is all to do with . . . saving all life on the mortal plane?" Lyzander asked dubiously.

"Quite so," Renata said icily.

"I am simply trying to grasp the parameters of the mission."

"The parameters of the mission are to get us to the Spiritsraad before Port Talaka falls to the forces of the Sudreik Kasar and their Casimiran allies. It is an *extremely* simple directive," Glaser said, his impatience frothing over.

"Aye, it certainly would be, if the place were not about to be overrun," Lyzander replied.

"Blood of gods, man, I shall strip you of your commission in a moment! And then you can take us into Port Talaka as a private!"

To everyone's astonishment, Lyzander simply shrugged. "Strip away. I expect we should all be killed inside of three days anyway."

There was something there, behind his confected indifference. Renata, her perceptiveness honed by her diplomatic training, could pick it out like a gannet plucking fish from the ocean. The man was heartsick. Heartsick to the point of recklessness, both with his physical well-being and his station. Something to do with the Empress, certainly.

She realised she was staring at him, for he briefly locked eyes with her, and his expression changed. Before Glaser could surrender fully to his apoplexy, Lyzander directed them all back to the map. "Naturally we will make for Fort Landulf. That will take two days in itself. We will approach Port Talaka from the west, over the bridge at Ahsia."

"What about from the north, here?" Glaser asked, pointing to a bridge on the map.

"No," Lyzander said, shaking his head. "It is too close to the ocean. It'll be one of the first pieces of infrastructure the Casimirs will reduce."

Glaser considered this for a moment. "All right. Carry on."

"There is little else to say. We can follow the Kayin Road all the way into the centre of the city if it is clear; for as long as we control the north, it should be a matter of simply riding to the Spiritsraad as if it were anywhere else. If the place comes under attack, then we should have to come via the north of the city instead, to avoid the Kasaraad." He tapped where the wolfmen's parliament building lay on the map. "That will be the focus of the enemy's attack. Quite aside from its political significance, it's a hundred feet tall. No artillery officer worth his salt is going to pass on that opportunity."

"The Spiritsraad is the same height," Maruska remarked.

"Well, there you are then. Both prominences are likely to form the kernel around which the rest of our enemy's operations are focused. But there are ways into and out of both places which I am aware of and which the enemy is not."

Glaser pursed his lips. "And why is that, I wonder?"

Lyzander spread his hands. "No nefarious purpose, Colonel. I was part of a detachment tasked with removing some politically and culturally sensitive items from the Kasaraad and delivering them into Sovan hands for safe keeping."

"A monuments man."

"Quite so."

"Hm," Glaser said. "And what about forces in the city? I have been told of the disposition, though it seems my briefing might have been somewhat *lacking*."

"Marshal Biskup is there with the better part of twenty thousand men," Lyzander said.

"Well, that at least seems to be accurate. It will be a bitter pill for the Conformists to swallow."

"The southerners will be slowed at Ten Dai, but they won't be stopped. Klossner hasn't the manpower nor the cannon. By all accounts the redoubt there is of poor quality. Their best chance was at Al Heri, which Klossner has now squandered. And whilst I do not share the colonel's tactical acumen, it seems to me that twenty thousand men is not enough to take on a hundred thousand."

Glaser rubbed his face. Renata felt sorry for him. It was difficult to overstate the ramifications of losing Port Talaka. Once the capital fell, the natural progression would be the loss of the rest of the northern Kyarai, and with it Port Gero, the only serious Sovan gateway to the New East. In many ways he would have been better off remaining in Sova, at arm's length from the conflict. At least then his political enemies could not have directly associated him with the failure.

Not that any of it mattered.

"We must not lose sight of our ultimate goal," she said after a few moments' reflection. "Even the loss of Port Talaka is meaningless when taken against a backdrop of wider events."

"I should like to hear more about these 'wider events'," Lyzander said, unable to keep the insufferable smirk off his face, as if this whole enterprise was some great game.

"I should be delighted to tell you, if you can spare any time between bouts."

Glaser frowned. Lyzander looked briefly alarmed.

"Bouts?" Glaser asked.

"Oh, just a jest," Renata said, not taking her eyes from Lyzander's. "I saw men fighting in the pits on my way here."

Before Lyzander could rejoin, Glaser interrupted.

"Enough of this silly sparring," he said. "We need to be about it. Captain, go and gather your things and inform your commanding officer that you will be accompanying me south post-haste. If there is an issue, tell them to find me here. Ambassador, I need you for another couple of hours. Secretary Rainer: I suggest you and the others try and steal a few hours of sleep. We leave at midnight."

"You could have got me killed, you know," Lyzander said as he and Renata left the headquarters and made their way into the sultry evening air. The sky was a dusky pink, the same colour as the old castle walls for which Kalegosfort was named. Wolfmen, soldiers, and the weary and much put-upon inhabitants of the township still bustled through the streets. It was impossible to escape the sense of doom here. Renata fancied she could almost hear the guns of the Casimiran Navy, even two hundred and fifty miles north.

"How's that?" she murmured.

"Sparring with the wolfmen is a hanging offence."

"Seems to me, then, that it is an activity best avoided."

Lyzander scoffed. "What confidence it must take, to come to this place and offer such opinions as yours." They passed under the southern gatehouse and out into the wider township. There, he briefly exchanged a few words with one of the wolfmen soldiers.

"You speak Kasarsprek?" Renata asked.

"A little," he muttered.

"I suppose you would need some, to fight in the pits."

"That left quite an impression on you, didn't it?"

She shook her head condescendingly. "Oh, I have seen plenty worse in Sova. The men shoot one another on Blackmarsh often enough."

"I thought duelling was illegal in Sova."

Renata looked at him askance. "You have been out of the city much too long. It was reinstated when Zelenka Haugenate took the throne."

Again that brief jolt of . . . *something* crossed his features. Guilt? Certainly an emotion akin to it. She found herself much more interested than she should have been in the nature of his relationship with the Empress.

"Well. Fancy men shooting to miss on the heath is not quite the same as taking a bludgeoning from a Kasar."

"A curious thing to brag about, considering you lost."

"Depends on what you are trying to achieve, I suppose," Lyzander muttered. This time, Renata missed the flash of heartsickness behind his eyes.

"A beating? To be embarrassed before your peers?"

"That's enough!" he snapped, but his features immediately softened. Still, he did not apologise, and Renata said:

"You will not speak to me like that. I am an ambassador to—"

"The mer-men, yes," Lyzander said mockingly. "What a lofty appointment. Forgive my impertinence, your *Excellency*."

Renata set her teeth. "Our mission could not be of greater importance. All of this, Port Talaka, the war in the Kyarai, it is but a bucketful of water in the Jade Sea."

"Yes, yes," he said, waving her off. "Saving the world. I am keen to hear what it is that has the captain of the 1st Sovan Legion running all the way down here. You have yet to tell me the full nature of it."

"And I shall not, at this rate. You are little more than a coach gunner. And an impertinent one at that. Fulfil your role and let more serious minds tend to the health of the mortal plane."

Lyzander scoffed. "As you wish, Excellency."

"And do not call me that," Renata snapped. "Damn you, sir!"

He offered her a very broad, very disingenuous grin, touched his forehead, and disappeared down a side street.

Renata eventually found her way to their lodgings, though she nearly got lost in the warren of streets. The house was a square construction of dark pink adobe with extruding wooden beams. The roof was simple thatch, home to a family of small, lime-green birds which chirruped incessantly. Above the front door was an alcove in which sat a crude stone idol of Nema Victoria, but rendered in a blocky, geometric pattern.

Renata opened the door and went in. There was one main living space. In the corner was a pile of rugs which she realised were beds. Next to them was a colourful wooden door, and much more jarringly, a set of pewter Sovan soldiers. Other crude furniture and trinkets lined the wall space. In another corner was a shrine to Nema Victoria, with a statue garlanded with flowers, several woodcuts, and a smoking stick of incense which did quite a good job of covering up the smell of dog. Truly, it was like being in an oversized kennel.

Ozolinsh was sitting on the pile of rugs, her back propped up against the wall, examining one of the pewter soldiers; Herschel and Guillot were praying quietly at the Neman shrine, in, or affecting to be in, a sort of trance.

"Remarkable, isn't it," Ozolinsh muttered as Renata sat down heavily next to her, nodding towards the shrine in the corner.

"Remarkable is one word for it."

"Sovan missionaries prattling on about Nema Victoria in the northern Kyarai; Casimiran missionaries prattling on about Neman Conformism in the south. Did you know the wolfmen used to be almost entirely secular?"

Renata shook her head. She was not well versed in the wolfmen, having dedicated her academic and professional life to the study of the Stygion.

"Aye. They were all converted," Ozolinsh murmured, not taking her eyes from the two monks in the corner. "Now they are going to destroy one another, and over a manufactured religion that was never theirs in the first place. Lunacy."

"You are not religious, then? Surprising, given your line of work."

"You will not find a greater concentration of atheists than in the engineering corps."

There was a brief pause. "I have been having dreams," Renata said eventually. "Disturbing dreams."

Ozolinsh shifted uncomfortably. "Oh aye?"

Renata turned to her. "Have you not?"

The engineer offered her a weak smile but said nothing.

"No," Renata said, shaking her head. "No, you will not do the same thing as Didacus. I swear I am going to lose my mind with all this obfuscation."

"I am not obfuscating."

"You told me in Balodiskirch you had become attuned to strange goings-on in the aether."

"I did."

"So why are you avoiding talking to me about it now?"

Ozolinsh scoffed, making a great show of being confused. "I am not avoiding anything!"

"Have you had any nightmares? Tell me directly."

"Hell's bells, *yes*. So what?"

"So ... so *what?*" Renata asked, astonished. "Plainly it is relevant!"

Ozolinsh sighed, seeming to deflate into the rough earthen floor of the house.

"I don't like to think about it," she said quietly.

"Why not?" Renata demanded, a little too aggressively.

"Because!" Ozolinsh took a moment to compose herself. "Because all of *this* ... " she hissed, "this mission, being here, saving the *world*, the 'Great Silence' ... it sounds so *ridiculous*. I have grown too used to these things being issues of academic speciality, not tangible matters with earthly ramifications."

"I think—"

"And so when I see or hear or *dream* things which give credence to it all, I . . . I don't *want* it to be true. Do you understand? I don't *want* this. I came here because I thought the journey would be interesting. It was a chance to see the canals. The Kyarai. Ever since I joined the Corps I thought I wanted this, but I don't. I, don't, *want*, this." She thumped the books chained to her belt. "I preferred it when it was just academia. Wards, thaumaturgical equations. Just another form of energy. Problems to be solved. We laughed at the Nemans, the Senators filing out of the Council of Bishops. Swinging their censers, wearing their funny clothes and silly hats and leading garlanded deer through the streets."

Renata's brow furrowed. "But you . . . but you *know* it's real. You are closer to the arcana than anyone."

"Yet it doesn't *feel* real," Ozolinsh said. "Even when you are in temple, listening to the sermons, it all feels so removed, so abstract. When you speak to a confessor, or take the sacrament, do you really feel like you are communing with the Angels? With Nema, and Savare? With the Deti?"

"No," Renata admitted.

"If it doesn't feel real in a temple, then how could it possibly feel real in an engineer's chambers? My job is mathematics and geometry more than anything else. And now I can hear all sorts of bloody noises in the air, shrieking and screaming and whispering and prattling on, and every night I have a dream in which I am standing on an enormous—"

"Wall!" Renata said excitedly. "So you *do* dream about it!"

"Aye, I dream about it. And of corpses," Ozolinsh added bitterly. "It is all much too lucid, though. It only feels like a dream when I wake up."

Renata looked at her levelly. "Who did you dream about? Azura?"

Ozolinsh glanced at her. She looked almost guilty.

"You dreamt about Didacus, didn't you?"

Ozolinsh nodded.

Renata felt her hands closing into fists. "But what does it *mean*?" she hissed. "It cannot be some sort of . . . *prognostication*."

That was her greatest fear; that whoever appeared in that strange liminal space, floating beyond the enormous bulwark, was marked for death.

Ozolinsh remained silent.

"Oh, say something, for Nema's sake. You would not shut up half a minute ago! What do your bloody books say on the matter?!"

Renata had spoken loudly enough to break the two monks out of their prayer trance.

"Ah, Madam Secretary," Herschel said in a slightly confused way, as though he had just woken up. Next to him, Guillot smiled weakly. "Did you manage to speak to Colonel Glaser? What is the plan?"

Renata took a few trembling breaths to calm herself. There was more she wanted to drag out of the reluctant Ozolinsh – for she wanted to hear it from a Sovan, and not these strange monks – though precisely what information she was hoping to glean she did not know. Either way, the matter was not going to be settled there and then. "Yes," she said. "We are leaving at midnight. The colonel recommended that we try and get a few hours' sleep; we will be travelling through the night and all of tomorrow. Captain Joseph Lyzander believes that Port Talaka is only a few days away from falling to the Casimirs, so haste continues to be our primary concern."

"I suppose it is too much to hope for a bite to eat?" Guillot asked. "Perhaps I shall see if I can turn up something."

"I don't think it's wise to be poking around after dusk," Renata said. "There will be time enough to eat tomorrow morning."

She stood, and gestured for Ozolinsh to stand too. Then she began to pull the pile of rugs out from the corner. They smelt strongly of wolf. "Here, lend me a hand," she said, and the four of them laid out the rugs on the floor so that they could all pretend to try and go to sleep.

∾

It was cold in the middle of the night. Renata did manage some sleep, and was woken, dry-eyed and exhausted, by Ozolinsh, who had kept time. She didn't look as though she had moved at all from her sitting position in the corner.

They made their way through the dark streets, stopped every now and then by patrolmen. They met Glaser, Maruska, Lyzander and the Life Guards at the southernmost extremity of Kalegosfort. With them, too, was a detachment of four red-coated wolfmen, soldiers who turned out to be members of one of the most élite and august Kasari regiments, the Grasvlaktekraag.

Beyond them, there was nothing except the darkened wildflower plains of the northern Kyarai.

There was no stagecoach this time. Everyone, even the Life Guards, rode on large, horned plains horses, which could go for much longer at a faster speed than regular horses. After a brief introduction in which Ozolinsh and the monks greeted Captain Lyzander, they set out under the ink-black sky, one brilliant with stars and bands of astral cloud.

South of Kalegosfort were more coal-mining operations, as well as a sequence of vast open channels, concreted and buttressed, waiting to be filled with seawater and so connect the Jade Sea to the Meridian Ocean. Continuing on seemed absurd given that they were likely to hand over any brand-new infrastructure directly to their enemies, but knowing the Sovans as she did, Renata expected they were trying to pilfer as much coal as possible from the ground in the time they had remaining. Every ton was another for the insatiable fires of Sovan industry.

They reached Fort Hildiwara in the middle of the morning, one of the largest Sovan fastnesses Renata had ever seen, an enormous bastion fort with a garrison of several thousand men; and then, after food, drink, loading supplies into their saddlebags and changing their horses, carried on across the plains south-east to Fort Landulf, which they achieved in the afternoon of the following day. This was an even larger fort than Hildiwara, and in most respects would be a harder objective for their enemy than Port Talaka itself.

On that hot, windless afternoon, they could finally hear the fighting south of the capital.

If Kalegosfort had been a place of frenetic activity, then the road between Fort Landulf and Port Talaka was something else entirely. It did not just have to contend with thousands of Sovan and Kasari soldiers pushing east into the capital, with all their horses and cannon and supplies, but with thousands of refugees fleeing west too. The result was an incredible jam of people and matériel kicking up great clouds of red dust. And in the heat of the sunbaked Kyarai, tempers were flaring.

Renata drank in the incredible view before her. This was what she imagined the final days of the First Sovan Empire to have been like, before the formation of the old Republic. There was an incredible sense of history being made in that hot, sultry air.

"The bridge is going to be nigh-on impassable," Lyzander said, his horse appearing next to hers. In violation of military dress code, and in spite of several injunctions from Colonel Glaser, which he had cheerfully ignored, his jacket was unbuttoned almost to the navel. Renata briefly traced the musculature of his chest and midriff with her eyes, glistening as it was with sweat in the punishing heat. She herself had taken to wearing a wet blouse wrapped around her head and neck, which made her look quite ridiculous, but at least it kept the sun off her skin.

"There is only the one?" she asked, squinting into the distance. They could see Port Talaka now, and its great stepped pyramids rising out of the metropolis. A few miles to the south, the enormous River Yaro, a brilliant, glittering blue in the hot sun, broke into its many dozens of distributaries. It was dismayingly fast and deep.

Lyzander nodded. There was no banter now, no spark of back-and-forth. He looked concerned. "Here, yes."

He kicked his horse forward, and Renata watched as he called out to a succession of humans and wolfmen, some soldiers, some civilians, in an impressive display of multilingualism.

"What is the matter?" Ozolinsh asked, taking the place where Lyzander had just been.

"He's worried about getting over the bridge," Renata said, not taking her eyes off the enormous mass of people ahead of them.

"We can't go north? Take the Gero Road, and the bridge there?"

Renata shook her head. "The captain thinks it will be one of the first things the Casimirs destroy from the ocean."

Ozolinsh sucked her teeth. "This feels like a mistake. Port Talaka, I mean. Coming here. I say we cut north and make for the Door to the Sea."

Renata shook her head. "No. We are here now."

The day wore on. They pressed east, the plains horses making good time across the rough ground. In the middle of the afternoon, they came within sight of the Jade Sea itself, a vast body of glittering green water. But it was not the ocean which Renata was entranced by; it was the armada of Casimiran ships, towering men-o'-war three decks high, bristling with cannon. This was the same armada that had destroyed the Sovan Jade Fleet off Oksanastadt.

"By Nema Victoria," Renata breathed. Occasionally the side of one of the ships would erupt in a great pall of bright white smoke, and several long seconds later, a thunderous report would chase it.

"It has already begun," Maruska said from next to her.

"Come on!" Glaser snapped, red-faced and perspiring in the heat. "We need to get about this before the whole bloody city is rubble."

A mile west of the Ahsia Bridge, the traffic reached a complete standstill. The clamour here was as loud and violent as the cannonade off the coast beyond. Refugees, desperate to be out of the city before it was sacked, had stampeded across the bridge to the point where a crush had developed. Now Sovan forces could not proceed east into the city, and no one could get out.

The bridge itself was easily two hundred yards in length and twenty wide, and spanned a treacherous section of the Yaro Delta. Here the distributary had carved a deep channel through the rock over hundreds of years, flowing so strongly and quickly that in places it frothed with whitecaps. It did not stop some people from trying to swim it in their desperation; more still would be forced in, either to avoid the crush or because of it. They were either drowned immediately, or swept out into the ocean and drowned there.

Just beyond the bridge, Port Talaka rose enormously and tantalisingly out of the evening haze.

Glaser, in as black a mood as Renata had ever known, was bellowing incessantly at the press of people. It was entirely ineffectual; even if he could be heard above the terrified clamour of refugees and the angry shouts of the soldiers trying to get them out of the way, no one was in any sort of position to follow his orders.

"What are our other options?" she asked Lyzander. She was in a sour mood as well, hot, sunburnt, dehydrated, saddle sore, her nerves overwrought.

Lyzander winced. "The Gero Road is no good. We would have to travel back west, cross the Yaro at the Ilker Junction, come back east between Talaka and Ten Dai, and then approach the city from the south." He shook his head. "It would add days to the journey."

"What about a pontoon?" Ozolinsh hazarded, though even she

did not sound convinced. Renata glanced at her. The woman's face was red and peeling from too much sun. Behind them, the two monks had copied Renata's idea and draped their heads with wet rags. Both looked utterly miserable. Only Maruska, a native Qareshian, seemed unbothered by the heat. Notwithstanding, there was something off about him. He sat pensively in the saddle, clearly preoccupied, and Renata resolved to speak with him when they had a quiet moment.

Lyzander didn't even bother replying to Ozolinsh. There was no way anyone was getting a temporary bridge over this part of the river.

Renata was about to say something else when she caught sight of Glaser. He was now on the north side of the road, directing a company of about thirty Sovan and Kasari soldiers. They marched in good order to the north-western end of the bridge and formed up in two ranks, levelling their muskets.

"Nema Victoria, surely not," Renata said, appalled.

"Good gods, he's going to shoot them," Lyzander snarled. He yanked his plains horse around, but there were too many people in the way for him to reach Glaser quickly enough – though even if he had, Renata was not quite sure what he planned to do. Murdering the man seemed a step too far, even for someone as offensively insolent as Joseph Lyzander.

Glaser barked out an order and the first volley smashed into the refugees. If there had been panic before, now there was chaos. Immediately several dozen people plunged into the water below, some of them corpses. The remainder of the refugees in the centre of the span entered into an almost dissociative state, in which some continued to try and force their way across the bridge, some tried to force their way back, and some did nothing at all. It was this latter group which fell prey to the next volley. Renata's hand went to her mouth as she saw one Kasar, a female trying to shepherd several pups, catch a musket ball directly to the side of the head and flop limply over the balustrade.

Renata looked over at Glaser. He was stern and businesslike, and could be impatient, but he was no murderer. Was he? Had she misjudged his character so thoroughly?

"The brute," she whispered, over and over again, trembling with rage. She turned to look at Maruska, who simply shook his head helplessly.

She turned back. Lyzander had finally fought his way through the jam and was screaming at the colonel. The latter pulled a pistol from his sash and aimed directly at the captain, and Renata heard herself scream "No!" – but Glaser was not so exercised as to blow his brains out.

She kicked her horse hard on the flanks, pushing her way into the screaming mass of refugees, who were now stampeding west. The horse snorted and bucked and threatened to gore several of the plainsmen with its horns, but Renata yanked its head back with the reins, and wrestled with it until they were through.

Lyzander was still screaming at Glaser, but the latter was now ignoring him, eyeballing the bridge, his face a mask of displeasure. Renata followed the line of his gaze, to where Sovan soldiers were now having great success in clearing the span at bayonet point. In their wake lay several bodies bleeding on to the flagstones. Many others had been transformed from refugees to walking wounded, and some of those would die. Every battlefield surgeon and corpsman for a hundred miles was in the city, preparing to salvage as many Sovan and Kasari soldiers as possible.

"There. Now get across!" Glaser said, ramming his sabre home into its scabbard.

"How could you?" Renata demanded of him. "You bloody ... How *could* you? You are supposed to be protecting them, not butchering them!"

"For Nema's sake, woman!" Glaser snapped, pushing past her. "What do you think happens if this bridge isn't cleared? Do you think these people would fare any better under the ministrations of the Casimirs? Perhaps they should take their chances with the naval cannonade?"

"You could have—"

"I need to get in. Now. *We* need to get in. We do not have time for these peacetime niceties, Ms Rainer."

"I *thought*," she said through gritted teeth, "you were a decent person."

"I *am* a decent person."

"Decent people do not order civilians to be shot en masse."

"Decent *people*, Madam Secretary, recognise that very large groups of very frightened refugees act in want of all sanity. What is better, two volleys to clear the bridge and" – he eyeballed the span – "a dozen wounded Kasar? Or the western arterial route into Port Talaka to be plugged indefinitely so that men and powder and matériel and supplies cannot be brought to bear in defence of the city, and the civilians within cannot escape in an orderly fashion? How many will die then? Nema Victoria, Ms Rainer, I thought the Imperial Office was a place of hard heads, not this *silliness*. Now for the gods' sakes, fetch the ambassador and that bloody engineer and those bloody monks and get over the fucking bridge before I turn the lot of you into the Yaro."

And with that, Glaser entered the capital city of the wolfmen.

XVII

An Infernal Prize

*"War is such a profitless endeavour that premiers will go
to desperate lengths to justify its expense. 'Just one more
mile,' they say, 'just one more brigade', as if each handful
of blood-soaked soil would turn to gold in their hands."*

POLEMICIST ISABELLA JOKUMSEN

Castle Oldenburg

COUNTY OF HAUNERWALD

The journey back to Castle Oldenburg was fraught. Von
Oldenburg was at pains to avoid everyone he came across, both
pagan and Sovan, though he need not have worried in that death-
benighted place.

Yelena folded in on herself. Some quality to the air around
them and the aether behind it had dulled her wits, lulling her into
a trance. Von Oldenburg was not pleased about that at all, but he
had long since given up on trying to coax her out of it. Whatever
it was, it could not be cured by his ministrations.

They journeyed relentlessly. Von Oldenburg and Yelena had
taken to riding the horses so as to avoid physical contact with

the fusilier, whilst the latter lay catatonic on the floor of the post-chaise. He seemed to have become dormant, and they had a devil of a time getting him to drink. Still, von Oldenburg splashed fresh water on his face and into his mouth every couple of hours, hoping that the man would swallow some even if by accident. He had taken to caring for this strange creature with a care and tenderness normally reserved for a child, though his motivations were entirely selfish. There was a great deal he wanted to achieve.

After several days of riding, they crossed the border into Haunerwald and then shortly after reached Castle Oldenburg itself. Von Oldenburg immediately dismissed any member of his extensive household staff who tried to assist; instead he wrapped the vacant with ropes and dragged him single-handedly into a chamber in the lower levels of the castle. This had once been a functioning fortress, after all, and had its share of dungeon suites. Many of them had been converted into things like libraries or stores, but there were still several which could double as holding cells.

He shepherded Yelena into his study, and sat her down with the same tenderness he'd shown his vacant captive. He had one of the servants make her the special herbal tea she liked.

"It's okay, Lena," he muttered in his gruff way. "We will soon have you back on your feet." It unsettled him to see her so affected. Nema, a part of him would have preferred her to be out cuckolding him. At least then she would have some signs of life about her.

With everything in place, he went to the post-chaise and recovered the prototype mechanism from the strongbox there. Then, out of a surfeit of caution, he directed one of the footmen to burn the carriage, slaughter the horses and lime the corpses. Who knew what arcane poxes they might have carried back with them from Draedaland?

Bustling back to the study, he began to retrieve books and scrolls from his extensive library. These were bits and pieces of arcane lore which he'd had grave robbers, argonauts and thieves steal for him; they were books he had lifted from libraries, pilfered from tombs and unearthed from castle ruins. They were notes hastily scrawled on pieces of paper from expeditions up to Draedaland, grimoires bought for exorbitant sums of gold-mark that would keep pagan villages in victuals for decades, and codexes traded or stolen from other nations considered to be entirely outside the scope of the civilised world. In his library was contained several centuries' worth of information, amassed and accreted from every conceivable source.

Von Oldenburg knew these works intimately, and yet could not immediately think of where he had read about men and women being rendered mindless before. Even the Neman Creed, the most authoritative text about the afterlife, did not mention it – at least not in such terms – and he had the unabridged tome with all the heresies and apocrypha the Conformists believed in.

He spent several fruitless hours poring through his various books and texts. At first he searched for explanations; then he searched for methods to possibly reverse the issue. Finally he turned to his most prized and dangerous possessions: manuals on magickal practice. These were not the dry tomes maintained by the Corps of Engineers, filled with mathematical and thaumaturgical charts on maintaining wards. They were grimoires, mediaeval codexes drawn up by Neman monks and Justices of the long-disbanded Magistratum.

"Lena, I need your help," he said, approaching her. She had not uttered a word since their return, though she had drunk her tea. She seemed to be in one of those periodic moods where she regretted ever having become associated with him.

"What is it?" she muttered tiredly.

"I want to try something," he said. He had a slightly feverish air about him, vexed after the fruitlessness of his search. He handed her an open grimoire, and tapped the relevant part of the page, where there were several lines of text in Old Saxan and a number of ideograms. Yelena squinted at the page for a moment, and then looked up at him.

"You wish to en-thrall him?" she asked.

Von Oldenburg nodded. The spell was part of a collection of verbal magicks which could be used to compel a person to speak or do something. Hundreds of years ago, Justices – itinerant law-keepers – had used these spells to determine the truth of matters from witnesses and criminals before rendering judgement. But the magicks were not limited to extracting confessions and testimony. At their core, they were about commanding men's minds in some way.

"I want to try to compel him to eat. Well, I want to neutralise him, as well, but I can't do anything until he learns to sustain himself. If we do not act quickly, he will perish for want of victuals in a matter of days."

Yelena considered matters for a moment. "Not this one," she said, licking a thumb and forefinger. She flicked through the tome for several long minutes, and then reversed the grimoire and held it back to von Oldenburg. "This one."

Von Oldenburg examined the ideograms there, complex runic symbols and their attendant magickal incantations. He looked up at Yelena. "You think this will work?"

She shrugged. "I know not. But with the afterlife in its present state, I should ward yourself very extensively and carefully. To open your mind to the holy dimensions at this time, after all we have seen in the north, seems like the height of folly."

He shook his head. "I've no intention of doing any such thing."

Yelena smiled darkly. "It is not *your* intention I am concerned about."

He thought for a moment. "Could the same wards which protect me also act in . . . " He paused, thinking of the right way to express himself and his ideas. "Listen to me. The man has the ability to drain the rational part of another person's brain, yes? We saw this in Draedaland. Like a communicable mind rot."

Yelena nodded, a little less affected now that they were several days and several hundred miles clear of their most recent misadventure. "Quite so."

Von Oldenburg liked it when Yelena employed these little Sovan verbal tics. Such mannerisms were anathema to native northerners, and signified a social break from her former countrymen.

"Such a pox is clearly aethereal in nature, correct? This is not an earthly malaise."

Yelena shook her head. "Certainly I have never come across it in all my years as a healer. Plenty of instances of insanity, particularly in the elderly, but not in such a way as to be contagious."

"In which case," von Oldenburg said, warming to his theme, "in the same way I might use prophylactic wards to defend myself against the various . . . *entities* inhabiting the afterlife, could those same wards not be used to imprison the mind rot, to contain it within the man's own body? As though we were putting a psychic cage around him?"

Yelena mused on this for a long while. "I think the theory is sound. The difficulty will be knowing if the wards have worked without exposing yourself to the same danger again."

"What do you mean?"

"Well, you will ward yourself first, yes?"

"Yes."

"Then you will use a ward of containment on the vacant."

"Yes."

"Well, the only way to know if the ward of containment has worked is to then remove your own magickal shield."

Von Oldenburg shrugged. "So we will get someone else to test it. Obviously I'm not going to do it myself, am I?"

Yelena snorted bitterly. "No, I suppose not."

Von Oldenburg softened, not because he actually cared about the idea of someone else getting killed, but because he needed

Yelena on his side, and her truculence was a barrier to his success. Not to mention it was just plain irritating.

"We will take what precautions we can. We can keep the thrall shackled, and perhaps bind his hands, or glove them in some way. Quite aside from the ethics of allowing a member of my staff to be killed, finding a replacement is always such a bore."

He had intended for his last remark to be a joke, though it wasn't really, and Yelena didn't laugh.

"I need rest before I can help you," she said. "And then reinvigoration."

Von Oldenburg's lips formed a thin line. "And you cannot take such *reinvigoration* from me?" He tried to keep the pathetic, plaintive edge from his voice, but it proved impossible.

Yelena was unfazed. "No," she said firmly. "I need someone younger. More vigorous."

"Hm," von Oldenburg grunted. He knew that these sexual escapades had some latent magickal quality to them, by which she subtly drew energy from her conquests to replenish herself. And so, occasionally, when he was feeling jealousy's bite, he would pretend that she was somehow sparing him. He also knew that if he committed to marrying her in a proper Neman ceremony, and made her *Countess* von Oldenburg, she would stop. In some respects – probably in most respects – it was her way of punishing him. What a stir that would cause in the Senate: Count von Oldenburg, head of the Palatinate of Nordenkova, one of the foremost lords of the Council of Nobles and a Senator to boot, marrying some country bumpkin Draedist witch-healer. The pamphleteers would run out of ink and paper satirising it.

He retaliated, of course, by visiting the most expensive and talented prostitutes in Sova, though it didn't bring him much satisfaction – neither the retaliation, nor the sex itself. Besides, Yelena didn't seem to care one jot. He had tried in the past to put a stop to her cuckolding him, but threats of violence achieved nothing, and locking her in her chamber . . . Well. If anything, she seemed to prefer it, and would spend days on end reading and meditating. In the end, it had just become the price of doing business with her. He could never divest himself of her, yet he was constantly at pains to conceal just how crucial she was to his efforts.

At least – thank Nema Victoria and all the saints – she had means to prevent herself from becoming pregnant.

"Well, be about it then," he said eventually. "Just find somewhere discreet."

And she did indeed leave, abandoning von Oldenburg to his books and his tired lust.

It took time to lay the preparations, and von Oldenburg didn't retire until the small hours. He needed to be sharp for the morning's sorceries, for to misincant the wards was to open his mind up to all manner of depredations from the afterlife. At one point he awoke to hear Yelena's enthusiastic coupling with some young suitor – a man fated to spend the following few days in an exhausted malaise not unlike a hangover – and he bit and worried at the flesh between his thumb and forefinger.

The following day, Yelena was much restored in body and mind, and together they turned to the task of preparing the wards. Armed then with the necessary spells, she began to prepare the cell and its immediate vicinity in much the same way she had prepared their bedchamber in Toutorix, salting the floorboards, burning herbal concoctions, and inscribing the door jamb with protective runic symbols. Whatever was to take place in that old dungeon, the arcane contagion would not spread beyond it.

"I have never seen someone invert a ward like this before," Yelena said, inspecting the grimoire one last time. "Truly, I do not know what will happen."

"We have naught to lose in the attempt," von Oldenburg said briskly, though they had a great many things to lose, not least their lives. Nonetheless, he found that sometimes you just had to get on with things. To not think about it too much, just press ahead. Bullheadedness could sometimes be a virtue if applied at just the right moment.

They stood in silence while Yelena incanted the wards that would shield him – in theory at least – from the predations of the vacated fusilier. These were simple pieces of arcane armour, some of which protected him in the same way a steel cuirass would protect against a bayonet, and some of which had the effect of rendering him invisible to any entities which might wish him harm. The words were uttered with the appropriate care and solemnity, though the effect was completely intangible. For a brief, fleeting moment, von Oldenburg wondered whether she might just be pretending to ward him, and so engineer his death; but Yelena had had a thousand opportunities to kill him over many years.

"It is done?" he asked, his mouth a little dry. He cast a brief glance at the door to the chamber.

"It is done," she confirmed.

"Right," he said, gripping his pistol. He had wrapped himself in rags in the same way a leper would and strapped on an old cuirass, and he was acutely conscious of how utterly ridiculous he looked.

He took a deep breath, and entered the chamber.

The fusilier lay motionless on the floor. He looked as though he were mere hours from death. His breathing was laboured, and his lips were dry and cracked. The urine which stained his breeches was such a dark yellow as to be almost brown. Von Oldenburg's attempts to hydrate the man had clearly been in vain.

Von Oldenburg gripped the grimoire in his sweating hands, and focused on the words written there. Then, slowly, he spoke the incantation.

He was not as skilled as Yelena. He did not quite have the right accent, the right enunciation. The room seemed to draw in slightly, and darken. Whisperings filled his ears, scratching at his brain. His efforts were inexpert, but to stop now, with the incantations half uttered, would be catastrophic.

He pressed through. Once he'd finished, he inspected the body of the fusilier. Nothing had perceptibly changed. In theory, though, the contagious aspect of the mind rot should have been contained. They could make that containment a much more permanent state of affairs by inscribing the ideograms in the grimoire directly on to the man's skin, either by cutting it with a knife or simply drawing them on, but he wasn't even going to attempt that yet.

"Lena!" he called through the closed door.

"Yes?"

"It is done. Fetch me Kyselý."

There was a pause as Yelena hesitated – no doubt baulking slightly at the casual sacrifice of a member of the household staff. But she knew better than to disobey him, and he listened to her footsteps retreat down the corridor. He watched the fusilier the entire time, though the man was facing the opposite wall, and only the sound of his laboured breathing filled that small dungeon.

A little while later, Yelena returned with a diffident old man, one of von Oldenburg's longest-serving and longest-suffering butlers. No stranger to odd goings-on in the castle, he nonetheless looked deeply unhappy as the doors opened and this bizarre sight greeted him.

"You wish to see me, my lord count?"

"Kyselý, touch this man."

". . . Touch him, my lord?" Kyselý asked, aghast.

"Yes. For Nema's sake, just touch his skin. Anywhere about the face or hands should do. In fact, make sure you touch his hands."

Kyselý did not move an inch. He looked at the prostrate form of the soldier with profound unease. Von Oldenburg, in a rare oversight, had not appreciated how this scene might look.

"There's nothing the matter with him," he said, though it was a ridiculous thing to say. Standing as he was trussed up in rags and literally holding a pistol over a man manacled to the floor, there was no statement on earth so patently untrue.

"Has he some pox?" Kyselý asked after a moment.

"If he did, do you think I would be standing here?"

"Why are you armed?"

Von Oldenburg let out a great snarl of frustration. "It is not for you to question! Touch him, now!"

Still Kyselý could not be compelled. "I do not want to, my lord. I am . . ." he cleared his throat, "sorry."

Von Oldenburg's features curdled. "Damn your apologies, man! I pay you – and handsomely, I might add – to do as I bid! Now take off your damn glove, and put your damn hand on *his* damn hand. And if I have to tell you one more time, your employment here shall be terminated – and I shall *not* provide a reference!"

In fact, he was more likely to kill the man, for news of this sorry enterprise could not be allowed to escape into Haunerwald. But Kyselý did not need to know that just yet.

The butler looked deeply unhappy. In fact von Oldenburg thought he might refuse again; but instead, he said, "What will happen to me if I do?"

Von Oldenburg relaxed slightly. "Nothing at all."

"Why will *you* not touch him, then?"

"Blood of gods, man, you are impertinent!" von Oldenburg exploded, his rage entirely unmanufactured. He brandished the pistol. "Get on with it! Or I'll shoot you like a dog!"

Kyselý had the temerity to give him one brief, venomous glance, and then shuffled with obnoxious slowness over to the fusilier. He paused, but the soldier did not stir. Kyselý looked at von Oldenburg one last time, and then, removing his glove, reached down to touch the fusilier's hand.

The fusilier jerked, and grabbed the butler's wrist.

"Oh shit," von Oldenburg said with profound dismay. The aether warped. An intolerable scream ripped through the space behind the mortal plane. Kyselý, an old man but much more vivacious than the fusilier, turned wordlessly to von Oldenburg and advanced on him.

"Shit, shit shit shit!" von Oldenburg snapped. "Lena! *Lena!*"

There was no time. Kyselý was still an old man – he had not been granted any kind of superhuman strength through his transformation – and so von Oldenburg could out-dance him; but the butler was interposed between him and the door, and there was the fusilier to contend with too, who could still lay a grasping finger underneath the garments around his ankles.

"Lena!" he roared. He did not want to shoot either man, for now he had *two* vacants, rather than one, and von Oldenburg liked redundancy. Still, a part of him was tempted just to put an end to this. To kill them both and warn the Senate of the danger. He shuffled round the far wall, in spite of the wards protecting him. After all, warding the fusilier had failed; what was to say that his own wards were not useless?

"Lena, for Nema's sake!!"

"What is it?" she demanded, voice muffled from the other side of the door.

"I could not ... *Nema*," he gasped, staggering backwards as Kyselý lurched for him. "I didn't ... It didn't work! Help me, damn you!"

"It's not strong enough, it must be the rune!"

"What?"

"The incantation is not strong enough alone, you need the rune!"

"How the damned fucking hell am I supposed to do that?"

He danced back again, but now tripped over the form of the fusilier. He clattered idiotically into the wall, landing on his buttocks, his left hand smacking on the floor. The pistol discharged point-blank into the top of the fusilier's skull, blasting it so viciously it was as though someone had taken a wine bottle and smashed it on the floor.

Still Kyselý advanced on him, as if nothing at all had happened.

Von Oldenburg snarled in frustration and rage. "I need your help!"

"I'm not going in there," Yelena replied.

"Lena! Damn you!"

He tried to make his way to the door, but the thing that had once been his butler made contact with his cuirass. "Gah!" von Oldenburg shouted, leaping backwards. Once again he clattered into the undressed stone of the old dungeon wall, the ill-fitting armour pinching his skin. "Lena! For Nema's sake, get in here and help me!"

With a sudden burst of recklessness, he grabbed Kyselý and shoved him backwards, so that the man tripped over the fusilier and crashed awkwardly to the floor. Such a fall should have incapacitated him, possibly with a broken hip – but Kyselý pressed himself up, relentless in his need to transmit the mind rot.

Von Oldenburg was about to make a swift exit when the door opened and Yelena came in. She had taken the time to truss herself up in rags, too. They both cut utterly absurd figures, like a pair of leper argonauts.

"So glad you could join me," von Oldenburg snarled, sweating and heaving in great lungfuls of air.

"Shut up," Yelena snapped. In her right hand was a knife and in her left was the grimoire, opened to the page of runic ideograms. "You will have to pin him down."

"You must be fucking joking."

"This is it!" Yelena snapped, the two of them parting as Kyselý renewed his slow but inexorable approach. They all made a circle around the chamber, as though locked in a baffling tripartite waltz. "You will not get another opportunity. If you intend to press this, then you must do it now."

"If he touches me—"

"I did not take you for a fearful man!"

Von Oldenburg gritted his teeth. He let out a shout of frustration as he closed with Kyselý, striking him quite unnecessarily with the butt of his pistol – it had no effect whatever – and then, checking he had not one iota of exposed skin on his hands, grasped Kyselý's wrists. Finally, using his greater strength, he pushed the old butler to the floor.

"I have him!" he shouted with the frantic desperation of a man who was much more accustomed to ordering the death of someone than performing the act himself. "I have him! Quick!"

Yelena was not quick. "It is *much* more important that I be precise."

"Damn you, Lena!" von Oldenburg shouted as Kyselý struggled weakly beneath him. The butler moved his head as though trying to bite him, but he had neither the strength nor the reach to get anywhere close. Yelena was right; with Kyselý pinned, there really was no great rush.

Von Oldenburg waited whilst she checked and double-checked the ideograms.

"Will a piece of charcoal not do the trick?" he asked her as she finished and brandished the knife.

"Do you want it done properly or not? You should fashion a brand if you plan on doing this more than once."

"Oh aye, I'll just have the local smith turn one out."

"And you call me impertinent."

"Where was this Lena when we were in Toutorix?"

Yelena endured a spasm of irritation. "Do not distract me! Pin his wrists with your knees and hold his head with your hands. I need him to be still for this. Nema knows we do not want to stuff him full of demonic energies."

Von Oldenburg looked at her sharply. "Is such a thing even possible?"

"Let us take the necessary precautions and we shall not have to find out."

They took the necessary precautions. Yelena set to work cutting the rune into Kyselý's forehead. Von Oldenburg held him with an iron grip, at one point using the man's ears as handles. Such was the heartless and wanton brutality of the enterprise that even von Oldenburg began to doubt himself. It seemed as though Yelena was a foil to him; where he was bullheaded, she was meek; but where he became doghearted, she drew on some deep reserve of callous resolve that he did not know she was capable of. She was a woman of two distinct parts, and that only served to deepen her enigma.

He watched with a ghastly fascination as she cut the ideogram into the man's head, a circular rune quartered like a compass, and in each of the quadrants a glyph. In order to achieve the detail required, she had to draw the rune very large, so that the entirety of the man's forehead was a red ruin by the end of it. But when the blade finally left his skin, the transformation was instantaneous.

The two of them exchanged a glance as Kyselý went immediately limp. As soon as Yelena withdrew the knife, he stopped thrashing and became docile – so docile, in fact, that for a moment von Oldenburg thought she had killed him.

"Is he dead?" he asked her.

She shook her head. "Get off him, and you will see him breathe."

Von Oldenburg obliged, and stood. Kyselý was indeed breathing – and blinking, von Oldenburg noticed now, for there was blood running into his eyes, and it was obviously bothering him. But it was bothering him in a very particular way. It reminded von Oldenburg of a man he knew who had suffered a head injury from a nearly spent cannonball, which had rendered him a simpleton. External stimuli bothered him – especially bright lights – but in a way that he could not quite himself comprehend.

Von Oldenburg approached Kyselý slowly. Yelena had not moved, and seemed to share none of his caution.

"Is it safe, do you think?"

She shrugged. "It is as safe as I am ever going to make it."

Not for the first time, von Oldenburg found himself cursing the failure of their mission to Verdabaro. What expertise from the Selureii had they denied themselves with their craven retreat?

"I should fetch another—" he started, but stopped – practically choked – as he watched Yelena remove her gloves and grab Kyselý's hand. "No!" he shouted, wincing, bracing himself for that horrible shriek as she discorporated and tried to kill him.

There was nothing. No fracturing of the mortal plane, no infernal babblings, no desperate, mind-rending scream. Just Yelena, holding the hand of a man who had lost his mind.

For the briefest of moments, he felt a stab of an emotion akin to guilt as he considered what it was he had done to his longest-serving butler.

"Yelena! For Nema's sake, *say* something!"

She looked at him, but there was no pleasure or satisfaction to be discerned in her features. "I'm fine," she said, dropping the man's hand unceremoniously. "It has worked."

Several thoughts and emotions clamoured for monopoly in von Oldenburg's mind. Elation that they had succeeded, anger and irritation that *his* inverted ward had achieved nothing in practical terms, relief that Yelena was alive, resentment that she would forever be a more accomplished practitioner of the Draedist arcana than him. The urge to inflict pain upon himself, to mortify his flesh, to transmute his emotional anger and anguish into physical agony and so dissipate it, was a strong one. But to do so there and then, particularly in front of Yelena, would have been embarrassing and ridiculous.

"Water," he said. "And victuals. Let us see if we can get him to eat."

They spent quarter of an hour taking off their makeshift armour and fetching some food and brandy from the castle's stores. The servants knew better than to enquire what had happened – for it had been impossible to conceal the noise – but there were plenty of inquisitive looks shot their way.

They returned to the old dungeon and opened the door.

"We need to get rid of this body," von Oldenburg said distastefully, looking at the corpse of the fusilier and the now extremely large pool of blood marring the stones of the floor.

Yelena ignored him. Kyselý had not moved from the floor – had not moved at all – and remained lying on his back, staring up at the ceiling. The blood from the wound on his forehead had run into the cracks and crevices of his face, giving him a ghastly visage. Yelena crouched down next to him and said in a stern, authoritative voice, "Sit up."

To von Oldenburg's utter astonishment, Kyselý did so, obeying her like a well-trained dog.

"How did you do that?!" he demanded.

"Try it yourself," Yelena said simply.

Von Oldenburg squatted down and held out a bread roll. "Take this," he commanded Kyselý, and chuckled in amazement as the man plucked it from his hand unquestioningly. "Eat it." Kyselý began to eat the bread roll. Von Oldenburg looked at Yelena. "Remarkable," he breathed.

Yelena stood. "That's enough excitement for me for one day."

"What do you mean?"

"I mean what I said. This whole business has drained me and frayed my nerves. I'm going to have a bath."

Von Oldenburg snorted in astonishment. "Lena, nothing of its like has been achieved for . . . Well, for all we know, such has *never* been achieved. Think of the *possibilities*—"

But Yelena was already leaving. "Later," she muttered. "With victuals he will keep. You play with your new toy. I need a wash, and rest."

"Lena!" von Oldenburg called to her back, but she had already left.

❧

They did not reconvene until much later in the afternoon. Von Oldenburg tasked the household staff with engaging the services of a new butler, and informing Kyselý's wife – Mrs Kyselý, he presumed – that the man had perished in an accident and that she would be reimbursed for her loss. He ignored the inevitable clamour of questions and retreated to his study, where he mused on the day's labours. Eventually Yelena joined him, at the same time that a bout of late-afternoon rain pattered against the windows.

"Feeling restored?" he asked her, a glass of brandy in his hand, his eyes not leaving the fire in front of him.

"Somewhat," she replied.

There was a silence. "We have known each other for, what, ten years?"

"Something like that."

"I feel as though I am no closer to ... *understanding* you. Your mind. Your thoughts."

"What is it you do not understand?"

Von Oldenburg considered his next question, chewing his lower lip as he thought. "Why are you here? Why are you with me?"

"I—"

"You do not love me. Let us not pretend otherwise."

Yelena considered this for a moment. "No, I suppose I do not. Not in the traditional sense, at any rate."

Von Oldenburg snorted with derision, though it caused him great anguish to hear it spoken, and he wished he had not raised the matter. "And what is the 'traditional' sense?"

"You want me to explain to you what love is?"

There was another pause. "I suppose I do not love you, in the traditional sense, either." He had hoped to wound her as she had wounded him, but her nonchalance did not seem to be affected. He cleared his throat; she did not say anything, nor did she seem to be about to say anything further. "But I feel a very strong sense of affection for you. I know I don't show it, or rather, I show it in strange ways."

Again Yelena was silent.

"Damn it, Lena, say something!"

She sighed. "I do not know what it is you want me to tell you."

"I want you to tell me, to *explain* to me, why you are here."

"I am here because that is what you desire."

Von Oldenburg shook his head, annoyed. "That cannot be the only reason. You have said yourself you do not love me. And clearly you are not frightened of me—"

"You mistreat me frequently."

"I have never raised a hand to you."

"You have threatened to."

"Threats I never intended to carry out."

"Well, then I am comforted."

"Whatever you think, I have still never struck you!"

"Mistreatment is hardly confined to acts of physical violence."

Von Oldenburg gritted his teeth. "I know I am not a subtle man, but if you consider my behaviour to be mistreatment, then know that I mistreat everyone equally."

"That is hardly an excuse for someone you consider to be your wi—"

"I have nothing to excuse!" he suddenly thundered. Yelena did not react at all. He took a moment to govern himself. "I have a purpose in life, Lena. A *purpose*. And this purpose is greater than so many things. It is greater and more valuable than life itself. I am trying to achieve greatness. Greatness for Sova. For the Empire. Greatness which is the Empire's by *right*. Look at who surrounds us; look at who bedevils us. Half-breeds. Conformists. *Pagans*. Men and women tepid of spirit. The wealth of their lands should be ours. The blood of their people should be *ours*, damn it! They owe us if not their servitude then their allegiance, yet they display neither! They—" He stopped suddenly, catching himself. This was a tirade Yelena had heard many times before. "What I do not understand is why *you* are *here*. You do not love me. By your own words I mistreat you. You are Draedist, and cannot love Sova by any measure. Why do you cleave to Castle Oldenburg?

You are like a ghost in these halls. You are not a prisoner. You are free to leave whenever you wish."

She looked at him for a long time. It was difficult to read her, as it so often was. Was there a hint of astonishment there? Did he assert some power over her that even he was not aware of?

"I do not have a simple explanation."

"Then give me the complex one! Nema knows we have enough time."

"Everything is so plain in your eyes, isn't it? You have never been troubled by adversity—"

"Blood of gods, Lena, I face adversity at every turn—"

"Of your own artifice!" Yelena suddenly snapped. "Yours has always been a life of wealth, and privilege. You face adversity only because you confect intrigues. You could have spent your time, your *life*, in unutterable luxury. Everything you have ever wanted is merely on the other side of a coin. You cannot *fathom* what my life is, what it is like to live it, who I am and where I have come from. You simply do not have the mental scaffolding upon which to build the thoughts. The complexity of my explanation is not something that can be picked apart and analysed and solved, it is one of emotion which is beyond your ability to comprehend. I am here for a thousand reasons which *defy* reason. And if you cannot turn your mind to it, do not burden me with the responsibility of educating you."

And with that, she left.

For the first time in a very long time, von Oldenburg was lost for words.

XVIII

A Sincere Desire to Go Home

"The Empire languishes in the grip of the elderly equestrian class of Sova. I think of these wizened and cosseted old fools as 'dragons'. Their sole preoccupation is to amass and hoard goldmark, and to shield it from public works; they bestir themselves not to enrich their fellow man but to see only that their wealth is unmolested by the tax-taker. A new generation of lawmen have made their sole concern to construct ever more elaborate contrivances, too, so that these vast sums may continue to evade the grasping hands of the exchequer, and instead remain in the custody of none but indolent scions."

SENATOR JULIJA PAVIČIĆ

Uncharted Foothills

GREAT NORTHERN BARRIER RANGE

Well. I am a long way from home.

Peter remembered writing those words to his father weeks before – or was it months? Time moved strangely in this place. Fort Ingomar had been a long way from Sova, twelve hundred miles as the crow flew, though the journey was almost twice that to avoid the interposition of the Principality of Casimir. Who knew how far it was now? Fifteen hundred miles? Two thousand?

It was cold up here, cold and wet. Although it was approaching summer, they were getting higher. The Great Northern Barrier Range was aptly named; it was a barrier, separating the known world, the civilised world, from ... from *what*? Nobody in Sova had the answer.

He was carried for a while, and then when it was clear he could walk, he walked. From breaks in the dense forest, he could see the now distant Lake Ena, so still it could have been an enormous plate of glittering blue glass stretching to the horizon. But mostly he kept his head down. The catmen may have been savage and terrifying in the heat of battle, but they did not seem to be given to random acts of violence. The prisoners, of which there were perhaps ten, were not harmed. In fact, the catmen took time to ply them with water, roots, leaves and berries.

Peter examined his captors during daylight hours. They were human-sized, a little larger, their bodies naturally powerful and muscular. They were clothed in pantaloons of woven grass, though many were naked, and unlike the Kasar, they wore no jewellery – not so much as a wooden bangle. Most of them had fur as black as ink, but there were some who were sand-coloured, their fur marked with splotches of black and white. There was no hierarchy based on colouring that Peter could discern during that long hike.

The catmen spoke very little, and when they did, it was almost exclusively in low growls that bore no parallel to Saxan. Would that there were some diplomats among the prisoners, or linguists from the University of Sova, they might have been able to make contact – even come up with some kind of creole language like Kasarsprek. For that was what these people were: *uncontacted*. There was no record of any race of catmen anywhere, certainly not that Peter knew about. The ramifications were profound.

They knew about the Kasar, of course, humans who had been fused with plains wolves during the ancient magickal cataclysm; and they knew about humans who had been fused with sea creatures, creating the Stygion mer-men. Clearly, at least to Peter, something similar had happened in this distant and untouched region. The magicks which had saturated the world during the primeval conjunction of the afterlife and the mortal plane had obviously merged together pagans and forest-dwelling cats. And if this distant, untouched, unknown civilisation could exist, what *other* civilisations existed? Were there bird men? Lizard men? Hybrids which defied taxonomy entirely?

They limped on, soaked by the rain, which seemed not to bother the catmen at all, forced to sleep directly on the forest floor at night without the comfort of a fire – the catmen did not light any – their clothes muddied and bloodied. Peter was plagued by insects. Flies buzzed incessantly around his face where the skin had been rent. The incisions were much too deep to heal cleanly without being stitched up, and as well as the physical pain, there was an uncomfortable heat to them now as the beginnings of a pox set in.

Perhaps a day or two after they had been captured, his face began to smell and suppurate and he felt himself becoming febrile. He slowed to a stagger as the heat enveloped his whole body, and the hike became a surreal, nightmarish forced march during which he was plagued by hallucinations. On one of the days he saw his father, and tried to speak with him; but then his father told him to shut up, and it wasn't his father at all, but Furlan, and he was being rude because he was frightened and did not want to be struck by one of the catmen.

Peter was convinced he was going to die then. One evening he lay on the forest floor, feeling the wet loam soak into his uniform, which was by now filthy and ragged, and he hugged his knees, burning and shivering and waiting for the pox to claim him. At one point he became aware of a catman standing over him, and assumed in his febrile state that he was about to be executed. Instead, some questionable unguent was applied to his face. The catman would chew on a plant, which he masticated into cud and then thumbed roughly into the incisions in Peter's face. Peter, in his sweaty, disoriented state, whimpered and cried out as pus and old blood was painfully expressed from the wounds, but the catman simply growled idly to his fellows, like a physician murmuring to his students.

The following morning, Peter awoke to find the pain at least had gone, and the fever was much improved. He went to touch the wounds on his face, but the nearby catman growled at him, and he immediately withdrew his hand. He still felt weak and nauseous, however, and the forced march, which had before been difficult, was now unendurable.

They travelled for two weeks, maybe even longer than that. He had lost all sense of where he was, until one clear day, when the sun was out and a warm wind was blowing, he saw that the body of Lake Ena was entirely to the *south* of them. They had walked the length of it, a journey of almost a hundred miles, to the point where the lake actually began to narrow again into the River Vida. He suffered a sense of powerful vertigo as, for the first time, he appreciated just how *far* they were from Sova and everything he had ever known. Hell, at this point it was a two-hundred-and-fifty-mile journey just to get back to Fort Ingomar.

Finally the journey ended. He had not spoken a word in weeks except to his own hallucinations. The party of ten prisoners was down to six; Olwin and Furlan remained amongst the survivors. Peter was pleased, initially at least, though perhaps it would have been better if they had died en route. Who knew what depredations awaited them?

The catmen lived in the forest understorey, which made sense, given their feline progenitors. The creatures had stripped the lower and middle branches off the surrounding barrier pines and beeches and encircled the trees with broad platforms, which themselves housed wooden shacks roofed with thatch. Some of these collections of dwellings were stacked two or three high, whilst rope bridges were strung between the trees. In the centre of this settlement was a large platform mounted on an enormous oak, containing a single structure, clearly a communal area of some sort, and it was around this which the rest of the village had been built.

Unlike other settlements, the place was quiet. Peter could see no fires, and there was no smell of smoke. If the village was occupied, then the inhabitants were not surprised, or alarmed, or even interested by their arrival – nor did they apparently cook their food. He realised, too, that there was still no birdsong, save for the distant caw of a raptor at high altitude. This place was marked by a total absence of life.

The wind, mild and wet, breezed through the trees like breath. Although his view was obscured by the surrounding forest, Peter had a sense of *height*. The ground to the east moved ever upwards, to the west ever downwards, which meant they had stopped somewhere on the side of a thickly forested mountain within the Barrier Range.

He contrived to sit next to Furlan, though the artillery captain did not say anything to him. Olwin was nearby as well, her features stern. The other soldiers looked freshly frightened, for the length and monotony of the journey had served to dampen their sense of fear and danger.

The catmen stood around. They did not seem to be engaged in particularly animated discussion; indeed, they spoke in a stilted, fractured way, their conversations marked by lengthy periods of silence. There was no urgency to their movements, or even any sense of purpose. Had they been Casimirs or Sanques, Peter and his fellow captives would have been corralled into a sentried billet and provided with victuals, and then taken away one by one for questioning. The catmen almost didn't seem to know what to do with them.

Peter took this time to examine them. As well as their obvious physical characteristics, they shared several peculiarities. The more obvious was the grotesque lesions, growths and tumours which marked all of them. On every one of the creatures, there were tumescent growths, like fungal rashes. The nearest catman had a huge batch of wart-like pustules that spread from one shoulder to the other and covered most of his back. The rest had similar disfigurements, some of which were dried, grey and keratinous with age, whilst others were fresh and glistened in the late-afternoon sunlight.

The second quality, harder to define, was a sense of repulsion. It was not to do with their gross biological disfigurements, though they were certainly arresting; nor was it the general fear and disorientation that came with being a prisoner. It was more innate than that. It was as though the catmen were surrounded by an invisible aura of repugnance, eliciting a feeling of dread and loathing in Peter from the same part of his psyche which produced such base instincts as hunger and lust.

"Do you *feel* that?" he whispered to Furlan when he was sure that none of the catmen were paying them any attention.

Furlan nodded subtly. He glanced at Peter's face, and quickly looked away. Peter wondered just how unsightly the three claw marks were which ran from the corner of his right eyebrow down to the left side of his chin.

"What are we doing here," he murmured. It hadn't really been a question, and Furlan didn't give him an answer. He wouldn't have been given a chance anyway; the catmen seemed to be possessed of extraordinary hearing, and one of them turned and growled angrily at them. They were quiet after that.

They sat there, waiting, as the light drained from the sky. With darkness came a cold breeze, and soon they were shivering and huddling together for warmth. Peter found himself pressed against Olwin, which was not the intimate contact he had been quietly daydreaming about for the past couple of months. She seemed less affected, both mentally and physically, than the rest of them, and Peter wondered what it was that enabled her to remain so calm.

Eventually – finally – movement. Peter realised that the forest was coming alive around them, not with wild animals and birds, but with more catpeople. They were emerging from the surrounding forest like returning hunters, though none of them were carrying anything. Peter estimated there were perhaps forty of the creatures altogether. They looked over at the prisoners, and traded a few words with their captors; then all of them clambered up the trees and into the dwellings above, making their way across the rope bridges to the central meeting place. Peter expected that it would soon be filled with the flickering orange light of fire, but there was nothing. The catmen seemed perfectly content to simply sit and converse in the darkness.

"We should run," one of the prisoners said, a private from the regiment. He looked pale and gaunt, his face half lost under several weeks of beard growth. He gritted his teeth. "We should run. We will not get another chance."

"Shut up," Peter hissed. "They can hear you."

"They are going to kill us all, whatever the fuck they are. If we stay here, we're dead."

"You won't make it twenty yards," Furlan growled.

"And it's better to stay here, is it? To wait and die?"

"You don't know what it is they want with us."

"They want to kill and eat us," the man said. Peter didn't like that; not because it was a ghastly thought, but because it was what he feared as well.

Still, it was strange how even though he was fairly certain they would all die, he still couldn't quite bring himself to mount an escape attempt. It seemed to him the difference between the risk of dying and the certainty of it.

"Just sit still and shut up," Furlan muttered. "Let us at least see what it is they—"

"To hell with you," the man grunted, pressing himself up. He broke into a sprint, though it was a rather anaemic movement, weak and malnourished as he was. He did make it twenty yards, in spite of Furlan's prediction, but not much more. A dark shape dropped on him from the trees, so suddenly and silently that it made Peter's heart leap.

The man was not given a chance to cry out, so quickly was he killed. But it was not his death which was the most shocking thing; it was what happened immediately afterwards. More catmen dropped out of the trees from places Peter couldn't even see, descended on the fresh kill, and proceeded to ferociously rip the man apart and devour him. The catmen engaged in a savagery they had thus far reserved, consuming the private so quickly that they ingested most of his uniform as well. And when they were finished, and had returned quietly to the meeting place in the centre of the settlement, smaller, runt-like creatures which looked like ghastly childlike malformations of the adult catmen picked at and fought over the remaining bones.

If Peter had been frightened before, now he was terrified. One of the other prisoners was physically sick, though they had little enough to retch up. Olwin looked miserable, her eyes rimmed with tears. Furlan, too, appeared to be on the verge of weeping.

"I want to go home," Peter said. Then he, too, started to cry. "I want to go home."

Well. I am a long way from home.

The words echoed around his head constantly. That the afterlife was a real, tangible place was broadly accepted within the Empire, though the consensus remained that it was strange and unknowable, and one was better off just focusing on matters earthly – at least until old age. Now, all Peter could think about was entering that deathless realm. Would he see his father again? Would he even *want* to? Given the nightmarish things that had happened in and around Fort Ingomar, it seemed that the immortal plane was in a state of flux. There was never a good time to die, but it also seemed like now was a particularly bad one.

They were left to huddle together on the forest floor overnight. Even in the small hours, none of them tried to escape. Peter sat, awake for most of it, catatonic with fear. It was one thing to face the lethal musketry of the Casimirs, whose motives were at least comprehensible; it was another to face an enemy that was utterly inscrutable.

No one dared speak or move, even when the sun rose and the air warmed and the mountains were bathed with light. It was the lack of noise which was the most intolerable thing. Who were these curious, savage automatons? Why did they not speak to one another? And where were all the animals? The deer, squirrels, foxes, rabbits, bats and birds?

Eventually, the catmen assembled. All of them were completely naked, having shed their grass pantaloons. Peter shrank away as they approached, and he and the rest of the prisoners were pulled to their feet. Then they were ushered wordlessly and with minimal force to the north, on another short hike. They left behind the hamlet and came across a second clearing, this one atop a small cliff which afforded them a breathtaking view of the steppes to the north, and to the south, the enormous Lake Ena.

But it was not this incredible vista on which Peter's attention was fixed. In the clearing was a stone circle, fifteen feet in diameter, which had all manner of runic symbols chiselled into it. In the centre of the circle was a large block, to which were affixed four manacles. There could be absolutely no mistaking the purpose of this place.

Now they did begin to panic, and the catmen were forced to restrain them. If they were in any way moved or affected by the prisoners' desperate entreaties, they showed no sign of it. Peter could offer nothing except trite pleas, and then, when it was clear that no amount of shouting and weeping was going to get them freed, he resorted to a refrain of "I want to go home".

It was Furlan who was singled out first. Weakened from want of food and water and his nerves frayed beyond repair, he was wrestled easily by a single catman to the stone block. Peter shouted and screamed until his throat was hoarse, because there was nothing else he could do. Of course, he was ignored.

Furlan was forcibly stripped of all his clothes until he was naked; then the manacles were clamped around his wrists and ankles. Peter and the other prisoners were dragged off to one side and forced to the floor. Furlan wrenched at the iron chains, but he had not a hope of escaping.

A new catman appeared now. Unlike the others, this one was bedecked in what looked to Peter like ceremonial garb. As he approached Furlan, he chanted in that guttural catman tongue. He held in his hand a curious object, a large golden spearhead, easily eight inches long, which seemed much too ornate and finely wrought for such basic creatures.

Furlan was swearing at the creatures now, ranting and raging with all his strength, the manacles cutting deep incisions into his wrists and ankles. The catman shaman paid this impressive display of rage absolutely no heed as he completed the ritual chanting. It might have been Peter's imagination – and he was now half deranged with fear – but the runes seemed to activate and glow slightly. It was difficult to tell in the morning sunlight.

He did not know what to expect from this ritualistic execution, but it certainly was not the thing that came to pass. The catman pressed the spearhead into Furlan's face – not point-first, but the flat of it against his forehead – and tied it there with a length of leather cord. Then, after this baffling opening, a second catman approached, and handed the shaman a large curved knife, which he used to open Furlan from the base of his sternum down to the top of his groin.

Peter screamed out one last time. At least the captain died quickly. A stronger man might have tolerated the wound for a minute or two as his blood left him, but they were all weak and frightened, and the shock of the injury ended Furlan's life almost immediately.

Except . . .

Except.

Furlan *wasn't* dead. His head had lolled forward, but he was groaning softly as the shaman began to excavate his abdomen. Using the knife, he parted the muscle and mesentery and cut Furlan's organs out of him one by one, handing them to another catman, who arranged them artfully on the stone circle. Peter watched in horrified disbelief as Furlan simply did not die, even as vital piece after piece of him was removed.

"*Estas neeble . . .*" Olwin said wretchedly from next to Peter. The others were crying out too, accusations of witchcraft, entreaties to Nema and Sovan gods and saints.

Finally, Furlan's heart was cut out, still pumping, and Peter prayed to Nema Victoria that it was finally over and the man's torment was at an end. But still Furlan writhed and groaned gently, and Peter realised that he was witnessing not just a brutal execution, but a piece of bleak and savage black sorcery.

"Why?" he moaned, his face streaked with tears and snot and drool. "Why are you *doing* this?"

Another catman now approached, this time with a parcel of what looked like oilcloth. The shaman opened it to reveal an armful of offal. He took these fresh organs one by one, continuing to incant in that guttural, growling tongue, and packed them into Furlan's abdomen as though performing some sort of insane vivisection. Then, when this sequence was concluded, he set to work knitting Furlan's abdomen back together with a bone needle and length of gut.

Peter had long lapsed to silence. Next to him, Olwin was repeating the same phrase over and over again, "*malpermesita sangomagio, malpermesita sangomagio"*, until she was wailing it like a widow.

The bizarre ritual was complete. Furlan was left there, held up by the manacles, very much alive, though he absolutely should not have been. The shaman disappeared back into the forest, paid only the most passing and minor obeisance by the other catmen. Then, after a pause, the length of which seemed to have no significance whatever, Peter and the rest of the prisoners were pulled to their feet and led back to the settlement, where they were corralled into a group and left on the floor. The catmen dispersed, and there was nothing left to do but sit and think about the dreadful fate which awaited them all.

XIX

The Knackerman

"'Sova in all things', declares our most celebrated political philosopher, Artem Managold – never was there a tighter intellectual ligature placed on the foreign policymaker."

AMBASSADOR ANETE JEKABSONE

Port Talaka

KASAR KYARAI

Port Talaka was in chaos.

If the scene on the bridge had been the appetiser, then the scenes in the capital were the main course. Here, the streets and roads were jammed up with wolfmen and humans trying to flee the city. They pulled wagons piled high with furniture and belongings. Renata saw one cart loaded with the elderly, infirm, small children, and one bloodied Sovan soldier lying on his back, trying to keep the flies away from the soiled bandages around his legs.

She saw human mothers with screaming children, Kasari mothers with mewling pups, a man carrying his elderly father on his back, a wolfman dragging what looked to be the corpse of a friend wrapped in a rug. People lugged armfuls of silverware and other valuable items to trade on the journey north, or just to keep them from falling into enemy hands. In one alley, she saw a group of soldiers getting blind drunk. In another, she saw a second group locked in an orgiastic tangle with local prostitutes.

"Nema Victoria, 'tis the *Fall of Gevennah*," she murmured, referencing the famous Kliner painting.

Faces were gaunt and drawn and sallow with stress. Behaviour was frantic, erratic. Fights were breaking out everywhere. And all the while, the cannonade from the Casimiran Navy thundered into the city. Shells launched from specialist shore bombardment ketches exploded in the streets and against the rooftops. The adobe houses, their thin earth walls perfect for the long Kyaran days, were smashed to pieces. Their beams, too, dried to tinder by the hot sun, caught aflame as quickly and surely as kindling. Soon, several housing districts were blazing in great conflagrations of boiling orange fire, filling the air with smoke.

"This is suicide!" Ozolinsh shouted as the plains horses carried them east toward the centre of the city. Here, apartment blocks and adobe and timber dwellings gave way to larger structures of stone, with pillared facades, ornate balustrades and pyramid-shaped roofs, whilst the dusty streets and back alleys were replaced with broad flagstoned boulevards and attractive hanging gardens. Stepped pyramids – now temples to Nema Victoria – were in great abundance, but none compared to the two which rose enormously out of the centre of the city. These were the twin peaks of the Spiritsraad and Kasaraad, the respective seats of the spiritual and secular governments of the Kyarai.

They looked dismayingly far away, lost in the haze and smoke.

"Keep up, damn you!" Colonel Glaser shouted over the thunderous report of errant shells. The cannonade from the Jade Sea was either poorly aimed or indiscriminate, designed to reduce the city and break the will of the occupants rather than destroy any particular fortifications. Or perhaps the shoreline fortifications had already been destroyed, and the sailors were bored and looking to use up their stocks. Occasionally a roundshot would whistle overhead, and collide with a building with a tremendous clang and explosion of stone chips.

"No, this way!" Lyzander shouted, urging them south. In the distance Renata fancied she could hear not just the general chaos of the city under siege, but . . . drums? The sharp rattle and tap of drummer boys' snares, and to accompany it, the crackling of musketry. Was the fighting so close already?

"I thought you said we had to avoid the—" Glaser began, but Lyzander cut him off.

"No time, no time! They are much closer than I thought!"

They urged their plains horses to a gallop, though with the amount of human and Kasari traffic jamming the roads they had to stop and start constantly. There were soldiers here, too, throwing up barricades, shoving people out of the streets, coalescing into defensive pockets to slow the enemy advance.

"Ten Dai must have been overrun," she heard Glaser say to Lyzander.

"Sounds that way," Lyzander replied grimly.

"The fortifications to the south—" Renata began, but Glaser shook his head.

"The walls will have been the first thing the Casimiran Navy reduced. Those bomb ketches can fire behind the lines anyway." He was quite for a moment. "Damn!"

"What does that mean?" Renata asked.

"It means we have even less time than we thought," Glaser replied. Then he turned his attentions to the refugees ahead. "Make way there, damn you! Make *way!*"

The mass of people was thinning. Here, there were few dwellings, fewer reasons for people to be in the centre of the city. They moved at speed through broad, pleasant streets, the flagstones cut into pretty and complex geometric patterns, or interwoven with images of serpents and other mythological creatures carved in bas-relief. The hanging gardens were fed by channels of water, themselves creating a multitude of square lakes, bubbling pleasantly with fountains. Sovans – especially in Sova – were often dismissive of other nations and cultures, but it was clear to Renata at least that Port Talaka was a place of great beauty and craftsmanship. Its masons and artisans were as skilled as any Sova could produce, its human diversity as rich and multifaceted, its buildings and streets as architecturally impressive. It was a beacon of culture and prosperity in the south – and it was very shortly about to be overrun by an army of Kasar radicalised by Neman Conformism and their Casimiran sponsors. Who knew what dismal fate awaited it then?

Who knew what dismal fate awaited all of them?

"Shit!" Lyzander suddenly shouted. To the south, they could see bluecoats. "Already?!"

Renata's heart fluttered in her chest as explosions of smoke and flame indicated where the Casimirs were firing great volleys of musketry into unseen Sovan and Kasari soldiers.

"This way!"

They thundered through a shallow set of water gardens, the plains horses kicking up sprays of foam. Renata let out an involuntary shriek as a shell screamed overhead and exploded against the eastern face of a nearby building. Chunks of stone were blasted out like debris from a dynamited cliff. One piece of shrapnel snicked the flank of Renata's horse, and it whinnied and reared up, sending her head-over-arse into the water below.

"Ambassador!"

"Ms Rainer!"

"Renata!"

Everybody shouted at once. She pressed herself up out of the water, soaked to the bone. Someone was next to her, strong hands gripping her by the arms, hauling her up. It was Lyzander. He peered into her face with great intensity. "Are you all right?"

"I'm fine," she snapped, shocked and embarrassed. In fact she had landed awkwardly, and the nerves in her right shoulder were crazed, leaving her arm weak and numb.

"Here, she can ride with me," Guillot said, pulling his horse next to them.

"It's okay, I can ride with the captain," Renata said immediately, but Guillot shook his head.

"He hasn't the space, look."

It was true; the back of Lyzander's horse was laden with packs and weapons, whilst Guillot had plenty of room.

"All right," she said, and allowed Lyzander to boost her up on to the back of the monk's horse.

"Hold on to me," Guillot said, though she did not, contriving to clutch the saddle instead.

They set off again, taking what looked to Renata to be a long way round, a sequence of back streets to the south until they could cut east again. Roundshot and shells continued to hit the Spiritsraad and Kasaraad – they were enormous targets, after all – but plenty sailed straight past to crash into the streets beyond. They came across the sitting body of a wolfman who had been decapitated by one such errant shot, cutting a gory but ultimately melancholy image in that deserted street.

They came to a stop perhaps half a mile south-west of the Spiritsraad. They could not see the base of it thanks to the interposition of dozens of buildings, but halfway up the enormous stepped pyramid were visible outposts of Sovan soldiers and Kasari troops from another élite regiment known as Hyernakryger.

"They're firing," Ozolinsh remarked. She was red-faced and sweating heavily in the smoky heat. Behind her, Maruska struggled with the reins of his plains horse. Renata privately considered that the old man should have waited for them to the north.

"What?" Herschel asked next to her, in a similar state to the engineer.

Ozolinsh pointed to the Spiritsraad. "The Sovans. They are firing."

"She's right," Lyzander said. The Sovans and Kasar there were aiming their muskets at steep angles down the steps of the pyramid. There was so much smoke it was as though the Spiritsraad were volcanic.

"Prince of Hell, can someone please explain—"

"If they are firing, it means the enemy is there. At the foot of the temple," Renata said.

"How in blazes are we supposed to get in, then?" Herschel demanded.

"Bloody hell," Glaser murmured as a roundshot slammed into a group of Sovans and Hyernakryger, violently dismembering them.

"There is a secret entrance," Lyzander muttered, rubbing the sweat from his face and taking a long draw of water from his flask.

"Don't you think you'd—" Herschel started, but Lyzander cut across him.

"Ah, shit."

Renata followed the line of his gaze, to where a Kasari soldier had appeared at the end of the street. It wore only a pair of pantaloons, which were ripped. Its muzzle was wet with blood, and more dripped from its claws.

"One of ours?" Glaser asked, but Lyzander was already levelling his pistol at the creature.

"Go."

"Go where? You can't possibly hope to—"

"Bloody go! Go east!" Lyzander shouted. "Head for the storm outflow at Nuadha Street. Look for the jade wolf!"

The Kasar let out a snarl and began to run the length of the street. Renata's heart leapt. She felt Guillot tense up in front of her. Both Ozolinsh and Maruska let out grunts of fear. It was extraordinary to think that a single wolfman could elicit such a response. What terror did an army of them instil?

"Wait!" she shouted as Guillot began to pull the horse around. The monk did not wait. He was urging the horse as fast as it would go back out of the street.

"Come on!" he called to Maruska, whose plains horse seemed to obey the young monk with a mind of its own. It seemed strange that he should single out the ambassador.

Renata turned to see Lyzander fire his first pistol at the Kasar, and miss. Glaser, too, offered a parting shot, before urging his horse after them.

"Joseph!" Renata shouted as they rounded the corner and he was lost from sight.

None of them had any idea where they were going now, nor the skill to properly guide the plains horses with much deftness. It had been easy to follow Lyzander's lead.

"The storm drains will be over there!" Glaser shouted from behind Renata, before swiftly overtaking her. He pointed to where a small distributary of the Yaro appeared to cut through the south-western closure of the city, but it was difficult to make it out in and amongst the jumble of buildings and smoke. A huge fire was eating large swathes of the city to the south, and vast clouds of black smoke were drifting through the streets.

"This way!" Guillot shouted to Maruska, suddenly cutting left back towards the Spiritsraad, where it was clear a savage firefight was taking place for the core of the city. Glaser, Ozolinsh and Herschel charged on ahead heedless.

"What the . . . Where the hell are you going? Turn back Nema damn you!" Renata shouted at him.

"Nema damn me?!" Guillot said with sudden savagery. He turned around, but he did not even glance at Renata; instead he was looking back down the street to where Maruska's plains horse followed as though enthralled by him.

"I said turn back! You're heading the wrong way!" Renata punched him on the back. "For god's sake, turn—!"

"Shut up, you bloody bitch!"

Renata's next words died in her throat.

Guillot wrestled the horse to the right into a dingy, dirty alley, the surrounding buildings long emptied of their occupants.

"Damn you, man, what is this idiocy!" Maruska called out, pulling fruitlessly against the reins of his horse.

Guillot said nothing. Instead, he turned and shoved Renata square in the chest, so that she tumbled off the back of the horse. She hit the ground hard, and lay there, winded.

The monk dismounted smartly and landed next to her. Renata scrabbled over to the side of a nearby building, her chest clenching and spasming painfully where the muscles of her diaphragm refused to relax. Maruska was shouting incoherently; she heard him dismount from the enormous beast, but she was utterly preoccupied with the advancing Guillot.

"What are you doing? What's going on?!" she croaked, coughing as her mouth filled with smoke and dust and dirt. The sounds of battle were terrifyingly close, perhaps only a couple of streets away.

Guillot ignored her. She noticed for the first time that he held a dirk in his hand.

She looked up, wide-eyed, at Maruska. He was running at Guillot with a speed and ferocity that defied his age and frame.

"No!" Renata heard herself scream.

Guillot punched the dirk squarely into the old man's throat.

Renata's world began to dissolve. A suffocating shock surged through her. Her vision constricted, focusing entirely on Maruska, as though her eyes wished to imprint the image of him dying on her brain for ever like some malevolent pamphleteer.

She couldn't breathe – Maruska couldn't breathe. His throat and lungs filled with blood. He fell to the floor, his wrinkled hands trying in vain to fend off Guillot.

He didn't stand a chance.

The young monk stabbed him again and again with breathtaking dispassion, as though he were nothing more than a mechanical press. Twenty, thirty times, in the chest, face and neck.

Renata's own chest constricted in sympathy. Loud animal moans escaped her mouth. She rolled over on to her side, her shoulder pressing into the hard, warm earth.

The dream. The nightmare. The wall, the fortress, Maruska's savaged form.

Not a dream. Not a nightmare. A *vision*.

An incredible shriek of terror ripped through the fabric of reality as Maruska finally expired, a final insult, his death robbed of any conceivable scrap of dignity.

"Do you have *any* idea what it is like?" Guillot said as he stood and approached her. His malignant nonchalance galled her into fury.

"How could you?" she asked, breathless with rage. "How *could* you?"

There was something about the way he moved, the way he held the dirk, the way he advanced on her.

Realisation hit her, a stab of ice to her gut.

"You," she said. This was the same man who had tried to kill her in Sova. The man on the Creus Road, and in the Dynast's Palace.

"Do you have any idea what it is *like?*" Guillot repeated. He took a step towards her. "*Watching* you?"

Renata's eyes flickered over to where Maruska lay motionless, his blood reddening the already red earth of the Kyarai. "W-watching me?"

"*Watching* you. It is like watching children trying to dam a stream. Throwing rocks in, trying to plug gaps with sediment. Idiotic minds, unable to grasp the fundamental physics of what it is they are trying to achieve. That is what it is like. The stream always wins. Even if you dam the channel, the banks burst. You can only hold it back for so long. Minutes. In our case, days, weeks. The briefest flickers of time."

"What are you talking about?" Renata choked out between angry sobs.

"This. You. The 'diplomatic mission'," he said with caustic sarcasm. "You think you can stop it. You think that through these actions, you can make a difference. But you can't. Because you don't even know what it is you are trying to stop."

"What *are* we trying to stop?" Renata asked. Her back was pressed against the wall. She should have run, and run immediately. She should have forced herself up and fled to the end of the street. The man was only armed with a knife. It was too late now. She had let him close the gap. Now he loomed over her.

"You will know soon enough."

"Who *are* you?"

Guillot paused, thinking. "*Guillot?*" he said out loud, as though asking himself the question. "*Gee—yo.*" He drew it out, savouring the feel of it in his mouth. He turned to her. "I am the Knackerman."

"The . . . what?"

"The Knackerman. And it is time for you to die."

Tears trickled down Renata's cheeks. "You monster," she breathed. "You ghoul. You . . . " Rage blossomed within her. "You *shit!*" and she punched the monk square in the centre of his face –

She froze. Something had happened to Guillot's face. It had . . . *distorted*. As though she had punched a mask made of soft clay.

She watched in horror, feeling her gorge rise, as it began morphing, breaking, creaking and crackling and popping. It sloughed away, and underneath, instead of a human face, was an oval of burnished gold, an inscribed tablet of metal covered in runic ideograms and script from an alphabet she did not recognise. There was no nose, no eyes, no cheeks or mouth or chin, no forehead or hair. It was as if someone had sliced the front of Guillot's skull off and sealed the wound with a tomb plate. He was a clockwork man, an automaton, powered by no earthly processes of life.

Renata couldn't breathe. She tried to shrink away from this

monstrosity, but Guillot – *the Knackerman* – seemed to grow, looming in front of her. An awful buzzing sound filled her ears, and the sickly, earthy smell of decay was in her nose.

"What are you?" she whispered, sweating, weeping, her heart struggling to withstand this assault on her sanity.

JUST A MESSENGER, a voice said in her head. AND THE MESSAGE IS: JUDGEMENT.

Her whole body stiffened as she waited for him to stick the dirk into her throat. She put out her hands instinctively, trying to press the monk away, trying to stop him from stabbing her, trying to do *something, anything,* to put some distance between them. Why did she not run? Nema Victoria, why had she not just *run* when she had the chance?

"Hey!" someone shouted from her left.

Renata turned. At first, her eyes blurred by tears, she thought it was Lyzander; but although this man had the same dark skin tone, it was not the captain. For one thing, he was not wearing any sort of military uniform, but rather a hooded poncho of Kyaran brocade.

Some discorporate screech of frustration echoed through the aether as Guillot lurched forward, trying to stab Renata quickly before this welcome interloper could do anything to stop him; but the man was too quick, bringing his pistol up and firing a single shot which caught Guillot somewhere in the midriff. Renata actually heard the ball impact the monk's torso, a great wet thump that carried with it the smell of burning fabric.

The man closed quickly, drawing a second pistol from his sash.

"Madam Secretary!" he shouted in a south-east Sovan accent. He levelled the second pistol at Guillot, but came up short with a horrified gasp when confronted with the inexplicable ghastliness of the Knackerman. "Wha . . . ?" he said dumbly.

Guillot snarled and threw a handful of sand in the man's eyes. The pistol discharged point-blank, and Renata felt Guillot's blood splash her face.

"Run!" the man shouted as he and Guillot tussled.

She did not need to be told twice. She lurched desperately out of the way, leaping over Maruska's corpse – something she would reflect on with profound melancholy in the days to come – and ran off into the tangle of streets.

She had been fleeing madly and without direction for perhaps five minutes when she heard her name being called.

"Renata! Renata! Madam Secretary!"

She looked up sharply to see Lyzander at the top of the street atop his plains horse.

"Help me!" she screamed.

He urged the horse forward, and in moments was in front of her, holding his hand out. She grabbed his arm frantically and was hauled effortlessly on to the back of the great beast. Seconds later, they were cantering away.

"What the hell happened to you?" he asked her. "Is that your blood?"

Her hand instinctively went to her face where Guillot's blood had sprayed it.

"No," she said, suddenly exhausted.

"What the hell happened?" he repeated.

She gripped him tightly, wanting nothing more than to be out of that cursed city for ever.

"I don't know," she said quietly, tears running down her cheeks. "I don't know."

XX

En-Thralled

"Thanks to the phenomenon of the modern newsman I can have the idiocy of my peers transmitted directly to me at the breakfast table instead of having to wait until I reach the Senate House."

COUNTESS RADMILA KLEMENT

Castle Oldenburg

COUNTY OF HAUNERWALD

He paid unsavoury men to dispose of the corpse of the fusilier in the old dungeon. He probably should have had them clean the room, as well; instead he simply had the maids from the household staff do it. With retrospect, that was a mistake, for however handsomely he paid his people, he could not control everything they said and did. He was subtle in his manipulations and delicate in his murders, but nonetheless had a reputation as an evil man. One day, one of these slayings was going to come back to haunt him.

Yelena absented herself, not from Castle Oldenburg, but certainly from his company. Even that he did not much notice. After the horror of first en-thralling Kyselý, which had left him suffering all manner of intellectual maladies, he had been desperate for her love and approval. But that initial self-revulsion had faded, as it always did – he had felt something similar after his very first murder decades before – and with it his desire for her validation. His relationship with Yelena was a mercurial and cyclical thing; the times he sought her affections coincided precisely with her utility to whatever was his current enterprise.

But with Kyselý docile and responsive to commands, von Oldenburg had become en-thralled in turn with this automaton he had created. He moved Kyselý to a larger chamber, an empty storeroom in the subterranean levels of Castle Oldenburg, and there began to perform experiments on the man.

At first, he brought Kyselý food and drink, leaving it at the far end of the chamber – he was still a little skittish about getting close to the man – as though his former butler were a wild animal he was hoping to tame. Then, in a clear voice, he would command, "Kyselý, eat the food", and the man would eat it. He did so mechanically, and choked often, especially on the drink. That was an issue, since this was no corpse; Kyselý was alive, albeit in an entirely autonomic sense, and required sustenance to remain so. And so von Oldenburg found himself cutting up his meals himself, making sure the pieces were bite-sized, and favouring foodstuffs that the man could easily digest – bread soaked in wine, poached apples, softened onions, creamed cheese, butter.

Another unwelcome byproduct of Kyselý's living death was the waste he produced, worsened in no small measure by the uneven diet. Von Oldenburg had chamber pots produced, and commanded Kyselý to shit in them – which he did – but then von Oldenburg had to empty them himself, for he could not trust anyone else in the castle to do it. For a Sovan count and member of the Council of Nobles, it was an unforgivable debasement. And besides, Kyselý seemed to shit whenever the urge took him, in the way an infant would, rather than at convenient times of the day. Eventually von Oldenburg had the idea of ordering him to take a cup of coffee first thing in the morning, which did not solve the problem entirely, but certainly made it more manageable.

With Kyselý's most immediate needs taken care of, von Oldenburg decided to broaden the scope of his experiments. Initially he simply had Kyselý perform certain actions, like walking in circles around the storeroom, or jumping up and down. Then he progressed to more delicate ones, like having him pick things up and put them down again. It seemed like the man could easily be commanded to do tasks that he had done in life, which as a butler was a great many things, from serving meals to darning ripped clothes and everything in between. Indeed, von Oldenburg did not even need to be particular with his language. Providing the man with needle and thread and simply instructing him to "repair these breeches" had the desired effect. It was as though there were a physical aspect to the man's memory which was residual, something ingrained within the fibres of his body which caused him to respond to commands even in the absence of mental capacity.

Late one afternoon, after perhaps a week of these experiments, he sat down with Yelena in the drawing room. It was a warm day by the standards of Haunerwald, and for once the fire was unlit and the windows were open. The room was filled with honey-coloured light.

"I need to make more," he said eventually. He was smoking his pipe, something he tended to do only in Haunerwald, where the air was clearer. The taste of it reminded him of the streets of Sova, and he felt a strange pang of nostalgia for that benighted city.

"What do you mean?" she asked, though his meaning was clear.

He was quiet for a long, ruminative moment. "I need more of them. Kyselý is nothing more than a proof of concept."

Yelena snorted. "But a few days ago you had frightened yourself insensible with that horror. Now he is, what, trifle of the week?" She nodded to the floorboards, where, somewhere beneath them, Kyselý languished in his chamber, an affront to the natural order of the world.

Von Oldenburg did not like that, but endured it with gritted teeth. "I have a plan, but it would mean leaving Haunerwald. Probably for many months. And I would need to take Kyselý with me."

"He will surely perish if you move him."

Von Oldenburg shook his head absently. "I do not see why. I need him only to create new thralls, not to perform any great feats of manual labour."

"You told me that you and Broz were tracking a Selureii scheme to stifle news of the plague in Draedaland."

"I did say that," he agreed guardedly.

"Well, can we not assume, therefore, that in creating more of these thralls, in communicating the mind rot to more people, you are aligning your goals with those of the Selureii?"

Von Oldenburg scoffed. "Do not be ridiculous. If they had their way, then presumably the whole of Sova would be filled with these vacants. I am simply ... looking at *synergies*. Efficiencies. It seems the Selureii wish for a good portion of the world to end. I wish for the House of Casimir to end. To that limited extent, our purposes *do* align." He smiled, pleased with himself and his logic.

There was a long silence. Eventually Yelena asked, "What is it you plan to do with him. *Them*, I should say. How many are you going to create? To what end?"

Von Oldenburg hesitated a moment. Then he stood with a grunt, and retrieved a map of the Empire and its abutting territories, which he unrolled and weighted down on a desk. "Here," he said, tapping a finger on a territory to the north-east of Hofingen, itself the territory north-east of Haunerwald. "Liendau. I wonder if the mind rot has spread across the River Kova."

"That is enemy territory."

"As far as I'm concerned, every territory outside of Haunerwald is enemy territory."

"I mean that is *Casimir* territory."

"I know. Liendau has long been a Casimiran province. Sparsely populated, its only strategic value lies in providing Casimir with a land bridge to the North Sea. But really, it's just five hundred miles of steppe. It has more in common with Draedaland than Casimir."

"And you plan to, what, invade it?"

He shook his head. "If Draedaland has all but fallen to the mind rot, it stands to reason that Liendau could fall just as easily. The question really is if the rot is able to be transmitted across the Kova. But we will not run into any enemy forces, not really. The bulk of the Casimiran Army is engaged in the Kyarai and the New East."

Yelena thought for a moment. "I still do not understand your plan."

"Our Great Enemy has a soft underbelly in its neglected north. I think an enterprising count at the head of a force of thralls could make a great deal of mischief there."

"A *force* of thralls?"

"Think on it. The mind rot is spread instantaneously and with incredible ease, and the resulting thralls are absolutely pliable – and expendable. In this way, a man could drain the number of men available for his enemy to draw on, whilst simultaneously allying them to his own cause. Every Casimiran man and soldier we infect is both denied to our enemy and added to our ranks. *Think* how quickly the rot would spread through an army of even ten or twenty thousand men standing shoulder to shoulder in ranks. And," he went on, almost shouting now, "it is not just battle. They are an endless source of free labour. Think of the great works the Empire is undertaking – vast canals in the south, thaumaturgic wind generators to power ships, mining operations in the New East. What do all of these things require? Vast numbers of workers. What do vast numbers of workers require?

Salaries, tens of thousands in goldmark. The work could all be done by thralls for a fraction of the cost."

Again, Yelena was silent for a long while as she considered what he was proposing. "Like Kyselý, though, every person so infected would need to be tended to and cared for."

"Would they?" von Oldenburg retorted. "Why?"

"Because they will die for want of water in a matter of days, or for want of food in a matter of weeks. And soldiers in the march require as much in the way of victuals as farm labourers."

"So let them die. That is our ultimate purpose anyway."

Yelena took in a deep breath, and let it out slowly. "What you are describing is a profound evil."

Von Oldenburg waved her off irritably. "'Tis nothing worse than what the Draedists have been doing to one another for years."

"What are you *talking* about?" Yelena snapped. "There is no precedent for this. I do not know what fables you have been reading—"

"I don't mean specifically this," he said angrily. "Do not twist my words, woman. I mean the practice of death magicks. The plague is spreading quickly and virulently. This way we may both control it *and* turn it to our own means." He thought about that some more. "Indeed," he mused, "we might even be able to *sell* the wards. There are plenty of lords and ladies who would part with significant sums of goldmark to be guaranteed protection from the mind rot. We would have to be careful about how we advertised. And then there is the question of how to control the flow of information about the plague itself. For all of the Selureii's efforts, such news will break out in the capital soon, if it has not already. The Privy Council is already aware, as is the Empress, even though they are all currently distracted with the impending loss of the Kyarai . . ."

If Yelena said anything else, he did not hear it. Schemes, thoughts of moneymaking, daydreams of his investiture as the new Emperor having single-handedly destroyed the armies of House Casimir, consumed him for the rest of the afternoon. In fact it was not until late in the evening that he returned to see Kyselý. Normally he would see the man standing in the corner of the chamber, the only sound in the room his quiet, slightly laboured breathing. This time, however, he could sense something was wrong. Kyselý was *sitting* in the corner of the room – something he did not tend to do unless instructed – and with each exhalation he moaned audibly. The sound had the most disarming effect on von Oldenburg. He was not a man naturally given to pity, and he had come to see his former butler as little more than a tool in a very literal sense. But there was something about that noise that humanised the man quite wretchedly.

There was also a pronounced smell emanating from Kyselý, and it wasn't excrement. Von Oldenburg had discovered, after much trial and error around precise wording, that Kyselý could be issued instructions for future behaviours as well – "shit in the chamber pot every time you need to go" – which had at least made the chamber slightly more sanitary. No, this was a different sort of smell; a sickly, pungent scent, like mouldering vegetables in the hot sun.

He stepped towards the man slowly, as though approaching a skittish horse. The smell grew stronger. "Kyselý, stand up," he commanded.

Kyselý stood up, an audible grinding sound coming from his left leg. As he did so, a great wave of stench was wafted over to von Oldenburg.

"What's the matter?" he asked, though Kyselý had no ability to answer. He simply regarded von Oldenburg with a sort of bovine incomprehension.

"Stop looking at me like that, damn you," von Oldenburg muttered, and was of course surprised when Kyselý did precisely that, averting his gaze to focus on some random spot on the far wall.

The smell was certainly coming from the butler's leg. Von

Oldenburg tugged Kyselý's breeches down – he was now as familiar with these indignities as a Neman orderly in Blackmarsh Asylum – and recoiled with a horrified grunt. Several inches of Kyselý's leg around the hip had completely necrotised. The wound was one great suppurating mess, like a lanced boil, oozing pus and utterly enpoxed. A shard of bone, clearly responsible for worrying the wound open over the course of von Oldenburg's experiments, protruded from the ghastly aperture.

"Nema Victoria," he murmured, hand over his mouth. Absently, he bit and worried at the callous there. He looked up at Kyselý again. The man was sweating and feverish. Von Oldenburg placed a hand against his forehead. "Shit," he muttered, and then again, "Shit, shit, shit, fuck and blast!"

He turned on his heel and marched smartly out of the room, closing and locking it, and then made his way up through the castle until he found Yelena in their bedchamber. "Kyselý's broken his damned hip," he said angrily, as though it were her fault. "He must have done it when we first en-thralled him. And I, like a fool, have been having the man march around and jump up and down perform all sorts of useless bloody exercises, and of course all the while he has not uttered one word of protest. Damn!"

Yelena's expression was one of alarm. "How bad is the wound?"

"Absolutely rotten. We'll be lucky if he lasts the night – 'tis a miracle he has not already perished."

Yelena leapt out of bed and quickly donned a nightdress, then left the bedchamber. Von Oldenburg pulled in her wake like a catboat being dragged by a man-o'-war. He followed her as she gathered up a fine leather case – one which von Oldenburg had gifted her, and which he knew to contain all manner of potions and unguents – and together they hurried downstairs.

Inside Kyselý's chamber, the man had not moved, and cut a pathetic figure, standing with his breeches around his knees in a half-crouch as though he were feral. Yelena opened her case and immediately began dousing the wound with carbolic acid. Von Oldenburg sneered at that; for all her pagan herbs and potions, poultices and unguents, even she could not deny the medicinal ingenuity of Sova's best physicians.

Kyselý grunted in pain as the acid was applied, though as a reaction it was automatic. Then she packed the wound with some acrid-smelling paste, and strapped it with a bandage. "Maggots will clean it. We should check the kitchens for any spoiled food. And then he must lie still so as not to worsen the break."

"Surely he will die," von Oldenburg said, desperately hoping she would contradict him.

But to his dismay, she said, "I should think so."

"We will need someone else, then. Another member of the household staff."

Yelena hesitated. "Lamprecht," she said eventually. That focused his attention in itself. She rarely used his Neman name. "I know you are taken with the potential of this—"

"We have not even begun to scratch the surface of its potential," von Oldenburg said immediately. It was a fragment of a well-rehearsed and entirely imagined speech he had been giving to large crowds at the Royal Exhibition Centre. "Imagine it, Yelena. Thousands of thralls, mining for coal, fighting our wars, constructing our temples, digging our canals. Never tiring, never complaining. They don't require pay, don't require coddling or praise or encouragement. Utterly compliant, utterly expendable. I can see a time when everybody has one such thrall in their house, someone to perform mundane tasks—"

"By Nema, Lamprecht, these are *corpses*! They are walking, breathing, eating and shitting *corpses*! They are *vacant*, waiting to die. Entirely liminal beings. You are so consumed by this you have lost sight of how *utterly* ghoulish it is."

Von Oldenburg shook his head, irritated, tired, disappointed, but not angry. "You have always lacked clarity of vision. Just leave the thinking to me, my wife." With slightly trembling hands, he pulled out the bottle of tonic from his breast pocket and took another mouthful of that bitter liquid. Then, with his handkerchief, he dabbed away the sudden and extreme oversupply of saliva that filled his mouth. "I need my mechanism, my amplifier. We might have as little as one night left to examine the thaumaturgic properties of the ideograms and how they interact with Kyselý's autonomic system. They may yet be a way to duplicate the effects of the mind rot without requiring its transmission from someone already en-thralled."

Yelena just looked at him. "You used to value my counsel."

"It is as it has ever been," von Oldenburg muttered, waving her off. "Tomorrow we shall have to have a brand fashioned. Take a quill and some paper from my drawing room and make as detailed a study of that ideogram as you can." He examined the cut which Yelena had made on to Kyselý's forehead, itself somewhat inflamed. "I wonder what happens if the ideogram is ruined somehow, or even obscured. Do its effects persist? Or must he be re-marked? Whatever the answer is, it is clear we are going to need someone else to take his place, and soon. If you have no stomach for it, then you will have the brand fashioned. Go as soon as you have drawn the diagram, and offer the smith a hundred goldmark to make it and keep his fucking mouth shut about it. Do you understand?"

Yelena understood. She said nothing, but she understood. She left, and von Oldenburg turned back to the old butler. "Rest now, Kyselý," he murmured; and then, as if to a dog, "Lie down."

Kyselý lay down. An alien emotion stirred within von Oldenburg's gut, a feeling that perhaps Yelena was right, and he should simply abandon this enterprise now. There was still a chance to end it, to turn back, to step away from the edge.

Instead, he shook his head, and took another drink of tonic, then left the chamber to find some brandy.

It was going to be a long night.

With Kyselý slowly dying – or rather, quickly dying – and Yelena occupied in copying the ideogram for mass manufacture, von Oldenburg returned to his study and began pulling out books from the shelves.

He had the mechanism next to him, and held it in his left hand in the same way a royal would hold an orb at their investiture. This nameless piece of equipment was the result of thousands of days of work and study. He knew that scientists at the University and the Corps of Engineers were working together to create "cells", metal-fluid mediums in which energy could be stored. It was these primitive experiments which had given him the idea to create this mechanism, his thaumaturgic equivalent. It was intended to harness and store the power of the afterlife, in much the same way Kyselý had, and was a conduit – or rather, it was supposed to be. It did not work, and never had done. But he was convinced that his latest run of experiences in Draedaland presented the key with which the mystery could finally be unlocked.

The main difference between electrochemical energy and thaumaturgic energy, to von Oldenburg's mind, was that the former was constrained by the laws of nature, whilst the latter was not. The former dissipated and died, much like the inefficient steam mechanisms he had seen in the Royal Exhibition. Thaumaturgic energy was infinite, and infinitely powerful, and seemed predominantly "bioaethereal" in nature – a term which von Oldenburg had concocted himself and which he was desperate to share. A great source of his frustration came from what he considered to be his unrecognised – and, thanks to the law, unrecognis*able* – genius in this cutting-edge field.

Bioaethereal energy was a type of energy which concerned the interaction of human beings, the immutable substance of their minds and souls, and the dimensional realities which existed beyond the mortal planes. Von Oldenburg, like some mediaeval scholars of the afterlife, considered that the so-called "holy dimensions" were not holy at all, but had simply been made so by unsophisticated minds trying to understand and taxonomise something which was to them inherently unknowable. Beings which had been worshipped as gods and angels and demons were not so; rather, they were just different and unfamiliar forms of life. It was one of the many reasons why he despised the silly pagan rituals which had infected human attempts at contacting and otherwise dealing with the afterlife. All that was required – all that had ever been required – was the scientific method.

Yelena was unconvinced, but then she was hidebound and shackled to the pagan way of thinking.

Von Oldenburg examined the texts and the mechanism, making notes, flicking through the pages, trying to see *behind* what Neman scholars had written. In his journal, he wrote:

Process:

1 *Instigation*
   a *Mind rot is transmitted through skin contact with nearest infected person*
   b *Infectee immediately loses conscious brain function*
   c *Unexplained sound (human scream(s)?) accompanies transmission but with no earthly source (<u>deeply</u> unsettling)*

2 *Intermediate stage*
   a *Infectee ("vacant") seeks fresh victim to transmit mind rot*
   b *If no nearby victim, infectee remains dormant & autonomic function persists*
   c *After c.2–3 days infectee dehydrates & expires*

3 *Further transmission*
   a *Infectee (infectee 1) transmits mind rot through skin*
     contact to new victim (infectee 2)
   b *Steps 1 a–c above repeat for infectee 2*
   c *Infectees 1 & 2 repeat 1 a / 2 b–c*

4 *Warding*
   a *Step 1 a etc. can be prevented with prophylactic*
     warding (see fig. 1)

5 *En-thrallment*
   a *Vacants can be en-thralled post step 1 b with*
     ideogramic binding (see fig. 2) applied directly to skin
   b *Vacants respond to spoken commands*
   c *Vacants will expire without victuals (NB 2 c)*

He paused for a moment, listening.

"Hm," he grunted. He thought he had heard something out of the ordinary, but decided he had not.

He turned back to his journal:

Conjecture:

Given 1 c above, the mind rot appears to be arcane in nature.

I speculate that it is direct exposure to the spirit realm which is stripping these brains of their sensibilities.

This being the case, the vacants are in essence open <u>conduits</u> to the spirit realm.

Akin to an uncontrolled / un-warded séance.

"Transmission" / "contagion" inappropriate terms.

More like "exposure".

But:

Sovan argonauts have been travelling to the afterlife for centuries with no reported cases of vacancy (cf. Case of Magistrate Resi August? Check G. V. Jadran hospice records).

   Mind rot = <u>not</u> the transmission of a thaumaturgic pox from one person to another, but rather some active force <u>within</u> the bioaethereal energy which deletes the essence of a person's mind.

   Theory: is the energy akin to an aethereal suspension, within which is some particulate matter deleterious to consciousness? (Akin to so-called "sub-scopic organisms" posited to create earthly poxes?)

He paused again. "Who's there?" he asked the empty study. He looked over to the window, but it was dark and quiet outside. He turned and checked the door, but it was closed and locked. "Is someone out there?" he demanded.

Silence.

He grunted, and returned to the journal once more.

Selureii: Draedist death-cult based in Verdabaro.

   Have been tracking Selureii activity in Sova for some time. Most recently they have attempted to destroy news of mind rot plague spreading.

   Selureii obviously keen to hasten & intensify ~~contagion~~ exposure.

   Exposure to mind rot in urban areas (e.g. Sova): uncontrollable & catastrophic.

   Selureii attempt to destroy the Empire? Or broader humanity? <u>To what end?</u>

   Task: given change in circumstances (wards, en-thrallment, & cetera), reattempt to make direct contact with Selureii in Verdabaro?

THE KEY IS BLOOD, a voice said from the far corner of the study.

Von Oldenburg looked up sharply. He squinted, but he could see nothing. It was the middle of the night, and the only light was provided by candles. It left much of the study, and its huge collection of curios and forbidden volumes, shrouded in deep darkness.

He was no stranger to the arcane and the horrors of its exploration. He had experienced many unsettling things – not least the aethereal screaming he had heard during his misadventure north. But there was something about this . . .

"Who is that?" he demanded. He managed to sound indignant, though his heart was pounding. What was it about the middle of the night that exacerbated these things?

The darkness seemed to deepen. The study had been quiet before, subject to the rustling of wildlife, the watchman's labours, the creaking and groaning of hundreds of tonnes of castle stone shifting and contracting in the night's cold. Now it was silent. So silent that the silence became an imposition. His blood sang in his ears, and he could hear the squirming and pulsing of his heart and guts.

He dared not move.

"Who's there?" he asked again, with the comparative volume of a cannon firing.

THE KEY . . . the voice replied, though it sounded more like three voices, speaking in unison, IS BLOOD.

Von Oldenburg had opened his mouth to once again make demands of this discorporate interloper, when an enormous deluge of blood crashed into the chamber like water through a smashed dam.

"Nema Victoria!" he shouted, leaping to his feet, the chair flying. He staggered backwards, connecting with another table behind him. The torrent was endless, a thousand thousand gallons of hot red blood, smashing into everything, shattering windows, filling the study more quickly than it could escape.

Surely he would drown, or be swept away on the flood to be dashed against the hard stone walls, or pinned there by the sheer force until his lungs filled with it.

DO NOT . . . SAY . . . THAT *NAME*! roared the voice—

≈

Von Oldenburg jolted awake and staggered to his feet, paper stuck to his face, the mechanism a sudden weapon in his hand ready to be shot-putted into the face of the interloper.

But there was nothing.

No one.

He took a few moments to steady himself, snatching the piece of paper from his face and setting down the mechanism with less care than it was due. It was dawn, and the candles had all burned down to the nub. He emitted a small, irritated noise; it was a waste of wax and money.

The castle was silent, but it was regular, corporeal silence; not even a true silence, but one filled with the distant sounds of the various processes of life. As silent as the real world ever got.

Already the nightmare was fading from memory like a stone dropped into a murky lake. The fear, which had consumed him so viscerally, felt like a distant, alien thing, like a description of a feeling relayed by someone else.

He shivered. Not quite distant enough. He looked over to the corner again, but it was of course empty. For all the dream had made him feel, nothing was as disquieting in the grey light of morning.

He sat down and picked up his pen, and began to make more notes. He had spent too long dabbling in the arcane to ignore the importance of such a nightmare, especially one which had felt so frighteningly real – even if, perversely, it was becoming already difficult to recall.

The key is <u>blood</u>???

His skin broke out in gooseflesh as he recalled the voice which had issued this prophetic message and then raged at him. There had been a *force* behind that anger, a tangible, elemental force so powerful it had warped the fabric of reality. It was best not to dwell on it too much. Von Oldenburg was keen to unlock the secrets of the afterlife, but he was not so bullheaded that he wanted to tangle with its more . . . *malign* elements.

"The key to *what?*" he asked the room.

His eyes settled on the mechanism.

A thought struck him.

He snatched it up, and hurried down into the depths of Castle Oldenburg, to seek out Kyselý before he died.

In spite of Yelena's ministrations, it was clear that Kyselý remained on the brink of death. The man lay on the floor, unmoving except for the shallow rise and fall of his ribcage. His breath was laboured, rattling his throat.

Von Oldenburg pulled the tonic from his breast pocket reflexively and took another swig, dabbed the drool from his mouth with a handkerchief, then replaced the cork and put the bottle back in his pocket.

"Kyselý, stand up," he said.

The thrall stood with a great grinding of bones and an expectoration of foetid matter which had escaped the poultice. Immediately he sagged dramatically to the left, collapsed to one knee, and then keeled over. In spite of his obvious inability to do so, he kept trying to stand, a slave to the instruction. This was too much even for von Oldenburg, and he said, "Kyselý, sit down, for the gods' sake."

Kyselý sat down. There was something so mournful about his former butler, von Oldenburg hoped that what he was about to do worked, so that he did not have to deal with the man further.

Yelena had left her physician's case in the cell – there was no danger of Kyselý interfering with it – and von Oldenburg rummaged through it until he found a razor. Then he advanced on the thrall, circling round to the right so as to avoid the worst of the smell, and squatted down next to him.

"Sorry, Kyselý, old chap," he muttered, as if by speaking flippantly he might trick himself into thinking he was not committing a profound evil, and with the razor sliced open Kyselý's left leg.

The thrall whimpered, but did not move.

His blood flowed sluggishly. Von Oldenburg opened the mechanism at its apex; inside was a container for a lodestone, a feature of the most recent prototypes, which he had developed as part of his thaumaturgic energy transmission theory. There was a thought: he had left one of those prototypes in his bedchamber. He made a mental note to retrieve it for redundancy purposes.

The blood flowed into the lodestone container as though he were filling up a flask of wine. All the while, the mysterious message percolated through his mind.

The key is blood.

Had the key always been blood? It stood to reason that the life-giving fluid, ritualised for the entire span of human memory, held some special significance within bioaethereal thaumaturgy; but precisely how to harness its power was something that had not yet occurred to either von Oldenburg or his many scholarly predecessors – at least, not the Sovan ones. He wondered idly how Broz was getting on. The diplomatic mission must have reached Port Talaka by now.

The container in the centre of the mechanism filled to the brim, and he closed the little hatch on the top of the brass orb and withdrew it. Then he laid a hand on Kyselý's right shoulder.

"Rest now, Kyselý," he said quietly, and the thrall duly lay down. "Not long now, eh?"

Underneath his leg, Kyselý's lifeblood continued to leak and pool.

Von Oldenburg hurried back through the castle to his study, where he carefully set the mechanism in its cradle, then went to find another of his servants. Of Yelena, there was still no sign; hopefully she had gone to the blacksmith as he had instructed.

He moved quickly through the many corridors and halls. For the first time in the castle's bloody existence, it seemed to be empty, and part of him briefly wondered if Yelena had warned the household staff away. Something had changed with her lately, something which was making her more . . . *compassionate*. She had always been something of a foil to him, but she had seemed even more so in recent weeks, and especially since he had en-thralled Kyselý. He would speak to her again, when there was time. Now, more than ever, he needed someone by his side who, even if they did not agree with his methods, understood them.

Eventually he gave up in the halls of the castle proper and went into the servants' quarters. He immediately ran into a young scullery maid, who looked very flustered to see him.

"My lord count," she said, curtsying so low her knees almost touched the bare stone floor. "W-we are just preparing breakfast . . ."

"What's your name, girl?" he asked. He was feeling a little ma-niacal, as sometimes happened after he ingested too much tonic.

"Ž-Žofia," she stammered. She could not have been older than twenty.

"Come with me at once," he said, and he turned on his heel and made his way back to his study. The maid was so diminutive that he had to check constantly to see if she was following him, for her footsteps made almost no sound.

"In here," he said, gesturing her into his study. Like Kyselý had been, she was hesitant to the point of impertinence. "Now, damn you!" he thundered, and she let out a small squeal and hurried in to what to her must have looked like a chamber of insanity.

Von Oldenburg walked over to where he had set the mechanism. It seemed to glow ever so slightly, shrouded in a pink-orange luminescence as though it radiated dawn's light. When he picked it up, there was a warmth to it.

"This is a thaumaturgic amplifier," he said, cradling it like the head of a newborn. He walked towards her slowly. "I designed it to hold thaumaturgic energy so that it could be released on command. See here the inscriptions? The ideograms of containment? Much like the wards we used to . . . Well," he said. He was not so given to madness as to be blind to the maid's obvious confusion and fear.

He licked his lips slightly feverishly, his heart pounding, and took another step towards her. "Here," he said. He spoke with a jarring, absurd levity that did nothing except make the maid extremely suspicious. "You should take it."

She shook her head, matching his step forward with a step back. "No thank you, my lord."

"There is nothing to worry about. I just want to show you something."

The maid cast about the study. "Is the Lady Yelena not available?"

Von Oldenburg gritted his teeth. "Do not mind about the Lady Yelena. I want you to take it."

The maid took another step back. "What is that on the side?"

Von Oldenburg looked down to see Kyselý's blood browning the mechanism. The stain had no plausible explanation beyond the truth, and he did not even attempt to give one.

"Just put it in your hand. Here, be careful to keep it upright."

"I do not want to," the maid said.

"Fucking *take it!*" von Oldenburg snapped, striding forwards to close the gap between them. The maid staggered backwards in a sudden blind panic, but ran into a desk and in her haste tripped and fell to the floor. In seconds von Oldenburg was above her. He grabbed her wrist roughly even as she began to scream, and slapped the mechanism into her hand like a grenade.

Her screams transmuted instantly from real to aethereal. As the real world fell silent, so the afterlife echoed with the maid's shrieking lamentation.

There was something else, too.

The sound of distant, malignant laughter.

Von Oldenburg was trembling with disgust and horror and excitement. The maid collapsed to the floor, her brain stripped of its sensibilities. She struggled fruitlessly to infect him, grabbing at him with her small hands, but of course with the wards that Lena had originally spoken to protect him, it had no effect.

After a little while, she lay still, and lapsed into dormancy.

She was ready to replace Kyselý as his next test subject.

"I've done it," von Oldenburg whispered, carefully retrieving the mechanism and setting it up on the desk. Again that small part of his mind, the salient of sanity, railed against this crime against the natural order of the world; and in a brief concession to this vestigial conscience, he vomited on to the study floor. *I should have used a man*, he thought. *I should have taken more time, sourced some criminals from the town gaol, men who were scheduled for execution.* Sickness and elation clashed within him. He was appalled with himself, and yet could not help but feel he was one of the most brilliant minds of his generation.

He went to the study door and closed and locked it, still shaking, his mind racing. So much to do, so much to *do*. He began immediately pulling out more volumes, freshening his pen, opening his journal to a new page, considering what new runes and ideograms might complement this new-found power.

Gone from his mind was how he had made this great leap of inspiration in the first place; who – or more pressingly, what – had set him on this path in the quiet dark of the night.

Indeed, in and amongst his frantic excitement, he did not think to ask *why*.

XXI

Rot Your Soul

"If strength is the measure of a soldier, let
compassion be the measure of a diplomat."

FROM MANAGOLD'S
THE GLASS SABRE

Port Talaka

KASAR KYARAI

They charged through the streets with reckless speed, until
they were reunited with the rest of their party on Nuadha
Street. By some miracle – for Lyzander's instructions had been
vague and rushed – Glaser, Ozolinsh and Herschel had found
their way to the storm drain outflow. It was a broad channel
of saltwater concrete, the sides sloped, the base flat, ten yards
across in the pan. On the northern side was a large stone embankment, whilst the southern side was open to allow the
floodwater from the Yaro Delta to overspill. This part of the
outflow channel actually delved down underneath a large
part of the eastern closure of the city, so that it formed a broad
tunnel that most people would have mistaken for overgenerous

sewerage. An iron grate, jammed up with tree branches and foul-smelling sludge from last time the river burst its banks, blocked their entry. Above it, perhaps in an effort to distract from the unsightly nature of the outflow, was a large statue of a wolf wrought from jadestone.

"Renata!" Glaser and Ozolinsh shouted.

"Madam Secretary!" Herschel added. He looked past her shoulder. "Where is Brother Guillot?"

"Much more pressingly, where is the ambassador?" Glaser asked.

And then they all cried out in shock and dismay as Renata plucked the pistol from Lyzander's sash and, trembling with ferocious anger, aimed it squarely at Herschel's chest.

"What are you people?" she demanded.

"Madam Secretary!" Glaser shouted. "What the devil is going on?"

"Renata, we don't have time for this," Lyzander said from behind her.

"These monks," Renata said, not taking her eyes off Herschel, "they are not human."

Glaser frowned. "Madam—"

"Guillot killed Maruska!"

"*What?*" Glaser thundered, turning to Herschel. Behind him, Ozolinsh's hand went to her mouth. Herschel looked at her, wide-eyed.

"What are you talk—"

"Shut up. Shut *up!*" Renata gritted her teeth, her finger tightening against the trigger. She thought of the way Guillot had stabbed the ambassador in that brisk, businesslike way, over and over again, relentless. The image would haunt her for ever.

"Renata," Lyzander said from directly in front of her. He spoke over his right shoulder, with his arms up as though the gun were pointing at him; now he gently rested his hand on her forearm. "Please."

"Madam Secretary, lower the gun," Glaser called out to her. "We need this man."

"If he even is a man!"

Glaser looked at Herschel. He gestured to Renata. "For Nema's sake, what is she talking about?"

Herschel spluttered in confusion. "Colonel, I do not know, I swear it!"

"The other one. The other monk," Renata sneered. "*Guillot*. He was not human."

"He was hardly a Kasar!" Glaser snapped. The sounds of battle were drawing closer. "Can we please rake over this later?"

Renata felt Lyzander slowly increasing the pressure on her forearm, pressing the gun down and away from Herschel. She resisted, but only slightly. The old monk *did* seem genuinely bemused.

"He had ..." she said, her voice failing, "he had no face."

"No face?"

She made a frustrated noise. There was too much to say, and not enough time.

"It was *him*, Colonel. It was him in Sova. On the Creus Road. In the Dynast's Palace."

In front of her, Herschel looked alarmed. "Colonel, I promise you I have no notion of what—"

"The man in the Dynast's Palace was not Brother Guillot, Renata," Glaser said. "I know we did not get a good look at him, but of that I am certain."

"He can change his features. His face, it was like a glamour. Like a mask, made from ..." Renata let out a great cry of exasperation, gripping the pistol tightly in her hand and re-aiming it at Herschel's chest. "I cannot sit here and explain it to everyone! These monks are up to something and they are not telling us!"

"Brother Herschel." Glaser spoke levelly. In the circumstances, it was an incredible indulgence. "Is it possible that Guillot was supplanted by an impostor?"

Herschel swallowed, sweating. "He has been out of sorts for some days now. Perhaps weeks. Ah! I have said it – I have *said* it! Didn't I say it?"

"He has said it," Ozolinsh called out, eyeing the city behind them as more and more of the streets filled with the rolling thunder of musketry and cannon fire.

"Please, Madam Secretary, I swear I do not know what is happening," Herschel implored.

"That's enough, I think," Lyzander said. He took the pistol from her unresisting hand and tucked it back into his sash. "We can discuss this later."

"Aye," Glaser said, dismounting. "Let us be about it, before we are all killed."

"Didi was murdered!" Renata shouted.

"And I am very sorry to hear it!" Glaser shouted back. He turned to Lyzander, and gestured to the storm drain. "Captain! Get on with it!"

Lyzander sighed and expertly dismounted the plains horse. Renata found herself being pulled off after him, caught in his arms, and deposited on to the ground.

"This is not done with," she said, levelling a finger at Herschel.

"Shut up, the pair of you!" Glaser roared. "Captain, I assume you mean for us to enter the sewer here?"

"'Tis not a sewer, but yes. The gate looks locked and that is by design, but it is not; here, all of you help me with the debris."

Renata spared Herschel one last venomous glance, and then set to dragging the muddy, effluent-smothered leaves and branches out of the rusty gate. As much as she wanted to fold in on herself over the murder of Maruska, there was simply too much to occupy her.

They cleared the blockage within a matter of moments, and then Lyzander and Glaser yanked the gate open, and they were running into that foetid darkness.

"You smuggled antiquities out of the Spiritsraad this way?" Glaser asked. The sounds of the Jade Sea and the thunderous barrages from the Casimiran Navy were dramatically amplified by the concrete tunnel.

"Just so," Lyzander replied, distracted.

They thrashed their way through the outflow, through water that was ankle deep and black with age. Renata saw other tunnels branching off from the main channel, and got the sense of a much broader network of outflows and sewerage. It made sense in a place like Port Talaka, given how interwoven it was with the Yaro Delta. A few good storms in the Reenwound, hundreds of miles to the west, would dump uncountable thousands of gallons of water into the river basin. If not for this massive and sturdy network of drains, Port Talaka would be washed away.

Without Lyzander they would have become lost, and exceptionally quickly. The tunnels were in no way designed with navigation in mind, and it was only thanks to the captain's recent history that they were able to find their way. It was not long before he was levering up a heavy metal grate leading directly into a storeroom beneath the Spiritsraad. Renata was beginning to think that they would have been better off leaving behind Ozolinsh and Herschel – and certainly Maruska – on the outskirts of the city, for they served no useful purpose except multiplicity of action. But halfway through thinking this, she cried out as Ozolinsh battered into her from the side and dragged her to the floor.

She was about to let out a cry of outrage when she saw an enormous Kasar, clad in a black cuirass and white sarong, wielding a halberd that was easily as tall as the wolfman himself. He had come very close to decapitating Renata, mistaking her for a Casimiran saboteur. It was only when Lyzander began shouting in hasty Kasarsprek and holding his hands out in a desperate gesture of placation that the wolfman calmed down.

"Ran-Juma, Ran-Juma, ik ben het! Je kent me!"

"Lyzander, wat doe jij hier in vredesnaam?!" the Kasar shouted angrily. Renata noticed he was wearing a necklace of braided leather, from which dangled a medallion of silver – the haloed deer's head of Nema Victoria. This wolfman, then, was a member of the Hyernakryger, the élite Kasari regiment responsible for the security of the Spiritsraad. Once a largely ceremonial force, they had found fresh purpose with the conversion of the northern Kyarai to Neman Victorianism.

The wolfman gestured, and Renata looked at where the blade of the halberd had smashed into the plaster of the storeroom wall.

"*We zijn hier om de Dwelkspreker te redden!*" Lyzander said.

"*De Dwelkspreker?*"

"*Ja!*"

"Damn it, man, what are you saying?" Glaser demanded. "Do you know this Kasar?"

Lyzander rounded on him, flushed and dripping with sweat. "This is Ran-Juma," he said, breathing deeply. "Yes, I know him, damn you." He turned back to Ran-Juma, and they exchanged further frantic discussion in Kasarsprek. The wolfman took in this band of filthy and bedraggled Sovans before him, and then, with a very human rolling of the eyes, indicated the door at the far end of the tunnel, and they all fell into step behind him.

"He is going to help us?" Renata asked Lyzander.

Lyzander nodded. "They have been trying to get the Dwelkspreker to leave for weeks. He does not think we are going to be able to."

"But he is going to let us try?"

"Oh yes."

They followed the Hyernakryger through the base levels of the Spiritsraad. The building was enormous, a stepped pyramid five hundred feet tall – and situated on a natural hill, making it taller still – filled with tunnels and chambers and vaults and all manner of chapels, shrines, and areas for the faithful to congregate. At the very top was the Spiritsraad itself, a drum-shaped and domed temple of ink-black stone, where the wolfmen's spiritual conclave resided.

"How do you know him?" Renata asked Lyzander.

"Same reason I know how to get into this place. Same reason he was guarding the entrance."

"From your smuggling of antiquities?"

"Under a letter of marque," Lyzander protested.

Ran-Juma led them to a staircase which went to the very top of the temple, an endless sequence of cramped, dark and stuffy switchbacks built in a shaft in the centre of the pyramid. Around them, the undressed stone walls transmitted the sounds of the battle taking place on the steps of the pyramid, as a rearguard of Sovans, Hyernakryger and other Kasari soldiers fought to hold off the Casimirs and their Sudreik Kasari allies and were slowly blasted to cinders by the constant naval bombardment from the Jade Sea.

Renata's thoughts dwelt entirely on the ghastly faceless visage of Guillot during the ascent. She had meant to keep an eye on Herschel, but he, unfit, and Ozolinsh, also unfit and certainly the shortest of all of them, lagged far behind. Even Renata, who was not much given to exercise for its own sake save for long walks around the royal parks of Sova, felt these labours keenly. She perspired abominably, the muscles of her legs were laced with fire and acid, and she felt as though she were going to be sick by the time they surmounted the final step and exited the shaft into the main hall of the Spiritsraad.

Beyond the threshold was a polished floor of cream-coloured stone shot through with veins of emerald, whilst a ring of intricately carved idols, each easily thirty feet tall, held up the vast domed ceiling. In the centre of the main chamber was a massive statue wrought from onyx, which depicted Nema Victoria – jarring and alien in that hot, distant land.

The place was packed with soldiers.

Dozens of Sovans from a mishmash of regiments were ripping the place to pieces, using anything they could find – barrels, sacks of vestments, pews – to make barricades. Statues wrought from jade and marble were toppled to create redoubts, doors were wrenched off their hinges, others were braced with iron braziers. The smell of smoke and brackish ocean air hung heavy, driven by the hot winds of the Kyarai.

"*Hier, hier, schiet op!*" Ran-Juma shouted. Their arrival drew absolutely no attention at all. Officers, both human and Kasari, directed soldiers and Hyernakryger to positions around the door. Renata let out a small yelp as the men at the main entrance to the temple fired frantically at bluecoats advancing up the sides of the Spiritsraad, clambering up the steps like apes in the Reenwound.

They cut through an ambulatory and past a side chamber that had been hastily converted into a field hospital, and finally Ran-Juma led them into a small chapel. This was little more than an alcove segregated from the corridor. At the far end was an altar with a human-sized statue of Nema, arms and wings spread, holding in her hands the altar itself, which had been decorated with a brocade runner and several candles. The smell of incense hung heavy in the air.

Sitting in front of the altar in some sort of meditative state was an elderly, stooped, grey-furred Kasar, clad in nothing except a white sarong.

"*Is dit de Dwelkspreker?*" Lyzander asked Ran-Juma.

"*Ja, dit is ze.*"

Lyzander clapped the big Hyernakryger on the shoulder. At no point did the priestess in the chamber turn.

"Thank you," Renata said to Ran-Juma, but he ignored her, instead speaking to the priestess in a rapid-fire stream of Kasari which not even Lyzander could understand. Still, it was clear to Renata that the Hyernakryger was imploring this shaman, this high priestess, this "Dwelkspreker", to quit the Spiritsraad whilst there was still time.

They all stood there in that hot, cramped chamber, parched and light-headed and nauseated by the cloying smell of incense. Renata willed this exchange to end, whether it yielded fruit or not. She was painfully, urgently aware of the enemy closing in – and more pressingly of their religious motivations, which might dissuade them from giving the quarter that the law of civilised warfare demanded. The urge to simply turn tail and flee and abandon this insanity altogether was a strong one.

Eventually the Dwelkspreker turned to face them. What figures they must have cut. For Renata's own part, with her blouse unbuttoned, her breast band was clearly visible and dark with sweat. She looked more like a peasant washerwoman from Blackmarsh than her Excellency the ambassador to the Stygion mer-men. To be so presented in Sova would have been enough to have her committed to a psychiatric institution, but such was her discomfort that even a number of unsubtle glances from Lyzander were not enough to see her cover up.

"What's she saying, Captain?" Glaser asked as the elderly priestess spoke.

"She says . . . she has seen us . . ."

"How can she have?"

"Colonel, please!" Renata snapped.

"Shut up!" Ozolinsh said at the same time.

" . . . in her . . . dreams? Visions? Like a . . . " Lyzander snapped his fingers impatiently.

"*Teken*," Ran-Juma said.

"Yeah, like a sign. An augury, a portent."

Renata could well believe it, given the horrors she had had to endure in her sleep.

"She says . . . she says it is coming . . . Like us, she has seen it, she and the other shamans have experienced a . . . "

"*Ontwrichting*," Ran-Juma said.

"I don't know what that means."

The Kasar grabbed his left bicep in his right hand and motioned up and down, making a clicking noise with his mouth.

"Dislocation?" Renata chanced.

"Yes," Lyzander said.

In the great hall behind them there was a huge blast of musketry and a cacophony of shouting and growling. Thanks to the domed roof and abundance of marble, the noise was calamitous.

"In the name of Nema Victoria, if she'll not come willingly, can we not just drag her out?" Glaser said through gritted teeth.

Next to him, the Hyernakryger bellowed his sudden outrage, having understood if not the content of Glaser's statement then certainly its tenor.

"Everybody shut up, I can't hear a fucking thing," Lyzander snapped. The Dwelkspreker continued to speak quite heedless of these many interruptions. "She says they haven't been able to ... com ... communi ... *commune* with the spirits for some weeks now ..."

"Is there a prophecy, damn it?! Ask her about the Great Silence!"

"*Ether* ... the ... Nema, *ziel?*" Lyzander murmured, wincing as he tried to hear, comprehend and translate, all whilst the bluecoats closed in. He snapped his fingers impatiently. "*Dwelkspreker, Grote Stilte? Grote Stilte? Ja?*"

The priestess nodded. "*Grote Stilte, ja.*"

"Yes, they have it – they know what it is. They have a, well, they have a phrase for it, if nothing else. Not sure how much further that ..." He paused a moment to listen to the Dwelkspreker's next words. "*Er is niets wat je kunt doen?*" he repeated.

"What is that? What does that mean?" Renata asked.

"There's nothing we can do."

"Nonsense," Glaser spat.

"There has to be something."

"*Verrot je ziel,*" the Dwelkspreker said. Then she shrugged.

"Rot your soul," Lyzander murmured. He turned to Ran-Juma. "Rot my soul? *Verrot je ziel?*"

"*Ja.*"

"Excellent. She's insulting us now. Fantastic. Damn and blast this nonsense, we need to go if we've any hope of getting out of here," Glaser said, grabbing the nearest person, which happened to be Ozolinsh. She aggressively pulled her arm out of the colonel's grip.

"Get off me!" she muttered angrily.

"Wait," Lyzander said, himself reaching out absently to grab the nearest person, which happened to be Renata. She instinctively slapped him away.

"Nema Victoria," Glaser breathed as the Dwelkspreker produced a ruby the size of a fist, wrapped in a piece of cloth and cupped reverentially in her hands.

"*Het Bloedoog*," she whispered.

The room darkened and drew in. Renata could hear distant screams, but screams which could not be accounted for by the closing battle. She went briefly cross-eyed, overcome with a sense of vertigo. It was clear that everyone else in the room was similarly affected.

"That's the Blood Stone," Ozolinsh whispered.

"What's that?" Renata asked.

"A sacred artefact. A powerful thaumic amplifier. It concentrates and channels the energies of the afterlife in ways which allowed for the Kasar to practise their death sorceries." Ozolinsh realised everybody was looking at her. "At least, that's what the legends say."

The Dwelkspreker wrapped the Blood Stone back in its cloth and then placed the parcel in a small, plain-looking chest that had been inscribed with a number of runes. Immediately the lid was closed, the chapel seemed to brighten, and the screams – at least those aethereal in nature – died away.

"She's telling us to take it," Lyzander said, and he did so, much to the obvious discontent of the Hyernakryger.

"That's it? Nothing more?" Glaser asked. "Our mission is to rescue these people ..."

"She will not come," Lyzander said. As if to punctuate this, the Dwelkspreker turned back to the shrine of Nema and resumed her silent vigil.

"Ik moet je iets laten zien," Ran-Juma said hurriedly to Lyzander.

"Wat dan?"

"Kom."

⁓

They followed the Hyernakryger through a few short corridors. These felt like serviceways, the sort that scullery maids would use, far removed from the grandiose ostentation of the larger Spiritsraad and its temples.

Shortly they came to a door with a large and thick glass panel embedded at head height. The door, Renata noticed, was heavily reinforced, strapped with iron and bolted from the outside. Approaching it gave her a strong sense of foreboding.

Ran-Juma gestured for them to look, and they did. Inside was a single Kasari shaman, naked by her own design – her robes lay shredded and strewn about the place as though she had been gripped by a fit of madness – and standing stock still in the far left corner. Her head drooped low as though she had been rendered insensible, and a streamer of drool dangled from her lower lip. In the room was the paraphernalia of séance, scattered about, destroyed.

Lyzander spoke to Ran-Juma in Kasarsprek.

"Quarantaine," Ran-Juma said at the end of the conversation.

"Quarantine?" Lyzander repeated.

"Ja."

"What did he say?" Glaser asked.

"After they lost contact with the spirits, one shaman volunteered to commune in isolation." He gestured to the door. "This is the result."

Renata eyed the Kasar with a feeling of profound distress bubbling in her gut. "What happened to her?" she murmured.

Lyzander spoke to Ran-Juma again, but the wolfman just shrugged. *"Ik hoopte eigenlijk dat je het mij kan vertellen."*

"What did he say?"

"He said he was hoping we could tell him," Lyzander said.

There was a loud explosion which seemed to shake the very foundations of the Spiritsraad. Dust tumbled from the rafters of the chapel. All of them traded one last nervous glance.

"Time to go," Glaser said.

They went.

XXII

Fate's Injunction

"Why must we ritualise and clothe the existence of the afterlife and its inhabitants in religious orthodoxy? They have the means to communicate with us, albeit in oblique and arcane ways. We beseech them, yet they do not intercede. If they have the means to affect matters on the mortal plane, we are yet to see any evidence of it. There is no difference between an answered prayer and blind coincidence. All of this Nemanist dogma is just mummery."

FROM GROSSO'S
THE GREAT ROT: THE RISE OF NEMAN CONFORMISM

Uncharted Foothills

GREAT NORTHERN BARRIER RANGE

In spite of his fear, Peter did fall asleep, though it could only have been for an hour or two, and it was so fractured and filled with hallucination that it barely qualified as such.

With Furlan gone in the most abysmal circumstances, and the rest of the prisoners enlisted men with whom Peter had little in common except the fact of their captivity, it was to Olwin he turned his attention. There seemed to be some quality to her, no doubt imparted by her paganism, which gave her an impressive measure of fortitude. "Hardy places breed hardy peoples" was a well-worn adage within the Sovan Empire, normally a reference to the Brigalanders across the North Sea, who mostly kept to themselves except when they were raiding their pagan brethren in coastal Draedaland. It certainly seemed to apply to her. She had been raised – one could only assume – in an environment a far cry from the townhouses of Sova, with their well-stocked hearths and larders, without a regimen of childhood sports and tutelage to occupy her body and mind. Enduring these hardships must have been second nature to her.

"We need to escape," he said. He was so close that his lips were practically touching her ear, and he spoke so quietly the breeze threatened to steal his words. But given the catmen's preternaturally good hearing, he would risk no more.

Olwin nodded. There was no argument, no hesitation. "Soon," she said.

"Now, while it is still dark," Peter countered. There was no doubt that the barbaric vivisection of Furlan was a fate that awaited all of them. A swift death in an escape attempt was immeasurably better than that horror.

"*Malpermesita sangomagio,*" Olwin whispered to herself.

"They will do it again. What they did to Captain Furlan they will do to all of us. We are better off trying to run."

There was no need to convince her; she had already agreed. Still neither of them moved.

She turned to him and leant in. "All go," she whispered, her lips brushing his ear lobe. "All us go. Run. Not you and me, all."

Peter nodded. "Yes. Better odds." *Of what?* the selfish part of his mind enquired; getting the message out, or his own personal survival?

"Now," he said again. Even then, a part of him wanted to believe that what had happened to Furlan was a one-off; that that was how the catmen operated, taking a single prisoner and vivisecting him and then . . . and then *what*? Letting everybody else go? It was absurd, but fleeing was still a difficult thing to muster up the courage for.

"We need to all run," he said to the man to his left. "We need to run, and we need to run now."

"They'll kill us," the man said, entirely too loudly.

"Shut up!" Peter hissed. The incisions on his face were itching abominably as they became scabrous, and it was taking all his willpower not to peel them off. "Shut up or they will hear us." He took a moment to check their surroundings, but could see nothing of their captors. "You saw what happened to Captain Furlan."

"Aye, I saw it," the private replied.

"They will do it to the rest of us."

"You can't know that."

"You want to risk it?"

The man began to weep softly. "Nema Victoria, just let this hell be over."

"There's nothing Nema can do for us now," Peter said, and surprised himself with just how earnestly he believed that. "It's up to us."

The private looked at him with resentment, his eyes red-rimmed with stress and fear. Still, he could not deny the reality of their situation.

The word was passed around the remaining couple of men and women – there were only five of them in total, now that Furlan had been taken – and once it was agreed that they would run, and once a direction had been chosen, Peter said, in a low voice, "Ready?"

None of them were ready, but they said yes anyway.

"Let's go."

The instinct had been to shout it, to make it a sudden and urgent injunction like the start of a race in the Sovan Arena. Instead he whispered it, and together they rose to their feet and stole toward the edge of the clearing.

Peter's heart thumped so percussively in that strange dead zone of silence that he was certain their captors would be able to hear it. But then, unthinkably, they were clear of the edge of the glade and making their way into the forest beyond.

Olwin, an expert in stealth and tracking, moved the most quickly and quietly. The four Sovans, to the contrary, rustled and pounded against the grass intolerably, crackling twigs, squelching in mud, breaking fern stems. But for the wind, it might as well have been a cannonade.

They dispersed at the forest's edge, but Peter followed Olwin slavishly. She took a course that would have been treacherous in the light of midday let alone the pre-dawn darkness, delving between sap-sticky pines and broad-leafed oaks, leaping between rocks, sliding down areas of loose loam. She ducked under low-hanging branches and skipped over tree roots and thick-stemmed plants, sure-footed and fleet and impossibly quiet. Peter tried to cut to her path with reckless haste, risking a turned ankle and worse to put as much distance between the settlement and himself as possible.

After perhaps one minute of running, and with a ridiculous sense of optimism – had it truly been that easy? – he chanced a half-turn to see how the others were faring.

He suffered such a surge of fear that it felt as though his heart would stop dead in his chest. The catmen had not only heard and observed them escape, but two of the three Sovans had already been caught. He could see their struggling silhouettes being lugged back to the settlement like sacks of flour. Even this break-out attempt had not bestirred the creatures to rage.

He renewed his flight with hysterical speed, making a calamitous ending all but inevitable. Surely enough, it came a few moments later: his foot slipped on a mossy stone, he turned sharply to the right and flailed, and hit the ground and rolled until the thickening ferns snagged him to a stop. Ahead of him, much further ahead, Olwin disappeared into the forest like a ghost.

He lay on the ground, dazed from the fall, half stupid with fear and burning with resentment at having been abandoned. Still he clawed his way onwards. Perhaps he would have done better to lie still, though surely the catmen would have smelt him.

He quickly lost any sense of direction, but he did not stop and take any sort of bearing. To stop was to die. Instead, he pressed himself back to his feet and ran madly, every second that he was not a captive a second closer to success.

He kept going for a few minutes until he realised that he wasn't running downhill. He must have turned east, or even north. He squinted into the dark forest, searching desperately for the right way. He tried four different directions, hoping to feel the ground underneath his feet slope downwards.

He began to weep as he traced lunatic squares through the trees. There was nothing now, no prevailing wind, no sun or stars, no nearby streams, no light by which to see lichen growing on trees – no navigational aids whatever.

This had to be some cruel trick.

He ran on, expecting at any moment to burst his way back into the catman settlement. He looked around constantly, but there was no sign of pursuit.

"Here," a voice said.

Peter stopped dead, his blood turning to ice.

"Here," the voice said again.

"Who is that?" Peter hissed. One of his men? It wasn't Olwin.

"Come closer."

He moved forward slowly, cautiously. "Who is that?" he asked again. Nema, but it was so bloody *dark*.

"Here," the voice said again.

Peter could see no one; he could barely make out the trees in front of him.

"Closer," the voice said.

"I can't see anything," Peter whispered.

Something seized his left arm. Peter cried out; another hand clamped down hard over his mouth. The hand was rough, like tree bark, and scratched sharply at his lips and nose. It smelt strongly of pine sap.

"Listen!" the voice croaked, and Peter was falling,

falling,

falling into oblivion.

❧

an old man, in the purple habit of a Neman missionary
    feet in soil, acid fear, thumping pulse
    ghastly, stooped mutants, catmen
    the man, foraging, cold rainwater on ferns
    salves for their wounds
    damming suppuration
    the tap of a hammer, hard-edged planks, a splinter, building treehouses
    midwifing fresh runts, amniotic fluid
    screeching
    grave rites, Neman rituals, the smell of incense and fire and burning flesh
    popping, fizzling tumours
    a large golden spearhead
    cutting the air, incisions in the fabric of reality
    tantalising glimpses of
    a golden city?
    thick toxic fog of malevolence
    wounds healed, knitted with gut
    bloodlines, husbandry, the span of geological ages
    rock and soil and blood and the pressing weight of the aether
    the missionary killed, impaled with the spearhead
    the rapacious stab of gold through the gut, stuck, chipped spine, sliver
    eternal life
    bark, ossification, morphing, trunk
    grasping hands, a frightened soldier, a memory of a life

a single purpose
Fate's injunction
judgement
And a splinter in Peter's hand

They came for him at dawn, summoned.

He wept helplessly as strong feline hands gripped the back of his jacket and the scruff of his neck and hauled him up.

The only consolation was that Olwin seemed to have made good her escape.

It was not much of one.

He wanted it to be him.

The ritual was performed again the next day. Of the four Sovans, one had been killed in the escape attempt. Once again she had been greedily devoured by the catmen, and once again her bones had been picked clean and fought over by the little mutant runts of the settlement, which only made an appearance in those circumstances.

Of the three of them left, one was manacled to the ritual stone in the early morning, and, screaming, subjected to the same horrifying and baffling rite. With the man's non-execution complete and his midriff freshly stitched back together, Peter and the remaining Sovan prisoner were led back to the clearing and once again left on the ground, unbound and unmolested.

If the day before Peter's mind had been racing with fear and a growing and urgent need to escape, now he was catatonic with despair. When he was not staring at the earth with profound vacancy, he ruminated obsessively on the skeletal horror of the tree-man. But the images and sounds and smells, so lucid in those dark and feverish moments, now refused to be perceived. It was like trying to recall a week-old dream; the visions had gone, but the fear remained, distilled and crystallised and filling him with a sense of unspent energy.

He scratched at the splinter which had worked its way into the palm of his left hand.

With his mind so focused, initially he felt no compulsion to run again – for what could possibly be the point? In the best case the catmen would contrive to return him to the same spot, to while away the rest of the afternoon waiting for death. But as the morning turned to noon turned to afternoon, and the catatonia waned and the fear returned – death was such a detestable thing to face prematurely – he resolved to run again. This time, if stopped, he would fight back and so precipitate his murder. The thought of being mindlessly consumed revolted him, but he was certain that he would not suffer the same fate as Furlan and the others.

Besides, there was a chance, however small, that he actually might escape.

He snorted out loud.

"What could possibly be funny?" the man next to him asked. He was lying on his back, his eyes closed. Gone was any barrier between officer and soldier. After all, what was Peter going to do, reprimand him? What formality could matter less?

"Thinking about running again," Peter said mildly, his face turned to the sun, as though they were two lovers passing an idle afternoon in Zobryv Gardens.

There was a pause. "That *is* an amusing thought."

Neither of them spoke quietly any more. What was the point?

"I'm afraid to die," Peter said eventually, helplessly. To say it out loud, to finally admit it to another person, to fly in the face of everything expected of him as a commissioned Sovan officer, felt so good it was euphoric. He chuckled; he'd surprised himself. "I'm terrified of it." He laughed again, a brittle thing. "I have been terrified since I set foot in the New East. The fear has never left me." A final trill of laughter, high-pitched and maniacal, and then there were tears in his eyes and his thoughts were flowing out of him like water from a ruptured dam. "I hate this. I hate it. Who could endure this? What is this horror? What is it that we have done in life to deserve this?" He looked at the private, his eyes wide with desperate entreaty, seeing none of his mania reflected back at him. "I want to go *home*," he said with the stubbornness of an infant. "Don't you see? I don't want to be here. I want to go home. I want my . . . Nema, I want my father." Now, broken, he sobbed with profound grief. "I don't want to be here. I just want my dad, all right? I just want to go home."

The private said nothing. What could he say? Eventually he stopped watching Peter cry, closing his eyes and turning away, trying to catch the last bit of sun before it disappeared behind the forest canopy and was lost to the evening. Peter envied him his resolve to die.

He made a second attempt to escape an hour later. Once again there was no one in sight, and once again his progress across the clearing was unhindered.

Once again he made it about a minute into the forest.

And once again he was stopped.

But this time, something was different.

XXIII

The Door to the Sea

"Nothing could stop the 'ball, neither feature of the field nor human contrivance. Fire'd obliquely, the thing jounced on and on, cutting thirty men down in a great long line over the span of a hundred yards. Even when it had slowed and roll'd gently, I saw a fool lose his foot below the ankle kicking at it. It reminded me of the Empire itself: unstoppable, irresistible, acting for want of everything except its own momentum."

FROM THE MEMOIRS OF
COLONEL THIETMAR GARRICK

The Gero Road

NORTH KYARAI

The Great Silence.

Rot your soul.

The Knackerman.

The Blood Stone.

Ten miles' hard riding north of Port Talaka, and the physical noise in Renata's ears had been replaced by a silent refrain in her head.

Here on the Gero Road they might as well have been in another country. Either side of that broad track of compacted earth, wild grassland stretched. To the west, there was nothing for two hundred miles until the Sigismund Line of forts which separated the Casimiran protectorate of Saekaland from the northern Kyarai. To the east lay gently undulating prairie all the way to the Jade Sea – even now, on a clear day, too far away to be seen.

It was a four-day journey to Port Gero and the Door to the Sea. She should have spent the time intensively preparing for the meeting with the Stygion. Instead, she once again found herself brooding, mourning the loss of a beloved colleague and father figure, and shaken by the sharp lurch of the diplomatic mission into matters arcane.

Just a messenger.

And the message is: judgement.

A warm wind blew constantly from the east, stirring the grass like a great green sea. The only sound was the clip-clop of their plains horses' hooves. Once this road would have been bustling with colonial traders; Port Gero was the quickest and easiest ocean crossing from Oksanastadt – now in Casimiran hands – and the big whaling stations at Maretsburg and Vitaney Island. With the imminent failure of the Kyaran war, the traders would probably be unloading at Fort Karl. Either way, the Gero Road was deserted.

No. That wasn't quite right; there was a solitary figure many miles to the south, moving slowly up behind them. Renata had the feeling she'd seen him somewhere before.

They had been so focused on escaping the city with their lives that they were ill-prepared for this part of the journey. They had only what they wore, what armaments they could carry, and what supplies were loaded in their saddlebags. Fortunately it was approaching summer, and the weather was clement.

"All right," Glaser said, bringing his horse to a stop. He dismounted smartly, his boots kicking up a cloud of straw-coloured dust from the road. "Let's have it."

The rest of them dismounted too and stretched their legs, and their plains horses milled about, idly cropping the grass in the late-afternoon sun. Ozolinsh, Herschel, Lyzander, Glaser, Renata: all of them looked dusty and dishevelled and tired, their faces and necks red with sunburn, their foreheads glistening with sweat. In an effort to cool down, they were in a state of partial undress, which had the effect of making them look like a band of pirates.

"What was that business with Guillot?" Glaser asked. He was like their weary, put-upon father, and they his difficult and unruly children.

Renata looked at Herschel, but he did not meet her gaze. He looked sweaty and miserable, and the bare circle of his scalp was a virulent red and peeling with sunburn.

"He murdered Didacus," Renata said, trying to keep her voice level. "Then he tried to kill me." For all she was becoming accustomed to this carousel of horror and action, enduring a second murder attempt had profoundly affected her. She was a diplomat, after all, not a soldier.

"Why?" Glaser pressed.

She gave her account of it; of the attack, of the man's insane ramblings, of his brutal murder of Maruska, of the bizarre golden plate behind his face, and of the arrival of her saviour, a random man with impeccable timing whose fate remained uncertain.

"The Knackerman?" Herschel asked as she finished her account.

"That's what he said," Renata replied. "Why? Does that mean something to you?"

"It's a Draedic legend," Herschel said, frowning. "A *Selureii* legend."

"Selureii?" Glaser asked.

"I feel like I've heard of them," Ozolinsh murmured.

"Yes, you would have done," Herschel said. "The Selureii are a Draedist death cult. They perform séances, like we do. Did," he added with a faltering, sheepish laugh. "I'm afraid there are a fair few such cults in our line of work."

"Your paths have crossed?" Glaser asked.

"In the spirit dimension, yes. Not here, not on the mortal plane. We have nothing to do with them, nor they us. They are . . . dangerous. Extremists."

"Extreme in what sense?"

"They believe that because life is eternal in the spirit realm, that is the natural state of man. That our time on the mortal plane is a mere prelude; that we should hasten towards death at the earliest opportunity."

"*Now* I remember," Ozolinsh said, snapping her fingers. "They are Rochusians. There was a Sovan scholar, hundreds of years ago – Justice Emmerich Rochus. He theorised . . . well, what you just said."

Herschel smiled and inclined his head politely, though it was clear he hadn't a clue what she was talking about.

"How is it that Brother Guillot came to be infected by this arcane parasite?" Glaser pressed.

Herschel shrugged. "I have no idea, honestly."

"How can you have no idea?!" Renata demanded. "You two have been inseparable since you left Reichsgard!"

"I do not know what to tell you. His behaviour has been off since we have been in Sova—"

"Off how? Describe it," Glaser said.

Herschel cast about as though he might conjure up an explanation from the grass plains. "I don't *know*! He has been out of sorts for a little while. Surly, withdrawn, combative. He was always eager, perhaps a little zealous, and it could make him easily frustrated. But he was not evil, just . . . quiet. He kept his own counsel. In Sova he became . . . Something about the city overwhelmed him. It is an oppressive place, full of sights and sounds, and I think it vexed him. He was obviously grappling with something. I put it down to fear of our being executed. Perhaps he was vulnerable."

"To what?"

"To whatever it is that happened to him. Perhaps his internal conflict made his mind ripe for the predations of the Knackerman. Perhaps they changed him somehow." He laughed with anxious exasperation. "I can assure you that Brother Guillot was a regular living, breathing human being at least at one point! To say nothing of a close friend!"

Glaser ignored the monk's brief anguish. "Are you saying he might have been *possessed*? Whilst the two of you were in Sova?"

Herschel sighed, pursing his lips briefly. "From what I know of the legend, the Knackerman is a sort of . . . patron saint of necromancers. A ferryman. Whenever a necromancer dies or becomes trapped in Limbo, the Knackerman has a special way of . . . moving them along. It's a northern thing. The moniker comes from shepherding."

"Could your abortive attempt at a summoning in Zetland have precipitated this?" Glaser asked.

"No. We had already left by then."

Glaser rubbed his chin. "Could the Sel . . . Sel . . . "

"Selureii."

"Sel-*ur-ree-eye* have summoned him? It? The . . . *Knacker*man?"

"I do not know."

"If they did so, they must have been in Sova at the crucial time."

"I suppose."

"You had no forewarning of their arrival?"

Herschel shrugged. "How could I have?"

"If you are in league," Renata muttered darkly.

"What were they doing there then?" Glaser asked, but it wasn't a question directed at anybody in particular. He turned to Renata. "Guillot, or the . . . *entity* which had taken possession of him, said he wanted to stop the diplomatic mission?"

Renata nodded. "That was the skin of it."

"And murdered Ambassador Maruska to that end?"

"Yes."

"And tried to murder you – well, *again*, if we are to assume it was indeed the Knackerman in the Dynast's Palace."

"Indeed."

"So the Selureii are aware of the Great Silence?"

"I should think so," Herschel said. "They are much more accomplished necromantic practitioners than we in the Bruta Sarkan."

"And they believe that our diplomatic mission to the Kasar and the Stygion will somehow prevent or even reverse it?"

"I couldn't say," the hapless old monk said. "But logically, that holds."

"And so to that end they are our enemy."

There was a silence as each of them considered this. Renata exchanged a look with Lyzander, who seemed very much out of his depth.

Eventually, Glaser sighed. "We shall have to be careful going forward. If Guillot is still alive, it is likely he will try again."

"If it truly is the Knackerman that is pursuing us, then Brother Guillot's death will make no difference," Herschel said.

There was another pregnant silence as those chilling words, delivered so offhandedly, filled the space between them.

"Prince of Hell," Glaser said, rolling his eyes, and remounted his horse. "Captain Lyzander: as our resident Kasarsprek speaker and wolfman expert, I should like you to turn your mind to the Dwelkspreker's words. 'Rot your soul' is just bizarre enough that it might mean something, though Nema Victoria knows we are overburdened with portents. And as for the Blood Stone . . ."

They all turned to look at the small chest, currently lodged in Glaser's saddlebags, as though it had called out to them.

"Madam Ozolinsh, as our thaumaturge, I should like you to think on its significance. Perhaps you can compare notes with Brother Herschel here. The Dwelkspreker gave it to us for a reason; perhaps there is some application to it."

"It is an attenuation artefact," Ozolinsh said. "There is plenty of mediaeval literature about its spiritual importance, but certainly within the Corps of Engineers we know it to be an amplifier of magick. That is to say, it increases the power of a given sorcery by orders of magnitude. As for what it does in and of itself, I know not."

"Perhaps there is something about it in the volumes you carry?" Glaser said, pointing to the books chained to her hip.

"Aye, perhaps."

"Well then. That is your task. And as for you, Ambassador—"

"I know," Renata said. "I need to prepare to meet the Stygion."

They journeyed on, a gloomy and introspective band.

"Tell me a little about them," Lyzander said to her. The two of them were some way off the rest of the group; Glaser was at the front by at least fifty yards, whilst Herschel and Ozolinsh's quiet conversation carried on the wind from the same distance but to the rear.

"The Stygion?"

"Aye."

"What would you like to know?"

Lyzander shrugged. "What are they like? What sort of reception can we expect?"

"Hostile." Renata snorted. The truth was, she didn't want to admit how little she knew, in practical terms. Oh, she could speak at length about their customs and history, or at least those things as recorded by Sovan scholars. But as for modern Stygion society, she was out of her depth.

"Will they even speak to us?"

"Honestly, I do not know," she said. Lyzander was hitting on her largest private fear: that there was a very good chance they would be completely ignored. Then the only fruits of their mission would be a gigantic ruby and the useless injunction "rot your soul".

"So we turn up to the Door to the Sea, and then what?"

Renata looked at him sidelong. "Are you jesting with me?" she asked tiredly.

Lyzander smiled in what he clearly considered to be a sincere manner. "Not at all. I have been *pressed* into the diplomatic service. I want to know what it is I can expect."

Renata sighed. "We have made contact before. Well, Didi – that is to say, Ambassador Maruska – did so some years ago. Their society is as stratified as ours, though not for the same reasons."

"What, then?"

"They grade themselves by magickal latency."

"Oh, I think I know this," Lyzander said, leaning back in the saddle slightly. He thought for a moment. "Something about sharks, no?"

"You are talking about Spears. That is their equestrian class. Sort of like ... if you took all the senior merchants and professionals and minor lords and ladies, and all of the senior officers from the Sovan Army and Navy, and bunched them together in a single stratum."

"But they control sharks."

Renata let out an exasperated noise. It was precisely the kind of silly, superficial aspect of the Spears that the pamphleteers focused on.

"Yes. They are bonded to white sharks."

"They use them as weapons."

She gritted her teeth. She should not have been surprised that Lyzander would be interested in such morbid details. He was, after all, a basic man.

"*Selachomancy*, it is called. The power by which the sharks can be commanded. But they are so much more than that. They are bodyguards and companions, proxies for duels, symbols of social standing ... "

"And?"

Renata rolled her eyes, but she smiled in spite of herself. "*Yes,* weapons of war, and execution and law-keeping and killing and maiming."

Lyzander winked at her. "Extraordinary."

"It is," she agreed with great sincerity.

"How did you get into it? 'Tis very specialised."

"My father was an accomplished linguist. He is a Zyrahn Dynast."

"Oh, my neck of the woods."

"I had you for a Balabrian?"

He looked at her with a smile. "Very *good*, Madam Secretary. Very unlike a Sovan to bother to learn the difference. Still, you do not have your father's colouring."

"No, my sister kept it all for herself," she said with a pang of guilt. She had left Amara to languish in Sova. "She is very beautiful."

"You are not exactly hard on the eye," Lyzander said, and then seemed surprised at his own words.

"That is not—"

"Appropriate, I agree. Forget I said anything," he added with an insolent smile.

Renata pursed her lips. "I am spoken for." She didn't know why she had said it, and it wasn't even true, not really. She had not spoken to Alistair for a long time, and had no intention of maintaining their courtship.

"And you think I am not?" Lyzander pressed his hand to his bare chest with mock affront.

"That reminds me," Renata said, her mood suddenly sour. She fished out the Empress' letter from her pocket and handed it to him. "From the Kammerfräulein's office."

Lyzander's expression collapsed. He snatched the letter from her hand. "How long have you had this?" he demanded.

"I . . ." Renata began, taken aback by the sudden intensity of his words. "It was given to me in Sova. But there has not been an opportunity—"

"To hand over a letter?" he snapped, brandishing it at her. "How long did that take? All of two seconds?"

She felt anger blossom within her. "I have given it to you, have I not? I am not a bloody messenger! After all I have endured, how dare you burden me with your impudence!"

Lyzander seemed to regret his quick temper. "Renata—"

"Madam Secretary to you!" she retorted, reeling from the breakneck turn in the conversation, and urged her horse ahead.

"Who is the leader?"

Renata looked back. It was perhaps an hour later, and with tempers cooled, Lyzander had caught up with her again.

"I hope you've come to apologise to me," she said, though she could not muster much in the way of indignance.

He held up his hands in contrition, and in so doing, his plains horse veered off to the right. It was so unguardedly ham-fisted that Renata actually laughed.

"I am sorry," Lyzander said as he pulled his unruly mount back up next to her.

"What precisely *is* the nature of your relationship with the Empress?" Renata asked.

"Complex," he said, and that, it seemed, was that.

"Well. I am sorry to hear it."

"I should not have shouted at you."

"You should not have."

"Thank you for bringing me the letter."

"'Tis no matter."

They rode on in silence for a little while. "So? Who is leader?"

"Of the Stygion?"

"Aye."

"The Thrice King. Actually, it's the Thrice Queen now."

"An odd name."

Renata shrugged. "It's a historic term. Essentially it means that she is the queen of all three estates: the executive, the equestrian and the commoners."

"What are the commoners called?"

"In Saxan, 'nulls', for their want of latent magickal ability."

"And what do they do? All the grunt work?"

"Same thing the commonfolk do in Sova. You have to remember, like the Kasar, these people are at least half human. They organise their society in similar ways."

"Can't be that similar, though. For one they live underwater. How do they even breathe? There's a point; how are *we* going to breathe? And how are you going to speak with them?"

"A lungfish," Renata said, with a note of dismay in her voice.

"What's that?"

"You'll see. As for speech, there's a lot of sign language. The lungfish will let me do some verbal communication, but it's quite limited."

"What does that sound like?"

"Loxica? It's made up of sounds designed to carry through the medium of water, so there's a lot of . . . well, humming, I suppose you would say. Humming and a sort of clicking sound. And some subvocalisation. Unlike humans, the Stygion have a very nascent, ah, sense of telepathy. It's not so much *mind*-reading as being able to read what's behind someone's speech in a perceptive way. Sound carries a long way in water, so the Stygion have developed manners of communication which are . . . "

"Secret?"

"Not so much secret as private. Ironically, the sign language we are forced to use as diplomats is to them the more personal, informal way of communicating."

"It all sounds rather refined for such a savage race."

"People used to say the same of the Kasar."

"Aye, well. Haven't seen the Kasar use a white shark to cut a sailor in half before."

Renata was quiet for a moment. She was beginning to re-member why she did not discuss her line of work outside of the Imperial Office.

"Understanding a people, their culture and customs, and what motivates them, requires us to look past the violence of contact."

"That from one of your books, is it?"

"It is. Written by Artem Managold. He was the head of both the Imperial Office and the Board of Trade, before they split them in two."

"Bully for him."

"Captain, you started this conversation. If you are uninter-ested in what I have to say, you are more than welcome to ride in silence."

Lyzander sighed. "I am in a strange mood," he said eventually. He gestured to the letter from the Empress, and looked as though he were about to say more, but instead added, "Forgive me."

Renata waved him off. "Just . . . If you want to talk, let us talk. I have enough on my plate without people trying to get a rise out of me."

"Just so," Lyzander said, inclining his head in apology. He made a show of looking around the endless wildflower plains that stretched to the horizon in every direction. "What a desolate place. By rights I should not even be here."

"Well. You are going to be here for some time, so I should make your peace with it. There is currently nothing else in this world of greater importance than our mission."

"Then where *is* everybody?" Lyzander asked with a measure of exasperation. "Where is the Army? Why are we not marching on the Jade Sea in force?"

"Because Sova insists on pissing away men and matériel in the Kyarai on an internecine war which only exists because a hundred years ago we decided there should be two versions of Nemanism instead of one."

Lyzander considered this for a moment, then spat. "What a bloody mess," he decided on eventually.

"On that we can agree. Now, let me concentrate. I have a lot to think about."

They rode on, day and night. Port Gero was a Kasari settlement, situated at the very north-eastern tip of the Kyarai – the apex of a spur of land known as "the Horn". But the Empress had paid for a thousand-year lease on the place, and constructed a large coastal fortification and naval base there, and it was a Sovan colony in all but name.

Renata eyed the fort as they rode past it down a coastal path. It occupied a commanding view atop the bluffs, and had a substantial battery watching the approach to the Horn, whilst two Sovan men-o'-war lay at anchor in the small harbour. Beyond, the view of the Jade Sea was breathtaking. It stretched in every direction, a rich blue-green colour, crystalline in the light of the sun and whipped to whitecaps by the wind. Above, huge banks of cloud sailed like airborne glaciers. The only visible land was that of the Horn itself, a peninsula almost a hundred miles long. From where they stood, it was little more than an insignificant coda of sand-coloured cliffs.

They rode south-west along the coastal path until they came to a set of treacherously steep stone steps cut into the side of the bluff. Here they left the horses to crop the grass on the clifftop and took with them only what they needed: weapons, a little food, and the Blood Stone.

"What are those?" Ozolinsh asked as they picked their way down the side of the cliff. She was pointing to a line of perhaps five or six indistinct shapes a hundred feet out into the water. They looked like wooden posts strapped with buoys, the waves foaming gently around them.

"Suffocation posts," Renata said.

There was a pause. "Suffocation . . . posts?"

"You'll see in a minute."

They reached the bottom of the cliffs and traipsed along the sand. Here the water thundered concussively against the bluffs, though it was calmer further south. It was warmer here, too, sheltered as they were from the scouring ocean wind.

They walked until they drew level with the suffocation posts. Beyond, a hundred yards from the beach, was the great monolith of the Door to the Sea itself, a rectangular frame of stone thirty feet proud of the water's surface. Either side of it, gripping the frame, were statues of mythical sea creatures, as though the whole thing were a heraldic device. The Door was centuries old, and its base was crusted with limpets and sea slime.

"Oh," Ozolinsh said, now realising the nature of the suffocation posts. Each had tied to it a mer-man in various states of decay. The corpses were united in their posture, necks bent forward as far as the post and bonds would allow, each having strained, futilely, to reach the life-giving brine and so breathe.

"As the tide recedes, they drown in the air," Glaser murmured.

No one else said anything. The five of them simply stood on the sand in the fading afternoon light.

"They do not look like . . . They are not what I expected," Ozolinsh said eventually.

Renata examined the corpses as best she could from the beach. Like the Kasar – and humans, for that matter – their skin was a variety of shades. Grey and blue-green were predominant, but there were some brighter markings, as one might see on tropical fish. The mer-men were certainly humanoid – jarringly so – but it was the heads which were most different. Great downturned mouths like that of a grouper; eyes that were golden orbs sheathed behind glassy nictitating membranes; an absence in the centre of the face where noses were forgone in favour of vertical slits; bony ridges on the forehead that swept back into crests at the top of the cranium, and then ears like great vestigial fins. Their chins dangled with fleshy, sensory protrusions like those of a catfish, whilst their necks were serrated with gills. Their hands were webbed to the very tips of their fingers, whilst there was a curious segmentation at the base of the sternum. There, anchored below their ribcages were pectoral fins; and another fin swept from the middle of the spine, hanging desiccated and slack between their legs. These creatures truly were the marriage between fish and man, the most bizarre and alien of the Magickal Cataclysm's manufactures.

"What of the nature of their transgressions?" Herschel asked.

Renata realised the question was directed at her. "I don't know." She shrugged.

"It is a sublime torture," Glaser said. "Suffocation. It must have been something bad."

"How does it work, then?" Lyzander asked. "We just waltz in?"

"Precisely that," Renata replied, surprising them all. "The Door is watched at all times."

"You mean to say that there are guards standing sentry right there right now?"

"Yes," she said.

There was another awkward pause.

"Well," Glaser said, clearing his throat. "We don't want to pitch up mob-handed. I suggest that the ambassador makes contact in the first instance. Then she can sound them out as to whether they are open to further, uh, guests."

Renata was about to agree with him – she had not envisaged matters proceeding in any other way – when to her surprise Lyzander took a step forward.

"We can't possibly expect her to go in alone," he said, brandishing his right hand at the ocean.

"She is the ambassador to the Stygion, Captain," Glaser said incredulously. "She is literally the only person in the Empire whom we can."

Lyzander turned to her. "I'm coming with you."

"They might kill you," Renata said, uncertainly, though she

was pleased at the prospect of some company. After all, Maruska should have been there with her.

"They might kill *you*."

She considered this. "They might," she agreed.

A curious stand-off ensued, until Ozolinsh said, "What are you going to *wear*?"

Renata chuckled. "Not much. Blouse and breeches will be fine. And I shall have to apply some markings." She pointed to the nearest corpse. "You see those stripes on his face? They are indications of rank."

"You have the necessary materials?" Glaser asked.

"I do," Renata said, and after rifling briefly through her pack, she took out a pot of what looked like boot polish and unscrewed the cap. Inside was a thick waterproof paste with a garish yellow colour.

"You mean to apply that to yourself?"

"Yes," she said, and she looked up to see everyone staring at her. "Why don't you all find something to occupy yourselves with whilst I prepare?"

The first marking was a chevron that went from the corner of one of her eyebrows to the apex of her forehead, and then down to the other eyebrow. This denoted her as a member of the equestrian class, the social equal of a Spear. The next was a thick ring around her left forearm, which put her within the political stratum; and the final one was a simple ideogram on each of her cheeks. This was not a signifier of class, but a reminder that she required oxygen to breathe. Maruska's predecessor had developed this piece of semiotic standard after her chaperone had neglected to provide a lungfish and nearly killed her.

Renata shivered. She had wanted this for so long. It represented the culmination of her academic and professional career. And now, standing at its threshold, she was frightened.

She removed her shoes and socks and knotted the sleeves of her blouse at her elbows. Her hair was already tied back, but she did it again more firmly. Then she put the greasepaint back into her diplomatic bag, and pulled out a pair of rubber-lined glasses that were bound by an adjustable leather strap.

"What on earth are those?" asked Lyzander, who had been watching her prepare.

"They were a gift from Ambassador Maruska," she said, taking a moment to indulge the memory. He had presented them to her in an engraved pewter case, not so much a gift as a promise that she would one day use them. That had been almost three years ago.

She stood and affixed the glasses, checking the strap to make sure there was a seal around her eyes. "They protect my eyes from the saltwater." She delved back into the bag and withdrew Maruska's pair. "Here."

"Thank you," Lyzander said, and put them on.

Renata took a deep breath. "All right. Leave your weapons here. Strip off as much of your clothing as possible."

Lyzander did so, until he was wearing nothing except a pair of breeches.

"What's next?"

The man really was quite muscular . . .

"Ms Rainer?"

"Hm? Yes. Right. Let's be about it."

"Is there anything we can do from here?" Glaser asked as she walked past him.

"Nema," she breathed, as the cold water of the ocean lapped around her feet. She turned to the colonel. "Not that I can think of."

"We shall try to divine the secrets of the Blood Stone and its significance, then," he said. "I should probably go and speak with the CO at Port Gero as well. Find some stabling for our horses."

"As you will."

Glaser grimaced, his eyes moving between her and the Door to the Sea. "Good luck then, Ms Rainer."

"Thank you," she said. She turned to Lyzander. "Watch your feet. Stay close to me."

She waded out into the ocean. The water was shallow for quite a long way out, though by the time they reached the Door to the Sea, it was at chest height. Beyond the Door itself was a drop-off, where the slippery rocks and coral ended in an underwater cliff. Out here – approaching a hundred yards from the beach, where Glaser and Ozolinsh and Herschel looked suddenly very small indeed – the currents were markedly stronger. Renata shivered; there was an incredible, terrible weight to the water.

"So we just go through, do we?" Lyzander asked. The stone frame was built atop two great plinths of saltwater concrete. The mer-men had not constructed the door themselves; rather, it was the work of Sovan hands. Nothing made this more apparent than the statue of the trident-wielding Sovan ocean demigod, Stygio, one of Nema Victoria's ten children and good luck charm of choice for the Imperial Navy's many thousands of sailors. It was for this god that the Stygion had been named – literally, in old Saxan, "sons of Stygio".

"We just go through," Renata confirmed, checking again the seal on her glasses. She performed a few arpeggios to warm up her voice. Although Maruska had told her that her Loxica was as good as any he had heard, she had yet to wield it outside of a classroom.

Lyzander looked as though he regretted coming with her.

"Here we go," Renata said, and taking a deep breath, she dived into the cold, brackish water.

XXIV

Ritual

"The envoy may threaten, but must do so judiciously. We might compare such to a sabre made of glass: it makes an impressive noise when rattled, but it is easily broken."

FROM MANAGOLD'S
THE GLASS SABRE

Uncharted Foothills

GREAT NORTHERN BARRIER RANGE

Peter fought desperately against the catman who stopped him, punching and scratching and even biting, trying to get himself killed quickly whilst his blood was up.

"Do it!" he screamed with lunatic anger. "Do it!"

The catman did not.

His nerve held only for so long. As he was carried back to the settlement, he struggled madly, insane with desperation; but slowly, it waned, crushed by the monumental imperturbability of the catman.

This time, however, instead of being shoved roughly back on to the ground next to the other soldier – who was watching these proceedings aghast – he was hoisted over the catman's shoulder and taken up one of the nearby trees. It was a broad pine, stripped of its lower branches, and the catman ascended it with feline ease in spite of the added burden.

They reached the nearest wooden hut and entered. Inside it was bare, with not a scrap of furniture to be seen. It was impossible to comprehend how sparse and bleak these creatures' lives were, how devoid of any and all human comfort – for they must have been at least partly human, at one time.

He was set down, sweating and panting and with his nerves ringing, on the crude wooden floor of the hut. Here at this moderate elevation, a mild breeze swept through the open sides of the structure, carrying on it a smell of pine sap.

The same smell on the tree-man's hands.

The catman, a black-furred brute a head taller than Peter, gripped him by the shoulders; and Peter felt that strange feeling of formless revulsion that came from being close to one of the creatures.

"N-nuh ..." the catman said. Peter looked up sharply, squinting into its enormous feline face. It really did look like a humanised jaguar, or sabrecat. "Nnnnnn ... *nnnnnn.*"

He fought the urge to crawl backwards. His fear was giving way to curiosity. All the other Sovans who had attempted escape had either been swiftly killed or simply dumped back where they started. Nothing about this encounter conformed to either.

For one, the beast seemed to be trying to communicate with him.

"Can you speak?" Peter asked hesitantly.

"Nnnngg. *Nnnnnnn!*"

He shook his head, studying the catman's mouth and face, his features creased in confusion, trying to understand. "What are you trying to say?"

The catman opened his mouth, and for a brief second Peter thought he was about to bite him. But instead, the creature worked its jaw and tongue, as though the latter were a foreign object, flopping about its palate and teeth slackly. "T-t-*t*," it said, then forced air through its cheeks and lips as though blowing a raspberry.

Peter winced, unable to shake the feeling that this contact, this nascent attempt at conversation was prohibited, and that the other catmen – wherever they were – would soon be upon them. But there was no one to be seen, either at the base of the tree or in the clearing.

"Tuh? Tee?" Peter tried. "Me?"

The catman shook his head, obviously frustrated. He batted the side of his face in the way an angry toddler might.

"*Nnnnnnnnuh*. Crruh. Thruh. Eet. *Eeeet* – er."

Peter squinted at the creature's mouth. It seemed to be desperate to make some sort of bilabial sound, but the best it could achieve was a sort of quasi-*m* which wasn't really an *m* at all.

"Eter," the catman said with more confidence. "*Eter*."

"Eater?" Peter tried.

The catman let out a snarl of frustration in precisely the same way a jaguar would, the same yowling that he had heard hundreds of times in the New East but which, like all other animal sounds, was absent from this encampment.

He reached out his hand again and poked a claw into Peter's chest. "Eter."

Peter pointed to himself where the claw had been. "Peter?"

The catman nodded vigorously. "Eter. *Eter*."

"How do you . . . " Peter began, squinting again into the creature's face, "know my name?"

Now the catman pointed at himself. "Uuuuurl. *Urrrl*-an."

Peter's eyes widened as horrified realisation dawned on him. "My god," he breathed. He looked once again at the catman, examining the features, trying to discern something, some essence of the former artillery captain. "*Furlan?*"

The catman let out a roar of triumph. "Urlan," he said, batting clumsily at his chest. "*Urlan*."

Of course; the shape of his mouth would allow for nothing less. He was a non-human creature trying to make human sounds. What a monstrous mental prison it must be, to be able to think lucidly, but be unable to speak.

"But how?" Peter asked, still examining catman-Furlan for any trace of the human he had been but two days before.

Even as Furlan began to clumsily charade the ritual at the execution stone, it dawned on Peter that, of course, it could only have been that. But the idea of it, the thought of taking a human man and with dark sorceries turning him into one of these . . . *things*, was abhorrent. Why? To what end? These catmen seemed to do nothing except exist. Mill about and rapaciously self-propagate, driven by nothing except a rather blunt set of basic instincts.

More to the point, at what stage did their humanity dissipate? Clearly there was some residual human cognisance within Furlan. Did it slowly burn off as a result of the sorcerous transformation? Or was it entirely behavioural, like those tabloid examples of feral human children being raised in the Kyarai? Would Furlan, forced to join in with this bizarre catman society, slowly abandon what he had once been as a way to spare himself the insanity of it?

Even as these thoughts vied for attention in Peter's head, the most pressing of all came to the fore: this was the fate that awaited *him*, if not tomorrow then the next day. Absurd thoughts filled his mind of turning up at his family estate so presented; his mother weeping, Leonie retching and fainting, his brothers hustling him back outside. Perhaps they would threaten to shoot him. Certainly Osbeorn would. Aldhard was kinder. Aldhard might give him some money and clothes, and send him on his way. Perhaps he could eke out an existence in Wolfsland . . .

But even as this bizarre reverie claimed him, his mind drifted back to his baffling and frightening experience in the forest with the tree-man. To what dark purpose had he turned these mutants? And on whose instruction? If Peter had taken anything from the visions, it was that at some point in the distant past, some Neman missionary had stumbled across these creatures; and that they in turn had killed him with the same golden spear they used for their ritual. In so doing, the missionary had . . . *fused* with the tree? It was such a bleak and dismal fate it made his skin crawl.

"What do you . . . can you . . . " He had so many questions they caught in his throat. "Can you think? Are you still *you*?"

Furlan performed a human gesture of equivocation with his hand. "Suh – *sun*," he said, gently slapping the side of his head. "Gone. Sun gone." *Some gone. Some of what made me Furlan has gone.* Peter shivered. It would have been better to die. This was a profound moral evil.

"Is this what all of them once were? The catpeople?"

"*Kato*," Furlan said, pressing a palm into his sternum. He pronounced it "Kay-tow".

"That's what you're called? Kato?"

Furlan nodded. "S – *ssss* – ear. *Stear*." He pressed a hand into his forehead, and then drew his fingers together into a conical shape and pressed it into his forehead again.

"Spear? The spearhead?" Peter asked, thinking back to the large golden spearhead which had been used to perform the transformation ritual, the same one which had been used to murder the Neman missionary.

Furlan clapped his hands once, pleased. "Yes, yes. Turn." *The spear turned me into Kato.*

"What is it?"

"Aowld, *aowllld* elic." *An old relic.*

"You are one of them now?" Peter asked. "You're going to . . . What's the plan? Are you going to live here with them?"

Furlan seemed to be overcome with a range of indecipherable emotions for a moment, anger, fear, horror, and a strange sense of acceptance. All of them manifested in a bizarre sequence of movements and sounds, his least human display yet.

"Carn't leave. *Can't.* H-hate. *Hate.* 'Ut can't leawve." There were actual tears in those feline eyes. *I can't leave. I hate this. But I can't leave.*

"But why?" Peter asked. "There are wolfmen. There are Stygion. Other races, other peoples. Sova will find a place for you. It finds a place for everyone."

Actually, he privately thought Sova might make an exception for the Kato, who seemed to have strayed entirely from their human roots and who exuded an aura of repulsion.

Furlan shook his head helplessly. "Stay. 'Othing 'ow 'ut life. Leave, die."

"There is nothing now but life?"

Furlan nodded. "Exist. All do. Exist then die."

"Why? *Why?*"

The frantic, half-whispered and deeply frustrating conversation went on for the better part of ten minutes, with Furlan trying and failing to produce any coherent response. He seemed to be gaining an increased mastery of his voice and mouth in how to substitute glottal stops and other letters for what previously would have been bilabial sounds; but concurrently his coherence seemed to degrade, as though mentally he were regressing in real time. Whatever had happened to him, the transformation had been much more than physical, and no matter how much Peter implored, and spoke of Badenburg and Sova and the Empire, Furlan could not be enthused about any of it. It seemed that as part of his vivisection, he had been infected with a fatal pessimism – to say nothing of some sort of inherited memory – that he must remain and propagate, as if the Kato served some special, as yet unknown cosmic purpose which forced them to continue beyond the base self-preservation instinct. Otherwise surely these creatures would be driven to starvation or mass suicide?

"Why do you feel . . . I'm sorry to say this, Captain, but there is something about you which is repulsive. I cannot bear to be near you. It is as though you have some quality which pushes me away." He felt wretched saying it, for Furlan hardly needed another knock to his confidence. But he might never get another opportunity to discuss these matters.

Nema Victoria, he might soon *be* one of them.

"Inert," Furlan said. There had to be some part of his brain that was transformed by the rite and filled with this knowledge. Or perhaps the catmen had stuffed him full of the brain of one of their deceased, so that this new creature was half Furlan and half catman. How else could he have assimilated this information so quickly? "We inert. The screaning has sto'ed."

The screaming has stopped. Peter had noticed it too. His time in the New East had been defined by its constant aethereal assault. Screams, visions, portents, hallucinations. Everyone had been plagued by them, everyone had been terrified – everyone. And yet out here, hundreds of miles away and deep into uncharted territory, there was nothing except silence.

We are inert. Inert to what? The tricks and machinations and predations of the afterlife? Were the Kato proof to those horrors? Soulless beings, invisible blanks, dark spots in the tapestry of life?

In which case, being here did not so much provide the answer sought by Major Haak, but rather simply broadened the depth and scope of the question: just what the hell was going on in the afterlife? And why did it not seem to be having any effect here, in this place?

"Who is the tree-man?" Peter asked. "The Neman. The missionary. Who is he?"

Something shifted in Furlan's expression. He took a step backwards, eyes wide with horror.

"Guh," he grunted.

"What? What is it?" Peter hissed.

But whatever the answer was, even if Furlan knew it, they had run out of time.

"You nust run," Furlan said, eyes twitching as he detected what Peter could not; the return of his people.

His people. *Peter* was Furlan's people. The regiment was Furlan's people. *Sovans* were Furlan's people. Not these horrors.

"Help me," Peter said, suddenly desperate. "Help me and I'll come back for you. I'll return with soldiers. For the love of Nema, Captain, get me out of here and we'll find you the best physicians and surgeons and thaumaturges in the Empire. We can turn you back, I swear it."

Furlan was already moving. He grabbed Peter and slung him over his shoulder, and in seconds they were descending the trunk of the tree.

"Go," Furlan said. "Head to the lake and then souwth. I will sto' then."

But it was futile. Peter saw with a sickening lurch that the shaman was back.

"No," he breathed. It was too late in the day; the ritual was supposed to take place in the morning. "No!"

But there was nothing he, or Furlan, or anybody could do.

Peter expended the very last of his mental and physical energy trying to escape from the iron grip of the catmen. Like all those who had gone before him, any attempt at resistance was utterly pointless.

In the fading light of dusk, they manacled him to the stone and the shaman produced the golden spearhead. Something felt different about this ritual; for one, there weren't nearly as many catmen there. During the other transformations, there had been a full audience from the members of the settlement. For another thing, they had not stripped him naked; instead, one of the shaman's assistants simply ripped open his jacket and shirt, exposing his midriff. It felt impromptu, rushed.

The splinter in his hand itched abominably.

The execution stone felt cold and damp against his back. He chafed and scratched his scalp as he looked around desperately for anyone or anything that might help him. But it was all in vain.

The shaman approached him, stooped and wizened, his skin arrayed with great constellations of tumours. Peter screamed and begged and writhed fruitlessly. There was chanting and rushed ritual, and then the spear was pressed into his forehead and bound there.

The moment it touched his skin, his consciousness discorporated. He was floating above his body, watching as it writhed and tried to scream and was brutalised. But it was like watching somebody else.

The world, the forested mountains of the Barrier Range, the clear pine-scented air, the distant screams of raptors disappeared. Now he was presented with a fresh vision: a creature of great malevolence was standing over him, a creature of coal-black skin, an eyeless face, three mouths stacked one above the next. A great plain of blood spread out beneath them like an enormous plate of red glass. Peter was lying strapped to a sacrificial table and the creature above was holding his heart in its hand. The air was filled with the sound of incredible moaning lament unparalleled in its anguish.

STOP THIS, the creature said. Its voice was everywhere at once, soundless and yet perfectly comprehensible, as though it wasn't a voice but a foreign thought that arrived in Peter's brain fully formed.

He could not say or do anything. He was a mere observer, without corporeal form or agency. He had the sense that he was witnessing something that had happened a very long time ago – thousands of years by the count of mortals.

I AM TIRED OF RELIVING THIS.

The voice was weary, imbued with volcanic anger as well as a depthless, incurable sadness. Peter had no idea what to make of any of this – he knew that he was terrified, but the vision was so impenetrable, so baffling, that his predominant feeling was one of curiosity. Was this the afterlife? The holy dimension? Something told him it was.

The vision was dissolving; as he began to feel a tugging, churning pain in his gut, something else filled his mind's eye. It was that same figure, the creature with black skin and three mouths, standing in front of an enormous circular door. The creature itself was the size of six or seven men standing foot to shoulder. The door, then, was ten times bigger than that, the better part of five hundred feet in diameter, cut into an enormous cliff face the colour of rust. The cliff formed one half of a chasm impossible to comprehend in its enormity. It ran infinitely in both directions. The chasm was filled with the skeletal remains of gigantic creatures encased in armour. Its floor was a forest of broken lances, swords and spears.

Peter knew in his marrow that nothing but the most exquisite horror lay beyond the door, something so abominable and terrifying that it threatened to flay his mind of its sensibilities.

And then the vision was fading, and he was coming back into his body, and something – something *else* – was wrong.

The ritual was incomplete.

His guts sang in agony.

He could feel damp mountain air on his *insides*.

The splinter in his palm pulsed with white-hot pain.

But . . .

He was free

And he was being spirited away from that hellish place.

XXV

The Violence of Contact

*"Here we arrive at the tendentiously named 'Sons of Stygio',
a people who have never referred to themselves as such. They
present an enigma to the Sovan envoy. Their preoccupation
is with neither material wealth nor the cartographic insult
of imperial expansion. Their lives are orders of magnitude
simpler, yet their intellectual fruits are surpassing. They
have made industry of poetry, song and storytelling, and
insofar as any race of creatures can achieve harmony and
equilibrium with their surroundings, it is the mer-men. In
the arena of foreign policy they make formidable opponents,
for – to put it bluntly – we have nothing they want."*

FROM A LETTER FROM AMBASSADOR ANETE
JEKABSONE TO THE IMPERIAL OFFICE

The Door to the Sea

JADE SEA

The drop-off yawned below. It must have been twenty fathoms deep.
At the bottom she could see colourful rinds of coral and streamers
of green and brown weed – the beginnings of a kelp forest. Beyond,
the Jade Sea stretched vertiginously, a deep, cold blue.

To the right, the suffocation posts jutted up from the sea floor like gruesome maypoles.

She should have taken a moment to immerse herself in an area of shallow water before attempting the Door. The urge to kick back to the surface was already a strong one. Maruska had taken her many times to the Sovan bathhouses to train her lungs, and she could hold her breath for over three minutes; but that had been in calm warm water, the only threat mild social embarrassment. Here in the ocean swell she was lucky to get thirty seconds out of her lungs.

She broke the surface next to Lyzander.

"Are you all right?" she asked him.

"I'm fine," he panted. "Just need to get used to it again. We used to swim in the Zyrahn Straits as childr—" He pointed suddenly, his eyes widening in mad, lunatic desperation. "*Fuh!*"

Renata's features creased in confusion. "What?!"

"Shuh – *shark!*"

Renata turned sharply. Closing quickly on their position was a large grey fin.

"It's just a Spear-mount, it's all right!" she shouted, for she could see the harness straps which the mer-men used to ride it. "It's all right!" she repeated. *Nema Victoria, Savare – gods, Stygio! – let it be all right.*

"For Nema's sake, Renata, get out of the water! That thing is going to kill us!" Lyzander babbled, grunting and spitting out mouthfuls of seawater as he bobbed up and down on the waves.

"It's not," she said. "It won't."

Please, sweet Nema, Mother of Gods, please, dear Stygio and the Deti and all the saints, please don't let it kill us.

"Oh, Nema Victoria!" Lyzander moaned, kicking madly beneath the surface, his face a rictus of abject misery. "Oh, blasted fucking hell and all the demons in it!"

Renata ducked beneath the surface—

She screamed immediately. A second shark, one they had not

even seen, was approaching her rapidly from underneath, eyes white, mouth open, teeth bared, throat dark and black and rapacious. An incredible, visceral prey-fear exploded through her blood like a shell from a bomb ketch. There was no experience even remotely comparable. She would have preferred any act of man-made violence, endured a hundred attempts on her life at the hands of human beings over this. She kicked and thrashed as the shark closed, the grey skin of its mouth peeled back, ghastly pink gums bristling with teeth, ready to cut through her legs as cleanly as a butcher's knife—

Seconds before she inhaled two deep lungfuls of brine, the shark twisted away. It passed so close to her that she felt the crazed water in its wake.

She broke the surface again, screaming, and Lyzander too was screaming like a madman, and in the distance Glaser was now waist-deep in the water, shouting at them and trying to find out "just what the damned fucking hell" was going on.

Of course, if the Stygion had wanted them dead, they would be dead. And as soon as this realisation was firm enough to take root, Renata managed to stop panicking.

"Stop," she said to Lyzander, who, to his credit, had remained treading water beyond the drop-off, rather than fleeing back to shore. "Stop, stop making that infernal noise," she added, as though she herself had not been making the same bloody racket but five seconds before. She knew she had to resubmerge before she lost her nerve. "I'm going back under."

"Nema, Ren, you can't—"

"Wait here."

"Fuck and blast—"

She plunged beneath the water again. This time, instead of two white sharks, there were two mer-men – Spears, she realised – floating *right there*, illuminated by shafts of golden sunlight in the same way a monastic manuscript might illuminate a saint.

<Who are you?> the leftmost demanded. Unlike the Stygion

tied to the posts, this one had milk-pale skin, so thin as to be almost translucent, with a hard elfin face and a long ribbed tail easily ten feet from hip to fin. He wore a shirt of mail created from flat, iridescent seashells and spiked conch pauldrons with trailing segmenta of stitched whalebone. The speaker had no helmet, but his fellow – a rich blue colour with yellow counter-shading – wore the skull of a hammerhead shark. Renata was reminded of mediaeval Sovan knights, who often wore sallets topped with wooden animal crests or other panaches.

<Ambassador Renata Rainer> she signed, the one piece of Loxica she had absolutely perfect. Then it was another trip to the surface for air.

"Who is that? Is that . . . *them?*" Lyzander asked, nodding his head towards the indistinct shapes a few fathoms below the surface.

"It is," Renata said, panting. "Just give me a moment to catch my breath."

She treaded water for another few moments, and then ducked back down again. The two Stygion had not moved, but some dis-tance behind them, their white shark familiars moved effortlessly and ominously through the water.

<What is your business here, soil-eater?> one of the mer-men signed to her with guarded curiosity. The Door to the Sea had been sentried for years, but like many far-flung forts in the Sovan Empire, it was probably seen by the mer-men as an undemanding posting.

<We need to speak with your . . .> *Damn.* She could not recall the signage for a Stygion thaumaturge. <Magicians> she set-tled on.

The sentries looked visibly confused, as well they might; she had just asked them to take her to the local children's entertainer.

<*Magicians?*>

Renata sighed inwardly. She had begun to swim to the surface again for more oxygen when a billowing cloud of blue started to flow towards her. It looked for all the world like a misshapen jellyfish, transparent and filled with bulbous organs, trailing long feathered fronds in its wake. She tried to remain calm as the thing slithered around her head, though it was a deeply alarming sensation. The fronds wrapped gently about her neck, and the transparent membrane of the creature surrounded her head like a slimy diplomatic bag. There was a tightening round her neck as the lungfish formed a greasy seal against her skin, and then the water was draining from the creature's interior, pumped out through tubes gated with double sphincters, until Renata's head was surrounded by a salty balloon of air like a biological diver's helmet.

<Thank you> she said.

<Yes> the guard replied. She got the sense that he had summoned the lungfish out of irritation, rather than altruism.

<I must speak with the Thrice Queen urgently> Renata said, deciding just to give them the message she had rehearsed. It was going to take a little time to get used to speaking Loxica in a dynamic way. <We have lost contact with the afterlife. The matter is of the gravest importance. I beg your indulgence>

The two Stygion regarded her.

<What of the other?> The guard pointed to Lyzander.

<He is my associate>

One of the white sharks stopped its lazy drifting and swam suddenly and directly at Lyzander. For a horrible moment, Renata thought it was going to bite him; instead it butted him roughly in the back, dragging him down underwater. Lyzander thrashed madly, a great white stream of bubbles rushing from his nose and mouth as the shark drove him ten fathoms deep with its snout.

"Stop!" Renata shouted reflexively into the warm bubble of air that smelt of fish and brine and her own hot breath.

They ignored her. Lyzander was about to drown – or worse, the two sharks were going to devour him. But after a short while, a second lungfish appeared, and enveloped his head like a marine strangler; and although he clawed madly at its stretchy skin, he relented the moment sweet life-giving oxygen flowed into his chest.

<Come on then> the guard said. He swam effortlessly to intercept his Spear-mount, gripped the harness, which was bifurcated by its dorsal fin, and motioned for Renata to follow him. Renata swam after him and took hold of the length of rein he held out for her, and the other Stygion did the same with Lyzander, who looked at Renata through his glasses with an expression of terrified wonderment.

Then they were taken away from the shore, and out into the deep water.

The sharks swam quickly, and soon they were out in the open ocean, with no sign of the sea floor even in full sunlight. Renata found the effect to be quite chilling; the depth of the water was frightening by itself, but they were towed for around twenty minutes, too, which put them at least two miles offshore from Port Gero. She had never felt so vulnerable in her life.

In the distance, large dark smudges began to slowly resolve into the outskirts of the Stygion tether city. These were clusters of spherical structures anchored to the seabed with long, sturdy cables, and buoyed by air-filled bladders so as to float within the epipelagic zone – the hundred-fathom depth to which sunlight penetrated seawater. The structures were made from an iridescent, resinous substance which had no terrestrial equivalent; they varied in size from small dwellings to large, communal chambers easily thirty feet across. Between them were lattices of ropes festooned with vegetation, whilst the structures themselves – to say nothing of the tethers – were increasingly amorphous thanks to the rampant growth of coral and crusts of barnacles. Above, great masses of sargassum drifted like clouds.

The entire city – and it certainly was a city, for even through the sapphire haze, Renata could see that the settlement stretched for at least a mile – was a hive of activity. Crustaceans scuttled across the surface of the buildings, as abundant as vermin, whilst herring dogs zipped around the tethers, clicking and squealing at each other. Everywhere drifted idle masses of fish, no doubt drawn by the great cornucopia presented by the tether city.

This was Ozeanland, one of the first mer-men settlements the Sovans had come across, and so the first to be burdened with the deeply unimaginative Saxan name of "ocean country". But whilst Ozeanland might have been significant for the Sovans, it was in fact one of the lesser Stygion settlements. The capital, Maris, was over a hundred and fifty nautical miles to the north-west, near the Iris Isles.

They drew an enormous amount of attention as they were towed into the city. Many of the entities that Renata had assumed were fish actually resolved into more Stygion. They moved with incredible grace, and made no secret of their curiosity – especially the children, who orbited the newcomers in an excitable cloud along with dozens of herring dogs and seals which tailed the mer-men young like pets. The water filled with a cacophony of spoken Loxica as they all chittered and chattered in a maddening chorus of clicks and atonal hums.

For all the excitement of the children, there was an undeniable air of hostility from many of the adults. Even though Ozeanland was largely unmolested by the Sovan Navy, their brethren in other coastal tether cities frequently tangled with Imperial sailors and fishermen; they had long ago learnt to avoid the men-o'-war sailing from Port Gero.

This hostility, taken with the looming danger posed by the white sharks, the endless breadth and depth of the ocean itself, the unswimmable distance to shore, and the fact that she was being kept alive by a fish slaved to the magickal whims of her hosts, conspired to provide a foil to the delighted wonder that Renata was desperate to feel. Instead, she felt vulnerable and intimidated, and missed Maruska and his confident expertise keenly. It made her grateful for the presence of Lyzander – even if he himself was deeply unhappy.

The two Spears who had brought them to Ozeanland had gone, and she and Lyzander floated aimlessly in the water, buoyed by their lungfish helmets, marvelled at like animals in a zoo. After several minutes of this intolerable limbo, another Spear arrived, and one Renata immediately recognised, thanks to the markings on its skin, as her diplomatic opposite number. This Stygion was female, and had blue and black tiger striping on her back and white countershading on her underside.

<Welcome to Ozeanland> she signed. She seemed to do so a little uncomfortably, and there was little wonder in that; she was speaking to Renata in the same way she would speak to a lover or family member. It elicited a great burst of amused excitement from the crowd of observers – which only served to irritate the diplomat further. <My name is Sina>

<Excellency> Renata said back. <I am Ambassador Renata Rainer. This is my companion, Joseph Lyzander>

Sina looked at Lyzander, the nictitating membranes over her eyes flashing glossy and gold in the sun's light. <You do not have Didacus with you>

<He is dead>

Sina considered this for a moment. <Bad>

Maruska had warned Renata that the Stygion could appear to be a cold and unfeeling people, and the superficial savagery of their society certainly suggested a race devoid of the empathic capacity of humans. But whilst it was true that the ocean had scoured away some of their softer qualities – "hard places breed hardy peoples" – they were just as capable of kindness and compassion as anyone else.

<Yes>

Sina paused, first to dissuade the approach of a large squid, and secondly to disperse the crowd of children, who for all their unaffected and delightful curiosity were becoming quite annoying.

A moment later, a large white shark meandered lazily through the water to appear at her right elbow. <This is Teulia> the ambassador said, running a hand over the rough skin of the shark's head with great fondness. To Renata it was like stroking the iron spout of a cannon. <She'll keep you safe>

Renata almost asked what it was they needed to be kept safe from; instead, she said, <Thank you>

<Come>

Sina signalled for Renata to grip Teulia's dorsal fin, and motioned for Lyzander to hold her hand – which he did, though with incredible reluctance. A moment later they were being towed again through the apparent chaos of Ozeanland, to a large chamber perhaps two or three fathoms below the water's surface. Renata could not help but notice that they were being trailed aggressively by a dozen or so Stygion, at least half of them Spears; nor could she help notice that Sina did not seem to be particularly invested in dispersing them.

Here they were at the extremity of the city, with nothing but the beautiful blue-green waters of the ocean stretching away into the distance, sparkling in the evening sunlight. Would the Stygion swim her back to the shore before night-time? It was something she had not considered, but it seemed like one of the few things that could make the experience even more unsettling: being in the water after dark.

Within the ambassadorial chamber – which was rather large at the better part of twenty feet in diameter – were all manner of trinkets. It reminded Renata of her own chambers within the Imperial Office, filled as it was with pictures and *objets*. Given that they were underwater, this chamber was laid out differently by necessity; it seemed that the predominant form of decoration was a colourful marine growth that was husbanded and shaped into attractive patterns in the same way one might indulge in topiary. Personal items were secured to the walls with an organic netting that looked to be some sort of braided kelp or sargassum, whilst the windows could be covered over with the same, presumably to prevent unwanted entry. But by the very nature of these structures and their society, the Stygion simply did not accumulate valuable material possessions in the same way that Sovans did, and had not developed the need to protect them with doors and locks.

<We were not expecting an ambassadorial visit> Sina said once they had arranged themselves. <I would have prepared something for you to eat>

<Please do not worry> Renata replied, though she was ravenous.

<The timing of your arrival is auspicious. My people have a very long list of grievances to air. Plenty would like to kill one or both of you to send a message to your masters>

Renata's gut surged. Sina had presented this with no apparent hostility at all, and that felt somehow worse; to be threatened with death, however tacitly, as a matter of emotionless fact rather than in anger.

Fraternalism, she thought, trying to conjure up in her mind Managold's five tenets of diplomacy. Except all she could think about was Guillot, and his bitter, sarcastic laughter.

<I am aware of the problems caused by the Sovan Navy> she said. Was this a test? To deny that they had done anything wrong seemed ludicrous, and was sure to inflame the situation. But then, her predominant injunction as a diplomat was *Sova in all things*. She was a representative of the Empire, not of the Stygion, and it was certainly not in the Empire's interests to acknowledge its own many and ongoing crimes. To admit wrongdoing, after all, was to create liabilities, either to diplomatic quid pro quos, or reparations, or both.

They had barely exchanged three sentences and already Renata was overwhelmed by the endlessly branching possibilities. Each thing she said was so freighted with unforeseeable consequence, each fresh route so marred with pitfalls and traps and unwitting obligations and grievances.

Sina moved quickly from professional neutrality to visible incredulity.

<Did I understand that correctly? "Problems"? Was that the word you used?>

Renata felt thoroughly out of her depth. She carried in her words the authority of one of the largest empires in the world.

<You must forgive my clumsiness> she said after a moment's thought. <I have not had a chance to practise my Loxica on a real Stygion>

Maruska might have praised her for that subtle piece of redirection – might have praised her if it had worked. But Sina did not take the bait.

<The Sovan Navy frequently kills our people. They fire their ships' cannons and harpoons into our cities. They kill our oyster farmers. They murder our whales and sharks for meat and herring dogs for sport. You have made industry of such slaughter on the place you call Vitaney Island>

What would Maruska have done? He would have acknowledged Sina's feelings on the matter, rather than the – alleged – crimes themselves. He would have nodded sympathetically, and prevaricated; he would have agreed with the central assertion – that killing was wrong – in a vacuum, robbing it of the crucial context. "Yes," he might have said, "it is always difficult to hear about one's countrymen being killed." In so doing, he would have given away nothing except superficial agreement. And he would have done it all in a foreign language, too.

And that was why Maruska had been the ambassador, and Renata had not.

<I know that there are many issues to discuss. Many matters to address> she signed eventually. Actually, she would reflect, it was another rather deft piece of misdirection. <But I am here because there is an issue which affects us all, as mortal peoples>

Clarity of will. Stay focused on the issue at hand.

For all the undeniable hostility radiating off Sina, even her interest was piqued by this.

<Whatever it is you wish to speak to me about, know that you will not get our cooperation on any matter without assurances that certain of your practices will stop>

Renata endured another wave of uncertainty, once again viscerally aware of the power vested in her. If the Great Silence was real, then the sensible thing to do was to agree to all of Sina's demands. After all, there was no point in aggressively protecting and consolidating Sova's position if Sova – and the rest of the world – would shortly not exist.

But even with that in mind, she found it difficult to yield up anything that could satisfy the Stygion ambassador. And besides, there had to be more formality than just what Renata said in one tether city to one person. There would need to be treaties, which would have to be witnessed and ratified. Perhaps there was more room for equivocation than she thought.

<Please hear what I have to say, and then we can discuss conditions>

Sina's dissatisfaction at this seemed to be shared by Teulia, for the great white shark was swimming rings around the chamber outside. Whether this was simply out of psychological tethering or an intimidation tactic, Renata did not know. What was much clearer was the intention of the crowd of mer-men who had followed them and now floated outside of the diplomatic residence.

Eventually, Sina acquiesced. <Why are you here, then, if not to discuss the many crimes of your people?>

<As you know, the practice of magicks in Sova is illegal>

<Yes>

<Some weeks ago, we were visited by a pair of monks from an order who have been secretly communing with the dead. With the afterlife>

<Yes>

Renata paused, confused. <You know of this?>

<I know that our Psychic Conclave are aware of it. They are in Maris>

Renata's blood surged. How was it that the Sovans were the last people to hear of this? Indeed, they might never have done had it not been for the reckless bravery of the Bruta Sarkan monks. Never before had the proscription of sorceries seemed like such a self-inflicted wound.

<The monks reported to us, on risk of execution, that they had lost contact with the afterlife. That this loss of contact aligns with an ancient prophecy known as the Great Silence. They are not able to tell us what the Great Silence is precisely, save that it portends the end of the world. We had hoped to speak with the Kasar about the matter, but Port Talaka has fallen—>

<Small wonder> Sina sneered. <You have infected the wolf-men with opposing branches of the same religious root. Now they kill each other by the thousand. We had missionaries from Ten Dai, did you know that? Shouting into the water, trying to convert the tetherers at Gyatso>

It was interesting to Renata that the Loxican for "wolfman" was "honourable brother".

She shook her head. <No, I didn't know that. What happened to them?>

<Killed, of course>

<Of course>

<What did the Dwelkspreker say?>

Again Renata paused. She had not expected the Stygion ambassador to know about the Dwelkspreker – but of course, the Stygion and Kasar had much friendlier and healthier bilateral relations than the Stygion and Sova.

<That our fears were well founded>

<But not the nature of the threat>

<Only that it is as acute as we fear>

The light levels in the diplomatic chamber suddenly dropped, and Renata turned to see a large white shark swimming slowly past the aperture that acted as a skylight. The noise outside the chamber was growing, a discordant and atonal collection of hums and clicks which seemed to reach her ears the moment they were transmitted. Directionally it was impossible to pinpoint them.

<Am I under threat here?> she asked, her patience fraying. <I am a formal ambassador plenipotentiary of the Sovan Empire. Whatever your grievance with my people, I and my associate should be immune from harm>

Sina looked annoyed, but her irritation was not directed at Renata. She swam fluidly directly into the outer chamber and shouted animatedly at her peers, in Loxican so quick and thickly accented that Renata could not keep up with it. Renata moved to the same exit, and saw beyond Teulia swimming in a short and aggressive circle with another one of the Spear's white sharks. She knew from her studies that this was classic aristocratic posturing, one with a very good chance of ending in bloodshed. Either way, two things were clear:

First, that a sizeable number of Stygion here wanted her dead.

Second, that Sina was not necessarily in a position to stop them.

After another angry exchange, Sina swam back into the ambassadorial chamber, and this time strung netting across the entrance – netting that looked as though it could be dislodged with a sharp glance.

<They are angry, and they have good reason to be> she said as she returned. <But I will not have it said that *we* violated diplomatic protocol. I will not give the Sovan Navy any more excuses to try and destroy us>

Renata looked up at Lyzander. He was pressed against the ceiling of the chamber like a piece of flotsam, eyes wide through the bulging transparent skin of the lungfish.

<Thank you> she said, turning back to Sina. <I would gladly hear all of your grievances, but right now I really must speak with your Psychic Conclave>

<*Must?*> Sina sneered.

<This is something which affects all of us>

<Are you so certain? You have rightly identified that your magickal ability pales in comparison to ours. Who is to say that we desire to make common cause? A world without Sova is a pleasant prospect for many>

Renata gritted her teeth. *Credibility in authority.*

<I have come here to work with you, but know that we have the ability to—>

<I should not finish that sentence, if I were you> Sina said. <A shark attack is not a pretty thing to witness, even for a Stygion. Certainly I have never become accustomed to the violence of it>

<We are into bare threats already, then>

<Does a Sovan know any other way?>

Renata paused a moment. It was getting darker and colder as the evening wore on.

<I do not have much more time> she said, gesturing to the surface.

<You can sleep here tonight>

Her blood surged at such a disagreeable prospect.

<We will get too cold> she signed quickly.

<We can warm you if needs be>

<You cannot imprison us>

Sina gestured in the general direction of the shore. <You are free to leave whenever you wish>

Renata swore inwardly. Her attention returned to the noise outside, which was constant now. The crowd swelled.

She gestured to them. <If I leave, they will kill us>

Sina seemed to consider this for a moment. If she agreed, she undermined her own authority. If she denied it, she would be lying. It would have been a neat lawman's courtroom trick, but Renata took little comfort from her own cleverness. She was too tired now, too overwrought, to maintain any kind of professional reserve.

<Besides, you know we cannot swim that far> she added.

It was this admission of vulnerability that seemed to bestir some sense of remorse in Sina, as if she had regretted her hostility. Renata and Lyzander were, after all, utterly dependent on the Stygion not only for their diplomatic protection but their literal lives. The burden of the diplomat – the moral imperative – was to treat with a person who in any other circumstances would be an enemy; and not just to treat with them, but to be professional, courteous, and responsible for their well-being. Maruska had likened it to accepting the responsibility of looking after another's children. Renata found the comparison an apt one.

Sina softened. <Forgive this petty sparring. My people speak of little else except revenge against the Sovans. A lot of it is just angry talk. But I have become coloured by it. I have seen firsthand the damage done by your countrymen: the deaths, the anguish of those left behind. A whale mother's lamentation for her dead calf carries for a hundred miles. We cannot protect our children from the song>

<We can speak about it when there is more time> Renata wanted to have compassion and patience – had always envisaged herself possessing those qualities – but it was getting darker, the water gloomier and chillier, the sharks moving in ever more agitated ways, the crowd outside getting angrier. <But I really just do need to speak with your Psychic Conclave>

She had not anticipated quite how physically and mentally taxing the encounter would be. She was exhausted already, kept artificially alert by the very audible anger of the crowd beyond the walls of the chamber.

<I will—> Sina began, and then Renata's heart leapt as an enormous mouth slammed into the door to the diplomatic chamber. A set of jaws two feet wide clamped around the net and ripped it out, and then began to bite ferociously at the resinous walls either side of it. The chamber filled with clouds of muck, as coral and other sea plants were dislodged and pulverised by the assault.

-◎ 391 ◎-

Renata let out a scream and backed away to the far end of the room. Lyzander grabbed her around the midriff and pulled her away, interposing himself between her and the shark's mouth – a piece of incredible valour. She gripped his back tightly, her overriding fear that the lungfish would become dislodged, or unwrap itself of its own accord and swim away, forcing her to surface.

There was a sudden rush of water, and she saw Teulia slam into the shark from the side, clouding the water with blood. A savage duel ensued between the two huge fish, whilst the noise of the crowd rivalled that of the Sovan Arena during the summer games. Sina, apparently not just an ambassador but an accomplished selachomancer and duellist, channelled several blasts of fast-moving water into the crowd, dispersing at least the commonfolk – "nulls" – and their much less impressive array of familiars. As for the other Spears, protocol forced them to step back and allow the duel to progress, though several of the more aggressive females were riding their sharks in wide circles around the outside of the diplomatic chamber. One of those sharks had a helmet of resinous segmenta – the same durable organic material which the tether cities were constructed from – denoting a Spear of the warrior caste.

The shark duel was appalling in its violence and ferocity. It did not take long for Teulia to see off the challenger, and its Spear with it, for each Stygion shared a psychic bond with their shark, and damage to one resulted in mental damage to the other. But then another shark breached underneath her, rolling her dramatically, Sina was becoming visibly agitated as events spiralled out of control.

Renata thumped Lyzander on the shoulder, and he turned, his eyes wide behind the glasses. She pointed manically to the surface. It seemed like lunacy to try to escape, but they had to do something. If Sina died, they would be killed immediately.

Summoning all her reserves of courage, she moved with Lyzander out of the chamber's farthest aperture, the one that looked out on to the open ocean. She glanced around constantly for signs of other sharks, but most of the attention was now focused on the fight between Sina and her challengers.

They kicked their way upwards until they broke the surface. The lungfish quickly slithered away as they were exposed to the cold evening air, leaving Renata and Lyzander coughing and spluttering amongst the waves. Above, huge banks of cloud had closed in, rendering the sky a dramatic tableau of purple and orange and grey. The same wind which had set the clouds to scudding had also whipped the water into an unforgiving chop, something they had not felt five fathoms below the surface.

Renata's heart dropped into her stomach. Port Gero was so far away, easily two or three miles. The intervening water was cold and grey and forbidding, and had lost the green lustre for which it was named.

"Nema!" Lyzander shouted after a lengthy scream. "What in the damned fucking hell is going on?!" He spluttered and spat as he struggled to keep his head above the waves. It was easy to forget that he could not speak Loxica, and had had nothing to go on except what he had seen and witnessed.

Renata didn't have time to give him an answer. She kept ducking back under the water, trying to see what was happening. It was remarkable how hidden Ozeanland had become; it was barely visible through the evening gloom.

She resurfaced, spitting out a great mouthful of brine. "We need to get back to land!" she shouted. It seemed ludicrous; even for a confident swimmer, it was much too far.

"Look out!" Lyzander shrieked. Renata looked down, just in time to see a huge shark's mouth opening directly underneath her feet—

She didn't even have time to scream. A second shape, an enormous black and white blur, smashed into the shark from the side. A huge patch of red blossomed in the water as the blackfish – easily twenty-five feet from nose to tail – rammed the white shark on to its side and tore out its liver in a great welter of cloudy guts and frayed rags of salt-bleached flesh. From the incredible cacophony of noise rose a spine-tingling howl of anguish from the Spear who'd just had half his mind burned away.

Renata quickly surfaced again to take one last gulp of air, ignoring Lyzander's frantic pleas for information, and then ducked back down. She tried to cut through the chaos of movement and noise – everywhere was just swishing tails and clouds of marine viscera – until the blackfish slowly cruised towards her through the gloom.

If the white sharks had been intimidating, the blackfish was in a league of its own. Not only was it four times the size, but it wore a ridged and horned helmet of black resin, hinged at the jaw, wrought into the visage of a furious grotesque. In sleek ridges across its back were further armoured segmenta, carefully contoured to its body, whilst cruel hooked spikes were strapped in rings to its white underbelly to deter any breaching sharks.

There was no question that this blackfish was the great bull Kaipatu, the Thrice Queen's personal familiar. The Queen herself was seated in an ornate saddle of iridescent resin that was strapped behind Kaipatu's dorsal fin. She wore an incredible suit of armour, the pauldrons smithed into detailed simulacra of crustaceans, the cuirass gnarled with intricate shells and barnacles, the helmet inlaid with mother-of-pearl and swept back to contour the bony ridges of her own skull. She herself was tiger-striped like Sina, but yellow and blue, with her facial fins a vibrant orange striped with black.

From Kaipatu's mouth floated rags of white shark flesh.

<You are the Sovans> the Thrice Queen signed, her elfin face a mask of disdain. With a flick of her hand, a lungfish slithered out of the gloom and reaffixed itself over Renata's head.

<We are, Ina> she gasped, remembering to use the Queen's Loxican honorific. <We must return to shore soon. We need food and rest, and we are cold>

<No> the Thrice Queen signed sharply, in such a way as to convey extreme displeasure. <You will come to Maris>

Renata found herself shaking her head in disbelief. It was a journey of over two hundred nautical miles. The sheer distance of it alone was intimidating enough.

And yet, was that not why she was here? She was a diplomat after all. This was the life, the profession she had chosen. She had been desperate for this sort of mission since before she joined the Imperial Office. And besides, there was nothing in the world more important. It was easy to forget in and amongst these petty conflicts that there was much more at stake than their own survival. Making contact with the Stygion was not an end in itself; it was but the very beginning of a much larger, much more important mission.

And so she gritted her teeth, and nodded her acquiescence. <We will come with you> she said in Loxica.

Again the Thrice Queen made her contempt known.

<It was not a request>

XXVI

The Key Is Blood

*"If you want to bear witness to foreign policy being made,
avoid the Senate House, the Royal Courts, the Imperial
Household, the Privy Council, and the Councils of Nobles,
Bishops and Princes altogether. The fate of nations is decided
at the dinner table, in the kaffeehaus, in the brandy hall."*

SENATOR JULIJA PAVIČIĆ

Castle Oldenburg

COUNTY OF HAUNERWALD

"Prince of Hell, Lena!" von Oldenburg thundered as she let the brand clatter heavily on to the desk of his study. "Nema – be careful!" he added, as though she had dropped a newborn.

"I do not condone this," she said. Something had changed about her. She had helped him with his projects before – admittedly none of them had been so freighted with potential – and had done so with alacrity. But with this ... She was grappling with something.

"I know that," he muttered irritably, taking a swig of tonic.

"You are losing control of this."

"I am not."

"You are losing control of yourself."

"I am not!" he shouted.

"There is a malaise within the afterlife and you are exposing yourself to it with increasing recklessness. Who knows what tunes you unwittingly dance to?"

"The only tune I dance to is my own."

Yelena looked meaningfully at the vacant that had once been Žofia the scullery maid. She lay quietly in the corner, though she had thrashed a little on Yelena's entry into the study, a slave to her single and overriding imperative to transmit the mind rot.

"What is your point?" von Oldenburg muttered, turning back to his notes. "I fully intended to en-thrall her."

"Why did you not take a condemned man?" Yelena demanded, hitting upon his own private reservations. "Why must you do this to members of your own household staff?"

"The more I can keep this within the walls of Castle Oldenburg, the better. It would not do to be wandering into town, picking gaols and taverns and whorehouses clean of drunks and criminals. Word would spread."

"You are a fool if you think word has not spread already. There are demons in hell who envy your reputation."

"Spare me your histrionics, Lena," he muttered, returning to the brand which Yelena had had the smith fashion. He would probably have to have the smith killed too – assuming the brand functioned as intended.

He examined it. Per his specification, the circular ideogram had been mounted on the end of a sturdy pole the same weight and length as a fire poker. The brand, after all, needed to be wielded as much as a weapon as a tool. The ideogram itself had been expertly and intricately wrought. Now, when heated and applied directly to the skin of a vacated person, in theory they should become en-thralled as effectively as when Yelena had cut the ideogram into Kyselý's forehead.

He picked up the brand and shoved it into the fireplace.

"If this works, we can make preparations to quit Haunerwald immediately."

There was a long silence. "You mean to go through with it, then?" Yelena asked.

He nodded his head. "I do."

"How did you get the mechanism to work?"

"The key was blood," he replied. "I'm not quite sure how it works yet, but I believe that the blood of a vacated person acts like a conduit between planes of existence. Harnessed in this way, I can store it like a fluid-metal battery, to be unleashed at will. It means that I no longer need Kyselý to vacate people."

"The mechanism will do it?"

"Aye. It still requires direct contact, though. And of course, we still need to imprint them with the relevant wards to bend them to my will."

He snatched the brand from the fireplace and walked smartly over to where Žofia lay thrashing. He stood astride her head and pinned it between his ankles, and then thrust the burning brand directly on to her forehead. There was a brief sizzle of flesh, a brief stink of the same, and she immediately stopped moving.

Von Oldenburg withdrew the brand. "It worked," he said with a brief, forced smile. He didn't feel happy. He felt no sense of accomplishment. To the contrary, everything about it disgusted him. This should have been a triumph of scientific achievement; instead, his mood was black – and it was Yelena's fault. Her *miserliness*, her constant doubt, questioning, undermining, was really getting under his skin. Of course, he couldn't expect her to appreciate the ramifications of the technology, nor to be excited about the prospect of the fall of the House of Casimir. Her Draedist origins would forever preclude her from such modes of thinking, no matter how much time she spent with him in Haunerwald.

But she might have at least been appreciative of his success, and impressed by his ingenuity and tenacity. Instead, she seemed . . .

"Disgusted."

"What?" Yelena's brow furrowed in confusion.

"You are disgusted with me and this work."

She did not refute it, as he secretly hoped she might.

"Who would not be?" she shouted. "Look at what it is you are doing! And Kyselý, dead in the basement? A man who gave you two decades of service, murdered!"

"And who helped me murder him!" von Oldenburg thundered. "Who was the one who cut the sigil into his head? Certainly I could not have done it without your help! How dare you stand there and judge me when you have been *instrumental* in this success! Foundational! Indispensable! Damn it, woman, I ask again, why are you *here*? What business do you have in this place? You *hate* me and my methods, yet you take steps to assist me, to preserve my life, to further my pursuits. You fuck me, but you will not bear my children. You say you love me, but you will not marry me. Who *are* you?"

To von Oldenburg's surprise, Yelena weathered this diatribe with impassivity. But if he thought he was going to wring an explanation from her, he was mistaken.

"Well?"

"I have nothing to tell you. You know everything about me there is to know."

"Nonsense!" he spat, taking a step toward her. He brandished a finger, opening his mouth to unleash another tirade, then paused, reached into his breast pocket, and took out the tonic there. He unstoppered it and took a large swallow of the bitter liquid, dabbing his mouth as the normal torrent of saliva followed. "You are ferociously fucking irritating, do you know that? Are you even here?" he demanded. "Are you even real?" He snatched the tonic back out of his pocket, examining the ingredients for hallucinogens. But there was nothing, just a bracing concoction of caffeine, mercury and heroin.

Yelena shook her head sadly. "Lamprecht . . . I *do* love you," she said, her eyes wet with tears. "You make it very hard to love you, but I do."

Von Oldenburg paused. That, he had not expected.

He turned to the prostrate, still and vacant form of Žofia; but of course, the scullery maid was not going anywhere.

"Well . . . you know how I feel about you," he said, suddenly on the back foot. He took a step towards Yelena, and she took a step towards him. Something stirred within him, a sense of lust which he frequently conflated with love and affection. He closed with her feverishly. She winced slightly at the smell of his breath –the tonic really was quite pungent – but he kissed her fiercely nonetheless, and she kissed him back, and did the small moan she knew he liked and which signified her surrender to the moment.

His ardour was suddenly and dramatically inflamed. He fumbled with his breeches and thrust them down to his knees, and she hitched up her skirt. In spite of her apparently enthusiastic reciprocation, it was clear she was not ready to take him. He rubbed her vigorously the way he knew women liked, though she quickly stopped him and redirected his hand to her breast, which he grasped eagerly. After a minute of this he grew impatient, and she took him inside her, and he began the brisk business of rutting away to climax.

He finished quickly, much too pent-up and overexcited to savour the experience. *Perhaps this time,* he thought idly, *she will conceive.* But some part of him knew she would not. And besides, his work had reached sudden fruition; to be thinking about having children now seemed most ill-advised.

His mood blackened quickly as the brief euphoric hit faded, not helped by the sight of the catatonic maid in the corner of the room, who had borne witness to their coupling with bovine incomprehension.

"Look away, damn you," he muttered to the girl – and she, en-thralled to him, complied immediately, which made him feel even worse. What had he *done*? What horror had he unleashed on the world?

The light was fading in the late evening, and he was tired, having not slept well. He rearranged himself so as to regain some of his modesty, whilst Yelena did the same. Suddenly he was eager to be out of her company.

"I am going to have a bath before bed," he said, shambling over to a drinks cabinet, from which he liberated a large decanter of brandy and a crystal tumbler. "I shall see you in the morning."

"See you in the morning," Yelena replied brusquely.

He left and made his way upstairs, seeing off the first brandy en route and pouring himself a second. There was neither hair nor hide of members of his staff, and he shouted incoherently for the better part of twenty minutes for someone to draw him a bath. Still no one attended him, and so he drew his own and climbed in.

The tonic was a powerful soporific when combined with a few charged glasses of brandy, and he nearly fell asleep and drowned. He managed to drag himself into his bedchamber, where he dried himself off and collapsed into the bed still naked. Within minutes he drifted into a wild fever dream, with the cracks and crevices and ridges of the duvet transforming into a god's-eye view of a mountain range. He heard himself mumbling instructions to Broz and watching the diplomatic mission's progress across the topographical sheets.

He slipped in and out of sleep in this way for what felt like hours, until eventually an impression of a person, like a deceased parent in the mind of an infant, swelled and monopolised his thoughts. It was a deeply unpleasant sensation.

Eventually he sat up. "Who's there?" he heard himself ask, still half asleep.

At the foot of his bed stood a figure shrouded in shadow. Von Oldenburg couldn't make out the spectral form, but by *Nema* its presence terrified him.

THE KEY, the ghastly apparition spoke in three overlapping voices, IS *BLOOD*.

∼

Von Oldenburg awoke with a lurch the following morning. His head pulsed with a painful headache. Instinctively he reached for the tonic on the nightstand, and took another large swallow – probably too much this time, after a decent volume the night before, especially since he had taken on so much alcohol, too. But he found it increasingly difficult to function without it.

He drooled uncontrollably for a few moments. This time he just let it soak into the duvet; he was much too preoccupied with a sudden fluttering of his heart, and a great bout of perspiration, which was not abnormal when drinking the tonic, though not normally as acute.

"The key is blood," he said aloud into the leaden air of the bedchamber. The sudden appearance of the apparition had been unwelcome and frightening, but it had had the same substance as a nightmare: unpleasant in the moment, fuzzy and forgettable in the light of day.

Still, that he had heard this bizarre declaration twice now could not be ignored. He thought of Yelena's words from the evening before: *Who knows what tunes you unwittingly dance to?* He had to admit, with incredible grudging, that she might have been right. What *had* he entangled himself in? In conducting his research and constructing his mechanism, had he become ensnared in the designs of some celestial creature? These sorts of stories were common within the Nema Victorian Creed and the many volumes that had been written on the arcana – Sovan argonauts being used as pawns in the great battle between the forces of Nema and of Kasivar, the Prince of Hell. Saint Helena of Muldau was a famous recent example he could call to mind, though there were many others.

"Yelena?" he called out, for she had not slept with him.

He threw off the duvet and pulled on underwear, a shirt and breeches. Outside it was a pleasant, sunny morning – and much too late. "Damn," he muttered. Normally he was up at the crack of dawn. Still, it was no great mystery; he'd had a difficult evening and a poor night's sleep, and Nema knew his household staff were no longer around to rouse him. That was something else that needed looking into; just precisely where the hell they had all gone.

"Yelena!" he shouted as he exited his bedchamber. He supposed it was rather pointless, given that she could have been anywhere in the castle. Notwithstanding, he continued to bellow her name again and again.

There was no response.

He moved through the corridors and halls, bristling at the continued lack of servants. The familiar scent of breakfast cooking was also conspicuous in its absence.

"Damn bloody fools," he muttered to himself. He was going to have to hire out of county.

He made his way to the great hall, but the table had not been laid and the drapes were still closed.

"Where the devil is everybody?" His voice echoed through the empty room.

A thought struck him.

"Hm." He chewed absently on the callous between his thumb and index finger. "Yelena," he said slowly. It was almost a growl.

He quit the great hall and moved, now with a vague sense of urgency, to the study.

The door was locked.

"Yelena. Yelena!" He rattled the handle violently. "Yelena, damn you, open this door!"

He pressed his ear to it, but there was no sound from beyond. Slightly unsteady on his feet, he took several steps back, and kicked the door. It did not move. He barged it with his shoulder, and it gave slightly, but remained locked. With an angry sigh, he took several decent steps back, and charged it like a furious bull.

This time the door gave way. Von Oldenburg lurched into the room, and then tumbled down the steps just beyond the threshold, landing hard on the floor.

He swore profusely, and grunted as he climbed to his feet, knees and ankles popping. His eyes traced his workbench, searching for the mechanism, the brand, his books.

It was all gone.

"No," he breathed, throwing open chests, yanking out drawers, scattering papers and scrolls and books, tearing down bookshelves—

It was all gone.

"No! No! NO! *NO!*"

He looked urgently to the corner to see that Žofia was still there, and he closed with her quickly. "Žofia, get up!" he commanded, but she did not move. "Get up this instant!" he thundered, but she remained completely motionless, staring glassy-eyed at the ceiling.

She was dead. Worse: the skin of her forehead, where the brand had been, was cut away to the bone.

"Yelena!" he roared, launching to his feet. "Yelena, damn, fuck and blast you, YELENA!"

The brand was gone. He checked the fireplace, using his bare hands to throw out fistfuls of ash, hot coals and lumps of old, charred wood.

"My notes, my damned fucking notes!" he raged, ripping open books, trying to find his journals, drafts, any scrap of paper that might contain something, *anything* that he had written down—

"*YELENA!*" he screamed, but of course she was gone, long gone, probably the moment he had got into the bath. By the clock it was ten in the morning; she had twelve hours on him, tens of miles with a tailwind, and with all his notes and—

"Prince of Hell, the mechanism," he breathed.

He charged back out of the study and through the corridors, making his way back up countless flights of steps to his chamber.

There he ransacked his drawers until his hand closed around the cold brass sphere of the prototype mechanism. He let out a shaky sigh of relief, which transmuted into a ferocious growl of rage.

He gripped the new mechanism in his hands, holding it tightly like an eight-pound cannonball as he laughed and cried maniacally. Of course, of *course*. Sova had got to her. What had they offered? What had her instructions been? Clearly she had been told to play out the rope, to see his mind, his plans, and above all what he could accomplish. He had been such a damned fucking fool to think that Sova had no magickal contingency beyond the engineering corps. Their magickal contingency was *him*. No wonder he had never encountered any real difficulty, no wonder his operation to amass so much in the way of curios and artefacts and grimoires had proceeded virtually unopposed. They had let him.

They had fucking *let* him.

"That damn woman, that damn bloody woman," he muttered, and bit the callous on his hand so savagely he tore it clean away. Blood dribbled down his hand and arm and pattered against the rug on the floor. "Fuck. Fuck!"

Would they come for him now? The Army? What authority did Yelena command? Where did she sit within the hierarchy? She probably had a direct line of communication to the Empress herself. She had been with him for ten years. She had to have been one of their most prized assets. Had she ever even been from Draedaland?

"Shit, shit, *shit*," von Oldenburg said, wiping his hand on his shirt. It was bleeding profusely. What a foolish thing to have done. It was precisely the sort of thing that would kill him, some stupid, reckless, self-inflicted wound which would become enpoxed. It was precisely the sort of pathetic end his enemies would wish for him

"How long to Sova?" he asked the air, walking through the corridors. "Five days with decent staging." He went down to the dungeon, to where Kyselý's body lay slowly decomposing.

Yelena's medical case was still there, and he fumbled through the various glass jars and potions until he found carbolic acid. He doused his hand in it, screaming with the pain, and then wrapped it in a bandage.

"Assume a week," he said, pacing the stinking chamber.

He stopped dead.

He slowly turned to the corpse of his former butler.

The ideogram was still carved into his forehead. In her haste to leave, Yelena had forgotten about Kyselý.

Frantically he ran back to the study and snatched up several sheets of paper and a pen, then returned to the corpse and made detailed copies of the ideogram. It was wretchedly scabrous, but von Oldenburg was a viciously intelligent man, with a very good memory, and it was not long before he had a decent facsimile.

More preparations needed to be made. A week to quit Castle Oldenburg; really, a matter of days. He needed to get north, give himself head start, lose himself in the anarchy of Draedaland. Perhaps he would make his way to Verdabaro, link up with the Selureii there.

"That *bitch*," he hissed furiously, nearly crumpling his drawings in a fresh rage. "That damned fucking . . . *turncoat shrew!*"

So much to do – too much to do. But Lamprecht von Oldenburg was a resourceful man. There was still time.

He was confident he could prevail.

XXVII

A Bigger Fish

"The children of the wealthy should be discouraged from joining the Imperial Office; they are frequently meritless as candidates. Such people have led privileged, frictionless lives, and are unserious by their nature. They make for very poor diplomats, having not had to work or compromise for anything in their lives, and are poorly equipped for the crucible of foreign policy, where empathy, understanding, negotiation, and concession are fundamental doctrines."

FROM AN IMPERIAL OFFICE INTERNAL MEMORANDUM

Maris

JADE SEA

They covered the distance much more quickly than just the fast swimming of Kaipatu could account for. Even though the blackfish was enormous, and the flex of his tail incredibly powerful, it was clear that the Stygion were using their channelling powers and their knowledge of ocean currents to speed them on their way.

They headed north-north-west, swimming long into the night. The Queen had with her a dozen Royal Spears, and Renata and Lyzander were saddled on to the backs of huge bull white sharks, bent forward so as to adopt the most streamlined position possible.

Being surrounded by a great mass of sharks and blackfish meant Renata was able to acclimate to their presence and shake off her innate fear of them, but the ocean itself remained a great source of anxiety. Ozeanland had been but a few miles from the shore of the Horn; now they were well and truly in open water, with no sign of land in any direction – not that there was anything to see thanks to the midnight darkness.

They swam endlessly. The ocean currents were warm enough to stave off hypothermia, but never quite warm enough to be comfortable. But in the event, the constant swishing motion of the sharks' tails, the darkness, and the monotony of the journey eventually conspired to lull Renata into a state of fractured and unsatisfactory sleep.

It was from this state of half-consciousness that she was rudely roused. Several hours out from Maris, the Stygion around her exchanged a sudden and frantic burst of chatter; and this was followed by a dive so quick and deep that Renata's ears and nose pulsed and clicked and the skin of the lungfish closed in around her head claustrophobically. There they floated, a good seven or eight fathoms below the surface. Above, the weak grey light of dawn rippled and eddied with the chop.

Renata was about to ask what was happening, imagining some monstrous leviathan known only to the Stygion that was about to devour them; but Lyzander, who was looking much more relaxed now that he had acclimated to both the ocean and their situation, pointed ahead and upwards. She followed the line of his finger, to see the copper-alloy-sheathed bottom of a huge warship moving ponderously above them.

All of them were very still and quiet for a moment; and then there was a flash and a great plume of smoke from the ship's bow chaser, and a cannonball punched into the water above with incredible force, trailing a great streamer of ferociously churned water. For at least four fathoms it maintained sufficient force to cut a mer-man in half, and enough energy to seriously injure someone for several more after. Following it were dozens of smaller musket balls, which had neither the weight nor the force behind them to do much damage beyond a fathom or so, though the psychological effect was quite terrifying.

The Queen scowled at Renata, though Renata was not sure it was even a Sovan ship – it was much likelier to be a Casimiran or Sanqish vessel this close to the Iris Isles. Either way, she wasn't about to argue; they could easily have kept moving, and been the safer for having done so. The Thrice Queen was looking to make a point.

It was a point well made, too. Renata's blood was singing, and every time a shadow appeared overhead, her heart skipped a few beats. The final couple of hours on approach to Maris were unbearable – though she took some comfort from the presence of sub-marine border forts, staging stations, and trading outposts that littered the approach to the capital.

And then, finally, they arrived.

Maris was to Ozeanland what Sova was to Port Gero. But although it was predominantly a massive tether city, Renata could see, through the mist of the waters, an enormous settlement on the sea floor as well. This part of the Jade Sea looked to Renata to be around twenty fathoms from floor to surface – certainly enough to be vertiginously deep, but nothing like the endless dark depths of the open stretch they had crossed to get here. Here the sunlight fell directly on buildings hundreds of years old, constructed in an almost human style no doubt when the Stygion were still trying to discover the precise nature of themselves and the lives they wanted to live. After all, the ancient mer-men, like the wolfmen, had been suddenly and catastrophically created out of the abrupt infusion of magic into the world. Those early generations, no doubt plagued with endless unviable mutations, would have been racked by physiological and psychological problems of a profoundly existential nature.

Whilst modern Stygion built their technically accomplished buoyed tether cities, which basked in the golden light of the sun, their pre-mediaeval ancestors had preferred a much more Saxan architectural style of building constructed directly on the murky sea floor. The buildings had – at least initially – cleaved to a jarringly gothick mode, though now only a little of it remained visible; the rest had been lost under a kaleidoscopic riot of coral growth.

Maris was therefore literally stratified, with the Royal Household and the equestrian Spear class living in ostentatious resinous structures in the tether layer, and the nulls forced to live on the ocean floor amongst the dull glow of bioluminescent fish. Access to light was their social currency.

It was to Renata's great surprise, therefore, that they were taken directly to the floor, to a structure that looked to her very much like a Neman cathedral that had once existed on land but had since become submerged and overgrown. Chasing them was a great cacophony of chatter from an orbiting crowd of excitable children and their fish, seal and herring dog familiars – though this was quickly dispersed by the Thrice Queen and her bodyguard, the members of which seemed to be looking for the slightest excuse to do violence.

The inside of the cathedral was filled with bioluminescent light, though there were apertures in the roof that allowed the distant sunlight in too. In spite of her excitement and awe at being in the capital, Renata knew from her professional training that this was the home of the Psychic Conclave of Channellers, the Stygion equivalent of the Spiritsraad – what the Sovans would once have called the College of Prognosticators back when such an institution had existed there. But unlike the College of Prognosticators, and indeed the Kasari Spiritsraad, the Psychic Conclave was a secular organisation. In fact, as Renata might have explained to Lyzander, really they were more like a much more powerful version of the Sovan Corps of Engineers.

The chamber was large and filled with artefacts, jarringly distinct from the mostly empty tether structures. To Renata's untrained eye, many of the items looked as though they had some sort of magickal significance. The Stygion were people who had been at pains to preserve, secularise and spread the teaching of magick.

The Conclave was assembled and waiting. There were five of them, a mixture of male and female. Like the majority of the Stygion, they had no need for clothing, armour or ornament, though each of them wore a golden circlet around their heads which Renata knew to be psychic energy attenuators.

<These are the ambassadors?> one of them asked, signing in a sharp, agitated way.

<Yes> the Queen and Sina said in unison, and then the former shot the latter an angry look. <I will speak>

Sina bowed her head in deference. <As you will, Ina>

<Tell the Sovans what you told me. I suspect they are here for the same reason. Certainly it is not to address the ongoing murder of our people>

The head channeller was a wizened old Stygion, his markings faded, his eyes cloudy and sightless. <I am Muirgen> he said to Renata. Although he signed, his accompanying vocalisations resonated inside her head via a psychic tether. Unlike Sina and the Queen, his Loxica was clean and comprehensible.

<I am Ambassador Renata Rainer> she replied. She felt like an impostor, a thief who had stolen Maruska's rightful title. <This is Captain Lyzander, my escort>

<We must speak urgently> Muirgen said. <The Great Silence has begun>

An intense, vertiginous jolt went through Renata.

<It's *real*?> she asked immediately.

<Yes>

For the longest time she had heard the Great Silence spoken of only by Guillot and Herschel, and in many ways they were the poorest possible emissaries for their cause. Guillot had been surly, immature, mercurial – and ultimately a murderer, or at least possessed by one – and Herschel was a kindly but diffident and bumbling fool. Even despite all the corroborative goings-on, the destruction of the mortal plane was a difficult thing to accept and comprehend.

<What is it?> she asked, not wanting to know the answer.

<It is a great deluge of death. Of consumption. Of rampant interdimensional gluttony. It is the end of every form of consciousness that we know>

Renata signed quickly and with greater confidence. Thanks to the psychic tether, Muirgen seemed to be able to understand her much more clearly.

<We were told by a pair of monks from an outlawed sect practising illegal death magicks that they had lost contact with the spirits of the afterlife>

<We know. The Bruta Sarkan>

<You *know* them?>

<Yes>

Renata's head became overstuffed with thoughts. There was too much to say, too many questions to ask, and not enough time. Why had they taken so bloody *long* to get here? Why had they not taken this more seriously? Suddenly the entire diplomatic mission seemed like an exercise in indolence. For Glaser it had only ever been an indulgence, a piece of political risk mitigation. For everyone else it had been the prospect of adventure. How stupid and arrogant they had been!

<What is this prophecy?>

<The Vorr>

A deep sense of foreboding filled Renata to the brim. <The . . . Vorr?>

<The Vorr>

<What are they?>

<Interdimensional devourers. They feed on aethereal energy. They eat it. Consume it. They are not evil; they do not torture souls, or put them to excruciation, or cannibalise their energy for infernal industries. They simply *eat* it. They are vast and insatiable, and they will pick a dimension clean.

<That is what we are contending with. The Vorr. That is why the afterlife has fallen silent. It is not because the spirits no longer wish to communicate with us. It is not because they have gone somewhere else.

<It is because there is no one left to speak to.

<The beings within it have been eaten>

Renata spent some time trying to comprehend this incomprehensible piece of information.

<Nema> she said eventually.

<Indeed>

And then she spasmed with horror.

Amara.

She remembered her dream; that enormous wall, an infinite fortification high above the clouds; she remembered hearing Amara's voice, discorporate, terrified.

They are coming.

Her spiritual essence had been made into chum for mindless interdimensional predators.

It was too much. All of it was too much.

<I need air> she said, feeling frantic.

<You have air> the Queen replied testily.

<No, I need ... I need to get out of here. Just take me to the surface, please. Just . . . I just need air. Nema, I'm going to be sick>

It was Sina, who seemed to have taken on the maternal mantle, who had Teuila spirit Renata to the surface. She broke above the waves, pulling the lungfish off and heaving in great deep breaths she did not need. The water here was only a little choppy, with a cool breeze whipping across the waves. In the distance, she could see the southern extremity of the Iris Isles, a rocky place of scrub and cypress trees bathed in bright light from the sun.

In spite of the cooling effect of the wind and salt spray, she retched, and then let out a great scream. A few moments later, Lyzander broke the surface.

"Renata, my God!" he shouted, tearing his lungfish off. "I heard it. I heard it all, in my head. I can understand him, Renata. I can understand everything Muirgen said." He looked profoundly shaken.

"But Amara was still alive," Renata said quietly to herself, features creased in confusion, kicking her legs to stay above the waves. "She was still alive. Isn't she?"

A dangerous thought took root in her mind: that her half-sister *had* been killed by the pistol ball meant for Renata; that she had died in Sova, long after Renata had left. That her immortal spirit had been *eaten*, chewed upon and swallowed like a morsel of food. It was a horror she could not even begin to approach.

"Amara," she whispered. But it wasn't just Amara: it was Maruska, too. She had seen him in a similar nightmare. The wreck of his body suddenly made horrifying sense; the damage had been done by teeth – huge, monstrous teeth.

It was already too much to bear.

And this was just the beginning.

Renata could get nothing sensible out of Lyzander, and they ended up simply holding each other amongst the bobbing waves until they calmed down. Spear-mounts appeared just beneath the surface, nudging at their legs with their blunt grey snouts, and Renata knew that they had to return. There was still so much more to discuss.

They affixed their lungfishes and were returned quickly to the Psychic Conclave.

<How are you feeling?> Sina asked Renata.

<My sister> Renata signed. <She was recently injured. I thought her to be still alive, but I had a nightmare—>

<Tell me about it> Muirgen interrupted, as though Renata had not been about to do precisely that.

She told them about Amara and the gigantic fortress she had seen, and the similar vision she had had about Maruska. When she had finished, the mood within the Conclave was tangibly glum.

<It is not just dreams> Renata continued. <I have heard things, too. Screaming, terrified screaming, but ... somehow discorporate>

<What you are hearing is the soul's anguish as it is devoured> Muirgen said grimly. <Not only the act of being eaten, but a life force, a cognisance, being extinguished from every possible form of existence across every possible dimension. You are hearing the destruction of not only it, but its *potentiality*>

<And these creatures, the Vorr ... They are waiting for us just beyond the threshold of death?>

<Indeed>

<So every person who dies now will end up straight in their gullets?>

<Yes. Well – perhaps not. We, too, have seen the large wall to which you refer. So perhaps a more accurate answer is: we do not know>

<How did this *happen*? How did it start?>

<We do not know how the Vorr came to be released from the prison dimension>

<The ... what?>

<She doesn't know what you are talking about> the Thrice Queen snapped. Above, Kaipatu's great grotesque visage loomed in one of the cathedral apertures. <You are going to have to explain it to her>

Muirgen turned his sightless eyes back to Renata. <You know of the afterlife?>

<Of course>

<You know that it is another plane of existence, one filled with entities, creatures, nations, and so on, which follow different natural laws which are alien to ours?>

Renata signed *yes* in Loxican.

<And that your aethereal essence, your soul, travels there when you die?>

<Yes, and if you have led a righteous life, you are taken to the Golden City by Nema, and if not, you are taken to the Halls of Hell by Kasivar>

There was a long, pregnant pause.

<We do not have time for this silly idolatry> the Thrice Queen muttered.

<Silly idolatry!?> Renata snapped in spite of herself.

<The beings within the afterlife, they are not more moral than us; they are not better or worse, they are not inherently good, or evil, they just . . . are> Muirgen interjected before the Thrice Queen had Kaipatu bite Renata's head off. <And your aethereal essence travels there whether you like it or not, whether you have been virtuous or evil>

Renata shook her head. <No>

< . . . No?>

<You cannot just deny the—>

<Sovan! Have your crisis of faith on your own time!> the Thrice Queen barked.

<Listen to me> Muirgen said. <There are multiple planes of existence, yes? This place, what we call the mortal plane, is where we live, but there are many others. Perhaps uncountable others. One of them, which is tethered to our plane, is the afterlife; and when we die, the aethereal energy which forms our consciousness travels there. Every plane of existence has various sorts of aethereal energy, and those of the afterlife behave very differently

when drawn to our mortal plane. They allow us to do things that our own natural laws do not. That is why they are so valuable, and why those energies have been so jealously guarded for all of human history. They go by many names – what you call the "arcana", or the "Draedist sorceries", or the "Saxan magicks", "necromancy", "death magicks", and so on.

<Long ago, the mortal plane and the afterlife became briefly conjoined—>

<The Magickal Cataclysm> Renata huffed. Children of three knew about the Cataclysm. Within the Book of Creus, foremost volume of the Neman Creed, it was the very first chapter – "The Cataclysmic Inception".

<The means by which these death magicks first flowed into the world> Muirgen continued as though she had said nothing. <That conjunction took place *here*, at the Eye of the Sea. One of the effects of this magickal deluge was *construction*, or constructive magick. It creates. The magick mixed with the living essences of the humans and animals it touched, and fused and transformed and mutated. It created the Stygion; it created the Kasar; it created dozens of other races which have failed for want of stability.

<Over the course of human history, both we mortals and those in the afterlife have sought to breach the skin of the aether that separates our dimensions. Names that will be familiar to you, that have long formed part of the Neman orthodoxy – Kasivar, Prince of Hell; the Muphraab of Ambyr; Malakh the Accuser; Ramayah the Progenitor – have tried to do this to harvest the energy of our souls for their own infernal industries>

Renata shook her head. <You just told me that none of it was real>

<I didn't tell you it wasn't real; I said they are not *gods*. They are not saints, nor angels nor demons – at least, not in the way the Neman Creed insists. They cannot be beseeched with prayer; they do not intercede in earthly affairs based on some . . . moral code of ethics>

<I do not believe that>

<I do not need you to believe it; I need you to listen to me>

<I am listening, am I not?>

Muirgen regarded her coolly for a moment. <Whilst it is true that Nema has interceded – has fought lengthy wars with Kasivar and his chieftains – to preserve the souls of mortals, to take them to the Golden City and shelter them there, this is less about beneficence and more about strategic necessity. If she does not, her enemies in Hell grow stronger>

Renata mulled this over, though she had no difficulty in accepting the bones of it; stories about these wars in heaven were in great abundance in the Neman Creed, and she had been reading them – and accepting them as gospel – since she was a little girl. As to whether prayer and worship were as futile as Muirgen claimed – well; that was a discussion to be had with her confessor, not these disagreeable mer-men.

<Where do the Vorr fit into this?> she asked.

<The Vorr are an ancient race that have hitherto been confined to an enormous psychic prison. We do not know how, why or when. Like you, we only have the Prophecies of Zabriel to go on, and the accounts are incomplete and difficult to follow>

Renata gritted her teeth. The Prophecies of Zabriel had long been winnowed out of the Nema Victorian Creed, and now formed part of the – illegal – Conformist Bible.

<But the thrust of it is they are a cataclysmic menace?> she asked.

<Indeed>

<How did they come to be released?>

<Again, we do not know. And it is much too dangerous to venture into the afterlife now to find out. But our theory is that someone, be it Kasivar himself or one of his lieutenants, opened the gates which kept them at bay>

<Why on earth would anyone do such a thing?>

<Perhaps they were tricked. Perhaps it was an act of insane,

wanton self-destruction – murder-suicide on a cosmic scale. Either way, our most pressing objective is to quarantine the Vorr within the afterlife. To permit them access to the mortal plane would be catastrophic>

<How could that happen?>

<There are two ways: directly through an extant portal, and indirectly>

<What do you mean, indirectly?>

<In theory, the Vorr could gain access to the mortal plane every time a necromancer travels to the afterlife. In so doing, the necromancer forms a bridge between planes and opens his mind to their predations>

<The practice of necromancy is forbidden in Sova>

<Yet the Bruta Sarkan practised. There will be others without the Empire, too>

<What happens to a necromancer when he comes into contact with the Vorr?>

<His spirit will be eaten>

<But what of his body?>

<His body will perish shortly after. A body cannot exist without a mind>

Renata thought back to the Kasar in the Spiritsraad, their quarantined necromancer there who had been trapped inside a chamber and left to rot. She shivered.

<And what about directly?>

<Directly, there is only one way: through the Eye of the Sea>

<But that is sealed?>

<Yes, and warded. And guarded day and night>

<By what?>

<That is not your concern>

<Where is the exit?>

<The Golden City, of course> That the mer-man could refer to literal heaven in the same way he might have referred to Sova left Renata briefly reeling.

<What would it take to open it?>

Muirgen shook his head. <A magickal artefact of incredible power>

Renata's guts knotted. She exchanged a brief glance with Lyzander, who seemed to have regained his sensibilities.

<What about the Blood Stone? Would that have enough power?>

<Certainly the Blood Stone would. But we need not trouble ourselves with that; it is being kept safe in the Kasari Spiritsraad>

Renata glanced at Lyzander again. <On that point . . .> she said slowly.

XXVIII

Into the Breach

*"'Tis a good thing the Stygion lay beyond our grasping reach;
I am convinced such a war would be catastrophic for the forces
of Sova. Who could hope to prevail against a race of creatures
who grapple daily with the elemental forces of the ocean itself?"*

AMBASSADOR ANETE JEKABSONE

Port Gero

NORTHERN KYARAI

If the journey from Ozeanland to Maris had been fast, then the speed from Maris to Port Gero was practically flight. The Queen, the Psychic Conclave, and Sina, not to mention two dozen Spears of the Royal Household, moved unhindered by the water. The ocean practically vibrated with the channelling of thaumaturgic energies.

Admonition hung heavy in the air, leaving Renata feeling hot with resentment. Would Maruska have known to bring the Blood Stone with him? Was it really as obvious a failure as they had suggested? To expect her to know the nature of these artefacts, and what they represented? Yes, Sova had possibly erred in cutting itself off from magickal lore and practice, but if these matters were so important, then surely the Stygion had to accept their share of the blame, too. They could have said something sooner.

They swam day and night. The Stygion spoke a form of transverbal psychic Loxica which Renata could not understand. Occasionally they would ask her a question to clarify matters, but there was not much more to tell them beyond what she already had: the Dwelkspreker had given them the Blood Stone in accordance with some augury, and they had brought it with them to Port Gero. She explained it to them again and again, but there were only so many ways to skin a cat.

It was after they had sped past Ozeanland that it became clear something was wrong; Renata could hear the thunderous roar of cannon and the rippling pop of musketry, and see the great leviathan hulls of ships above, the spaces between them wreathed in clouds of white smoke. Occasionally something would plunge into the depths: an errant cannonball, a great spray of wooden splinters, a body.

<What is happening?> the Queen demanded of her.

<I don't know!> Renata replied, and she didn't; her thoughts dwelt now entirely on Glaser, Ozolinsh and Herschel, whom they had left on the beach.

After a few moments, one of the guards from the Door to the Sea swam up to them.

<What news?> the Queen demanded.

<Ships, Ina, from the House of Casimir> he said.

<How many?>

<Four, Ina, two large and two small. They are attacking the fortress atop the cliffs. There are soldiers on the shore, too>

<What about—> Renata started.

<Be quiet!> the Queen snapped. <When did this start?>

<Only just this morning, Ina. They have been fighting all day>

<The Blood Stone> Muirgen said to Renata, his voice frantic. <Where did you leave it?>

Before Renata could answer, there was a loud crackling sound from the beach fifty or so yards away, and the water above and around them began to fizz and churn and spit with musket balls.

"They're shooting at us!" Renata shouted in Saxan. She looked over to Lyzander, who was using his Spear-mount as a sort of rudimentary biological cover.

The Queen let out a snarl of anger. Kaipatu shrieked his own vicarious rage. The Spears and their sharks frothed and chafed, itching to answer this injustice.

<Wait> she commanded. Spears readied their weapons. Those of means and high status within the Royal Household bore sleek rapiers of steel-hard resin with handguards in swept simulacra of conch shells. All carried blowpipes and had pouches filled with spines from sea urchins husbanded over generations for their toxicity. They could stop a person breathing in half a minute.

The Queen turned to Renata. <You and your man must recover the Blood Stone. It is of the most vital importance. The security of both our nations depends on it. Do you understand?>

Renata nodded, feeling the weight of her failure keenly. For now, it was strong enough to override her sense of self-preservation.

"We have to get the Blood Stone back," she explained to Lyzander, keenly aware of the ridiculous image they both cut within their lungfish breathing bubbles. She could feel the creature's organs nestled against the hair on the back of her head. The key was not to think about it too much.

Lyzander accepted this wordlessly. He gestured to the drop-off where the foundations of the Door to the Sea sat, crusted with barnacles and marine flora. Before she could say anything more, he swam to it and broke the surface just above a bank of colourful coral. Renata did the same, and they both did away with their lungfish.

Being in the open air filled her with a vertiginous feeling. It was late in the afternoon, and the beach where she had left

Glaser, Ozolinsh and Herschel was bathed in golden sunlight. There was no sign of any of them; instead the beach had transformed into a staging area for blue-coated Casimirs. The sand was churned beneath dozens of shoes as men and women lined up in an orderly fashion – and this in spite of the cannonade from the northern fortifications of Port Gero which was targeting the beach quite effectively – whilst several landing boats bobbed amongst the surf. Off to the right, a detachment of riflemen were firing at the water in the vague direction of the Queen and the other Stygion.

"By Nema ..." Renata swore. Approaching rapidly was a large enemy fifth-rate, which was in the process of furling its sails. To the north of Port Gero, rolling in the light swell, were two towering Casimiran men-o'-war firing directly on the fort, whilst bookending them were two bomb ketches lobbing shells over the walls. Further to the south, half a mile off the Horn, another three Casimiran vessels were locked in an exchange of broadsides with three similarly sized Sovan vessels, whilst a fifth Casimiran was hull-to-hull with another Sovan ship and engaged in a raucous boarding action. What Renata had initially taken to be an outcrop of rock was in fact the aftercastle of a further Sovan ship as it sank. Around it was a cloud of debris and sailors.

"They must have come from Port Talaka," Lyzander said, grimacing.

There were more landing boats being lowered over the side of the closest three Casimiran ships, each laden with dozens of soldiers. Taken all together, the landing force must have numbered in the hundreds, perhaps half a thousand. The foremost elements were already moving up the steps to the coastal path, which effectively shielded them from the attention of the Sovan cannons.

"How are we going to get through all of this?" Renata asked breathlessly. She flinched as a roundshot from the north wall slammed into the group of Casimiran riflemen, blasting one of them to ruin with a great wet thump and taking the leg off a second before ploughing a deep furrow into the sand. "We are as like to be killed by our own people!"

"Watch!" Lyzander yelled. The riflemen – those who had survived – had spotted them, and a sudden hail of fire peppered the water and the stone of the Door around them.

Renata ducked back under the waves, out of range of everything except all but the most carefully aimed close-range cannon fire. The Queen had evidently called for reinforcements; their numbers had swelled suddenly and dramatically as mermen arrived from nearby Ozeanland. The drop-off had quickly become a sub-marine staging area, crowded with armoured blackfish of the Royal Household, dozens of Spears and their sharks, and many more nulls and their herring dogs. All in all there must have been close to a hundred Stygion soldiers.

With a flick of Sina's hand, lungfish were quick to reattach themselves to Renata and Lyzander's heads.

<We need a distraction> Renata said. <We cannot achieve the fort as matters stand>

<What is going on?> the Queen demanded.

<A force of Casimirs, from Port Talaka we think. They're attempting to take the Sovan position here>

"Tell them more Casimirs will be coming," Lyzander said from next to her, and Renata passed on the message in signed Loxican.

The Queen's expression – naturally one of apparent displeasure thanks to her downturned Stygion mouth – seemed to curdle even further.

<Where is the Blood Stone?> Muirgen demanded. Thanks to his psychic attenuation, his frenetic aura filled the brine around him.

<My guess is it has been taken up to the fortress> Renata said. *My hope.* <But we cannot reach it>

<We will create a distraction as you require> the Queen said. <When you retrieve the Stone, do not try and return it to us by

hand; you will be killed. Just throw it from the fort into the water. We will find it>

Renata nodded, her blood surging. <I understand. Good luck, Ina> she added, but the Queen had already turned to her Spears, directing some of them to the approaching Casimiran fifth-rate – which had just dropped its anchor and was already lowering landing boats into the ocean – and some to the beach itself.

"Are you ready?" Renata asked Lyzander, and then swore; the Queen and her Spears were moving with frightening speed to-wards the beach, seeking out gaps in the coral and rock beyond the drop-off until they and their blackfish and sharks were in little more than a few feet of water. So positioned, they were dangerously vulnerable to musket fire, and the next volley to hit the water filled it with clouds of Stygion and white shark blood.

"Shit! Come on!" Lyzander shouted.

They both tore off their lungfish and broke the surface once again, making for the drop-off. Renata gripped the sharp coral at the edge, watching as the Casimirs had their attention split between the guns of Port Gero and the Stygion. There followed a brief period of indecision in which several more soldiers were felled by roundshot; then hasty volleys were being fired at the mer-men, and Casimirs were charging into the water with their bayonets brandished.

Renata turned, heart pounding. The Casimiran frigate had lowered two shoreboats into the water, each full of dozens of marines. Like the frigate itself, the shoreboats were lined with anti-mer-men spikes like upturned hedgehogs, whilst on the far side of the frigate she could see sailors tossing pails of what looked like offal into the ocean.

"What are they doing?" Lyzander asked.

"They're chumming the water," Renata said with dismay. It was an anti-Stygion technique that the Sovan Imperial Navy had developed. It overwhelmed the white sharks' senses, triggering their predatory instincts and untethering them from their Spears.

By luring the sharks to the side of the frigate, they could pick them off with harpoons and even muskets if they were close enough to the surface. "They will be trying to distract the Spears from the marines."

She ducked briefly under the water. Already some of the weaker-willed Spears were struggling to control their familiars as they gave in to their bloodlust. The sharks moved at ferocious speed towards the offal the Casimiran sailors had dumped into the ocean, and were soon ripping into it. The chum was poisoned – it was all so abysmally cynical – whilst harpoons and musket fire was quick to follow. In seconds, half a dozen white sharks were lying motionless on the surface, and the water filled with the screeching lamentation of their riders.

"Here, help me look for an opening," Lyzander said, and they both took in the chaos of the beach, waiting for the right moment to exit the water. Renata watched, mesmerised, as a gruesome melee developed over to her right, where the tide was up and men and women stood, sometimes up to the mid-thigh, in the ocean. Kaipatu had already dragged one man under the surf and gored him against the sand; several more men and women had lost great chunks of their calves and thighs to white sharks, turning the surf crimson. Renata could see at least two soldiers foaming at the mouth on the beach where urchin spines had nicked their skin and stopped the nerves in their lungs working.

The bluecoats in the staging area were now paralysed by indecision, in spite of the shouted orders from sabre-wielding officers. Many continued to surmount the cliffside steps; more still seemed to want to engage the Stygion. Those who did nothing fell prey to the Sovan cannonade.

"Nema," Renata breathed as the Thrice Queen herself joined the melee in the shallows, sending a hail of channelled water like brine grapeshot into the bluecoats, flaying skin, rupturing eyeballs, bursting eardrums and stinging like salted hell. One woman staggered backwards, blinded by these saltwater bullets, and was grabbed by two armoured mer-men and stabbed re-peatedly with iridescent resin blades. Another soldier had his leg raggedly severed by the bite of a white shark. He clutched the stump and fell, pale and screaming, into the water, where he was violently disassembled by several more of the armoured fish. A hurried volley of musket fire killed one shark and perforated the armoured segmenta of another, before a blast of channelled water battered the Casimiran survivors and arrested their momentum.

But for all the martial skill of the mer-men, they had no answer to the Casimiran cannon. A shot from the frigate's bow chaser hit one Stygion just below the waterline, ripping his lower half off in a great spray of saltwater and guts. His shark, consumed with insane grief, beached itself in an attempt to kill one of the few remaining soldiers. For its efforts, it was bayoneted to death. The officer darted forward with his sabre, too, and put three great, deep cuts into its dorsal fin and back. It reminded Renata of fillets at the Sovan Fischmarkt.

"What is our plan?" she asked Lyzander frantically. They were still submerged up to their shoulders, still gripping the coral riming the drop-off. "This is getting out of hand."

"I'm not sure it was ever in hand," the captain murmured, scanning the shoreline for any opportunity. "We are going to have to move soon, before those marines reach the shore."

"Why?"

"They will ease the pressure on the regulars. *Their* goal is the fort, not this lot." He gestured to the Stygion. "If these officers are worth their salt, they will remind everybody of that in short order."

Renata watched as the shoreboats coursed through the surf, propelled by frantic oarsmen. Armoured blackfish were attempt-ing to overturn them, but simple and effective modifications had made them nigh-on impossible to capsize. They had sturdy out-riggers, festooned with spikes, and the marines were well spaced out around the edges, distributing their weight. They fended off repeated attacks with harpoons and bayonets, and fired carbines and pistols point-blank into the Stygion, handing the weapons to several men in the centre who spent all their time reloading. Renata had to appreciate the martial ingenuity.

"For Nema's sake, we have to do something soon," she said. She gasped as Muirgen exited the water and channelled a great spray of brine grapeshot into the nearest boatload of marines. One was finally put overboard by a herring dog which leapt out of the water with incredible speed and agility and hit the man square in the chest. The moment he was in the ocean, he had his head bitten clean off by a white shark, to the audible dismay of his fellows.

"Renata!" Lyzander shouted for what must have been the third or fourth time.

"Hm? What? Yes?"

"Now!"

Dazed by the appalling violence, she allowed herself to be dragged by her bicep around the left side of the Door to the Sea. They scraped and scratched their hands and arms and legs as they clambered up the serrated coral and slimy rocks until they were wading free of the surf. Without the buoyancy of the ocean saltwater, she felt suddenly weak, as though someone had strapped all her limbs with lead weights. She had eaten nothing of substance for several days, and the constant swimming – to say nothing of the mental stress of communicating in an unfamiliar language, in an unfamiliar environment, under the threat of death – had left her profoundly exhausted. If her blood had not been charged with excitement from the chaos of the battle, she would have collapsed.

"They are going to shoot us," she said as they approached the beach, her whole body rigid with anticipation. It was lousy with bluecoats, and although most were distracted, several had noticed them.

"No they aren't. We are wearing nothing which marks us as Sovans. Just move with confidence." He gestured to the ships off the Horn. "Fewer than half these crews will be native Casimirs. We will not be suspected."

"Do you speak Kòvoskan?"

"Enough to get us past these dolts," Lyzander replied. "Just pretend you have been shipwrecked. Nema knows you look like it."

They waded through the water, stumbling frequently on the uneven surface, until they achieved the beach. In spite of Renata's misgivings, Lyzander was right; the chaos was so total that they were not challenged. They made their way briskly to the steps, and simply began to ascend, boxed in front and back by bluecoats. The soldiers were much too preoccupied with their mission and their own survival to even notice them.

After a few minutes, they reached the clifftop. The scene before them was only slightly less chaotic than that on the beach. The northern approach to Port Gero was a hundred yards of open ground, and the only natural cover was a three-foot defile running parallel to the wall barely fifteen yards beyond the cliff stairs. There, hundreds of Casimiran soldiers pressed themselves hard into the ground, sheltering from the thunderous cannonade which had left ten of their number killed and the ground a ruin of turned earth, waiting for the wall to be reduced sufficiently to storm it.

Renata and Lyzander ran forwards before they were blown to bits, and took up shelter in that pathetic earthen defile. Renata could smell soil and saltwater and gunpowder, whilst her eyes stung from the thick palls of white smoke which seemed to resist the scouring efforts of the Jade Sea winds. The noise, too, was constant; not only of the Sovan guns, muskets and rifles from Port Gero, but of the percussive explosions of shells lobbed from the bomb ketches and the naval roundshot from the Casimiran broadsides, all of which were conspiring to reduce the north-facing wall. The air was a hail of boiling iron and shattered stone.

"Another couple of minutes, I'd say." Lyzander spoke directly into her ear. They had to be careful not to shout out in Saxan, unless they wanted to be shot as saboteurs.

"And then what?" Renata asked, rolling into as tight a ball as she could manage. This was unendurable.

"And then they will have an opening."

"An opening?!"

Lyzander hazarded another glance, and ducked back down quickly as a lucky rifle shot clipped the soil three inches from his cheek.

"The only way we are going to get into that fort is by storming it with everyone else."

Renata looked him directly in the eye. "Are you quite fucking mad?"

"Is our purpose not the salvation of the mortal world itself?"

Renata gritted her teeth. It was frustrating to be reminded that there was no task too reckless, no act too bold, no measure too drastic when one considered the consequences of inaction.

"They will ransack the place," Lyzander continued. "Once the defenders are killed, they will go through everything. They will turn it upside down, looting. They will *kill* each other for a ruby the size of a fist. Our only chance is to get to it before anybody else does. We get in, we find it, we get out. If we're lucky, we make off before the battle is even over."

Renata swallowed, her guts churning. "I'm not sure I have the courage for this," she said in a moment of unguarded honesty. "I'm not like you, Joseph. I'm not a soldier."

He looked over the lip of the defile again; there was a great clamour going up, a cacophony of shouting, of men fixing bayonets, of a calamitous landslide of stone.

"This is it!"

"Oh Nema," Renata moaned, every muscle in her body tense.

"May I kiss you?" he asked her suddenly.

"What?"

"May I kiss you? I should like to know what it is like to kiss you, before the end."

"Uh . . . of . . . I mean . . . all right?"

He kissed her. His lips tasted like saltwater, his mouth like smoke. His beard scratched her skin.

She kissed him back, and for a moment, everything else seemed to be far-off and inconsequential.

Then he pulled away. "Thank you," he said.

"Uh . . . that's . . . quite all right," Renata said back.

"Right. Stay close behind me. This will all happen very quickly."

XXIX

Leaving the New East

*"Why not let trust and respect be our first instincts
when encountering a foreign people? In either event, the
likelihood of our making war on them is all but assured;
at least in this way, we can say they started it."*

SATIRIST AND PAMPHLETEER BILIOUS JOSEPH

Uncharted Foothills

GREAT NORTHERN BARRIER RANGE

"You must get away from here," Furlan said to him. "Go back to
Sova. Tell them what is happening here."

Peter was too insensible to appreciate that he could understand
the captain perfectly.

He was aware of movement, of being carried. He could smell
the forest air at night, but all his earthly concerns were focused
on his midriff. There was tangible *absence* there which he dared
not examine for fear of what he might find.

Or rather, not find.

Dear Father, I am a long way from home.

His thoughts drifted. What was home, anyway? What

was Badenburg to him? What was the regiment, the city, his countrymen?

Each jolting step that Furlan took sent spikes of agony through his gut. His eyes felt gummed up and blurry, his head stuffed full of cotton wool and foreign thoughts. His splintered hand pulsed with pain.

I am a long way from home. Here in the distant New East . . .

But it wasn't distant, not for those who lived here. Not for the Kato. Not for the pagans. Not for the Black Mountains, the Red Coves, the Kestrelli, the Daedii. There were entire confederations of people who called the New East home. There were Sovan colonists who called Davorstadt home, farmers and frontiersmen who called Linasburg and Valerija home. Slavomire and Maretsburg and Vitaney Island and Tajanastadt . . . these places would swell and grow, filled with prospectors and their families, soldiers, farmers, merchants and traders, whalers and miners, and the settlements would expand and bleed into one another and become contiguous, and the pagans would be driven back, ingested or integrated or killed, and soon tens of thousands of people would call this place home. Soon there would be nothing "new" about the New East, not even for Sovans.

What *was* home? If it was a physical place, then for Peter it remained Imastadt. But if home was a spiritual place, a place of intellectual growth, of maturation and loss of innocence, of experience – experience of wonderment and of terror, where the soul flourished or calcified or both in unequal measures – then the New East was his home. This place, unknown to Sovan cartographers, of thousands of miles of forest and mountain, of lakes and streams and rivers, of savage monsters slaved to ancient magicks they did not understand, forgotten by time.

The Alda River Valley had changed Peter even before the Kato got their hands on him. The foothills of the Great Northern Barrier Range had changed him. They had conspired together to break him apart like the digestive tract of an enormous creature, turned him into sludge, mixed him and reconstituted him like a golem. It had not made him whole; indeed, it had cut away parts of him entirely. Mentally, he could never go back. Like Furlan, his spirit had become bonded to the land here, fused with it.

As he was carried down the steep slopes, Furlan's feet turning great divots of loam, crackling twigs and snapping ferns, slipping over wet roots and branches; as he listened to the distant cry of wild cats, the high-altitude screech of raptors; as he felt the cold, damp mist fill his lungs, or the warm sun on his face, or smelt the undergrowth, he realised that he was held to this place by an unbreakable, invisible tether. He always would be.

Dear Father, I am a long way from home.

Except he wasn't a long way from home.

This was his home now.

Fever dreams claimed him. He thought of the door he had seen during the ritual. He dreamt of Olwin, tending to him. He watched as she examined his belly like a midwife, her pale face a mask of horror. He saw the flash of eyes at night, the growl of Kato, the distant screeching of the wounded. He tasted bitter medicines, stews made of roots and leaves, cold and clear mountain freshwater. He rejected it all. His throat closed, and he choked and gargled and retched it all back out immediately. He smelt soil and blood. He felt magicks curdle within his soul, unsure of him and what he had become.

His hand hurt. His palm roughened around the splinter and grew calloused.

He was moved through the forest slowly. At times he saw Olwin moving with him between the trees, he a buck, she a doe. At night when he rested, snatching a few hours of half-sleep nestled amongst hard tree roots like bones, feeling the wet loam soak what remained of his uniform, he spoke to his father. In the twilight hours between, he spoke to Furlan.

"The skin of the aether is thin here," Furlan said, and Peter knew this. He did not know how he knew it, but he did. It was inherited memory, ancestral recall. The ritual, even interrupted, had given as much knowledge as it had removed.

"It is the golden spear," Peter mumbled.

"It is," Furlan agreed.

"It cuts the air."

"It does."

They reached Lake Ena, vast and blue, its waves whipped to whitecaps where a fast, cold wind had cut across the Gvòrod Steppe to the west. Here, Furlan left him. They exchanged few words; there was little to say, and what there was to say they both already knew.

From there, Peter headed south. He staggered like a drunk, his uniform, once pressed and starched and neat as befitted a Sovan officer, ragged as a vagrant's.

He realised then that the screaming had stopped.

"It's quiet," he said to Olwin. He turned to her. There was still fear and suspicion writ large on her face. "The screaming; it's stopped."

She shook her head. "*Ne*," she replied.

Peter stood still for a long time, listening to the rhythmic wash of the waves, the wind through the trees.

"I can't hear it. It's stopped."

"*Mi povas aŭdi ĝin*," she replied. "I hear."

He thought back to what Furlan had told him. *We are inert.*

They *were* inert. Psychically inert. Spiritually inert. The spear had taken his essence, and in return it had made him null. The screams persisted; but he was shielded from them.

How? Why?

To what *end*?

Olwin left him. Had she even been with him? He felt her absence keenly. It made him heartsick.

He made his way to the Ena Split alone. How long had it been since he had fought the Sanques here? Weeks? Months? How many times had the indifferent world turned since he had left his fellows in the comfort of the known?

He drank from the lake and chewed on roots and his throat closed and it all came back out of his mouth again. He walked through the night. The scabs fell away from the cuts on his face, and he could feel the skin there, the rents stretched and glass-smooth. As for the rest of him, he dared not check. He had not turned into a catman, but he had changed. He coughed frequently; his hand grew stiff, the skin rough and discoloured. It was not long before he could not make a fist.

He reached the Split after a week of travel. He expected to find the place abandoned, or back in Sanquish hands; instead he found, to his great bafflement, the Sovan colours flying over a decent polygonal fort, bristling with cannon and encircled by sturdy breastworks.

For a moment he thought he had strayed even further south, to Aldaney Island, all the way to Fort Ingomar, for he remained quite insensible. But no; there was no question that this was the Ena Split.

"Who goes there?" a soldier called out to him from the northeastern rampart. "Here, it's a Sovan officer. Bloody hell, look at his face."

"Blimey," another voice said. "You don't think it's one of Lieutenant Kleist's men, do you?"

Peter walked forward slowly with his hands out in front of him. It was not in supplication; it was to check that the fort was real.

"Look at the epaulettes," the first voice said. "I think that *is* Lieutenant Kleist."

Peter stopped as his hands came into contact with the breastwork.

There was a pause. "Nema Victoria. Fetch the major, quick!"

He took one more shuddering step forward, and then collapsed.

❧

He continued to drift in and out of consciousness. Occasionally he would sit up, hot and sweating and gasping for air, convinced it was his turn at the execution stone. He was given brandy, which he rejected, and some of his blood was let from his forearm, and cold compresses were applied to his forehead.

He heard voices throughout the afternoon and evening. He spoke with his father, and Furlan, and Olwin.

Everything else was nothing except deep, unbroken silence.

"I am going to watch over you, Peter," Olwin said. She appeared to him several times; twice as a human, once as a white deer. The white deer of Nema Victoria. *"Ne timu."*

He felt her hand in his, two people bound together by unthinkable horror.

Just a dream.

All of it just a dream.

❧

It took him a few days to regain his wits, and even then only partly. The moment he opened his eyes, he heard the scrape of chair legs against the floorboards and rapid footsteps making for the door.

He looked around. It was an infirmary, one surprisingly well appointed, with beds which must have been brought up from Slavomire. It smelt of freshly cut pine logs, and was empty save him.

It was late in the evening, and a solitary candle guttered by the window. He heard voices outside the door, and expected Major Haak to enter; but to his surprise, it was a man he did not recognise, though certainly he wore the rank of major. Accompanying him was a green-jacketed artillery officer, an Imperial Engineer, as well as a pair of lieutenants. None of them were from the 166th Badenburg Regiment; these men were the 18th Kamarian, from the Prinzpatriate of Mirja.

"Good heavens," the major said slowly after a few moments' silence. "How do you feel, Captain? Lieutenant, I should say, now that your brevet has ended. You look as though you've had an encounter with a bear!"

What could he possibly say? Who were these people? When had they arrived? How long had he been *gone*?

"Where is this?"

"This is Fort Kleist," the major said with a twinkle in his eye. "You of all people should recognise the name."

"Fort Kleist," Peter murmured.

"Where have you *been*, Lieutenant?"

Home.

"Who are you?"

The major bristled slightly at the informality. "I am Major Hanna," he said. "18th Kamarian Infantry Regiment."

Peter shook his head as though he might dislodge the great cloud of fog that had taken the place of his brain. "Where is Major Haak?"

Hanna and the other officers exchanged uneasy looks. "Major Haak is dead, son. Shot himself some time ago now. 8th Company has been relieved of Fort Ingomar." He turned to one of the lieutenants next to him. "Where did they go, David?"

"Maretsburg, sir."

"That's right." Hanna turned back to him. "And you of course brought 10th Company with you here. Ingomar is being held by colonials. Three companies of militia from Slavomire."

Peter felt himself growing frantic. "Why did Major Haak shoot himself?"

"He was quite mad. Beckert seemed half gone himself, to

say nothing of the men. Seems to be endemic in this part of the world," Hanna murmured in addendum.

"'Tis no wonder with this bloody screaming," the artillery captain muttered, sticking a finger into his ear and scratching it. "I do not know how you all put up with it for so long."

Peter could hear nothing. "Listen to me," he said, trying to focus, trying not to succumb to the incredible panic he felt.

Major Hanna did not. "What we *don't* know is where you went after that. Captain Beckert said Major Kulkani ordered Haak to make for the Split and capture this place. Those orders are in evidence, for here we stand. But we have no notion of what came next. You must have taken the 10th with you into the forest. We had assumed you were all killed by some action or misadventure."

Peter felt himself begin to hyperventilate. "I left forty men here," he said.

Major Hanna shook his head in gentle chastisement. "I'm afraid not, Lieutenant. The place was empty when we arrived. Empty of the living, at least."

"The blood moon," Peter breathed. There was an incredible crushing sensation across his chest, as though someone had strapped a belt around his ribcage and was tightening it as far as it would go. He wanted nothing except to return to a life he recognised, one in which he understood the rules of the physical world and his place within it. But at every turn there was fresh insanity. "They came during the blood moon. Three days after we left, they must have come down."

"Who came down?"

He tried to sit up, but was struck by an incredible sense of nausea and vertigo.

"Just stay lying down for a moment, there's a good man. The physician says you haven't taken a morsel to eat or a sip to drink the entire time you have been here," Hanna said. "Don't babble; take a moment to gather your thoughts."

"Cathassach," Peter breathed. "I sent him back. Captain Furlan sent him back. Was there no one here?"

"Cathassach ..." the artillery officer mused. "I wonder if he means that pagan who pitched up at Fort Romauld a month ago."

"The one who was hanged?"

Peter's blood surged. "No! A Black Mountain pagan. Cathassach! He was our tracker, our interpreter!"

"That's the fellow," the artillery officer said cheerfully. "Hanged for desertion. Pitched up with not a hair nor hide of any one of you. Kulkani had him executed. If memory serves, he was prattling on about something – cat-monsters or some such."

"Foolishness," Hanna muttered idly. "Now, Kleist, what's this about a blood moon?"

"And what's all this bloody screaming?" the artilleryman added.

Peter began to suck in great, deep lungfuls of breath. "I sent him back," he said, feeling the world closing around him, fighting back tears. "I sent him back! Me! I ordered him! I took thirty men into the foothills. I left forty behind. Fifty? It matters not. We were attacked – a race of catmen. Like the Kasar, you see? But they are ... Nema, mutated! Warped, in all manner of states of ... metamorphosis. They sustain themselves by taking the innards of men—"

"Now see here, Kleist," Hanna said. He and the other officers wore expressions of distaste. "I know it's been a hard few weeks—"

"Nema Victoria, listen to me, damn you! Catmen, they call themselves the Kato. They have a magickal artefact, a golden spearhead ..."

"Hell's bells, I'll not listen to this Conformist nonsense."

" ... use it to transmute men into catmen ..."

"No wonder Haak shot himself, Prince of Hell."

" ... The screaming stops when they are close, they are magickally inert, the ... the ... Nema, the precise nature of it escapes me, but ..."

"I'll have you shot as well at this rate!"

" . . . they are taking men and they will take you the second you set foot outside this fortress on the next blood moon—"

"Confound you, Lieutenant! Stop this nonsense this instant!"

Peter fell silent. It was not possible. It was not *possible*. How could they not believe him?

"Look at my face, damn you," he said quietly. "Look at my hand!" *Look at my gut*, he might have added, if he'd had the fortitude to examine it himself.

There was a long and uncomfortable pause. The junior officers would not meet his insane, pleading eyes.

"You want to know what I think, Kleist?" Hanna said eventually. Gone was any warmth in his voice. "A young and inexperienced lieutenant arrives in the New East. Has a touch of the nerves in his new posting."

Peter opened his mouth to protest, but Hanna silenced him.

"Freshly breveted to captain and after a brief and successful action, he ill-advisedly takes a light company into the uncharted foothills of the Barrier Range. Doubtless the man is keen to prove himself and his command."

"But that's—"

"Inexperience causes the young captain to become disoriented and lost. Inclement weather and" – he looked pointedly at Peter's face – "wild animal attack reduces the company to below effective numbers. Easy pickings for pagans and expeditionary Sanques. The young captain abandons his men like the pagan before him, with only some half-baked concoction about monsters as an excuse. And here you are, the better part of two months later. How's that, Kleist? Cut to the kernel of it, have I?"

Peter fell to weeping. He wept because he knew that no matter what he said, they would not believe him. He wept at the sense of utter, all-consuming helplessness. That he could experience so much, for it all to be written off by the tired arrogance of a senior officer. Any experience needed the oxygen of external validation to be truly lived. It was like they were taking a part of it away from him.

"Tell me what really happened, Kleist."

"Catmen—"

"If I hear one more damned thing about catmen, Lieutenant, I'll have you blown from a gun."

Peter sagged back into the bed. He needed to get out of this place. He felt a sudden and consuming urge to jump up and run.

"It is as you say, sir," he said eventually. No point in saving face. Escape was all that mattered.

There was a pregnant pause.

"Not exactly the first lieutenant to be undone by his ambition," the artillery officer muttered. "Strange, though. Mark Furlan was with him. Man had an excellent reputation. Seems unlikely he would have got turned around in the woods."

"Perhaps he was killed here at Fort Kleist. What happened to him, eh, Lieutenant?"

"He was . . . " Peter stopped. To bring dishonour on himself, to accept judgement for his own ineptitude and cowardice, that was one thing. But would he really allow the memory of Furlan to be so dishonoured?

He gritted his teeth. "Captain Furlan is still alive."

"And you abandoned him, you rogue?" the artillery officer snapped.

"Please, just listen to me for a moment. There is a race of magickal mutants to the north-east—"

"What rot!" Hanna thundered.

"They harvest organs and use some sort of arcane artefact to create new catmen! Captain Furlan has been turned into one of them! He lives still and he needs our help!"

"Oh, for Nema's sake, get him out of here," Hanna snapped. "I am sick to my death of hearing about bloody beasts and sprites and ghosts in this valley. The only thing our men need fear is pagan insurgents and the fucking Sanques!"

"You have to listen to me. *Please just listen to me!*"

"Shall I have him escorted back to Maretsburg, sir?"

"Gods, no. Get him to Tajanastadt. The man belongs in Blackmarsh Asylum."

"Sir?"

Hanna shot the captain a venomous look. "I'm not serious, David. His mother is Lady Magdalena Kleist."

"Who, sir?"

"The Baroness of Imastadt."

"Good lord."

"Good lord indeed. Just put him on a ship back to Sova, for God's sake. If he's any sense, he'll do us all a favour and resign his commission."

He convalesced. He shaved, and washed, and was issued a new uniform. But there was a madness in his head which these trappings could not shake loose. He thought of nothing except the forest and the mountains and the catmen, the Neman missionary and the tree-man in the forest, and the vision – the demon and the huge door and the infinite valley filled with the armoured skeletons of long-dead giants. He thought of Furlan and Olwin. He thought of Cathassach, and felt a desperate guilt at what had happened to him.

Perhaps the thing to do was to leave. To leave the New East entirely, to resign his commission and return home to Badenburg. To see his mother, to rekindle his love affair with Leonie, to take a job as a banker or stocks trader like his brothers and friends. The thought practically suffocated him with its banality. How did anyone do it?

He was taken by mule back to Slavomire, and then by canoe by a silent old Black Mountain down the Long River all the way to Tajanastadt. Several times he fancied he saw Olwin moving through the trees at the river's edge. But it could not have been her.

He hoped she lived.

He hoped she remembered him.

Three hundred miles between him and the Kato was not enough.
It was as though their forest settlement were not deep in the
Barrier Range but in his brain itself, so utterly did it occupy his
thoughts. And if ever he turned his mind to something else, even
for the briefest moment, the scars on his face were an ever-present
reminder.

Slowly Furlan will change, he told himself as he boarded a
requisitioned coffee clipper in Tajanastadt harbour, a merchant brigantine loaded with furs and tobacco and a number of
wounded Sovan officers who had the rank and means to have
themselves repatriated. *He will forget his human nature, and with it
his agonies, and I shall remain the sole emissary to the Kato.*

He kept to a small corner of the deck where he was out of the
way of everybody, and breathed in the cold salt air as though it
might scour his brain of its malaise. He did not speak to anyone,
though he overheard plenty talking about the fall of Port Talaka
and the destruction of a good portion of the Jade Sea fleet to the
south-east. Whatever successes Sova was enjoying in the New
East – and there was no question it was the dominant force in
the region – the reversals in the land of the wolfmen were catastrophic. If they lost the northern Kyarai, they would lose access
not only to the Jade Sea itself but to all the coal and iron ore there
and all the gold and diamonds and lumber in the Reenwound.
The officers on the brigantine were convinced Sova would sue
for peace.

The clipper was much faster than the fifth-rate he had taken
from Port Gero, and the journey across the strait between
Tajanastadt and the Horn was only three days. At dawn on the
final day, just after the seventh bell, he accosted the captain. The
man, who was from Venland – one of the secessionist Western

Kingdoms which had, centuries before, formed part of the First Sovan Empire – was a Neman Conformist; and despite such being illegal in Sova, seemed unashamed in owning a pocket copy of the Conformist Bible.

"Is there anything in it about a golden spearhead?" Peter asked him. The captain had handed the Bible to him, and he idly flicked through it, as though its forbidden knowledge would leap off the page and lodge in his brain like a musket ball.

The captain looked at him sidelong. Although it was late spring, the Jade Sea was cold in the early morning, and he had a thick greatcoat on with the collar pulled up about his ears. He smoked his pipe and thought for a moment. "Could be something like that in the Prophesies of Zabriel. Lots of magickal artefacts in there. But you are not allowed to read them. Not as a Sovan. They will hang you."

"Will you not tell me, then?"

The captain took a moment to size him up, as though he were some kind of witchfinder. "The only member of the Deti pantheon I pray to is Stygio, Lord of the Sea," he said.

"Something you and the mer-men have in common, then," Peter said eventually. It took every ounce of his mental strength to conceal his dismay.

"Funny old world."

He handed the Conformist Bible back, as though holding it for any longer might start to burn him. The fuzziness in his head was returning: thoughts of enormous doors and dead giants, of ancient quarrels between demons and men, of savage, undiscovered races in the dark, deep places of the world.

"Not long now," the captain said, nodding to the horizon. "Why don't you join me for lunch before we put in? We can discuss these matters further if you'd like."

Peter, who hadn't eaten a thing in two weeks and whose body continued to reject the intake of any and all food and drink, declined politely.

"Suit yourself," the captain replied.

Peter resumed his solitary vigil at the bow.

⥲

They pulled in to Port Gero and unloaded. Soldiers came down from the fort to help bring off the wounded officers, whilst the sailors and dockworkers began to unload the cargo. Others – a miserable collection of wives and children – waited for news of their husbands and fathers.

The place was abuzz with chatter, and there was a sense of foreboding in the air. Peter made his way out of the harbour and into the town, a small seaside settlement overlooked by the fort on the bluff above. Here the air smelt of saltwater and fish, and seagulls trilled in the cold ocean air. Above, bruise-purple clouds scudded across the afternoon sky. The fort itself was a hive of activity, and he could see soldiers moving briskly atop the walls and officers with spyglasses watching the ocean to the south-east.

"Excuse me, madam," Peter said, stopping an elderly woman in the street. "Is something going on?"

"Talk of Casimirs making their way up the coast," she said, eager to be getting on. "There's going to be fighting in the next day or two. More of it," she added bitterly.

"I see," he said quietly. "Thank you."

She briefly appraised him. "Are you all right, mister?"

No.

"Yes, thank you," he replied. "Good day."

"And to you," she murmured, and bustled off.

He made his way through the settlement to the gates of the fort. He was stopped by the sentry, who saluted him smartly.

"Good afternoon, sir," the man said, doing a good job of not gawping at the claw scars on Peter's face. "Just come in on the clipper, have you?"

"That's right," Peter said. He felt as though his head were filled with a constant buzzing sound, an intangible, soundless vibration

⥿ 447 ⥿

that made him want to squeeze his head between his hands. His mind was on the forest again, always on the forest, and the execution stone, and the golden spear.

"It's all happening here, sir. Have you any orders?"

"What's going on?" Peter asked, feeling light-headed. His own voice sounded like a distant thing, something he was hearing but not producing.

"Your guess is as good as mine, sir. Casimiran Navy, heading up from Port Talaka. Haven't heard anything beyond the skin of it."

"I need to . . ." Peter swayed, and staggered. "Sova."

"You and everyone else, sir," the sentry said uncertainly.

"I don't—"

He collapsed.

The last thing he heard was the sentry crying for help.

XXX

Matters Slip
Beyond Control

*"The ambassador is more warrior than any member
of the general staff. By the power of his words
alone are entire nations disassembled."*

ARTEM MANAGOLD

Port Gero

NORTHERN KYARAI

There was recklessness, and there was this insanity.

They ran behind several lines of bluecoats. So many were killed – by Nema, so many. The Sovans on the northern wall loaded their remaining cannon with grapeshot and the effects were devastating. They cut down a dozen men and women at a time. One Casimiran sergeant was atomised in a great red cloud. More fell with huge holes erupting from their backs. Limbs were punched clean from torsos; heads were blasted apart like smashed wine bottles. And still they carried on.

Renata kept running only because she didn't want to be left

behind by Lyzander. The fort was obscured by enormous clouds of white smoke, which made it easier; if she had been able to see the guns, she would have lost her nerve.

Her lungs filled with that same smoke as they achieved the lee of the northernmost wall. Casimiran soldiers and marines poured into the breach created by the naval guns, clambering up the ragged slope of smashed stone like apes. They were easy pickings for the Sovan defenders. The latter were in better shape than Renata could have thought possible after the shelling from the ketches.

She watched as black- and blue-coated soldiers exchanged musket fire at short range and blades at shorter. The smoke was incredible, soup-thick, stinging her eyes and closing her throat and lungs. The noise, too – gods, the *noise*. It was like being in the centre of a thunderstorm.

Casimiran sergeants and officers were urging their men forwards into this most desperate and forlorn assault. They exhorted madly from the front, brandishing sabres. They were killed very quickly. It seemed to Renata that success in storming a fort called for a critical mass of men. Those first into the breach were certain to be cut down more or less immediately; it required, then, a solid block of soldiers right behind to press on and overwhelm the defenders. In this case, there were simply not enough Casimirs. This truly had been a gamble. Why had they rushed so?

The answer would come.

She shrieked as a body landed next to them – a rare Sovan casualty, a soldier who had fallen from atop the wall.

"Perfect," Lyzander grunted. He immediately began to unbutton the man's jacket. "Help me!"

Renata helped, or tried to; the body was trussed up in all manner of belts and straps and frogging, and she achieved very little.

"*Qu'est-ce que vous foutez tous les deux?!*" a Casimiran sergeant snarled at them as he appeared through the smoke. He carried what looked to Renata like a spear, which he brandished at Lyzander.

"*Nous ne sommes pas des Sovans!*" Lyzander shouted back.

"*Quoi?*"

Lyzander lurched forward, getting inside the range of the spear. The sergeant snarled and dropped it unexpectedly, leaving him to stagger off to the right.

"No!" Renata, jumping at the man. To her utter surprise, he punched her square in the nose. Pain exploded through her face, and a stunning, soundless blast of stars swirled in her vision. She staggered backwards, heedless of the incredible danger – for the air was filled with a horizontal rain of lead – until she hit the north wall and slid down to her buttocks.

The temptation then was to give up. To wait until the fight was over, one way or the other. If the Sovans prevailed, she could be on her way; if the Casimirs won – well. What use did they have for her? She was a diplomat and a civilian, untouchable by every law of warfare in existence. Either way, she didn't have the stomach for this.

❧

And *yet.*

❧

She let out a cry of frustration.

She pressed herself back to her feet.

She staggered over to the sergeant, who was wrestling with Lyzander on the ground.

She kicked him in the side of his head as hard as she could.

She let out another great cry, this one of pain – for she was certain she had broken a toe in the process. But she had done it. She had given Lyzander just enough time to get the sergeant on his back.

He stabbed him directly through the heart with his own spear.

He knelt there panting for a few moments, filthy and bloody and sweaty, catching his breath. "Thank you," he said. Then he nodded to the top of the fort. "Now: up there."

They clambered up the rubble. "Don't shoot! We're Sovans!" they roared over the din. They held their hands up whenever they could. It didn't seem to have much effect; at least two soldiers tried to shoot them through the thick gunpowder fog.

They scraped their hands and knees and shins on the smashed stone and brick. Renata very nearly impaled her palm on a spar of splintered arm bone. But they achieved the wall, where so many Casimirs had not. Here, they were a little safer; Lyzander looked visibly Sovan thanks to the jacket, and nobody was about to shoot an unarmed woman – at least, not on purpose.

With the defenders preoccupied with defending, few paid them any mind. They climbed quickly down the steps into a broad staging area where soldiers moved frantically to plug the gap in the north wall. The guns overlooking the eastern approach fired ceaselessly on to the Casimiran ships rolling in the ocean. The evening wind was picking up, and it was getting harder for them to fire with accuracy.

"I'm looking for Colonel Glaser!" Lyzander shouted to a succession of soldiers.

"Get out the way!"

"Fuck off!"

"Watch, there!"

Renata tried as well. Everyone ignored her.

They looked around, increasingly frantic. Were the others even here? Was this a fool's errand? The idea that they could have been so insanely irresponsible with their lives for no reason at all was intolerable.

"Let's try the infirmary," Lyzander said, wiping his forehead on a loose jacket sleeve. He pointed to where a sizeable field hospital lay against the south-western wall.

"Renata!?" someone shouted.

They turned sharply. It was Herschel; he was standing atop the parapet of the south wall, the side of the fort looking out on to the settlement of Port Gero. It was one of the only parts of the fortress not to be under direct attack.

"Viktor!" Renata called out.

She and Lyzander hurried across the staging area and up the steps to the parapet. Herschel had a spyglass in his hands. But for the circumstances, he might have been an indulged tourist.

"Where the hell did you go?" Herschel asked. "We haven't seen you for days!"

"We went to Maris, to the Iris Isles," Renata said breathlessly. "Watch!"

"Take cover!"

"Look out!"

They turned sharply. Men were shouting from around the fort. Everyone clasped their tricorns and ducked, or ran to find some rudimentary cover. Beyond the east wall, Renata could see great blooms of smoke and flame erupting from the mortars on the Casimiran bomb ketches, whilst another broadside from a man-o'-war thundered into the cliff face and eastern wall. It was poorly aimed; the swell was too high, and from where they stood, Renata could see that the crew had been forced to shutter the lowest row of gun ports.

They hurried down from the wall, and all the while Herschel gabbled over his shoulder.

"We thought you'd been killed!" he shouted over the intoler-able timpani of exploding shells and rock-smashing roundshot. "We tried to speak to the guards at the Door to the Sea, but of course that led nowhere. The colonel decided we should give you a day or two to turn up, failing which we would make back for Sova with the Blood Stone—"

"Where is it?!" Renata demanded as they once again sped across the staging area. Herschel led them through a door cut into the drum-shaped concrete casemate which sat in the centre of the fort, and into a cold, damp tunnel. Here was the fort's magazine, as well as sundry operations rooms and quarters. The occasional embrasure allowed some of the late-afternoon light to enter; the rest was provided by candles which guttered under the shelling.

"Colonel Glaser has it," Herschel said. "Here."

They entered a small chamber where Glaser stood with another officer and several men.

"Ambassador! Captain! By Nema, we thought you'd been killed!"

"Colonel, I need the Blood Stone," Renata said, trying to keep her voice level.

"What?"

They all flinched as a dud shell landed in the courtyard outside with a great metallic clang.

"I need the Blood Stone. Now. We need to return it to the Stygion." In spite of her efforts, she sounded desperate and impatient, not helped by the lunatic figure she cut, her clothes muddy and sooty and dripping wet. "There's no time to explain; you are just going to have to trust me."

"She's right, Colonel. We mustn't tarry," Lyzander said.

Glaser turned to him, nostrils flared, index finger brandished. "Mustn't? *Mustn't*? Prince of Hell, who do you think you are talking to, Captain? You do not tell me what I must and mustn't do! Now get out of here, the pair of you. We can discuss matters when this is all done with."

"Colonel, for Nema's sake, the Blood Stone is one of the only magickal amplifiers which can open the Eye of the Sea. It must be given to the Stygion before it can fall into the wrong hands."

The other officers in the chamber followed this exchange with expressions of utter bafflement.

"Madam Ozolinsh has already discovered and explained to me the nature of the Blood Stone and its importance. I'm afraid

I cannot give such a powerful artefact into the custody of the Stygion. The security of the Empire—"

"Damn your eyes and the security of the Empire! I am talking about the security of the *world*! Have you forgotten why we are here? What all of this has been about?"

Glaser could not be moved. "Ambassador, we really do not have time for this. I will speak to you about it when—"

"When everyone in this fortress is dead!"

"Stop *interrupting* me! You impertinent woman!" Glaser thundered. "Gods' death, get her out of here, somebody!"

Renata felt her hands bunch into fists. Before anybody knew what was happening – least of all her – she had leapt forward and was attacking him.

"Where is it?! Where is it, you fool?! Give it to me! Get off me!" She snarled, rabid, as several officers dragged her away. How could he be so stupid? How could he be so obtuse?

Sova in all things. Of course. A directive that had been hammered into them relentlessly. Sova in *all* things.

She was hauled out of the operations room. At least Lyzander had had the good sense to say and do nothing; he accompanied her back into the corridor unmolested.

The doors slammed closed and Renata rounded on Herschel. "Where is it. Tell me now. And where is Ozolinsh?"

"Madam Ozolinsh was badly injured in the bombardment," Herschel said, looking nervous. "She was taken to the infirmary. What was it the mer-men said about the Blood Stone?"

"How badly?"

Herschel shook his head and hands, as if trying to banish this line of enquiry. "Very. Something about her backbone. Ambassador: what was it the mer-men said about the Blood Stone?"

Renata made a frustrated noise. "What I have already said: that it can open the Eye of the Sea."

"Why would anybody want to do that?"

"Well, perhaps the Selureii for one, you numbskull!" She let out a trill of maniacal laughter. "Do you know what it is?" She took a step forward, her expression feverish. "Do you *want* to know what it is?"

"Wh-what?" Herschel asked, his back against the tunnel wall.

"Enormous, trans-dimensional thought parasites. *Mind vampyres.*" She jabbed a finger at the floor. "They are waiting right there, ready to eat your soul. They are like sharks in the aether, just below the surface, and they have, eaten, *everyone.* There. *That* is why you can't hear them. Do you understand me? That is why it has fallen silent. They are all dead! The deathless have died! Is any of this getting through to you?"

Herschel looked as though he were about to cry. "Blessed Nema," he whispered.

"Now," Renata said through gritted teeth, "*where* is the Blood Stone?!"

They were out in the open when the second assault came. Dusk was falling, the wind was picking up, and the sky was the colour of slate. Off the coast of the Horn, it seemed as though the Sovan Navy was slowly gaining the upper hand. This would be the Casimirs' last chance to take the place.

The breach in the north wall was once again wreathed with smoke from musketry and cannon fire. Blackcoat defenders two ranks deep fought desperately to hold off the final enemy incursion of the day. Screams and the ringing of swords and bayonets filled the air.

Herschel led them out of the staging area and to a barracks block near the western wall. Inside was a chaotic mass of injured where casualties had spilled over from the field hospital. They swept through like indifferent physicians to a partitioned area for officers, and Herschel gestured to a locked door. Lyzander kicked it in. Beyond was a chamber containing a bed, a chest of drawers and a wardrobe, which they promptly ransacked.

"Here it is," Renata said, clutching the small chest.

"I thought I might find you rogues in here."

Renata turned. Glaser was standing in the doorway, pistol in hand. He was breathing deeply where he had evidently run after them.

"Colonel, for Nema's sake, please—"

"Shut up!" he snapped. "Put that box down this instant. I should have you flogged for going through my personal effects, let alone hanged for thievery."

"Colonel, you cannot have lost sight of—" Lyzander tried.

"I've lost sight of nothing!" Glaser roared. "It is you who are blinkered by your love of the bloody fishmen. Sova is home to the greatest minds in the civilised world – to say nothing of one of the greatest concentrations of force. The Blood Stone will be safer there than anywhere else."

"Safer than the bottom of the ocean?!" Renata squeezed her face between her fists as a violent frustration filled her. She felt as though she could weep, crushed by the monumental feeling of impotence. "The Great Silence—"

"Gods rot your prophecies!" Glaser brandished his hand in the direction of the Jade Sea. "Of course they are going to *say* they need it! With an artefact like this, who knows what damage they could do to the Navy? To our trade? To our—"

Renata thought Lyzander would be the one to attack the colonel; but to everyone's surprise, it was Herschel. He charged into Glaser's side, grasping madly for the pistol. Glaser grunted, more annoyed than angry as this portly – and hitherto cowardly – middle-aged monk tried to disarm him.

"Stop it!" Renata shouted.

"Come on, gentlemen," Lyzander added.

"Nema damn the lot of you!" Glaser shouted back. They tussled madly, inexpertly; it was a bar-room brawl, and in other circumstances might even have been amusing.

Then Glaser fired his pistol, and the front of Herschel's throat exploded.

There was an incredible silence. The small chamber filled with the smell of gunpowder. Renata sat staring, blood-flecked, as the monk collapsed backwards, both hands clutching his smoking, ruined neck. Lyzander had frozen in place mid-intervention. Even Glaser seemed shocked – but not so shocked that he was not tugging a second loaded pistol from his sash.

Herschel looked terrified as his life's blood cascaded out of his opened throat, a terror doubtless exacerbated by the knowledge that his immortal soul was about to be consumed. Renata's paralysis broke, and she darted forward, casting about with trembling hands for something – anything – to stem the flow of blood, though it was hopeless. Herschel writhed and thrashed for no more than a handful of moments before he was still.

There was a brief pause; then Glaser, Renata and Lyzander were all jolted from their horrified stupor by the sound of Herschel's immortal soul screaming in anguish.

Renata felt faint. The horror was too much to endure. She turned to Glaser, eyes red-rimmed, her expression venomous. "How could you?" she whispered. She shook her head in disbelief. "How could you?"

"I . . . He . . . There was . . . "

"Lower the gun, Colonel," Lyzander said, his hands splayed in placation.

Now Glaser turned the weapon on Lyzander. "Get back," he said. He was not a man given to self-doubt, but even he could tell that this had been a fatal miscalculation.

"Colonel: the number of people who appreciate both the severity and the true nature of our situation is small" – Lyzander looked meaningfully at Herschel's corpse – "and *dwindling*. For the love of Nema, please."

"I don't have time for this," Glaser said loudly, nervously, tucking his pistol back into his sash. "We can discuss it later."

Lyzander opened his mouth and closed it again, his brow furrowed. "Er . . . right," he faltered.

Glaser squatted down next to Herschel, laying a hand on the man's chest. "That was ill-advised," he said quietly – a remarkably understated admission.

They would be the last words he spoke for some time.

Herschel's eyes snapped open, and with powerful, grasping hands, he clutched either side of the colonel's head and dug his thumbs deep into the man's eyes.

Renata screamed, scrabbling away from the appalling scene.

"What in the damned fucking hell?!" Lyzander shouted.

The light in the room dimmed. The air filled with a great droning buzz, like the wings of an enormous demonic fly. Glaser thrashed madly, gripping Herschel's wrists and trying to unplug his eye sockets. Lyzander briefly overcame his horror to kick Herschel in the face, and in so doing fouled a great portion of it as though it were clay.

Underneath was the same golden plate that had been beneath Guillot's.

The Knackerman.

"Good gods," Lyzander breathed.

GOOD GODS, the Knackerman said noiselessly, causing the exposed folds and cords of Herschel's neck to squirm and tremble. He turned his ruined visage to Lyzander. GOOD. GODS.

"For Nema's sake, run!" Renata shrieked.

"Don't leave me," Glaser moaned.

They left him. Renata and Lyzander scrabbled to get out of the chamber. Renata danced and squealed as Herschel's bloody hands grasped at her feet and ankles. Lyzander kicked and stamped relentlessly on Herschel's face and neck, but he might as well have been stamping on a mannequin.

They fled back through the barracks, chased by Glaser's terrified moaning. Renata would have taken her chances with anything the Casimirs could throw at the fort over the ghastliness of the Knackerman – which was just as well, because there were plenty of them within the walls.

"Shit," Lyzander said with profound dismay. The Casimirs had gained the north wall, and turned it and part of the staging area into a battlefield. "The gate!"

"We can't leave Azura," Renata shouted back, charging past him.

"Where the hell are you going? The infirmary is right here!"

"To throw the Stone into the ocean!"

"Oh, fuck and blast," Lyzander groaned behind her.

Renata dodged and ducked between clashing soldiers as she scrambled her way to the east wall. Several times she had to pause as surprised bluecoats stopped themselves from running her through with bayonets. Lyzander had a harder time of it; he had to fight off a number of Casimirs with a pilfered sword. He left two men bloody and wounded on the paving in his wake.

Renata scrambled up the steps to the banquette. The thunderous cannonade continued relentlessly in spite of the fighting as artillerymen answered the final broadsides from the Casimiran man-o'-war. Only the artillery crew of the north-easternmost cannon had been forced to abandon the enterprise and fight off Casimirs there.

Renata hit the parapet bodily in her haste to cross the banquette. There she fumbled madly with the clasp of the strongbox.

Of course.

"It's locked!" she shouted as Lyzander appeared next to her.

"So throw the box in!"

"It'll . . . bloody . . . float!" Renata gasped, breaking a fingernail as she tried to prise the thing open.

"Give it here!" Lyzander snapped, snatching the box off her and hammering it into the embrasure repeatedly. The thing was so strong it might as well have been made of iron.

"No, just ... get off," Renata said, wresting it back off him.

I'LL TAKE THAT, THANK YOU.

They both turned sharply. The Knackerman was standing there. His face had sloughed away entirely. His hands were still dripping with Glaser's blood. The fate of the colonel remained uncertain.

Renata's breath caught in her throat. She turned to throw the box over the side of the cliff. The Knackerman grabbed her hand by the wrist. Again that buzzing – and a great stink rose off him too. Renata was overcome by an urge to peel off her skin and bathe her body in vinegar.

Next to her, Lyzander landed two strong chops with the sabre on the Knackerman's right arm. He would have taken it off entirely with a third, but he was punched so forcefully in the chest that he was knocked off the banquette and sent tumbling back down on to the staging area.

I SHALL BE SURE TO PERSONALLY REPATRIATE THIS TO THE SONS OF STYGIO, the Knackerman said over the tremendous demonic buzzing. He plucked the box effortlessly from Renata's hand.

"Please," was all she managed. As an epitaph it was pathetic, and yet it was meant very sincerely. How quickly her sensibilities had abandoned her when presented with imminent death.

NO. WE MUST NOT KEEP OUR VORACIOUS FRIENDS WAITING.

Renata closed her eyes, wincing, waiting for the fatal blow; and then there was a rush of hot air, and a whistling sound, and a great wet thud. Her arm was released, and she pitched forward on to the banquette.

She opened her eyes.

Herschel's body – or rather, its constituent parts – lay in a great red ruin strewn across the courtyard. The roundshot which had hit it sailed on for another fifty yards before ploughing a deep furrow into the earth near the Port Gero settlement.

Renata expected the ghastly rags of flesh to begin coalescing and advancing on her again; but it seemed even the surpassing sorceries of the Knackerman could not overcome this mortal obliteration. That she had come within a whisker of being smashed in half herself was something to compulsively dwell on later.

She climbed shakily down the steps, trembling and nauseous and wanting to do nothing more than curl up into a ball and wait for this hell to be over. But something had changed. Confronted so relentlessly by direct threats to her person, she had failed to appreciate the broader picture within the fort. Blinking through the evening gloom and the roiling clouds of smoke, she noticed for the first time that there were *wolfmen* now – dozens of them. They were clad in red Sovan-style military jackets and black pantaloons, and bore enormous falchions whose scabbards hung from sashes of orange, yellow and black silk.

"The Grasvlaktekraag regiment from Kalegosfort," a familiar voice said from behind her. Renata turned, half expecting to see that the Knackerman had possessed someone else; but she remembered Herschel explaining that only necromancers were subject to possession. It explained why no one from their party but the Bruta Sarkan monks had fallen prey to it.

"You're alive!" she breathed, her heart fluttering, as Lyzander stood before her.

"Just about," he said. "One of these unlucky fellows broke my fall." He gestured vaguely to a pile of Casimiran bodies.

Renata stepped forward and grabbed him into a tight embrace, and then, giddy and overwhelmed by the horrors of the day, kissed him ferociously.

"Well, that was—" Lyzander said, and then stopped as a massive explosion ripped into the evening sky where a heated roundshot had perforated a bomb ketch's magazine. Port Gero, it seemed, would remain in Sovan hands for the time being.

"The Blood Stone!" Renata shouted, jolted back to reality. She pushed herself away from Lyzander as the last of the Casimirs, faced with the incredible brutality of the wolfmen, surrendered en masse.

They picked amongst the sick ruin of Herschel's body – Renata had grown dismally accustomed to the gore occasioned by modern warfare – and then, finding nothing, broadened the search. The box was not large, and there was a huge amount of debris within the courtyard for it to be lost amongst. But the shadows grew longer, and the noise and activity died down, and still it could not be turned up.

"Where is it?" she asked breathlessly, frantic. She looked at Lyzander. "Where is it? It cannot have gone far!"

"Do you not think I would have said something if I knew?" he replied, not taking his eyes from the floor.

Renata's heart pounded. They searched everywhere they could in the short time they had, for the fort was being locked down now that the battle was won and provision needed to be made for the prisoners. By the time darkness fell, they had still not found it, nor could anybody else be turned to the task. Lyzander's captaincy was not enough to order a general search: he was from another regiment, and out of his uniform, and nobody recognised him. Only Glaser had had the necessary rank and authority.

After several hours, it became clear that the Blood Stone could only have been missing by design.

"Someone took it," Renata said helplessly. They had scoured every inch of the courtyard and were now standing outside the south wall, in case the box had been flung completely clear of the fort. But even out here amongst the windswept salt grass and wildflowers, there was nothing. "Someone *took* it."

"But who could have known?" Lyzander asked, hand on his forehead. It was cold and getting colder. Even in summer, the night-time ocean breeze was unforgiving. "Who could *possibly* have known?"

Renata said nothing. What were they going to do? What were they going to tell the Stygion?

"Who could possibly have known about it?!" Lyzander repeated.

XXXI

A Convergence of Unwitting Souls

"The plenipotentiary is the most dangerous of all agents of the executive; imbued with the full power and confidence of the Emperor, they are a walking, breathing extension of the nation state. It is vital that persons so invested enjoy the fullest trust and confidence of all strata of the government; the scope for calamity is vast."

FROM J. P. COOK'S
IMPERIAL FOREIGN POLICY & INTERNATIONAL RELATIONS

Port Gero

NORTHERN KYARAI

"It is no different than if the Kasar had lost it in the fall of Port Talaka," Lyzander said in the weak grey light of the following dawn.

"I'm sure they will accept that explanation with alacrity."

It had been a long night. With their search for the Blood Stone foreclosed by the darkness, they had eventually announced themselves to the commanding officer of the fortress – Major

Matovesian – and imparted scant details of their mission and status. Matovesian was much too preoccupied with the blinding of Glaser – who had, by some miracle, survived the Knackerman's attack, albeit in a dire state – but still Renata went out of her way to explain the helpful presence of the Stygion, for which the major expressed his guarded and insincere gratitude. But with the fort piling up with casualties, and with dozens of Kasar from the Grasvlaktekraag regiment to billet – to say nothing of rebuilding the northern wall in short order – he had little time for them, and certainly not the manpower to divert to search for the Blood Stone.

"I will say this," he had remarked upon their parting. "If a soldier finds that ruby, you shall never see it again."

After a brief trip to the infirmary to see if Ozolinsh was still alive – she was, though unconscious – they had found some food to eat and a place to sleep, which ended up being in an old woman's spare bedchamber in the Port Gero settlement. Now, barely two hours later, they were trudging across the cold, damp sand, delirious from exhaustion and with heads full of fresh nightmares, ready to give the worst possible news to the Thrice Queen.

"You think they will be there? Waiting?" Lyzander asked.

"What choice do they have?" Renata replied, feeling crushed by the weight of their failure.

"Perhaps the ruby was obliterated by the same ball that killed Herschel?"

"Perhaps." She affixed her glasses. "Wait here. This will be over quickly, one way or the other."

Before he could say anything in protest, she ran into the frigid ocean water and waded out to the Door to the Sea. Beyond, swaying at anchor, were the several victorious Sovan warships from the previous day's naval engagement. Port Gero would soon be lousy with such ships as Sova consolidated its toehold on this distant part of the world.

She plunged beneath the waves before she could think too much about what she was doing. The water was gloomy in the dawn light, but the striking white and black hide of Kaipatu was starkly visible in the grey water. Either side of him were two white sharks mounted by Muirgen and the ambassador, Sina.

<Ina> Renata signed, waiting for the lungfish to affix itself to her head.

<I am to take it you have failed?> the Thrice Queen said. Renata could barely see her above the drop-off, which plunged darkly underneath her legs. Any moment now she expected a great set of open jaws to rocket up from below. Or perhaps they would drown her; command the lungfish to withdraw, and drag her down to the dark depths to expire in agony.

<Yes> she replied. Better to be honest. Better to get the news out of the way quickly. <There was a battle. In the chaos I lost the stone> She explained what had happened in prosaic terms. The temptation to provide a lengthy mitigation was a strong one. But she was tired, and the Thrice Queen would not care. The end result was the same: they had lost one of the most important magickal artefacts in the world. What did it matter if it was through bad luck or sheer incompetence?

<Who is "the Knackerman"?> the Queen asked Muirgen.

<Some sort of trans-dimensional agent?> he replied. <I know not, Ina. It is interesting – and telling – that his power is limited to manifesting within those who have made conduits of themselves between planes. I have never come across this being. I shall speak with the rest of the Conclave. It is likely that he poses great danger>

<Then see that you do it quickly!> The Queen turned back to Renata. <Who has the Stone now, soil-eater?>

So: they were back to epithets.

<I do not know> Renata said. <We searched for it for many hours>

She yelped as Kaipatu lurched forward, snapping his great jaws within a few feet of her. Was this what it would be like to face the Vorr?

<You must recover it. *Nothing* is more important> the Queen barked. Displeasure radiated off her like a physical force.

<I understand, Ina> Renata signed.

<If you truly understood, you would not have lost it in the first place>

Renata shook her head. She had not the wit nor the will to rejoin.

<What will you do now?> Sina asked.

<I need to inform the Empress what has happened here, and the Corps of Engineers. It will take all of us working in concert to solve the problem of the Vorr>

<Solve? Such arrogance> Muirgen scoffed. <To think that you have anything even close to the knowledge and abilities required>

"For Nema's sake! We are going to have to try and do something, aren't we?!" Renata shouted into the stale air bubble of the lungfish.

<Then I bid you good luck> he said after a little while. It was as though he respected her more for being obstreperous.

Renata took a moment to calm herself. It was cold in the water, and she was keen for this to be over.

<Will you help us?> she asked. <If you discover anything, will you share your knowledge with us?>

<That depends> the Queen said. <Will your Navy stop killing my people for sport?>

<I will push the Empress for such an injunction> Renata said. <I swear it>

<They will never agree. Sova is too vile a nation>

<It is capable of great viciousness> Renata agreed. <But we are nothing if not a pragmatic people. If I can impress upon the Senate the nature of the threat, they will turn their minds to the task>

<If>

Renata thought for a moment. There had to be something more concrete she could come up with. Diplomats were problem-solvers if nothing else.

<As ambassador I have plenipotentiary power> She stumbled slightly over the Loxican word for "plenipotentiary", and both signed and subvocalised it. <I am authorised on behalf of the Imperial Sovan Senate to make treaties>

It was a stretch; *Maruska* certainly had been invested with such power, though he would never have used it without close consultation with the government, and it was perfectly likely that the government had forgotten he had been so sanctioned. She was authorised in a technical legal sense, since she had inherited the ambassadorship, but she certainly had no de facto mandate to negotiate any such agreement.

<We could agree a treaty. Here and now> she said. <I do not know if such an agreement would hold, but it could make life very awkward for the Imperial Office to have to formally renege on it>

<It is not in your interests to say this> Sina said.

Sova in all things.

<It is in everybody's interests to preserve the mortal plane. We are all mortal, after all>

<You could lose the ambassadorship>

<There is no one who could replace me>

<They might decide they have no need of a replacement>

Renata paused. In fact that was precisely the sort of thing the Imperial Office would do.

<With the loss of the northern Kyarai, Sova will be less reckless with potential allies>

<We are not your ally. We are natural enemies> the Queen said.

<No. There is no need for us to be enemies. It is true, the Sovan Navy kills your people; but you kill our people too. Our fishermen, our sailors, our traders. Irrespective of who started

it, there is a mutual cycle of violence which it is in both of our interests to break>

<"Irrespective of who started it"?> both the Queen and Muirgen said in concert. Behind them, Kaipatu and the white sharks stirred in vicarious fury.

Renata held out her hands. She had worded that clumsily. <The point I am making is that we are both faced with an existential threat. If there was ever a time to make peace, it is now>

There was a pause as Sina, the Queen and Muirgen conversed in trans-verbal Loxica.

<Your primary mission must be to find and return the Blood Stone> the Queen said. <I do not think your superiors have the clarity of will to agree to peace terms, but an end to the wanton murder of my people would certainly give us time and space to consider the issue of the Vorr. Here>

A Spear approached Renata, and handed her a pearlescent oyster the size of a large grape. Inscribed upon its surface was the warrant of the Royal Household.

<It will take me time to get back to the capital, and longer still to bring you news of my success. There may be slayings in the interim>

<We have weathered your iron for many years now, Sovan. A few more weeks will make no difference>

<Thank you for your patience, Ina>

<That is not something I am often accused of having>

A joke? Was it possible? Renata chuckled good-naturedly, though across from her in the water she saw nothing that could be taken for Stygion laughter.

<I take my leave, then> she said.

<I suggest you do. Before I have you eaten on both sides of the mortal plane>

Again, it was possible that the Queen was being wry, but Renata did not wait to find out. She began to move back towards the Door to the Sea, pausing briefly at the edge of the reef. <If I need to speak with you . . .>

<We will have our sentries here as we always have done>

<Thank you>

The Queen did not respond; instead, Kaipatu and the surrounding Spear-mounts turned away, and were soon lost in the murky water.

She sat on the beach with Lyzander. He had procured a greatcoat which he wrapped around her shoulders whilst she explained what had happened. Around them, a work gang of Casimiran prisoners of war, under the watchful eyes of Sovan riflemen, picked amongst their dead, turning out pockets, collecting personal effects and valuables, and stacking the corpses for burning. Seagulls pecked and plucked incessantly at the cornucopia of human entrails, whilst beached in the shallows, the corpse of a large blackfish was worried at by dozens of crabs.

"Can I ask you something?" she asked after a long period of silence in which they had both watched the flotsam from the previous day's naval battle bobbing in the surf.

"Of course," he said.

"What was – or is – the nature of your relationship with the Empress?"

Lyzander's expression collapsed. "Ah."

Renata immediately regretted her question. "Never mind. I'm sorry I raised it."

Lyzander sighed mightily. "No. I should tell you. Last year, I . . ." He sighed again. "I was . . . that's to say, Zelenka and I . . ."

"You were lovers."

He smiled weakly. "We were lovers."

She waited for him to continue, resolved that she would not prompt him further.

"The Royal Household – to say nothing of the Senate and Privy Council – absolutely did not approve of our courtship."

Renata found herself nodding along to this; it was deeply unsurprising. "Do not tell me they expelled you from Sova?"

"Nothing as dramatic as that. The regiment was posted to Kalegosfort and then to Port Talaka. I could probably have remained in the city. I think Zelenka would have seen to it, if I had pressed her." He shrugged. "But I knew which way the wind was blowing."

"You took the decision out of her hands."

"Hm. Yes. I left – rather abruptly." He was quiet for a few moments. "I'm not really sure why; only that I felt a great . . . *pressure* to leave. It is a rum thing when the institutions of state are arrayed against you."

Renata snorted. "Aye, well. I know that feeling."

Lyzander glanced at her, and they exchanged a brief smile.

"Ultimately, I knew our relationship could not continue, but I still think I resented her for caving to the pressure. Even though I knew – I *know* – that she didn't really have a choice. I know it and yet I still feel bitter. That's a funny thing, is it not?"

"The human soul is certainly capricious."

"Hm. Well, anyway. The letter you brought to me has reopened the matter somewhat."

"That is . . . well, it is what it is," Renata said. She thought of Lyzander's kiss – kiss*es* – and felt a curious pang of jealousy; but then he put his arm around her, and she rested her head on his shoulder.

They watched the waves for a while.

Half an hour later, and Renata was sitting with the fortress's surgeon, a stern Vennish woman by the name of Ms Íñiguez, who explained to her the nature of Ozolinsh's injuries. They were sitting in the woman's quarters in the fortress. Her sleeves were rolled up the elbow, and she smelt strongly of carbolic acid, which again reminded Renata of Amara.

"A piece of femur," she said, holding her two index fingers up six inches apart. "Severed her lumbar spinal cord during the shelling. I have irrigated the wound and knitted it, and she has been provided with opioids."

"What is her prognosis?" Renata asked, chewing her fingernails. She had finally dried off and changed into some fresh clothes, but her hair was split and tangled from the saltwater, and her skin was dry and chafed.

"Very poor," Íñiguez said. "Frankly. If I had the equipment and the personnel, I would perform a laminectomy to reduce the pressure on the spinal cord – though there is a growing body of evidence that such a procedure is redundant," she added, her brow furrowed. "Either way, the biggest risk is renal failure. The urine in the bladder will turn sour and infect the renal tract. If the kidneys fail, she will die."

Renata felt sick. "Is there nothing you can do?"

"No. Not here. You will have more luck in the Royal Naval Hospital. She will need quinolone preparations. Give her plenty of clean water to drink; I recommend a good porter, too, for the constitution. You must also look out for sores."

"Sores?"

"Bedsores. Ms Ozolinsh must be kept immobile for the spine to knit. Lying on one's back over time leads to areas of the body becoming compressed, where the bone presses into the flesh. The flesh necrotises and suppurates, and will then become enpoxed."

"So we must move her?"

"As little as possible, but enough to keep the blood flowing around the body and to relieve pressure on the skin. Keep the head and neck aligned with the spine when you do so. When the wound is healed, she can be mobilised."

"Right."

"And of course she must be kept clean. Ms Ozolinsh has no voluntary bladder and bowel function any more."

Renata felt flushed with guilt. Ozolinsh would never have been here were it not for her.

"How soon can she be moved?" she asked eventually.

"Not for at least four weeks," the surgeon said. "And preferably even longer."

"That's not possible," Renata said. "We need to leave for Sova immediately."

Íñiguez shrugged. "I suspect we are all going to have to leave Port Gero in the coming days anyway, given the state of the Kyarai. Nonetheless, movement will only aggravate the wound."

"We need her. Alive. Sova needs her."

"I believe you, Ambassador. This is an instance where medical needs and political necessity do not align. It is not the first. It will not be the last."

Renata sighed. She was exhausted, and heartsick, and still there was so much to do.

"Ms Íñiguez?"

The physician looked up. Renata turned. Standing in the doorway was an orderly, a large man wearing an apron. He looked more like a butcher.

"Yes?"

"Young lieutenant off the 'Keith from the other day. Collapsed out the front gate. I brought him into the infirmary, but haven't had a chance to give him a going-over yet, what with all the action."

"Yes?"

"It's . . . best if you come and see, ma'am."

"As you will."

"May I see Azura?" Renata asked, making to stand.

"Yes, yes," Íñiguez muttered, and Renata fell into step behind her.

They made their way to the infirmary. Inside was a groaning mass of fresh amputees. Every bed was occupied; the smell of blood and death hung heavy in the air.

"What is it?" Íñiguez asked the orderly as they went to the relevant bed, which happened to be the one next to Ozolinsh's. The engineer looked pale and sweaty, and lay in the grip of a fever dream. Renata took her hand and stroked it.

"Take a look at this," the orderly said next to her. He lifted up the young lieutenant's shirt, exposing his midriff.

"What on earth . . . ?" Íñiguez murmured.

Renata knew she should not look, for decency's sake; but she had been so plagued by mysteries and horrors over the past six weeks that it was impossible not to see threads of aethereal connective tissue running through everything.

Íñiguez traced a finger over what looked like an enormous incision running from the base of the man's sternum to his pubis. "Whose work is this?"

"I know not, ma'am."

She spent a moment examining the wound, palpating the lieutenant's midriff. "Roll him on to his side," she said to the orderly, and he did. She continued to palpate. "Where are his . . . ?" she murmured. "Roll him again."

The lieutenant was rolled once more. Íñiguez examined him for a long time.

"It's not possible," she said, her features creased in absolute perplexity. "How is he breathing?"

"His lungs are still—"

"I don't mean physically. I mean . . . How is this man alive? He is missing half his vital organs."

Renata stood up next to them, overcome by curiosity. Íñiguez was so baffled she did not even dissuade her.

The lieutenant was probably in his early twenties, though he had been aged prematurely by Imperial warfare. The skin around his eyes was dark and wrinkled and gaunt, his face was marked by a dark shadow of stubble, and there seemed to be ingrained dirt in his pores. All of that was to say nothing of the three enormous claw marks which ran diagonally across his face from eyebrow to chin. He looked as though he had had a near-fatal encounter with a bear, and recently. In spite of all of this, though, someone had made a good go of cleaning him up. Whatever he had been wounded in, it was not the uniform he currently wore.

The scar running the length of his abdomen looked ghastly, but it was knitted expertly closed and was not enpoxed. It was as clean an incision is it was possible to make.

"This man walked here, you say?" Íñiguez asked.

"Aye, ma'am. Collapsed at the gate. Perhaps for want of water?"

She gestured roughly to the lieutenant. "And what is he to process it with? The man has no digestive tract, to say nothing of his missing kidneys."

"It is magick," Renata said. There was something about this man ... She could not put her finger on it. Being around him made her deeply uneasy.

Íñiguez and the orderly turned to her sharply. "What manner of magick can sustain a person in this way? I have never come across anything of the sort. And even if it is possible, it is illegal."

"What else could it be?"

They all turned back to the lieutenant, who stirred briefly and muttered something.

"What did he say?" Íñiguez asked.

"All in?" the orderly offered.

"No," Renata said. "Olwin."

"A pagan name."

"He has recently returned from the New East?" she asked.

"A day or two ago," the orderly said.

"What is this on his hand?" Renata asked. They all looked to where a large grey callous had claimed the man's palm. It was rough, and contoured like ocean cliff rock.

"Is that . . . " Íñiguez bent down and examined the skin closely, "*wood?*"

She scratched at the bizarre skin, peeling off a splinter, then held it up so that both Renata and the orderly could see it.

"What on earth . . . ?"

Renata looked at the man. She thought about the northern lands which abutted the Empire. That this man had been subjected to some sort of magickal transformation was beyond doubt – at least in her mind – which meant something was happening there, too, amidst the roof of the world, those vast unmapped places hitherto the sole preserve of Sovan argonauts and pagan natives. This man should have been dead ten times over, yet he was living, breathing.

"Have you seen any other cases like this?" she asked Íñiguez.

"Never," the surgeon replied.

Renata once again examined the man. There seemed to be something about him that was quietly repulsive, and it had nothing to do with his wounds. There was an aura of darkness about him. It unsettled her.

She looked at Íñiguez. "I should like to take him to Sova with me," she said. Something about this felt like an augury. If they were to find a way around the predations of the Vorr, then every arcane matter, every instance of sorcery, every inexplicable phenomenon had to be triaged, examined, considered, documented.

"You will do no such thing," Íñiguez replied, though she seemed to say it more because she felt duty-bound to say it as a physician. The man clearly made her, too, uneasy.

But Renata's resolve was iron. "I will," she said.

Íñiguez looked flabbergasted. "I am a warrant officer within the Sovan Navy—"

"And I am a Sovan ambassador," Renata said, cutting across her. "You will release this man into my custody."

There was a deadly silence, but it was clear the physician was keen to be shot of the young lieutenant.

"As you will," she said eventually.

"Have him brought up with Azura. We will take him in a coach until he is fit enough to ride."

Renata met Lyzander in the marshalling yard of the fort later in the morning. Together they walked up the steps to the parapet where it looked east across the Jade Sea. Here, the artillery crews manning the big coastal guns diced and drank and otherwise sheltered from the biting trade winds. In the distance, she could see the sails of approaching Sovan ships.

"Well?" Lyzander asked.

Renata told him about both Ozolinsh and Kleist.

"What in hell's name . . . " he muttered quietly, not taking his eyes from the ocean.

"I must write letters to the Imperial Office and the Empress. Then we must leave." Even in spite of everything she had witnessed and been told, here, now, surrounded by corporeal, tangible things – sea and stone and sand, terra firma, cold wind, cannon and human men – the Great Silence was a difficult thing to countenance. The mind rejected what it could not see and feel directly. Convincing those in power to act was not going to be straightforward.

Lyzander nodded. "Aye. You mean to bring Madam Ozolinsh with us?"

"We must. She is a practitioner of the arcana, and she knows what is at stake. Such people are rare indeed."

"What if moving her kills her?"

Renata shook her head. "We will take care. We will be careful. But she must come back to Sova, and now. We must look beyond the needs of individuals."

"That is a cold way to think."

"I think we are all going to have to cultivate that mindset in the coming weeks."

She turned at the sound of whinnying. There in the courtyard below was a stagecoach which they had requisitioned from the settlement, and the garrison's ostlers were hitching it to six plains horses on the orders of Major Matevosian. Their journey back to Sova would be significantly faster than their journey to Port Talaka, but it would still take several weeks. A great deal could change in the world in that time.

"And this . . . walking corpse-man?" Lyzander asked.

"If he is of no use whatever, then we can deposit him at the nearest Sovan outpost. But . . . "

"But?"

"Anything like this. Anything bizarre. Anything that is obviously the consequence of sorceries. Any visions, nightmares, auguries – all of it we should be attuned to and mindful of. We need *information* now, more than anything. We need to understand the afterlife and how it works. We need to undo two centuries of wilful blindness. And we need to do it very quickly."

Lyzander sighed. "Do you want to know what I think?"

"What?"

"I think Sova is very fortunate indeed to have placed you where it did, when it did."

Renata grunted, uncomfortable with the compliment. "Yes, well. They respected Maruska a lot more than they respect me."

"Aye, but you have the benefit of many voices speaking in concert."

There was another silence.

"We shall see," was all Renata said.

The journey was fraught. Renata's attention should have been focused on their mission; instead, she found herself utterly preoccupied with keeping Ozolinsh strapped and still and comfortable. As for the mysterious young soldier, he remained locked in some sort of fugue state. In many ways that was preferable.

Íñiguez had given her some laudanum to keep Ozolinsh's pain at bay, though it rendered her insensible. They had to make frequent stops to ply the woman with water and brandy, and to change and wash her as often as was necessary given the debilitating nature of her ailment. When she was not so occupied, Renata wrote a great many letters – "the diplomat's first and best weapon", Maruska had taught her. Some of them, especially those of a sensitive nature, were in diplomatic coding, and these were dispatched from staging stations with liveried messengers. She hoped that, in so doing, she could at least get the best scientific minds of Sova turned to the problem of the Great Silence ahead of her arrival.

And, of course, forewarn the Empress that she had legally bound Sova to a peace treaty with the Stygion.

After a week of travel, they reached Zetland again.

"Well," Lyzander said. The fortress lay a few hundred yards away, the only feature on the plains for miles in every direction, sitting beneath a low ceiling of dark grey cloud. Summer thunder had been rolling on the horizon for a while; soon there would be rain. "You know what happened to them."

She did, now. If the Bruta Sarkan monks had indeed attempted a summoning, and had exposed themselves to the afterlife en masse, then it stood to reason that they had all been killed by the Vorr. Herschel and Guillot couldn't have known it, but the explanation fitted.

"You don't have to go in," Lyzander said.

There was movement to Renata's right, and she turned

sharply, heart fluttering; but it was just the plains horses. The postilion had unhitched them, and they were cropping the grass.

"I just do not see what purpose could be served by it. Based on what you have told me, in the very best case you might catch a pox. See there: a yellow jack."

Renata followed the line of his finger to the doors, where an enterprising pedlar had daubed a yellow square there; in international semiotics, "quarantine".

"And in the worst?"

"Do not be facetious. Who knows what is lurking in the darkness?"

Renata took a deep breath. It trembled only slightly. "That's why you're going to come with me," she said, and began to walk towards the fortress before she could change her mind, leaving Ozolinsh and Kleist in the stagecoach in the care of the postilion.

If it had given the impression of abandonment before, now it was positively desolate. The livestock had long wandered off, and the doors remained sealed and undisturbed, still marked with that macabre signage:

DO NOT ENTER
ALL DEAD INSIDE

She had not heard the aethereal screaming for some time now – or at least, had stopped noticing it. But here in this dead, silent place, it returned. It was as though the sound was carried on the wind – like listening to a ship full of burning sailors two miles offshore.

She and Lyzander approached cautiously.

"Hello?" Lyzander called out, hand on the grip of his pistol.

"They cannot be alive," Renata said. "Even if their bodies had persisted in some sort of autonomic sense, they would have perished for want of food and water weeks ago."

"They cannot be alive in the *traditional* sense," Lyzander replied.

Renata did not have an answer to that.

"Hello?" he called out again. But the only sound was the wind across the plains grasses. "You are certain you want to do this?"

"I'm just going to have a look around."

Lyzander grimaced. "Let's get this over with, then."

The doors were not locked, and they opened surprisingly easily on well-oiled hinges. The air beyond the threshold was stale and smelt faintly of decay. Renata pulled her blouse up around her nose and mouth to ward off the worst of it.

The fortress was gloomy. There was an antechamber, an old mediaeval disarming room, and beyond, a larger great hall. That was empty, though the smell was stronger the further in they went.

It was clear that the ritual had taken place below ground. Following the smell, they found a staircase that led away from the great hall and into a basement level, one that was accessed via a large double trapdoor. Opening the latter released a great waft of rancid, soup-thick air, and instigated a cacophony of chittering and buzzing where the chamber had become a bustling colony for vermin and putrefactive insects. The darkness was profound, and obscured what had to have been a scene of visceral horror.

Renata let the shirt fall away from her nose. It was doing nothing against the stench. "Fetch a torch, would you?" she said to Lyzander.

"Aye," he muttered, and disappeared off, his footsteps receding back into the fortress.

Renata stood in tense silence for a moment; then she took a step back to put some distance between her and the reeking darkness below.

Her heel clipped the top of the step.

She stumbled, arms windmilling. She cracked her wrist on the lip of the trapdoor.

Her heart lurched; her breath came in ragged gasps. She fell backwards and slid down the stone steps.

Above, the trapdoor slammed closed.

"Captain!" she screamed, overwhelmed in the sudden pitch darkness. "Captain!"

The silence was total.

She pressed herself against the wall, filling the basement with the sound of her frantic breath. She should have been able to find the stairs again with one step to her left, but her foot landed on something soft, and she gasped and withdrew it.

She took several long beats to try and calm herself down. Lyzander would have heard her scream and the calamitous banging of the trapdoor and would be on his way to open it very shortly. And as ghastly as it was to think about, everyone was dead. It was a chamber full of corpses. They could not do anything to her.

Then she heard movement.

Something shifted at the far end of the sanctum.

And it was not rats.

Her heart leapt with such violence that she was worried it would falter and sputter out like a candle flame. Every inch of her skin roughened with gooseflesh as she was overcome with a vertiginous feeling of peril.

"W-who's there?" she stammered.

Silence again raged in that suffocating chamber.

"Who's there?" she repeated, her fear cloaked as anger.

There was no answer.

She reached out her hands – and immediately came into contact with someone standing directly in front of her.

Their eyes and mouth exploded into sudden golden radiance.

It was Peter Kleist.

"I don't want to be here any more," he moaned through mouthfuls of glowing ectoplasm like molten copper.

And Renata screamed and screamed.

It took Lyzander a long time to calm her down. He insisted the trapdoor had never closed – only that she had started screaming. Peter Kleist had not left the stagecoach; he was as catatonic as ever. And after she had bolted from the fortress, he had examined the basement chamber to find that, whilst it was a macabre scene of several hundred skeletonised corpses and an enormous rat colony, there was not a trace of anything eldritch.

Renata trembled in the warm afternoon breeze. With its huge wildflower plains and broad open skies, it should have been a place of great beauty and tranquil serenity. Instead it was a place of skin-crawling horror.

"What happened?" Lyzander asked her when she had eventually regained herself with several stiff measures of brandy from his flask.

"I told you, I saw him—" She pointed at the stagecoach, and then yelped in fright. Lyzander turned sharply, hand on the hilt of his sabre.

He relaxed.

"You're awake," he said uncertainly.

Peter Kleist blinked in the gloomy afternoon light.

"Where am I?" he asked. "And who are you?"

They repaired to the stagecoach, for it began to rain. Renata was doubly wary of Kleist, though the postilion assured her repeatedly that the man had not left the back of the stagecoach the entire time they had been in the fortress.

"Would you like something to eat? Drink?" Renata asked, a little disingenuously given what she knew.

He shook his head. "No thank you."

"You haven't had a drop of water in over a week," Lyzander remarked.

Kleist evidently didn't know what to say to that, and so said nothing.

"I am Ambassador Renata Rainer," Renata said after a while. "You were taken to the infirmary in the fortress at Port Gero. We are on our way back to Sova."

"Where are we?"

"Reichsgard. We've just crossed the Reka."

Kleist rubbed his face and eyes.

"I've just returned from the colonies," he said.

"We know. Did the Army repatriate you?"

He shook his head. "I am resigning my commission."

"Not something most give up so young," Lyzander said. Renata noticed that his hand was resting on his pistol.

"Aye, well," Kleist said. When he spoke, it was quietly. "I have had my fill of it."

"Saw some action, did you?"

"And more besides."

Renata exchanged a look with Lyzander.

"Something is happening to the world," Kleist said. He looked at his left hand, almost all of which had gone rigid and grey-brown. He quickly hid it behind him. "Either that or I am going quite mad."

"Something is indeed happening to the world," Renata said carefully. Her eyes kept flicking to his abdomen, as though she might glimpse something through his shirt and jacket. "What is it you have seen?"

"I'll not be mocked again!" Kleist suddenly shouted, making them both start.

"Govern yourself," Lyzander warned, grip tightening on his pistol.

Kleist seemed to deflate slightly. He took in a deep, ragged breath. "There are monsters in the north."

Outside, the postilion, water cascading off his waxed greatcoat, hitched up the last of the plains horses. A few moments later, they were on the move.

Renata turned back to Kleist. "Why don't you tell us what you saw?" she said gently.

He looked at her with red-rimmed eyes. "You aren't going to believe me."

"To the contrary," Lyzander said, leaning back and releasing the grip of the pistol. "We are probably the only people in the world who will."

XXXII

Devouring Gods

"In the same way that we would not tolerate a man walking up to our house and smashing it down with an axe, so must we find intolerable the actions of a man who would destroy the scaffold about which we construct our society."

SIR KONRAD VON VALT, FIRST LORD
REGENT OF THE SOVAN REPUBLIC

The Horn

NORTHERN KYARAI

He forsook the Gero Road entirely, preferring a goat herders' path that mostly cleaved to the western face of the Horn. Behind him, the sounds of battle faded away – a distant timpani carried on the ocean wind, and eventually, nothing.

He rode for several days until he reached Fort Karl, and then smuggled himself across the Sigismund Line into Saekaland. From there he crossed the River Saeka and rode into Grunhaven, an old mediaeval Templar fortress long reclaimed from Sova by the Saekas. Here was a quiet settlement and port, popular with smugglers; he sold his plains horse and hired a ship to take him up the coast.

Favourable trade winds saw that part of his journey completed in three days. He was deposited on the south coast of Sanque, and was able to cross into Casimir without incident – the former was a client state of the latter, after all, and their mutual border was undefended.

He could speak Kòvoskan comfortably enough, and had no difficulty in securing passage across the interior of the country. Here in the north, the principality was mostly given over to tenant farmers anyway, people who happily took his coin and did not ask too many questions. A succession of horses, donkeys and cart beds took him across the neck of the country until he reached Hasse – another member of the Kova Confederation, famous for nothing except its picturesque mountain ranges.

It was summer now, and the snow had melted, and he found the mountains' reputation well earned; they were pleasant and cool and filled with wildflowers. He hired a guide to get him to Lowestadt, and from there he took a boat down the River Kova to the north-eastern corner of Hofingen. There he quietly murdered the boatman and hid his body in the rushes for the blowflies, and then allowed the currents to carry him another hundred miles in the direction of the North Sea until he was more or less parallel with Verdabaro. He abandoned the boat, and once again cut across the country due west.

There was a darkness here, a darkness and a silence, and the natural order of the world could account for neither. The sky was persistently gloomy, and there was a general . . . *absence* of the processes of life. It was as if the whole of the country had descended into some liminal, interstitial space, airless and lifeless, a mere simulacrum of nature. This was not Draedaland; this was a theatre, the trees cut-outs, the grass a rug, the sky a painting, he a mummer.

Was this a sign of things to come?

The Blood Stone felt suddenly heavy in his satchel.

But he had not made a habit of questioning his master hitherto, and he was not about to start now.

Verdabaro sat on the edge of an enormous forest known as the Velykšuma, which stretched all the way to the north-western coast of Draedaland. The Draedist confederations in this part of the world had opted for an architectural style that was plain, a deliberate rejection of the colonial Saxan gothick of the First Sovan Empire. Verdabaro, then, was a town characterised by boxy buildings, either of undressed grey stone or clad in white plaster, with shallow sloping roofs of red-brown slate. And whilst hewing to guild closures had been inescapable, there was a much greater focus on coexisting with the natural world rather than supplanting it. Most structures were covered in creeping vines, the roofs lost under moss. The streets were lined with trees, there were public gardens and wildflower meadows, and watercourses were built around, not dammed and diverted and made iridescent with chemical pollutants. It was a place of great beauty.

It was also completely empty.

He moved slowly and cautiously through the broad streets. Like much of the rest of the country, the silence hung in the air like a physical force, oppressive and frightening. Would this be the fate of Sova? He shivered. He was not a fearful man, but the prospect filled him with dread. Whatever the Selureii were up to, whatever the nature of this contagion, there was no question it was a profound horror – its deliberate propagation a humanitarian crime.

For want of a better plan, he made his way to the city hall in the centre of the settlement, Verdabaro's only concession to architectural ornament. The building had once been a Neman temple, added to and extended over the course of centuries, with the result being structural motley. He gripped the strap of his satchel tightly and pushed open the door. Beyond the threshold stretched the main part of the old Saxan temple, an enormous, vaulted space once dedicated to the worship of Nema. It was a godless space now.

Standing at the very far end, facing away from him, was Lamprecht von Oldenburg. He was clad in a large brown duster, with his gloved hands clasped behind his back.

"*Kiu estas tie?*" a voice called out, in equal parts frantic and indignant.

"I told you, if you do not speak in Saxan, I will cut your fucking tongue out," von Oldenburg snapped. He turned. As he did so, his face lit up in a maniacal grin. "Broz! Good gods! You made it all the way here. You have a gift, my friend, for the most preternatural timing."

"My lord," Broz replied uncertainly.

Von Oldenburg approached him down the aisle. He was uncharacteristically bearded and looked slightly deranged. "What news of the south?"

Broz peered over von Oldenburg's shoulder, trying to discern the source of the second voice.

"Oh, don't worry about him," von Oldenburg said. "We'll get on to him in a minute."

"I followed them all the way south as you instructed. Of the diplomatic mission itself, I know not the outcome. The woman, Rainer, spent some time at least in Ozeanland. I can give you the full account, of course. There were some rather strange goings-on, too, in Port Talaka. Didacus Maruska was murdered by a . . . somewhat demonic gentleman."

"Most intriguing," von Oldenburg said, frowning seriously.

Broz swallowed, nodded. He was not a man of great scruple, but suddenly he found himself regretting this course of action. "The reason I abandoned the task was for a much greater and unexpected prize. I know you have made it your ambition to unlock the secrets of the arcane. I have something which should assist you in that enterprise greatly."

"Nema, Broz, what have you got?" von Oldenburg asked, his eyes darting to the satchel.

Broz withdrew the strongbox and opened it.

Von Oldenburg made a strange noise, something that sounded like a strangled grunt of pleasure mixed with a deep and abiding pain. Broz noticed for the first time that the bottom of his master's glove was brown and crusted with dried blood.

"Is that what I think it is?" von Oldenburg whispered feverishly.

"I'm not sure of its precise nature," Broz said truthfully. "Only that a lot of people seem very interested in securing it."

Von Oldenburg said nothing; with trembling hands, he reached into the box and withdrew the large ruby.

"The Blood Stone," he breathed. There was a gleam of madness in his eyes. "I cannot begin to tell you how good a thing this is."

Broz felt a thrill of pleasure at his master's words, even though a sizeable part of him continued to feel that perhaps this had been a grave mistake. Both feelings were subordinated to a much more immediate revulsion at the smell of his master's breath, which was quite rancid.

"What will it do?" he asked, his throat dry.

"Accelerate," von Oldenburg almost snarled, gripping the ruby tightly in his fist. "It will *accelerate* my plans greatly."

"Your plans remain at odds with those of the Selureii?" Broz asked, seeking some reassurance that he had not just doomed the world.

Von Oldenburg cackled. "Indeed, Broz, indeed! By Nema, do I have a story to tell you! Come here and see for yourself!"

Broz followed the count, past the altar and towards a small chapel at the rear of the ambulatory. The stones beyond the threshold were glossy crimson with blood.

"In here," von Oldenburg muttered.

The first thing that drew Broz's attention within the chamber was a scrawny pagan strapped to a large wooden X. Either side of him were two figures wrapped comprehensively in rags and masked with emotionless iron visages. They stood stock still – so still in fact that they might have been tailor's mannequins.

On the floor beyond was a stack of corpses.

"You have been busy," Broz said grimly. Every one of the bodies bore the hallmarks of torture.

"Oh indeed, indeed," von Oldenburg muttered.

Broz shivered. It was not the sight of corpses – something he was intimately familiar with – but rather the quality to the air in the chamber. This place, this chapel, filled him with a very tangible sense of dread.

"Who is he?" He gestured to the man, who was quite naked, strapped to the X.

Von Oldenburg took a step back and indicated the living victim and the pile of bodies. He brandished his hands in the same way a showman would.

"May I present the Selureii!" he said with a ghastly flourish. He pointed closely to the prisoner's neck. "See the tattoo there? That is the Draedic ideogram for 'Ascension'."

"This is . . . You killed them?"

"Well, I killed these ones. They are a death cult, see? So they *welcome* death." He turned to the still-living prisoner. "Except that isn't quite the case, is it? Not so keen on it all now, are you? Eh? Not on another's terms!" He surrendered to his rage, hitting the pagan three times in the face. "You . . . *stupid*" – punch – "*fucking*" – punch – "bastard!" Punch.

Broz noticed that the other two men, weird silent sentries, remained completely still.

"Who are they?" he asked, pointing at them, trying to interrupt and distract his master.

"Oh, I shall explain. I shall explain it all. It's the most remarkable tale, Broz," von Oldenburg said, panting. He reached over to one side and retrieved a sizeable spherical contraption from nearby.

"What is that?" Broz asked.

"This is the most extraordinary piece of thaumaturgic engineering you will ever see," von Oldenburg replied. "Let me describe to you the process."

He opened a large flap on the top of the sphere. Within was a compartment that seemed to contain a small reservoir of blood, and it was into this compartment that the count unceremoniously jammed the Blood Stone. "This mechanism will vacate a body of its thaumaturgic load – its 'soul'." He bunched his fingers together and then blew on them, as though he were holding a dandelion. "And then once the soul is vacated, a bloody great scream is going to tear through the aether. We'll all be able to hear it – or certainly you and I will, not these two fine fellows." He pointed to the motionless men. "Their days of hearing anything except my commands are over."

Broz did not quite know what to make of this, and so said nothing.

"Then the person will become what I have termed a 'vacant'. This is the first of two stages. Vacants know only one thing: some nameless, irresistible directive to spread the contagion further."

"The contagion?"

"The *contagion*," von Oldenburg said, raising his voice, "is a transmittable mindlessness which has its roots in the arcane. This man here knows its precise nature, which is why he is now so keen to avoid it." He turned to the strapped pagan. "Don't worry; I myself can be susceptible to hypocrisy!" he shouted with lunatic brightness.

The prisoner stared at him with incredible venom.

"He has told you the nature of it?" Broz asked.

"He has indeed. Do you want to know what it is, Broz? Do you want to know what it *is* that the Selureii have done pursuant to their idiotic death cultism?"

Broz was starting to get the feeling that perhaps he did *not* want to know what it was.

Von Oldenburg swept in close and gripped two fistfuls of

the front of Broz's jacket. "*Vampyres*, Broz. *Mind*-eaters. A race of trans-planar soul-suckers. That is their judgement. Their Ascension. Can you believe it? Can you *believe* it? The lunacy of it? Imagine willingly giving your soul over to interdimensional vermin to be eaten and thinking that was holy."

"That's—"

"Totally fucking mad?! Yes!"

The Selureii shaman snarled something long and unintelligible.

"We'll get to you in a minute," von Oldenburg snapped. He turned back to Broz. "The contagion, Broz, is people having their sensibilities stripped away from their brains by alien creatures who have flooded the afterlife and are consuming every soul that has the misfortune of ending up there."

"Everyone who—"

"Dies, yes. *Everyone*. Every soldier, every murder victim, every poor old man on his deathbed, their souls are sliding directly into the keeping maw of the vampyres. Someone let them in. Do you see? Someone *let* them *in* to the afterlife, and now these fine fellows, through some spectacularly ill-advised ritual, have let them in to the mortal plane. It's their fault. It's not a plague, Broz. It's a *feast*."

"They wanted it to spread to Sova," Broz said, as the mental tumblers clicked into place. "That is why they were stifling the news of the plague. They wanted Sova's inaction to abet the spread of the contagion."

"Aye, you have it."

"And the Stygion?"

"The Stygion are the most experienced magickal practitioners in the world. Their knowledge of the arcane is unparalleled. The purpose of the diplomatic mission was for Sova to make common cause with them; to discern the nature of the contagion and so stop it."

"That is why they tried to murder the diplomats in Sova."

"Right. A bit of a cackhanded attempt, but so often is the case with last-minute plans."

Broz thought a moment. "They tried again in Talaka. And in Port Gero. They did something to the monks." He shook his head helplessly. "I know not what it was, but it was arcane in nature. Seemed to me to be some sort of . . . demonic possession. I have never seen its like," he added, shuddering.

Von Oldenburg seemed untroubled by this. "Well, it's not going to possess me. I am warded." He looked at the pagan. "Who is this demon you are in league with, eh? Or is it all some shaman's trick?"

The pagan said nothing.

"How do we stop it?" Broz asked. "The contagion?"

"How do we *monetise* it, do you mean?" von Oldenburg asked. His expression was deadly serious for all of three seconds; then he burst into a fit of roaring laughter, thumping Broz hard on the shoulder. "I jest. Well, in part. Listen, I have not finished talking about this mechanism yet." He brandished it. "Phase two of the process involves en-thrallment. At the moment I have to use this." He pulled what looked like a fire poker out of the inside of his duster. At the end of it was a brand. "It imprints an old Draedist ideogram directly on to the skin. This rune slaves the vacant to me, and the vacant is now a thrall. And the thrall will do whatever I command it to do.

"What is *really* quite *excellent* for me is the Blood Stone. Because it is a thaumaturgic amplifier, I can actually use it to vacate souls at *range*. It's like a gun, except it doesn't kill the person, it enslaves them to me. Isn't that fantastic?"

"A marvel, my lord," Broz murmured.

"So in this way, we might slow and even prevent the spread of the 'plague' by instead redirecting the victims to my service."

Broz shook his head in confusion. "Should we not be focused on solving the . . . I mean, *problem* feels like too mild a word."

"Oh, let Sova worry about that. They will be turning their great minds to it."

"They *know*?"

"Yelena will tell them, if she has not already."

"*Yelena?*"

Von Oldenburg waved him off, irritated by the distraction. "I will ask you to track her down and kill her – naturally."

"Uh . . . naturally."

"But I do *want* them to solve the problem. I cannot achieve my ambitions in a world that no longer exists. Still, I am confident they will. Which gives me a chance to get a night's march on things."

"A . . . night's march?"

"It is easier if I show you. Words will not do it justice. In fact, speaking of demonstrations . . . "

He returned his attention to the brass sphere and the detained pagan. "Are you ready for your apotheosis?"

The Selureii gnashed his teeth in rage. "You are mad," he said in heavily accented Saxan.

"And you are not?!" von Oldenburg thundered. "To seek the destruction of every living being in the world because of the prattling insanity of Conformist orthodoxy? A pox on your Great Silence. You have lost. Take your licks with good grace."

"You can't stop it."

"You can't start it," von Oldenburg shot back. "Your *Ascension* is ended."

The pagan shook his head slowly, his expression venomous. "No."

"Yes," von Oldenburg said simply. "But let us not argue about it. Let us put it to the test." He held the orb and began to quietly incant.

"What are you doing?" the pagan asked, starting to struggle.

"Giving you what you've always wanted," von Oldenburg replied. The Blood Stone within began to glow. Von Oldenburg's eyes turned black, like crystal goblets filled with ink.

"Wait," the pagan stammered. "Wait – wait a moment, damn you. I can tell you more. Demon, eh? Just let me—"

"Be quiet," von Oldenburg muttered. "You had your chance with that, and I've a lot to get done this evening."

"Wait, damnfuck, wait—"

And then he went slack, and a great scream ripped through the chamber, nearly giving Broz a heart attack.

"Perfect," von Oldenburg said brightly. He turned to Broz. "Now come. We can talk further outside."

They left the hall and walked into the cool evening air of Verdabaro, flanked by the two lepers – or rather, *thralls*.

Deeply unsettled, but propelled by curiosity, Broz allowed himself to be led unresistingly out of the northern extremity of the town and into the forest beyond.

They followed a path for a little while, but that soon disappeared. Von Oldenburg moved with great purpose, even as the ground began to fracture and rise. They moved over moss-covered rocks and slippery tree roots, picking their way upwards like a pair of recreational hikers – though the swaddled corpses following them spoiled the illusion.

After a while Broz could hear a persistent thumping sound, many thumping sounds in fact, knocking and hammering and the rhythmic scrape of saws. The sounds grew in volume and density, until they reached the edge of a clearing and he was confronted with an incredible scene.

"Mother of gods," he breathed.

Thousands of Draedists were excavating the earth, cutting trenches and redoubts and breastworks, chopping down trees and creating palisades and log structures. More cut and hammered and chiselled stone, and chain gangs passed the blocks along, where they were mortared into walls. They sweated and grunted, but not one word was uttered, not one command issued. It was a vast, silent encampment of slaved thralls.

"Magnificent, isn't it?" von Oldenburg said, looking out across the scene like a man admiring a vista. He absently pulled a bottle of tonic from his pocket and took a long draw. Then he put it away again and made a dismissive gesture. "But this is just a trial run."

Broz noted that many of the thralls were dead or dying, and the ground in and amongst the foundations of this rude fortress were littered with corpses.

"A trial run, my lord?"

"Mm. I wanted to see if I could put a large number of people to work simultaneously, on a number of complex tasks. Only the smiths can smith, the masons mason, the mortarers mortar. But carrying a bucket? Cutting down a tree? Sawing a log, lugging a stone, digging a trench? Anyone can do these things. It is all about having the *numbers*. Feeding and watering them is going to be the next big task, but I'm thinking that I can get some of the thralls to forage and prepare food and water for the rest, see? So it all becomes self-sustaining."

"To what end?" Broz breathed.

"*Think!* Think what a man could achieve with an army of these thralls. Not only an inexhaustible supply of free labour, but an actual *army*. Not only will I bring the pagan lands back into the fold, but I will re-assimilate the Western Kingdoms and destroy both Conformism and the House of Casimir once and for all. Then I shall take the New East and the Kyarai and the Stygion Sea. They call this the Second Sovan Empire; well, mine shall be the Third."

Broz listened to this with a profound sinking feeling.

"That is ... quite the endeavour," he said.

Von Oldenburg looked at him askance, his face splitting into a grin. He took another quick swig of tonic and then laughed heartily.

"Quite the endeavour indeed," he said, and laughed again. Then he put his arm around Broz's shoulders. "Come, then. We have a great deal to do."

Epilogue

A Message from Beyond

*"It is in the name of the commonfolk that foreign policy
is made, and so one would think that a polity would be
exuberantly concerned with what inter-national measures
were being taken in its name. In fact, the opposite seems to
be the case – the further away one strays from the organs of
state, the less engaged and intelligent the worldview becomes.
The relationship is in fact entirely inverse; by the time we
descend to the level of the man on the street, he thinks that
to step across a border is to step immediately into enemy
territory, to look upon a foreigner is to look upon a belligerent,
to hear his language spoken is to hear perfidious code."*

FROM CHUN PARSIFAL'S
THE INFINITE STATE

St Slavka the Martyr Highway

SOVA

"Plague spreads in north! Travel restricted! Draedaland quarantined! Other pagan lands to follow! Find out more in the *Herald*!"

"Here," Renata said, handing over a goldmark bit.

"For the latest, always choose the *Herald*," the news-crier said, doffing his cap as he handed her a copy. She gave him an insincere smile and stood off to one side of the highway and read it.

It was a pleasant summer's day in Sova. The weather, indifferent to the trials of empire, bathed the capital in hot sun. It did not match the mood of the city, which took its cue not from the untroubled blue skies but from the criers and newsmen and pamphleteers. The tabloids had spread the news of the loss of Port Talaka and the greater part of the Kyarai with self-flagellating glee, pillorying senators and army and naval officers and insisting – implausibly – that older, better generations would have kept the unruly territory.

Facing the loss of massive industrial and mining operations, to say nothing of the new canal system, Sova had yielded. The House of Casimir had won this bout. A hasty treaty was signed to prevent the loss of further landholdings and preserve Sovan access to the Jade Sea via Port Gero – overstuffed as it had become with Sovan soldiers and ships. The threat of a bitter pill, and a quiet and significant payment of a million goldmark, had been enough to sate Casimiran designs on the Horn.

But the pamphleteers were voracious, and it was not enough to simply spread stories of martial misery. The people had to be kept fearful of fresh miseries too: now a mysterious and virulent plague in the north – at least, mysterious to most. Ignorance, for the majority, was bliss. She had been given a strict injunction to keep it that way.

"They are ready for us," Lyzander said, appearing next to her with a paper bag of pork rinds in his hand. He was a far cry from the figure he had cut in the south: freshly washed, shaved and clothed. He looked smart and certainly attractive, though Renata privately preferred the roguish figure he had presented in Port Gero.

She folded the paper and tucked it under her arm. She herself was clad in a light summer dress, though she sweated, and it was not solely down to the smoky summer heat.

"What do you think they will say?"

He shrugged. "They authorised the diplomatic mission in the first place, did they not?"

"Well, Colonel Glaser did."

Lyzander shook his head, finished his mouthful. "They are blinkered, but they are not foolish."

"We shall see," Renata replied. It felt like an increasingly common refrain.

They travelled down the highway, and entered the Imperial Palace. Their destination was not the throne room – the historic Hall of Solitude – but rather one of the committee chambers of the Privy Council. This was a sizeable state room, something one might have excised from the Admiralty; walls of patterned green paper, dark wood panelling, portraits of statesmen and women. Enormous windows looked across the Sauber to the Library of Sova and let in copious quantities of sunlight. They were dismally familiar with it, having spent many hours over the past several days presenting their findings.

A very large rectangular table took up the greater part of the space. At it sat four people; the first was the acting colonel of the Imperial Life Guards, a woman by the name of Lydzia Atanasov, who had inherited the position whilst Glaser convalesced; the second was Zénaïde Gagnier, who was the current director of the Corps of Engineers; the third was Emmanuel Bosko, the Empress's spymaster; and lastly was Zelenka Haugenate herself.

"Come in and sit down, please," the Empress said. She could not have been more than five years older than Renata. She had the pale skin and famous auburn hair of the Haugenate line, and wore a gown of light blue silk, off the shoulder, lined with glazed white cotton. Around her neck was a necklace of yellow diamonds, rubies and sapphires – the Imperial colours.

"I trust your companions are being well taken care of?" she asked, a reference to Ozolinsh and Kleist, who had been repaired to the Royal Naval Hospital.

"As best as they can be," Renata said. The weight of their combined testimony still hung in the chamber like a cloud. In fact, bringing Kleist back to Sova had turned out to be stunningly prescient; his ailments – which had no earthly explanation, as verified by serious moustachioed naval surgeons – had been a vital piece of corroboration.

The Empress's eyes flickered briefly to Lyzander. Renata wondered if they had spoken privately. If they had, Lyzander had not told her.

"The man who hears but one voice speaks with one," the Empress said.

"The man who hears a thousand speaks with all the world," Renata replied. "Karl Rothsinger."

Next to the Empress, Bosko, a quiet and jarringly avuncular old man, smiled. "You are well-read."

"It was one of Ambassador Maruska's favourite quotations."

"You are the ambassador now," the Empress said. There seemed to be a hint of displeasure about her. "I wonder if we shall come to hear some of your favourites in due course."

"Perhaps," Renata said.

There was a pause.

"I should like to clarify whether I have grasped matters before we proceed, if I may," the Empress said. There were no objections to that. "According to the Stygion mer-men, a portal between the so-called 'prison dimension' and the afterlife has been opened, and this has ... released an incomprehensible species of spirit vampyres known as the Vorr."

"Correct."

The Empress briefly looked either side of her, but no one had anything to add at this juncture.

"These Vorr have consumed all and sundry within the afterlife and rendered it silent, fulfilling a prophecy known – appropriately – as the Great Silence. That is the news that the two monks from Reichsgard brought to the Privy Council some months ago."

"Yes, Majesty."

"A diplomatic mission to the Stygion, mounted by Colonel Glaser at the instigation of those monks, has confirmed the . . . well, to be frank, horror of the situation. And we have no reason at all not to take their explanation at face value?"

"Certainly they have no special or specific reason I can think of to invent a lie so elaborate," Bosko said.

"Except to force a peace treaty," Colonel Atanasov observed drily.

"We shall come on to that in a moment," the Empress said. Renata felt her cheeks flushing.

"I can—" she started, but the Empress held up a hand for silence.

"No, wait a minute. Let me finish my précis before I lose the thread."

Renata acquiesced with a nod.

"During the course of the diplomatic mission," the Empress continued, "the Kasari Dwelkspreker handed you a powerful artefact known as the Blood Stone, which was subsequently lost to . . . Now, here is where I start to flounder. Let me see if I have it: a discorporate demonic agent known as 'the Knackerman'."

"Actually, Majesty, we do not know where the Stone ended up."

"Most unfortunate," the Empress said, and those around her nodded and grunted and otherwise signalled their agreement. She exhaled long and loud. "The detail I am most interested in at this point in time is the state of the monks in Reichsgard. You say they were all dead?"

Renata swallowed. "Yes, Majesty."

"To a man?"

"Yes, Majesty."

"And according to this Brother Herschel, they died in the process of some necromantic rite?"

"That is what I am given to believe, Majesty."

There was a pause. The Empress turned to Bosko, and said quietly, "Fetch her in, would you?"

The spymaster left, leaving the rest of them to sit in awkward silence until he returned. When he did, he had a woman in tow. She was tall and pale-skinned and strikingly beautiful, clad in a demure summer dress of pastel blue. Renata guessed her to be in her late forties or early fifties, and she was clearly northern by her facial structure and tattoos.

She carried with her a leather satchel and had a serious, businesslike air about her.

"This is Yelena Tesařik," the Empress said.

"Hello," the woman said briskly in accented Saxan, nodding to them.

"Ms Tesařik has acted as Count Lamprecht von Oldenburg's consort for around ten years now. *Acted* being the operative word."

"Count von Oldenburg?" Renata asked, bemused. "The senator?"

"The very same."

"Why?"

"Because much like your monks, Lamprecht von Oldenburg has been secretly practising magick too," the Empress said with false brightness.

"Well . . . what has he been doing?" Renata asked.

"Amassing a formidable collection of arcane books and curios," Tesařik said. "His stated aim has long been the restoration of magickal practice within Sova – to say nothing of the restoration of its former Imperial borders."

"So why monitor him? Why not arrest him?" Renata asked. Bosko chuckled softly opposite her, but said nothing.

"And so, what? You work for Sova?"

"I do not work for Sova," Tesařik said. "But I do work for an organisation *based* in Sova. We are a collection of undesirables: Conformists, Draedists, Tolls, Manaeii, and so on."

"To what end?"

She considered this for a moment. "We monitor the spiritual health of the mortal realm, quietly and discreetly. A little like the Bruta Sarkan, I suppose. Sova's size, diverse population, and ready access to funds has made it a natural home for our work, but we do not consider that we owe it any special allegiance. Count von Oldenburg came to my attention during one of his many illicit trips into Draedaland. He has repeatedly tried to make contact with the Selureii in order to gain their knowledge of the afterlife." She shrugged. "I insinuated myself into his life."

"You yourself are a practitioner?"

Tesařik inclined her head. "I have not sought to commune with the dead for some time, though I am . . . shall we say, psychically attuned."

"Tell the ambassador what you told me," the Empress said testily.

Tesařik looked briefly uncomfortable. "There is a plague in the north."

"So I have heard."

"It is not a normal plague." Something about this woman's words filled Renata with dread; and that feeling only intensified as the telling of her account went on – her trip to Toutorix, the en-thralling of Kyselý and the chambermaid, and the ideogramic brand. By the end of it, she had to grip the table as the implications of it settled on her.

"Now you see why I asked about the monks," the Empress said.

Renata nodded, her mouth dry.

It was Lyzander who said it out loud. "You mean to say that the plague in the north is the Vorr?"

"I cannot see what other explanation fits, based on the extraordinary testimony I have heard," the Empress said. "Which means that not only is the situation utterly dismal, but it is also significantly worse than any individual one of you thought."

Tesařik's brow furrowed. "The ... Vorr?" she asked, and it was Renata's turn to explain the situation and leave her reeling. "Good gods," she said quietly. "That is ... so very much worse an explanation than I had anticipated."

"Verily," Bosko muttered.

"Sounds as though von Oldenburg might just be doing us a bloody great favour, if you ask me," Colonel Atanasov said. "One wonders whether we should let him tear through the Kova Confederation first and then stop him."

"You are talking about a critical mass of thralls," Tesařik said before anybody else could speak. "The mind rot is communicated by touch, but with this mechanism, Lamprecht will be able to vacate vast numbers of people very, very quickly. Once a person has been vacated, they seek out another victim and so propagate the consumption. One becomes two, two becomes four, four becomes eight and then sixteen and then thirty-two and so on. Lamprecht can vacate them in enormous numbers, but he can only en-thrall them one at a time with the ideo-gramic brand. There are a frightening number of opportunities for him to lose control of the situation, particularly when he exposes them to a battlefield – as is his stated intention. We could very quickly be looking at the devastation of the entire continent."

The Empress considered matters in the silence that followed. Eventually, she said, "This is the very last thing we need right now. I'm about to sign the Treaty of Kalegosfort, which will lose us the northern Kyarai." She gestured to Renata. "You have another treaty for me to sign with the Stygion. But," she added, before Renata could speak, "there is no point in being Empress of a realm of ash. I will be honest with you, I do not have the faintest idea how to begin to deal with this matter. But it is clear to me that we must tackle it quickly and decisively; and experience tells me that the most important thing when faced with such exigencies is to *make* a decision, even if it might later transpire to be the wrong one. So: I want you, Ambassador, and you, Ms Tesařik, to establish a task force. Get everybody you need, women and men of great competence; take them from the University, the Argonauts' Society, the Corps of Engineers, other *nations*, for Nema's sake. Send emissaries to I'Kamataxia, the Shōgunate, the Tegsh Tal. If this is a global problem, then let us make it a global problem. *Pool* knowledge. Work together. Find out precisely what is going on, and not only how we can stop it, but reverse it. It may well be that we have to work with the Stygion. Ambassador, I shall leave such matters to you. I was not aware that we were at war with the Stygion, but to the extent that a peace treaty assists you in this endeavour, I will sign it.

"Colonel Atanasov, Count Lamprecht von Oldenburg is *persona non grata*. He is to be stripped of his titles and holdings. All of his merchant, trading and bank accounts are to be frozen, all his assets and funds seized. If he has ships, I want them impounded, if he has men, I want them arrested. I want soldiers pulling Castle Oldenburg apart brick by brick. And I want the man himself in chains before the week is out. Do I make myself clear?"

"Crystal, Majesty," the woman said unhappily.

The Empress turned to Renata. "I suggest you be about it. You have a tremendous amount of work to do, and in a very short space of time. At some point within the next day or two, I shall expect to hear of your plans."

"Our plans, Majesty?"

"Your plans, Ambassador, to save the world."

That evening, Renata went to Milankagate Cemetery to visit her sister's grave. It was a large and overgrown graveyard in the north of the city, sandwiched between the Summit of the Prefects and the Temple of Nema Victoria. It was a quiet and peaceful place, boxed in and shaded by umbrella pines and filled with a motley of gravestones, statues and mausoleums.

She had been absent for – well, everything. Her sister's death, funeral and burial. But Amara's linguistics colleagues at the University had told her about the service, which had been beautiful and well attended.

She spent a little while speaking to the grave and weeping quietly. Not only was Amara gone, but she had been destroyed in the most incomprehensibly vile manner imaginable. It was a source of profound heartsickness and guilt for Renata, and it was only now that she was back in Sova that the grief began to bite in earnest.

She left at dusk. She decided to detour through the enormous Temple of Nema Victoria before heading home, and made her way through one of the many side entrances. It was quiet and warm in the temple, the bustle of Sova blocked out by its thick walls. Somewhere in its labyrinth of halls, chambers and chapels, a choir was singing evensong.

She walked through it slowly, savouring the tranquillity of this holy space. Within the Taxonomy of Heaven, the Detian patron saint of siblings was Akhaber, and she made her way to his shrine after asking for directions from a helpful matria.

The shrine was a small, vaulted, incense-perfumed space no more than a few yards across. In it was a life-size statue of Akhaber himself, rendered as a winged man with a bird's head. In his marble hands he held an iron rack rimed with candle wax; Renata plucked a fresh one from a nearby store and lit it, and set it on the rack.

"Please," she said, her hand tracing a worn divot in the marble arm where generations of bereft siblings had beseeched him. "Watch over my sister."

And then, in an instant, everything was silence and darkness.

Renata screamed and stumbled backwards as the statue threw aside the candles and lunged at her, gripping her shoulders with his marble hands. As he did so, the shrine vanished, to be replaced by a vision of an enormous bulwark of white stone. There, soldiers ten feet tall, clad in gleaming golden armour and armed with weapons that seemed to be made of pure sunlight, were locked in a desperate struggle with creatures that defied perception and comprehension.

The Vorr.

"She is here, in the Golden City!" Akhaber hissed.

"Wh-what?" Renata stammered.

"Amara is here! Nema rallies all remaining souls to her banner! We must make common cause in the fastness of heaven! Quick, before it is too late!"

"I don't—"

But she was sitting alone, on the floor, in the candlelit shrine.

Slowly her breathing steadied. Sound returned to the world: temple bells tolling the sixth hour, the soft footfalls of the faithful, distant evensong echoing through the vaulted halls.

In front of her, the statue of Akhaber held the rack of candles, unmoving.

Renata staggered to her feet. The vision was fading quickly, refusing perception, falling away from conscious thought like a stone dropped into a murky lake.

"I need to . . . " she murmured, leaving the chapel and making her way briskly through the temple.

"Miss? Are you all right?" a passing nun asked.

"I need to . . . " Renata murmured again, walking straight past her, hurrying back through the temple halls in a daze.

"Amara . . . "

As soon as she was outside, she broke into a run.

The story continues in...

Book TWO of the Great Silence

Acknowledgements

As always my grateful thanks go to my agent, Harry Illingworth; to my editors at Orbit, James Long and Bradley Englert; to the rest of the Orbit team (Joanna Kramer, Nazia Khatun, Angela Man, Serena Savini, Lauren Panepinto and Nick Burnham, and everyone else at Orbit UK and USA behind the scenes); to my cover artist, Philip Harris, and map designer, Tim Paul; to life-long friends and beta readers, George Lockett, Will Smith and Tim Johnson.

Special thanks also to Gabriel Beecham, Robin Waas, Cécile Perrault and Chihiro Haraguchi, for your kind, thoughtful and patient help with translations. Any mistakes that appear in the text are mine and mine alone.

Finally, thanks to my darling wife Sophie and my three sweet boys, Scott, Leo and Max – if there's a better cohort of cheerleaders, I don't want to know about it.

Richard
Sydney, June 2024

extras

orbit

meet the author

Matthew Duchesne

RICHARD SWAN is a critically acclaimed British genre writer. His debut fantasy novel, *The Justice of Kings*, was an instant Sunday Times bestseller and has been translated into seven languages. His other work includes the Art of War and Great Silence trilogies, as well as short fiction for Black Library and *Grimdark Magazine*.

Richard is a qualified lawyer and, before writing full-time, spent ten years litigating multimillion-pound commercial disputes in London. He currently lives in Sydney with his wife and three young sons.

Find out more about Richard Swan and other Orbit authors by registering for the free monthly newsletter at orbitbooks.net.

if you enjoyed
GRAVE EMPIRE
look out for

THE RADIANT KING

Astral Kingdoms:
Book 1

by

David Dalglish

Six immortal siblings: five sworn to peace and one who demands a throne.

Radiance, the mysterious power of life and creation, is theirs to command. Death cannot claim them. For hundreds of years, the ever-living ruled with ease. Yet when the world is nearly broken beneath their reign, the six siblings swear a vow: They will sit upon no thrones, wear no crowns, and no longer teach humanity the gifts of radiance.

But after centuries of peace, Eder rejects their vow, anoints himself Voice of Father, and spreads a new, cruel faith across the land.

Faron cannot allow such indiscretion. Returning from a self-imposed exile, he swears to crush Eder's kingdom, and he will not do so alone—Sariel, their cold and calculating brother, knows all too well that an ever-living's dominion is bound for brutality and destruction. But to overthrow a nation, they will need more than each other. They will need an army.

PROLOGUE

SARIEL

Deep within a forgotten cave, Sariel's brother knelt in the heart of an unlit pyre. Sariel stood before him, an oil-skin in hand.

"Are you certain of this?" he asked.

"I am," Faron said. Though he was a kind soul, his voice was firm, and it reverberated throughout the cave.

So pure, thought Sariel. *So foolish. So broken.*

Sariel poured the oil across Faron's brow. It flowed through his brother's short black hair. Rivulets continued along the sides of Faron's handsome face and then splashed across his muscled chest and back. The drops continued down to the eulmore logs, stacked in preparation for the coming fire.

"You'll forget things," said their sister Calluna. She sat some distance away, her back pressed to the cave wall. She wrapped her pale arms around her legs and pressed her knees to her chest. Her long black hair formed a blanket around her. Protecting her. Hiding her. "It's been getting worse."

"It's what Faron wants," Sariel said, his voice soft and nothing like his brother's. He dropped the empty oil-skin on the logs. "To forget."

"Will you judge me for it?" Faron asked.

"No judgments, not for my kin." Sariel lifted his hand,

summoning the innate power of radiance he and his five siblings all possessed. A blue flame burst to life in his open palm.

"Eder will be angry," Calluna said, referring to their absent brother. The flame's blue light flickered off the faint tears in her eyes, adding depth to the cold starlight that forever shone within her irises. Eyes they all shared. The mark of radiance.

"Let him be angry," Faron said.

"I'll miss you," she insisted.

Faron smiled, so warmly, so miserably.

"I know. Be well, Calluna. I'll see you soon."

Sariel almost extinguished the fire in his hand. He didn't have to do this. He need not participate in his brother's attempts to forget those he'd loved and lost. The idea faded as instantly as it had come. No, he would be here for his family, whatever the cost. He looked down at Faron and saw his brother's head tilted away from Calluna so she could not see his own tears.

"You're too soft for this world," Sariel said as the fire grew stronger in his palm.

"Then do it," Faron commanded with a tone that had rallied armies and frightened kings.

Not yet. Not until he checked with Calluna, who looked ready to shrivel into herself. His sister sensed his unspoken question.

"I'm here to the end," she said, her will strong despite the timidity of her voice.

Then let the damned deed be done, thought Sariel.

He tilted his hand. The fire flowed like liquid from his palm and fell to the stacked logs below. The oil caught. The fire spread. Smoke filled the cave as flesh began to blacken and peel.

"Until we meet again," Sariel said as, for the third time in his agonizingly long life, he burned his brother alive.

PART ONE

AWAKENED

CHAPTER 1

FARON

When Faron awoke, he was blind, and he could feel worms crawling through his flesh and organs. An overwhelming sense of loss and sorrow pierced his mind like a spear, receding as his senses returned. Whatever the cause, he could not remember it. Let memory fade as he focused on the now. Where was he? What had happened?

The pyre.

Yes, the pyre. Its ashes were beneath him as he lay on his back. The worms, the carrion bugs, they shouldn't...

The cave. Sariel and Calluna must not have properly sealed the cave. That, or humans had broken their way in...but no, they would not. They feared the qiyan too much for such a risk.

I do not know how long you have feasted, but it comes to an end. Leave me.

The thought echoed through him, projected by his radiance. He instantly felt the change. The carrion insects cut, bored, and ate their way to the surface of his skin. Faron clenched his jaw against the pain. Worms slithered like snakes from his wrist and belly. A beetle retreated out his nostril. He breathed softly and shallowly, not wanting to disturb whatever creatures occupied his lungs.

Blood, his blood, mixed with the ancient ash. The pain receded, and he slept again.

•

The next time Faron awoke and opened his eyes, he saw the barest hints of light. It seemed his sight had recovered. The stone was cold, and it felt pleasant against his bare skin. He pushed himself to a sitting position, crossed his legs, and bowed his head.

Warning was given, he told the smallest and simplest of creatures occupying his body. Maggots, squirming in his stomach. Unhatched eggs, laid upon his skin. He clenched his fists and let radiance shine through his body. It burned the invading creatures like fire, shriveling their bodies and popping their eggs.

He gasped when the effort was finished. The pain of it slowly ebbed away. Faron stood, stretched, and then tested his limbs. His balance was wobbly at first, but improved as he shifted his weight from foot to foot. Next he ran a hand through his hair, found it slimy with moisture and dirt. He desperately needed a river or lake to cleanse himself.

The cave was pitch-black, but that did not bother the eyes of those touched with radiance. Faron looked about and found a tightly wrapped leather bundle, poorly hidden underneath a pile of stones. Beside it was a plain but finely sharpened sword. Faron smiled. Little Calluna, always watching out for him.

Within the bundle, he found a fresh set of clothes, remarkably clean after an unknown amount of time spent waiting. He dressed himself in the dark, the measurements correct as expected, and then took in the new style.

A white shirt, lacking the ruffles along the neck and top buttons that had been popular when last he visited the markets of Araketh. Long stockings, and atop them, a pair of leather trousers dyed black with the bark of eulmore trees. Most impressive was the brown leather coat. It had a high collar, thick copper buttons, and six pockets, three to either side. A belt was sewn directly into the sides of the waist, allowing him to buckle it shut should he be marching or riding.

A jingle alerted him to a heavy coin purse in a pocket. Faron pulled it out and undid the drawstring. Within were dozens of silver coins, and he examined one of them. There was a tower on one side and five stars on the other, the designs unfamiliar to him. A new currency, then, minted during his recovery. He put it back, pocketed the purse, and then continued dressing.

The boots Calluna had chosen for him were plain enough, brown leather with adequate padding, the color matching his coat. He slipped them on and adjusted the laces across the back to tighten them. That done, he grabbed the sword and headed for the cave's entrance.

It seemed he was wrong to doubt his siblings' diligence. The cave was sealed with a heavy stone, and what cracks remained must have been filled with mud. Time, though, was merciless, and wind and rain had worked away the mud until it was mostly gone. Little streaks of daylight peeked through, as did a hint of wind.

Faron placed his shoulder against the stone, braced his legs, and pushed. Leaves crunched and twigs snapped as the boulder rolled several feet before stopping against a thin eulmore tree. Its branches shook from the impact, its many violet leaves shivering in protest. Faron breathed in the clean air and felt his lungs heal away the last of the damage.

"How many years has it been?" he wondered aloud. His brother Eder could calculate that with a glance at the night sky. Tracking the movements of the moon and stars had always come easy to him. For Faron, there would be no answering that question until he reached civilization. The idea excited him as it always did when he reawakened. With the passage of time, language would be shifted, clothing would be changed, and homes would have adopted new styles or improvements. Even the meals might be different, should new spices become favored or the wandering feet of merchants build new paths between various portions of the grand island.

The reminder of food set his already ravenous stomach to grumbling. Of the several reasons he'd chosen this cave, one had been a field of raspberries to the north. He started that way, the violet canopy above him thinning, then stopping entirely as he exited the forest.

What fruit grew on the bushes was not ripe enough to eat. Not summer. Early spring, then, he guessed, as he skirted the outer edge of the bushes. If it were close to fall, the leaves of the eulmore trees would have been drained of their lovely color, shifting from violet to an ashen white. It seemed he'd have to make do with a bloodier meal.

Faron returned to the forest and gathered the occasional fallen branch or twig. Once they were piled together, he placed his hand in their center, summoned his radiance, and set them alight. For such simple tricks, he felt nothing, but this next one would put a strain on him and leave him winded. Still, it would be better than spending hours hunting.

Faron sat beside the fire, closed his eyes, and let his mind drift. His consciousness slipped through his boots into the dirt below and then spiraled outward. The world around him grew more vivid, more real. He heard the faintest clatter of red squirrel claws clutching black bark and birds whistling their songs as they flitted about the canopy. Blue-breasted robins, building fresh nests to impress mates now the winter was over. Purple-and-gold woodpeckers, thudding their beaks in search of grubs and worms.

Should have checked my body first. You'd have found a much easier meal.

No bird or squirrel would be enough, not for his hunger of untold years. Farther and farther he searched, until he sensed it: a wild hog, foraging among the underbrush.

Come to me, he said, pushing his will into the beast. He saw it in his mind's eye like little silver threads arcing between his body and the hog's. *Like a spider*, Calluna had described them once, and as much as Faron disliked the comparison, he could not deny the similarity.

Minutes later, the hog arrived, docile and quiet. Dirt caked its hooves. Two flies zipped about its deep red hide. Faron lifted his sword, turned its edge, and pressed it to the hog's throat.

"A victim of circumstance," he told the beast. "Know that I appreciate you for it, nonetheless."

A single cut, and the blood flowed.

•

Come nightfall, and with a full belly, Faron cast his will once more into the forest. This time he meditated for an hour, the focus of his mind spiraling beyond his immediate surroundings. As he took stock of the wildlife, he debated. In his last lifetime, he had befriended a hawk, and before that, a raven. Birds tended to be his favorite companions, but when his mind skirted across a nearby coyote, her loneliness struck him.

Come to me, he told her, and minutes later, she arrived, having crossed half a mile of forest to do so. Her fur was a tawny brown intermixed with white. The gangly state of her limbs and chest provoked a frown. She was not eating well, but why? He beckoned her closer so he could put his hands upon her. Contact allowed him a better understanding. Radiance flowed, silver threads connecting, and he peered into the coyote's mind.

A mother. Six pups. Four pups. Then three. Then none. Poor food. A poor hunter, abandoned by her pack. She was a failure. A failure. A failure.

Faron withdrew his mind, but his hands remained, and he looked deep into her yellow eyes.

"You do not understand me yet, but you will," he said, bracing for the strain. This would be harder than lighting a fire or sensing for nearby hogs and squirrels. Little wisps of silvery light floated like smoke from his hands and into her body, shaping her, changing her. What mind she possessed sharpened. The speech of humans would no longer be gibberish. Her eyes widened, and he sensed fear and excitement overwhelm her in equal measure.

"You will not remain this way," he told her. "It is a change too drastic, and a strain too great, but I would receive your answer amid true understanding. You will visit lands beyond this meager forest. You will walk the cities of man and see their nations and people. Sometimes I will feed you, and sometimes you will hunt for me. The way will be dangerous, and mankind's trust of you fickle and wary."

Those round eyes of hers stared into his. Her entire body locked stiff. The concepts he spoke of were grand and foreign to her, and yet she understood them now. It was cruel, in a way, but Faron was no stranger to cruelty.

"Will you join me, and see the wonders beyond this forest?" Faron asked, releasing her. "Stay, if you accept. Run and be free, if you refuse. I will harbor you no ill will should you reject me. The choice is yours, little coyote."

The connection between them faded, but he sensed faint echoes of her emotions. Her loneliness warring against her pride. The loss of her pups. Her vicious anger at a pack willing to leave her and her offspring to starve.

She turned away, just once, and then sat beside his fire. Her head tilted slightly. He could almost hear her voice in his mind.

What now?

"The intelligence I granted you will ease away," he told her. "But rest assured, you'll still be wiser than all other dogs, coyotes, and wolves. I suppose I should have your name. I would not demean you by calling you 'little coyote' forever."

His new companion glanced at the fire and the butchered hog beside it. Faron grinned.

"Go ahead," he said. "I've eaten my fill."

She tore into it with glee. Faron sat down, crossed his legs, and rested his chin on his hand. All animals had names, or concepts close enough to be usable as names. He closed his eyes and focused upon her.

What are you called? he asked.

She did not answer, not knowingly. Instead, a scent came to him, for that was how all coyotes knew themselves, and others.

Leaves, half covered in mud, wet with rain, bitter with a splash of blood, and yet, hovering about it, the final note of a wild iris bloom.

Faron chuckled at her.

"Quite a mouthful," he said. "Might I call you Iris, if only to save us time?"

The coyote cracked a rib free, chewed it twice, and then nodded.

"All right, then," he said. "Iris it is."

527

orbit

Follow us:

/orbitbooksUS

/orbitbooks

/orbitbooks

Join our mailing list
to receive alerts on our
latest releases and deals.

orbitbooks.net

Enter our monthly
giveaway for the chance
to win some epic prizes.

orbitloot.com